From the archives of the Comptrollerate-General for Scrutiny and Survey

THE SPIDER OF SARAJEVO

Robert Wilton held a variety of posts in the British Government. He was advisor to the Prime Minister of Kosovo in the lead-up to the country's independence, and is now helping to run an international mission in Albania. *Treason's Tide* won the Historical Writers' Association/Goldsboro Crown for best historical debut; in addition to his novels he writes on international intervention and translates a little poetry. He divides his time between Cornwall and the Balkans.

D0581390

Praise for *Treason's Tide*:

'Robert Wilton... has discovered a fresh vein of literary gold with this dense, superbly satisfying novel... beautifully written, wonderfully clever, this is another triumph' *Daily Telegraph*

'A sparkling gem of a novel; not only a gripping espionage thriller that has the extra thrill of being grounded in genuine history, but a beautiful, lyrical novel alive with the sheer joy of language... Not since Hilary Mantel's *Wolf Hall* has a novel been so drenched in a sense of time and place' M. C. Scott

'Brilliant invention, the ideal vehicle for a narrative revealing hidden conspiracies behind one of the turning points in British history... a compelling thriller' *The Sunday Times*

'This lively, intricate tale will satisfy many, especially those who enjoy riddles and puzzles' *Historical Novel Review*

'Robert Wilton's sensational thriller is set in 1805 as Napoleon's Grande Armée is about to invade England, but the real pleasure is the detail on London, a city teetering on the edge of revolution... With confidence and sureness of touch, Wilton handles the multiple strands of a narrative that moves inexorably towards denouement as the defunct and dandified British establishment quakes... Bernard Cornwell meets Ken Follett in a Southwark pub and someone gets coshed. That is to say, great, intelligent, fun' *Time Out*

'Excellent spy thriller [that] keeps you on the edge of your seat' www.historicnavalfiction.com

'The strength of the novel is based on this tangled web of spying, treachery and deceit... the novel keeps you guessing right to the end. The overall feel and mood of the book is one that I can imagine giving much pleasure on a long winter evening in front of the fire, a glass of good malt whisky at hand. It is that sort of adventure, thoughtful, complex and politically intriguing' www.novelsuggestions.com

Praise for *Traitor's Field*:

'Sets a new benchmark for the literary historical thriller. He achieves that Holy Grail of utterly absorbing, edge-of-the-seat thriller with a book of ideas that lays bare the convolutions of the English Civil War with a panache unmatched in modern writing. It's exhilarating, passionate, inspiring and literate and will garner new readers from lovers of Mantel and Cornwell alike... As a spy story, this is exceptional; clever, literate, thoughtful, life-enhancing. But read it first for the prose, and weep' M. C. Scott

'A thoroughly satisfying read... it is done so well that one feels no resentment about being tricked' *Historical Novel Review*

'Yet again he's done the seemingly impossible by bringing more documents to the fore and then bringing the time period to life right in front of the reader. The prose is sharp, the storyline even sharper and when added to characters that feel fully realized and believable really generates something special. Finally add to the mix a wonderful sense of mystery that blends danger alongside intrigue all round gives you a book to savour with your favourite tipple' *Falcata Times*

'Brilliantly written, *Traitor's Field* brings the sense of melancholy and paranoia – as well as a page-turning plot – familiar to fans of classic spy fiction' *Birmingham Post*

'A mystery meticulously plotted... what makes *Traitor's Field* such an engrossing and riveting novel is not just the excitement of the hunt, the intellectual pleasure of solving a clue or unraveling a thread, or even the chase through dark streets or across marshes, it is the characters... The writing itself is stunning... *Traitor's Field* is a thoroughly rewarding and engrossing read. After I finished it, all I wanted was more. Much, much more' www.forwinternights.wordpress.com

Also by Robert Wilton

Treason's Tide
Traitor's Field

From the archives of the Comptrollerate-General for Scrutiny and Survey

THE SPIDER OF SARAJEVO

ROBERT WILTON

CORVUS

First published in Great Britain in 2014 by Corvus,
an imprint of Atlantic Books Ltd.

This paperback edition published in Great Britain in 2015 by Corvus.

10 9 8 7 6 5 4 3 2 1

A CIP catalogue record for this book is available from the British Library.

Paperback ISBN: 978 1 78239 194 4
E-book ISBN: 978 1 78239 193 7

Printed and bound by CPI Group (UK) Ltd, Croydon, CR0 4YY.

Corvus
An imprint of Atlantic Books Ltd
Ormond House
26–27 Boswell Street
London
WC1N 3JZ

www.corvus-books.co.uk

To the Albanians
in gratitude for unfailing hospitality
and the hope that they may escape historical fictions

840. If a person goes to ambush a fellow-villager, taking with him other villagers as accomplices, and he kills that person, both the leader and his accomplices incur blood with the victim's family.

The law code of the Albanian Chieftain Lekë Dukagjini

1. If France is attacked by Germany, or by Italy supported by Germany, Russia shall employ all her available forces to attack Germany. If Russia is attacked by Germany, or by Austria supported by Germany, France shall employ all her available forces to attack Germany.

The Franco-Russian Alliance Military Convention, 18 August 1892

Introduction

MOST URGENT. SERIOUS... AGENTS... NEPTUNE CONSOLIDATE...
ALTEMARK MINOS HARM... ALL MUST REPORT TO EMBASSY.

This peculiar message, transmitted in June 1914, may have turned the
course of the First World War – before it even started.

The discovery of the secret archive of the Comptrollerate-General for
Scrutiny and Survey, under the Ministry of Defence in London, has
transformed our understanding of more than one drama in British history.
(A garbled version of the research and the continuing revelations reached
the press in May 2013.) From Elizabethan manuscript to Edwardian
typeface, its pages reveal the darkest aspects of national policy and
manoeuvring, at the moments when Britain and her empire were at their
most vulnerable. The records from the Napoleonic period, which formed
the foundation for *Treason's Tide*, showed the desperate gambits attempted
when the country was hours from invasion and defeat. Those from the
mid-seventeenth century – published in semi-fictional form as *Traitor's
Field* – show how this extraordinary organization survived and controlled
the transition from divine-right monarchy to republic.

This new episode from the Comptrollerate-General archives focuses on
another crisis for Britain and British Intelligence: when Europe waltzed
to the edge of the precipice, looked, thought about it, then leaped gleefully
over. Most schoolchildren know that the assassination, on the 28th of June
1914, of the heir to the Austro-Hungarian Empire sparked the First World
War. The month that followed, before armed conflict actually began in the
first days of August, is one of the most minutely analysed in all historical
writing – but also the most predictable. The Great Powers of Europe had
spent ten years or more establishing rival defensive alliances. A series of

squabbles had cemented those alliances. Each government had justified inflating military budgets by inflating the threat and the cause of national honour. Competing general staffs had wound up their political leaders to the imperatives of pre-emptive action. In the space of a generation, a Europe in which the shared interests of peace were protected by collective diplomacy had been replaced by one in which individual national interests were protected by bravado and defiance. 'War' had ceased to be a threat, and become instead a solution.

Once the Archduke Franz-Ferdinand had been murdered in Sarajevo, by Serbs with links to Military Intelligence in Belgrade, it was surely unavoidable that the Austro-Hungarian Empire, insecure and weakening, should take the opportunity to punish Serbia, the most troublesome threat to imperial stability. After a series of embarrassments, Russia could not but defend Serbia, her one remaining client in a region she wanted to influence. Germany felt the need to prove her international credentials and distract her population, had no reason to stop Austria teaching Serbia a lesson, and knew that if the inevitable war against Russia was to be fought, it was better fought when Russia was also trying to fight Austria. France was obliged to support Russia, and knew that if the inevitable war against Germany was to be fought, it was better fought when Germany was also trying to fight in the east. Great Britain, typically, was looking the other way and trying to deal with her own imperial troubles, but realized that after a decade of defensive posturing she couldn't afford to let Germany defeat France and dominate western Europe.

Such was the clockwork of July 1914 – and of innumerable student essays since. Less studied and less known is the background in the months before July, particularly the secret intelligence activity. The papers reproduced in this volume, never before published, reveal that background. In passing, they throw new light on more than one overlooked but significant incident of those mad months, and on one of the most remarkable careers in the history of the British Army and British Intelligence.*

The most significant developments in the evolution of British Intelligence machinery took place in the decade before the First World War. Alongside the existing Naval and Military Intelligence offices, and the police Special Branch and Criminal Investigation Department, in 1909 the Secret Intelligence Bureau was formed. Its home department would become Military Intelligence (M.I.) 5, today's Security Service; the Secret Service Bureau was born in the same year, and merged with the S.I.B. in 1911, its foreign department the beginning of M.I.6, the Secret Intelligence Service. But they were still in their infancy in those critical years of European politics, and in many respects behind their counterparts in the other Great Power capitals. What follows in these pages helps to explain how they survived that infancy, and also explains the great coup achieved by British Intelligence at the start of the war, which did so much for the reputations of the institutions involved and for the British war effort.

The usual debts and caveats apply. *The Spider of Sarajevo* has benefited from the wise guidance of Angus MacKinnon and Clare Conville, guardians of a greater age of British publishing, and that of Sara O'Keeffe and Anna Hogarty, heralds of a greater future. The strategic framework of events for this account is common knowledge. The detail is drawn directly from the archives of the Comptrollerate-General for Scrutiny and Survey, along with other relevant sources currently available (specific documents are referenced with the SS prefix, or equivalent; references are not given here for the many other documents that have contributed colour and background). The exact play of dialogue and emotion is of course my conjecture, consistent with the data and tending, I hope, to illuminate rather than distort what happened. If my fictionalization of these incidental elements inspires the reader to their own investigation of the facts, so much the better.

R. J. W., *May 2013*

*See also the introduction to *Treason's Tide*.

INDIVIDUALS NAMED IN THIS DOSSIER WHO ARE THE SUBJECT OF
SEPARATE FILES/ON OFFICIAL LISTS:

The agents
R. Ballentyne

J. Cade

D. Duval

Miss F. Hathaway

Major V. Knox

In London
Col. J. Mayhew, Secret Intelligence Bureau

Superintendent F. Thomson, Metropolitan Police Special
Branch

W. Palmer, clerk in the Ports & Consulates Office

Miss E. Durham, Ethnographer

In Berlin/elsewhere in Germany
Col. W. Nicolai, Chief of Military Intelligence

Col. H. Bauer, Military Intelligence

Maj. K.-H. Immelmann, General Staff

A. Niemann, writer

Baroness B. von Suttner, peace activist

Dr E. Müller, Director of the Frühling Sanatorium

D. Eckhardt, German Foreign Ministry

Freiherr G. von Waldeck

Fraulein G. Waldeck, his daughter

H. Auerstein

O. Auerstein, his son

In Constantinople
O. Riza, Ministry of Finance

R. Varujan, Financier

A. Charkassian, sister to Varujan

J. Radek, clerk in the Russian Trade Legation

K. Muhtar, Banker
H.H. Burley, H.M. Diplomatic Service

In Paris
G. Hamel, British aviation pioneer
Count M. von Cramm (also in Germany), aviator and sometime
Intelligence operative

In Saint Petersburg
G. Lisson, H.M. Diplomatic Service
R. Frosch, smuggler, and no doubt worse
"Anna"

In the Balkans
"Apis", Chief of Serbian Military Intelligence
W. Pickford, resident in Belgrade
R. Malobabić, conspirator
Count L. Castoldi, Italian Foreign Ministry (Durrës)
O. Rossi, Italian Foreign Ministry (Durrës)
Countess I. di Lascara
Assorted villagers, unknown to official records

ESPIONAGE ACTORS OF UNKNOWN OR FLUCTUATING ALLEGIANCE
Count P. Hildebrandt (alias Henschler)
Perez, V. (alias Peresa alias de Paresa alias di Bollino alias
the Marquis de Valfierno)
H.-P. Belcredi, anthropologist
E. Krug

A Table of Events

1899–1902
Second Boer War

1903
Erskine Childers publishes *The Riddle of the Sands*

1904
Entente Cordiale signed between Britain and France
August Niemann publishes *The Coming Conquest of England*

1905–6
Moroccan crisis follows Kaiser's visit to Tangier

1906
Launch of H.M.S. *Dreadnought*, and a new era of battleships

1907
Anglo-Russian Convention completes the Triple Entente

1908
Revolution forces Ottoman Sultan to reinstate the constitution and parliament
Austria–Hungary annexes Bosnia–Hercegovina

1911
German provocation at Agadir
Theft of Leonardo's *Mona Lisa*

1912
First Balkan War: Balkan states defeat Ottoman Empire
Declaration of Albanian independence from the Ottoman Empire

1913
Second Balkan War: victorious Balkan states fight among themselves
Coup in Constantinople

1912–13
London Conference arbitrates after Balkan wars and delineates Albania

1914

7 March	Wilhelm of Wied arrives in Durrës as King of Albania
16 March	Henriette Caillaux shoots *Figaro* editor Gaston Calmette
20 March	Curragh Mutiny: British Army officers refuse to act against Irish loyalists resisting Home Rule
24 April	Larne gun-running delivers arms to Irish loyalists
17 May	Protocol of Corfu: Albania grants autonomy to Northern Epirus
21 May	Third Reading of Government of Ireland ('Home Rule') Bill
22 May	*Berliner Tageblatt* publishes details of British–Russian naval conversations
23 May	Gustav Hamel takes off from Paris for London in new Morane-Saulnier aeroplane
	King Wilhelm abandons Durrës temporarily
26 May	Kaiser Wilhelm II meets Archduke Franz-Ferdinand, Konopischt
29 May	R.M.S. *Empress of Ireland* sinks in the St Lawrence River
23 June	Kiel Regatta of British and German navies begins
28 June	Assassination of the Archduke Franz-Ferdinand, heir to the Austro-Hungarian Empire
6 July	Germany guarantees support to Austria–Hungary
23 July	Austrian ultimatum to Serbia
26 July	Howth gun-running delivers arms to Irish (nationalist) Volunteers
28 July	Austria–Hungary declares war on Serbia
30 July	Russia begins general mobilization against Austria–Hungary
1 August	General mobilization ordered by France and Germany
	Germany declares war on Russia
3 August	Germany declares war on France
4 August	Germany invades Belgium
	British ultimatum to Germany expires; war
3 September	King Wilhelm leaves Albania

Spring 1914: Blood

The mountains were a palisade all around him, and Ballentyne thought: *I have escaped from the world.*

From somewhere nearby: gunshots, and shouts, sharp into the sky, and instinctively he started to turn; then stopped and smiled.

Whichever way he might look, the wall of mountains would be in front of him. The village, and the vivid green plain in which it had grown, nestled up here among the eagles. The Cursed Mountains, they said, but the mountains kept the village hidden and safe from the world.

The snow had shrunk away early this year. *A secret Eden, a fertile—* and then something thumped into his back and Ballentyne stumbled forwards a step.

'Ehh, English! Have you drunk too much?' A heavy hand clenching on his shoulder, and he turned. The face now thrust close to his was itself a mountain: craggy bones, and fissured, wind-blasted skin. Ice-clear eyes gazed into his.

He smiled. 'O Adem, I have not started to drink yet.' The old man chuckled hoarse. 'And then I'm afraid you're going to make me dance, or no?' Again the chuckling from the old man, and Ballentyne laughed softly at himself too. The language, the dialect of the northerners, was back with him now, and he enjoyed its taste like the air. A badge of exclusivity; a shared secret.

Ronald Ballentyne let the old man link arms and lead him back through the village: a dozen timber houses and three towers, squat and yellow-stoned in the afternoon sun, tiny black eyes peeking down from the blank faces.

The civilized continent, with its machines and its fancies, had fallen off behind him like an uncomfortable coat too heavy at the shoulders, as he'd trekked up from the sea and into the Albanian highlands: it was several weeks away now, and at least a century.

Gunshots again; the usual celebration of the young men in the mountain villages. *And, indeed, everywhere.* Venerable rifles, Italian Mannlichers and German Mausers fifty years old and gnarled Turkish contraptions, the debris of decades of feuding and skirmishing on the edge of Europe. Adem was wearing two pistols at least, their intricately decorated butts sticking out of the sash around his waist and nodding to each other as he walked.

A cramped wooden staircase in one of the towers, and the smell of men. A foreigner and a guest, Ballentyne had a more honoured place among the older men than his age warranted. It was Adem's privilege as head of the village to play host to the English visitor, and Ballentyne sat next to him, settling his tweeds and his Jermyn Street boots down among the patterned woollen trousers and goat-hide slippers. As usual, the surreptitious effort to pull his shins into the cross-legged position adopted easily by men twice his age.

Adem reintroduced him – 'our good friend Ronaldi, who is back with us this year and will always have a home here' – and Ballentyne watched the faces: the lighter hair and eyes and the eagle noses of the highlanders, played out on men from twenty to eighty, slow, watchful, serious in the counsel room. Boys came in with coffee, dark and sweet, and *rakia* distilled from pears, and the questions began, sober and incessant. Had Ballentyne come through Shkodra, and was the town recovered yet? Had the bridge ten miles down the valley been rebuilt? Was it true about the priest in Shoshi? No one seemed interested that they were now living in an independent Albanian kingdom with an imported German king, until someone asked about the Turks, and Ballentyne explained that with independence the Turks had gone from Albanian life; the faces seemed sceptical about this.

From outside, the friendly patter of drums and the twang of the two-stringed *çifteli*, and Adem led the men out. The sweet smell of burning fir-wood easing him towards evening, Ballentyne watched the dance begin, the snaking line of young men with arms around shoulders kicking and swooping in unison, felt his legs begin to catch the rhythm.

He settled on a log to watch. The bridegroom was an open-faced youngster at once proud and uncomfortable at his celebrity. Ballentyne had spoken to him two or three times, the guileless humourless answers helpful for research. He danced well, an eagle lost in flight. There were women watching now too, emerging with the evening to share the entertainment and to observe the newcomer.

The bride was a heavy-browed strong-featured girl, the ritual emptiness of expression coming easily in the strange village. Tonight would be her first night here, and it would be a hard living until she produced a son. Ballentyne watched her, with interest and sympathy. More rifle shots into the evening. Extremely unlikely that the couple had met before today.

Another pair of eyes caught his. One of the village girls – he recognized the face – watching bride and groom carefully. With Ballentyne's eyes clearly on her she turned her head slightly, but her glance was fixed for a few moments longer. Not the Turkish-taught submissiveness of the townswomen, but the self-containment and discipline of the mountain girls with their old codes. Ballentyne felt his professionalism slipping. The large dark eyes, the high cheeks and the full lips were typical – and lovely.

Besa – that was the name. A face in the fields or at a window, glimpsed two or three times during his stay and noticed. She would be... yes, the groom's sister. Hence her watchfulness of the couple. Her glance flicked back to Ballentyne, and away, and she pulled a strand of hair back behind her ear. Older sister. Professionalism again: small household – father dead, mother bed-ridden, two daughters but only one son; two cows, so doing well enough, but until the new bride produced a son the family would be fragile.

Beautiful women.

A thump on his leg, Adem's paw: 'Ehh, my friend! We find you a lovely Albanian wife and you take her to London, or no?' They both knew it was inconceivable that Besa or any other village girl should marry a foreigner. 'Make her princess, or no? He-eh heh heh!' The corroded chuckles echoed away, and Ballentyne watched the eyes and the wind-scraped parchment face and smiled. Beautiful women, and the best of men.

A pause in the dance, cheers of approval, and the young men began to drift away from their circle towards drink and meat; the musicians stopped only for sips. The groom, flushed and happy, was walking towards Adem and Ballentyne.

The warm restless tricks of firelight, the last of the day cool in the sky, the mountains dark beneath it, the pit-pat of the drums and the strained melody, the smell of wood and earth, the heat of the *rakia* in his chest. More shots, and shouts, and Ballentyne felt himself smiling at the sheer abandoned happiness of it all, and then a single shot and the groom's chest went scarlet and he pitched forwards into the dust.

Now the shots came fast, snapping from all sides. The shouts becoming screams. The circle breaking into chaos; a frenzy of running. Ballentyne had one moment of stupefaction, the echo of the groom's elation and his own dumb happiness still in his head and amid the madness a point of clarity: the face of Besa, the woman, staring cold at her dying brother.

Then a hand clutching his shoulder and pulling him up and backwards and away. He scrabbled for balance, for control, the gloom crackling with shots and cries, and then he was scrambling down a path after Adem, the rough walls of the houses scratching at shoulders and fingers as he went. At a corner the old man stopped, turned, grabbed him by the arm again and pushed him onwards down another path. Ballentyne hesitated, turned, saw the old man pulling the two pistols from his sash and levelling them deliberately the way they had come. Silence; the narrow eyes of the eagle; then he fired one of the pistols and began to stride after Ballentyne, gesturing him onwards with the gun.

'Kelmendi!' he spat as he came level. His hand, still holding the discharged pistol, was pushing Ballentyne. 'They are vermin, but why this?' A shot suddenly loud, and dust spattered into Ballentyne's face and Adem had pushed him forwards again. The old man turned, levelled his second pistol and fired and there was a cry. Hurrying on again: 'They will surely—' and a shot roared from ahead of them and the old man staggered back and Ballentyne spun to look – the old man sprawled, face angry-pale – and then a crash in his brain and gloom and nausea.

The nausea thumping and stabbing through his head, and his feet scrabbling over the ground, ankles kicking at stones; he was being dragged, an arm under each of his shoulders. Mind still confusion. Body a mess of sensations: strain in the arms, battering in the feet on the rough ground.

Another corner, he was flung against a wall, head and shoulders knocked on timber, and cloth thrust into his mouth – retching and gagging at the intrusion – a blow across his face; stupid surprise, and then the arms under his shoulders and being dragged again.

The twin breaths and pounding of feet were joined by a third, and something sharp was pushed into his back. 'Fast! Fast!' – Albanian, hissed at him, and Ballentyne's feet scrambled to keep pace.

They hurried for perhaps ten minutes: ditches, rocky ground, and then a thin stone track and the sound of water below. Had he walked this path? The shock was fading to conscious confusion, the pain to persistent aches and the rhythm of trotting. Had he walked this path?

Ten years of visits to the wild lands of south-eastern Europe. Robbed three times? Four? Nothing like this.

The last of the light; pale sky and a grey world of cliffs above and below. Boots blending into the stones beneath him. The river a ribbon of darkness off to the side and down.

His escort were breathing hard now, with their own heat easing and the ungainly effort to run and drag. Somewhere in Ballentyne's throbbing clarifying head the flicker of an idea: escape? Then the stab of metal against his spine again, bump and stab as they ran.

The path opened out, and they slowed to a walk. The arms steering him now, towards the ravine, opening up before him, the rush of water, his legs fighting for control and trying to stall before they pushed... and he was thrown down into the stones at the brink.

Clutching at the stones, arms and legs shivering, finding himself looking down into the ravine, on all fours, turning, looking up, arm instinctively in front to ward off – looking up into the muzzle of a pistol.

Is this what death is?

The end of the world: a little unseen barbarity somewhere in the Balkans. The great hole of a pistol muzzle.

A word, and the cloth was ripped out of his mouth and the muzzle and the pistol and the man holding it pulled away. Another man stepped forwards, two other men nearby.

The path had widened into a kind of clearing against the cliff face, stony and patched with grass.

Kelmendi, Adem had said. Kelmendi, the men of a village a few miles away, described with hatred or humour according to circumstance. The man with the pistol, and the two men now standing back – a glance showed that all three looked Albanian in face and dress. The few words had been spoken in Albanian.

But the man walking forwards did not look or dress like an Albanian. Ballentyne took him in, from the dust upwards: boots, puttees, trousers, jacket; good outdoor clothes that could have come from any European capital. A European face flushed by recent exercise; dark hair. His own age.

'Good evening.' He didn't sound like an Albanian either. 'Mr... Bahl-en-tein.' The ugly vowels of English cleaned, the syllables delivered evenly.

He looked and sounded German.

'Who the hell are you?'

A moment's consideration, and then a little smile. 'My name is Hildebrandt.' The head came forwards slightly. 'I am the man who shortly will kill you.'

Is this what death is? 'But – but for God's sake, why?'

A boot came up and, before Ballentyne's fuddled head had realized the intention, the sole pushed him hard in the shoulder and sent him sprawling towards the edge of the path. When he had scrambled round again, the man was crouching near him.

'Mr Ballentyne, I... I urge you' – the 'urge' was pushed out emphatically – 'that you make this easy. I will shortly kill you, yes, I will; but first I will ask you some questions, and' – a shrug – 'it were better – cleaner – if you would answer directly. These people' – he nodded back to the three Albanians – 'their habits...' A shake of the head, the teeth clucking sadly. 'We can be more civilized, yes?' The head forwards again, a pained frown. 'May we... behave as gentlemen?'

The two heads level, close, eyes searching each other.

Ballentyne launched himself forwards from the crouch, memories of school bullies who'd pushed him too far, hands scrabbling for face and neck as the German fell back under him. Then a thump across his head and the daze and hands under his shoulders and once more he was flung away to the edge of the ravine.

By the time he was staggering upright again the Albanians were on him, two of them pinning his arms and wrenching his head back. An unseen signal and the third moved in fast. Ballentyne glimpsed the flash of a blade and then his face seared in pain.

They dropped him. His whole world was his burning cheek, the panic for his eyes, blinking them clear, scrambling in the dust and one hand coming away from his cheek doused with blood.

Pain scalding. 'I don't – know – who you are!' He heard the desperation in his voice, hoped that the German heard it, hoped that it would overcome this mad horror, the irrational implacable violence. 'I don't know what you want!'

Again the sorry cluck of the teeth, but this time the eyes were fixed and cold; no theatrical shrug or shake. 'Let us be direct, Mr Ballentyne.' The voice was low, hard. 'You are an officer of the Comptrollerate-General. You are in these mountains on some mission of espionage or provocation. You will tell me your mission. You will tell me the name of the Comptroller-General. Or you will have much pain... and then you will tell me.'

Madness. 'Compt... This is – I don't – I don't know what you're talking about!'

Hildebrandt's eyes narrowed. 'I hope you appreciated the rifle shot that killed the dancer. That was mine. Hardly a challenge – not a great distance; but he was moving, and in a crowd. A little exercise. I hit what I aim at, Ballentyne. I get what I want.'

'He was barely more than a boy. It was his wedding day.'

'I know. We have a pair of spies in the village. All planned, you see? And the youth was a gift to my friends here. One less father of their enemies. They took little enough persuading to attack.'

'Why – why would you do all this?'

A sigh; almost a growl. 'Ballentyne: you are an officer of the Comptrollerate-General for Scrutiny and Survey. You are in these mountains on some mission of espionage or provocation. The mission, Ballentyne. The name!'

'I – don't – know!' Hildebrandt's eyes burned angry. ''Fore God, I don't know!' A gesture, and the Albanians were moving in once more. Ballentyne lunged forwards at the nearest, pushed him back, turned to the German. 'I don't know!' The arms clutching at him, pulling him, twisting his head back. The third Albanian coming for him again, knife high and flashing towards his face. Ballentyne was twisting his whole body against the restraint, terrified, angry, straining to see the knife: 'Listen, you bastard! I don't—'

A shot, echoing along the ravine.

The knife never came; somewhere below his vision a body collapsed into the stones. Now the other two were turning, loosing their grip, scrabbling for weapons, Hildebrandt turning surprised, and at last Ballentyne could see what they could see.

It was Adem. The old man, his host, striding into the clearing with bandaged arm and pistols levelled and, as Ballentyne watched, the second of them cracked and one of his captors yelled in pain. The old man dropped the used weapons and reached for his sash, but now another weapon fired and he flinched and broke stride and his shoulder dropped, scorched. The wounded man on the ground had a pistol out too and it came up towards the old man and Ballentyne threw himself sideways as the trigger strained. He landed on the man as he fired, and the ball just clipped Adem's arm. Still he came on, a ghost in the evening, two more pistols out of his sash and coming up and Ballentyne rolled away and the old man picked his shots and, one after the other, the two remaining tribesmen died.

Hildebrandt was alone, a smile of interest at the indomitable old man as he staggered forwards, and his pistol coming up to finish him. Another shot, ricocheting off stone, his smile dropped and his gaze lengthened and he saw other figures hurrying in behind the old man. He spun towards Ballentyne with the pistol raised and Ballentyne ducked his head away and heard the shot roaring in his ear and felt the world opening beneath him in a rush of scree and he was falling.

⊶══⊷

An old man, at a desk in London, reviewing the failures of many years and trying to construct, once again and perhaps for the last time, the possibility of success.

His hair had lost its colour but not found the distinction of whiteness. His face was pale with age and exhaustion. He was an insubstantial thing, and as the net curtains drifted dusty behind him he seemed to drift with them, to fade and to resolidify as if unsure whether he was, after all, alive in this time.

Through the window came the crunch of boots marching along Whitehall, but he did not hear it. He sat upright, and still.

Intermittently, a sheet of paper would rustle under his fingers.

He'd known that the scheme had not produced victory; now he knew that it had been turned against him, and produced defeat. Under his left hand was the report – which he now had almost by heart, from the date the previous summer at the top to the unique 'SS' reference at the bottom – detailing the attempt to use the festivities surrounding the marriage of Princess Victoria Louise of Germany to arrange a meeting. While the King-Emperor George V of the United Kingdom, and the Tsar Nicholas II of all the Russias, and the Kaiser Wilhelm II of Germany had blessed the pageantry with their greatness and manoeuvred jealously for pre-eminence, in meaner corridors behind the masquerade the old man's agent had been about to spring a trap prepared over a decade. Only a meeting, but it would reveal the identity of the greatest of the spies.

It is one of three men...

The meeting had not happened. The bait – the hint of a scandal at the top of the British Army, set against the appealing backdrop of all that royal show – had not been enough; or perhaps it had been too much, and his prey had considered it, hesitated, and withdrawn.

Now, under his right hand, the confirmation of the extent of his failure. In an empty attic in Brussels, a man had been found stabbed to death. The increasing elusiveness of the old man's agent was now explained. A line of reports stretching back over six months was almost certainly fabrication. And, once again, he was nowhere.

The image came unbidden, as it always did. A village in southern Africa; and a memory from the turn of the century. *Springfontein*. The wind blowing up the dust; a door banging; a face thick with sweat; the chaos. A defeat, and an education. A lesson in the brilliance of the man against whom he had set himself.

His opponent only used violence when absolutely necessary. It was becoming necessary more often.

In the reports around him on the desk, the chaos of Europe gathered. Not only in the games of Empire, in Persia and Africa. Not only in the territorial squabbles of the Balkans, and the economic fevers and the elaborate intrigues of the continental powers. But at home: Ireland divided and ready for civil war; espionage and sabotage in factories, military bases and dockyards across Britain. The country was being eaten away from within, while her enemies gathered without. The greatest peril for more than a century, and he was nowhere.

And then, from more than a century ago, an echo. A scheme of one of his predecessors. Might that serve to lure out his enemy? What had he left, against the Spider?

The Old Man

The Revd R. T. Satterby
Grange House
Buxton
26th March 1914

My dear _____,

I recall you saying when last we met that you had difficulty finding good and intrepid researchers, particularly women, and that I would oblige you if I should happen across some promising young person and bring them to your notice.

If this concern of yours holds, I wonder if I might recommend to you Miss Flora Hathaway.

You may understand something of the daughter through the parents. He is a doctor, whose assiduity is matched only by his suspicion of the novelties of his profession (I once joked that he probably found Harvey's work unproven and Jenner a veritable charlatan, which he found not at all amusing), she is a woman of the most energetic devotion to deserving social cases, and the severest judgement of the ills that cause them. They incline more, I may say, to the Old Testament than the New, and the girl has been raised in an atmosphere of uncompromising – one might say puritanical – rigour. The lack of sentiment of the parents has meant that they have made no allowances for their eldest child being of the gentler sex; a first-

21

born son would have had no more robust an upbringing.

That these two should produce a daughter of unusual determination and steadiness is no surprise. But it is only to providence that we may ascribe the force of her intellect. (There is a younger brother, but he enjoys neither the strength nor the strictness of critical reasoning to transcend the limits of his world.) She is highly perceptive, and Amazonian in power of logic. The generosity of a local benefactress enabled her to study a year at the University of London, where I believe she did very well.

She is in her later twenties, I should say. There was to have been a marriage to a doctor, but he died; now there is talk of clerical work in Manchester. If the young woman should prove fit for some academic or administrative work of benefit to you, I should be delighted to have been of service; and I must confess it would please me to see her out of this place and stretched, for otherwise I fear her lot will be marriage to a man stupider than she, or governess.

Are you out and about much these days? From up here in the wilds I confess I still assume the life of you London chaps positively Babylonian, even a guarded old elephant such as you. I have ordered young Rolfe's new Suetonius, and I hear that Stanislaus's boy is off to Antarctica ("young people are in a condition like permanent intoxication", indeed). Beyond these, and the sheep-centred insights of the local quidnuncs, I am ignorant – while yet remaining,

Yours ever,

Satterly

[SS G/I/894/I]

How many carriages on the train? Six, was it? And eight compartments to a carriage. Assuming—

James Cade caught himself. Supposition multiplied by supposition equals gross error. He stood, stepped over the outstretched legs of the other inhabitant of the compartment, yanked down the window and stuck his head out. The whole world roared and he recoiled, as the windows of another train flashed past in front of him. Out again. But the track was too straight to—

A tapping nearby, and he looked down. The other man in the carriage, tapping on the window and looking none too chirpy. He pulled his head in, smiled, offered a placating gesture and returned to the sixty-mile-an-hour wind. Fifteen seconds of gulped breaths and whipping hair and at last the track made an obliging concave bend.

Six passenger carriages. He pulled in his head and closed the window with deliberate completeness. 'Do beg your pardon. One must be sure, you see?' He smiled at the frown, stepped back over the legs, slid open the compartment door and stuck his head into the corridor. Not eight compartments but ten.

He sat. Sixty compartments; maximum three hundred and sixty passengers. How many termini were there in London? Half a dozen? How many long-distance train journeys a day? Ten thousand passenger up-journeys a day? What would they want on a train? Food, surely. A hot drink. Soup? Available at stations, of course. But on a longer journey... Longer journeys often expresses, and therefore a higher proportion of richer passengers. But now problems of supply and storage; potential mishaps at point of sale. Pretty girl in an apron?

The door slid open, and a soldier's distinctive uniform cap thrust in. Young face. Military supplies? Cade smiled, the other occupant frowned, and the soldier murmured something to a companion in the corridor and moved on. Cade pushed the door shut. Something to read. Newspapers? Delivery and licensing. Books? To sell or borrow? Average length of journey...

He turned to his fellow resident, and smiled. 'Pardon the interruption, but I noticed the size of your trunk up there. Is it a long journey you're making?' London. 'Yes, of course. And we're fearfully under-supplied, aren't we? Something to eat, perhaps. Something to read.' A grunt of acknowledgement and, as if to reinforce the point, the other man pulled out a copy of the *Glasgow Herald* and walled himself in with it.

Cade skimmed the advertisements on the front page – surely a ludicrously low price for a pair of boots; where had the false economy been made? – and settled back into his seat.

A conversation between two strangers. A conversation in the Philosophical Club that had become a supper. The older man's interest in the firm of Cade & Cade; interest in his ideas; sympathy for the limitations of commercial life in Edinburgh.

And then a letter from London; a business proposition for the firm of Cade & Cade, and in particular for Mr James Cade.

Nine times out of ten a bust: someone wanting money, or a partner to do all the work. But he was due a trip to London anyway. How many termini in London?

＋＝＝＋

David Duval drained the cup, licked the taste of cold tea from his teeth, and surveyed the wreckage of the bed-linen. Through the half-open door, the sound of plumbing.

Cheap plumbing; an ugly counterpoint to her singing. Cheap plumbing, threadbare rug, an early night, cold tea and a familiar unease.

It might be time for tears; for a letter and a rose. He was becoming over-critical and sentimental, both of which were rather nauseating. She was becoming habituated and faintly desperate, both of which were alarming. Any more of this would be futile and unfair; destructive only. He saw his jacket on the chair-back, his bag beneath it; a pretty shabby total of a life.

He pulled himself up against the pillow, felt the cold thrill of the bed-frame on his neck, and forced his shoulders back against it. Sentiment was bad; self-loathing was worse. He ran a hand over his jaw, then smoothed the moustache with finger and thumb. A touch of Victorian melodrama in the moustache; life needed a bit more of the spirit of that moustache. *Must keep moving.*

The jacket, and consequently the thought of the letter inside it. *Hadn't forgotten our entertaining conversation over drinks* – Duval had; *rather festive evening* – which might explain it; *but thoroughly enjoyed talking to you* – of course; *a scholar but not one of these stay-at-home chaps* – no indeed; *and wondered if you might be the man for a job* –

Always.

Under his hand, the residual warmth from where her rump had recently been, and from the bathroom the singing. Dark against the net curtain, his jacket, with the letter.

From the chair beside the bed, David Duval picked up a sixpence. He settled it precisely on finger and thumb, brought it in front of his face, and flicked it high.

⊹⇒⇐⊹

Ronald Ballentyne reached Whitehall early, and did one circuit of St James's Park to fill the time. The lake felt like a lung in the middle of London's monumental greyness, where the smallest building was an institution. He weaved among the prams trying to keep his eyes on the water, the trees, the white morning sky.

The porter in the Foreign Office lobby, all sleepy mahogany, took a second glance at his face while checking the list of visitors, and Ballentyne ran an instinctive finger along his cheek. The scar was fading, but felt tender and wide.

As he moved towards a bench, a man in uniform stood up in front of him. A flicked glance in the direction of the porter, and then: 'Mr Ronald Ballentyne?'

Ballentyne hadn't had much to do with uniforms. This one, sickly brown, looked like army.

He nodded.

The soldier – officer, presumably – something in the face and the confidence – held out a hand. 'Knox. Major Valentine Knox.'

A face about his own age, dark eyes under dark brows, and a splendid Kitchener moustache. Ballentyne shook hands and, to fill the silence: 'I'm... pleased to meet you.'

Major Valentine Knox seemed to consider this, as if unused to the reaction. The eyes narrowed a fraction. He said: 'I'm your liaison officer, Mr Ballentyne.'

'Liaison... for what?'

<hr>

The old man had a room of his own in the Foreign Office; a plaque on the door – one of the opaque titles favoured by bureaucracy, as if faintly ashamed of itself; the old man's name not mentioned. Near the end of a corridor; not among the carpets and vast allegorical paintings of the great men, but not far away.

Mayhew knocked. The location reflected the role: an occasional word of wisdom from an age now passing. He was bidden to enter.

Mayhew had the impression that, if the old man were to rise from the high-backed leather chair, he would leave his shadow precisely marked in the dust.

'They'll be starting to arrive shortly,' he said. One always seemed to speak quieter in these dusty bureaucratic places. He wished himself back in an officers' mess. 'The businessman first. At... ten.'

The old man took a moment to consider, as if recalling himself to the twentieth century. 'Thank you, Colonel.' He stared into the empty blotter on the empty desk. 'Good of you to keep me involved. Cade. I'll sit in on that one. Might stick my head in on the ethnographer; touch of the old don. Duval you should do yourself; I fancy he'll feel cleverer on his own with you. And you could let him think that, couldn't you, Colonel?' The eyes flicked up at him; Mayhew was piecing together the implication. Back into the distance. 'Hathaway... I shall do myself. All right with you?' The eyes into his again. 'Merely suggestions.'

Mayhew found himself nodding. He was a soldier. He recognized decisions; he recognized commands.

<hr>

Half a continent away, two men looked down from a gallery onto the audience chamber of an emperor – a Kaiser, the second Wilhelm of the Hohenzollerns of Germany.

Below them, a final platitude from the emperor's Austrian guest. 'To it! To it!' from the emperor, and silence. A moment of uncertainty as the protocol faltered, and then he led the party from the room in procession, German paired with Austrian. The slam of the door echoed around the marble.

In the gallery, movement at last.

'Why thank you, Colonel; that was most entertaining.'

'You are my honoured guest, sir. Yet I hope you realize the unique privilege you have been afforded.'

The honoured guest was dressed in a frock-coat, and he ran a palm down over the lapels as if checking his own sleekness. 'Indeed, Colonel. Indeed I do. Not, of course, that we heard any surprises. One of your emperor's many... virtues is his honesty. So no surprises. But two men of the shadows do not need to be reminded that the importance is not in the information itself, but in the perspective from which the information is gained.' A finger slid along the marble balustrade. 'Most impressive, Colonel.' A smile. 'Like so much in Germany.'

Colonel Walter Nicolai removed his cap, pushed his hand over the bristles of his head and down the back of it – *even those shaven hairs*, his visitor thought, *must be kept down* – and covered up again. The perpetual frown, the world a constant affront, and a stiff nod. 'We must be ready to crush them.'

'Them? All—'

'The British. The British Empire. There will be war in Europe.' A gloved fist thumped on the balustrade at the end of each sentence, stamping it as official. 'In the end Britain will be our greatest enemy. We must be ready to crush them.'

'Indeed.' Again the smile. 'Yes indeed, Colonel. And yet the British will take some crushing, will they not?' Another glance after the official party below. 'As great men have found before, the Channel is not easily crossed. That empire is not easily overmastered.' He saw the frown, saw the fist ready to have another go at the balustrade. 'Which is why you and I, the men of the shadows, must do a little business, is it not? Why you come

27

to me.'

'Correct. A great blow. A great coup of destabilization or sabotage—' Nicolai stopped; the lines above his nose sharpened. An elegant hand had been held up in front of him.

It withdrew to cover a discreet cough. 'Perhaps. And perhaps not, Colonel. If I may suggest, the weakness of Great Britain is... her greatness itself. So vast an empire – so many sheep to watch, so many threats in the night – it is easily distracted.' The hand conjured its truths out of the air. 'Your colleague von Tirpitz may anchor his fleet opposite the Royal Navy and have them make faces at each other. Your armies may be ready to throw the British back into the Channel if they should cross it. But we... we shall be where their forces are not. We shall be... at once everywhere.'

<hr/>

James Cade took in the character of the office: formal; leather-topped desk, kept well polished, but it wasn't in regular use. He took in the two men opposite him: man in army uniform, lots of ribbons and brooches and what-not, good shoes; and an older man half hidden against the wall, face in shadow next to the window. And he took in his own position in this room.

Am I buyer here or seller?

The front man at the desk, the pitch man. And the chevy behind. Give him a top hat or a tattie, he's still trying to sell.

Hie away, old Dad of mine, where's the deal here?

'Very good of you to come here today, Mr Cade. Quite a journey.' *And this is the British government. Puts up a good front, don't he?* 'My name is Mayhew; I'm a soldier, as you see. This is Mr – Robertson.'

And I'm Wullie Wallace. He said something appropriate. Lord, was this real? Was this how the government men did their business? And Jimmy Cade round for tea.

'Mr Cade, I won't waste your time reciting your abilities to you. You're a businessman; you know your own worth, I dare say. From various recommendations, we have a sense of that worth too.'

I'm to be a buyer, it seems. Oh aye, keep it coming, pitch man.

'We keep an eye out for men – men in all walks of life – with a certain resourcefulness; initiative. We have a particular need for men of business. It's a world that has its own qualities, of course. But we want a man who can also, under his own name and credibly, sustain a position as a businessman of repute and success. We could spend time and money setting up someone or other with a business front. Or we could take a man of established name; a name like Cade & Cade.'

Could you now?

Rather a frolic, though, wasn't it?

'You don't take the low road, do you, Mr Mayhew? You come right out with it. Is this how you normally do these things?'

The ghost of a smile from the chevy behind.

The front man again. 'To be honest, Mr Cade, it varies with... well, at root you're a salesman, aren't you? You know well enough how it's played.'

Cade smiled encouragingly.

'To come straight at it: we want to set you up – you as James Cade, known representative of your family firm – in a business situation abroad. Let you run it as you choose, run it as a going concern. And at the same time you would act as... as agent, for His Majesty's Government, keeping us in touch with... with—'

Cade leaned forwards. 'With the business climate as it affects your interests?'

Again the smile from the shadows – patronizing sort of smile – and this time it stayed. *Aye, keep smiling, old man.*

'Quite right, Mr Cade.'

Long as you fellows don't think you've got a fixed price.

⊱⊰

'Frankly, Mr Duval, we need men who are bit... a bit out of the ordinary. Who take the initiative.'

Duval took a moment before answering. There was something about the soldier's manner – snooty, maybe. With him, authority figures always were a bit. 'I'll be honest, Mr Mayhew.' He fancied a flinch across the desk. *Gotcha; you'll get no ranks and sirs from me.* 'I'm not much of a boy for following orders.'

'Mm. Creativity, Duval, takes different forms.' No 'Mr'. *Fifteen-all, is it?* 'Your architect's training means an eye to perceive and an eye to envision. We need both.'

'Do I get one of those uniforms?'

'No.' Stronger than intended. 'No, Mr Duval. No uniform, no rank. You will be who you are: David Duval, travelling student of architecture.'

He's uncomfortable. Not only disapproving, but uncomfortable. The world of the Colonel Mayhews was not supposed to involve being polite to the David Duvals. *Things must be getting bad, mustn't they?*

'Is that who I am? I'd often—'

'Mr Duval.' Hard, and then strangely a smile across the soldier's face. *You're not stupid, are you, Colonel?* 'Your lack of deference suits me as much as it amuses you. A man who unthinkingly accepts and does what he's told in this office will do the same in Rome or Berlin. That man is useless to me. I need a man who questions, who challenges, who's always looking beyond what he sees and hears.'

Duval nodded slightly. 'Mayhew, I love old England dearly, but I can't—'

'Thirty pounds a month.'

'Not enough.'

The eyebrows rose slowly under the careful haircut. 'Not enough for what?'

'To live. To live... as flexibly as I'd need to. Cultivate useful friendships. I won't corrupt the Kaiser's wife from a railway hotel, will I?'

Again the smile. 'You're even more impressed by your potential than we are. What's the going rate these days, then? For a corrupter of queens?'

'One hundred.'

'Fifty, and you'll get three months of it in advance.'

'Taking rather a risk with me, aren't you, Colonel?'

'The benefit of a rank and a uniform, Mr Duval, is that one is less likely to get hanged as a spy.' He stood. 'If at any time, on reflection, you decide you'd rather join the regulars, you'll find we've always room for enterprising young men there too.'

The world of men.

Flora Hathaway sat with deliberate poise, and considered the waiting room. Mosaic floor; dull rug. Furniture solid; functionality as done by an affluent people wishing to impress others and reassure themselves. One chair a piece of ludicrous baroque; some imperial souvenir. Fire laid economically but burning steady – that hadn't been done by one of the elegant sons of glory who glid along these corridors – and the hearth swept immediately afterwards. A clock on a dark stone mantelpiece, grotesque and thumping the seconds at her. Two portraits: middle-aged men in the formal wear of two decades ago. To help the awestruck visitor know what to look for; like the signs on the cages at the zoo.

The letter had been a surprise. Unexpected, of course. But also the style: neither patronizing nor commanding; courteous; frank about her achievements and frank – albeit in opaque terms – about what would be expected of her. *Research, requiring a high degree of discernment and initiative, while remaining directed and in the service of a wider object.* It appealed to her, certainly.

It had been written by someone who understood people. Someone who understood her.

Her parents' reaction: once again the weary hope that their troublesome-but-beloved might find something to meet her unrealistic standards; and then, unspoken after too many past missteps but still clear in their faces – the sudden formality in her father's, her mother's glance at her clothes – the admonitions to propriety and to the highest achievement.

Her parents in their distant parlour, set against this palace of national greatness.

I shall be worthy of the rare chances I am given.

Glancing down into the courtyard – and this time she thought of an aquarium – she watched two of the resident creatures striding across it, two men.

Ballentyne felt the odd dislocation washing over him again: the sense that the familiar world was unfamiliar, as if he were seeing it in a mirror, or in a dream.

The delirium of the fall, of the pain of rocks and the icy water, of unknown hands and a week of fever, of emerging weak and bewildered from the Albanian highlands; of huddling on station platforms, drowsing in night trains. Then England at last, the details of the dream fading with each full night's sleep, each familiar face. But now the soldier, this Knox: into his world of colleges and mountains a uniform, the lunatic distortion that convinces you you are dreaming.

'Easier if I explain as we walk,' Knox had said, ushering them into movement. Which might have been true, and yet he had not taken advantage of this easiness. Ballentyne walked across the Foreign Office courtyard in expectation, head half turned, waiting for words that never came.

They strode up the steps and into the porch – and moved as promptly backwards again, as the double doors swung outwards and a woman emerged. Murmured etiquettes from the two men, then: 'Why, young Ronald Ballentyne!'

Ballentyne focused properly on the face. 'Miss Durham. Good to see you.'

Knox frowned slightly; the visit was already even more public than he'd feared. Woman in her fifties. Solid-built and caped, a strong face under a tam-o'-shanter. Ballentyne's courtesy seemed genuine.

She glanced critically at Knox, and back again. 'Been in the mountains yet this season?'

'Yes. Yes – in the valley of Shala, and thereabouts.'

'How do our friends?'

'Well enough. I stopped with the priest in Breg Lumi.'

'And off there again, I hear.'

Ballentyne hesitated. 'No – well, I haven't planned—'

She flicked at him with a pair of gloves. 'Quite right, Ronald Ballentyne. No good shouting about it before you've got the thing worked out yourself, eh?'

'Well, I...' He gave up trying to understand. 'And how are you, anyway?'

The mighty torso heaved. 'Oh... Well enough, for myself. Mustn't grumble. But Albania! It's grim. Have you heard what's happening in the south? Ghastly. Ghastly.'

Ballentyne nodded.

'And trying to get these people to—' She shuddered, and shifted her shoulders under the cape as if trying to shake the whole of Whitehall behind her. 'I've just come from Terrence, and that was a waste of time, of course. I don't say he's half-witted, though he might be, but the most insipid, wheedling little excuse of an official you ever saw.' Another shudder. 'And now I've got this young woman along with me' – she gestured over her shoulder, and the voice didn't make clear if it was help or hindrance – 'wants to follow in my footsteps, or something.' A jolly guffaw. 'Well, if she's that determined!'

In the shadow, Ballentyne saw a younger, slighter version of Durham herself: the handsome profile, the close-bobbed hair, the strong shoulders; in her thirties, perhaps, and festooned with bags.

The gloves flicked at him again. 'Have a go at Terrence yourself, will you? He might take it better from you. Tell him it's not cricket, or straight shooting, or whatever it is men say.' The eyes were grave. 'They must see, Ballentyne. Those poor folk in the villages.'

Then she pulled herself straighter, and set her profile towards the courtyard. 'Come along, Miss Gowing!' she said over her shoulder. 'They'll be waiting for us at Precha's.'

She strode off, the younger woman following resolute in her wake and glancing at Ballentyne with a warm, distracted smile.

Where does she think I'm going? Ballentyne watched the two women sailing across the courtyard; then turned back to the porch and to Knox. *Where am I going?*

Knox was looking the question.

'Edith Durham. Sort of the... patron saint of those of us trying to open up and understand south-eastern Europe. And a heroine to the Albanians, for all she's done for them.' He reached for the door, and hesitated. 'Well, Mr Liaison Officer? Do you know what she seems to know?'

Knox pushed the door open for him. 'Better not keep this Foreign Office johnny waiting, eh?'

Terrence, departmental sub-chief for the Adriatic and south-eastern Europe, was slumped in his chair, fingers pressed into his forehead. On the blotter in front of him, a pair of scarlet knitted objects.

The fingers came away as Ronald Ballentyne was shown in with Knox a pace behind him, and the head lolled back against the chair. He glared at Ballentyne.

'I've just had Mad Edith in,' he said bitterly. 'It's all terrible and it's all my fault, apparently. Gave me these... these slippers.' He waved a hand towards the objects on the desk.

'*Opinga*,' Ballentyne said. 'Rather a good example. You give them to guests to use in your house.'

'I...' Terrence was clearly trying to recapture a picture of whatever suburban villa was home. 'Look, Ballentyne, I won't waste your time. You're off again, I know, and I've been told I've got better things to worry about.'

'But don't you want to hear—'

'Love to, old chap. But no point you doing it twice. You're down to meet someone else; not sure I had the name...' – he looked warily towards his desk, reluctant to disturb the slippers – 'military involved, somehow.' He nodded towards Knox.

Ballentyne turned, face grim. Knox, neutral smile, had the door open and was gesturing him out.

<hr />

For as long as he could remember, James Cade had loved ports. From Whitehall he followed the open sky the short distance to the river, and on the Embankment he turned left, for the heart of the City and the sea.

Fresher air and the sense of the world's possibilities. No better place than a port to make a decision.

As he walked, juggling the balance sheets of enterprises present and prospective, watching the crowds around him and wondering as always at London the great market, the ships got bigger. Bridge by bridge they evolved, sprouting funnels and the funnels multiplying, as if the river was itself a parade of the history of maritime engineering.

Risk. Some drop of impetus and activity at home; brother Tam must compensate. The image of a dwindling office; the old 'un would present it as expansion. Financial loss; beyond the negligible effects of the above, limited. The government investment in setting him up would make stock his only net outlay; and a Cade who couldn't make a running profit in one of the world's great bazaars didn't deserve the name. *Personal risk?*

He found himself slowing. Impossible to quantify. A calculation he wasn't used to, algebra with unfamiliar variables.

Fifteen minutes' walking had brought him into the City – the old London, the London of merchants and bankers and insurers that pre-dated by centuries and pre-conditioned the London of imperialists and diplomats he had just left. Across the water, the wharves and warehouses of the great merchant houses. To his left, the ground rising, up to where the Romans had had their forum and where the Bank of England now ruled the world. Still he went east. Now the ships soared up beside him, three- and four-masters, fully 500 feet long, bringing the world to London for men like the Cades to deal. The fat squat bow of a cargo steamer darkening the day next to him, a dribble of smoke escaping from her funnel into the jungle of masts and spars beyond. Below, between the behemoths, tugs and single-sailed traders and ferries chanced the swell.

Return. A potential new sector for Cade & Cade, with the risks underwritten by others. The possibility of turning a profit on it. And – he tried to scold himself, tried to hear his father – in a way, a little bit of a spree.

He came clear of the steamer and gasped in the pleasure of the sight: a windjammer, a four-master, six spars to a mast, able to unfurl an acre of sail: among the dark funnels a queen of elegance. *Careful, old lad. In business, money can buy a dream but a dream can't buy money.* Beyond her, her sea grey making her a ghost against the morning, a warship.

No better place than a port to make a decision; but not necessarily an even-minded decision.

As Duval stepped out into the corridor in front of Colonel Mayhew, another soldier rose from a bench to meet him. Perhaps his own height, his own age or a bit older; bigger built. Duval took him in, polished leather peak to polished leather boots. This one wore the uniform well; fit sort of fellow.

He glanced back at Mayhew. 'Now that,' he said, 'is the moustache I want. If not a uniform, do I at least get one of those?'

'This is Major Valentine Knox. He'll be your liaison officer.'

Duval mouthed the first name, and then stepped forwards. 'So what does that mean? Bodyguard, prefect, nursemaid?' Knox was still; his face was still. Duval held out a hand. 'You're the fellow who'll stop me getting into trouble, is that it?'

The moustache chewed on this. 'I like trouble, Mr Duval. I might be the man who gets you into it.' And at last he shook the offered hand, holding it and the glance a little longer than Duval expected.

'We have things to discuss, I take it.' A grin. 'And I've a hell of a thirst.'

Knox considered this. 'Come along, then.' He gestured Duval towards the marble stairs. Before he turned to follow, a last glance of shared meaning between the two soldiers.

⊹⟆⟆⊹

Lectures from men. Her father. The vicar. The MP. (What had he wanted? A daughter-in-law? A *wife*?) Professors. Ralph, trying a pose of gravity like an outsized hat. The policeman, after the march. Her father again. All so wise and so uncertain. Hopeful because strange, precocious Flora's dominant characteristic is her intelligence, *ergo* she is halfway a man; but then uneasy, because Flora does not follow the languid rules of chat, and watches, and challenges, and has breasts, and is all in all a most peculiar sort of man.

This man sat with his back to the net curtains, which glowed white around him and left his face in shadow. As if he were an absence. She'd not stifled a gasp at the cheapness of the attempt at advantage.

Then she'd entertained a vague fancy that he was embarrassed – perhaps disfigured, even. And now she realized it was probably one of the habits that men adopted in their strange world of deceit and intrigue.

'I shan't try to appeal to patriotism or duty, Miss Hathaway; I think you—'

'And yet by invoking them you have tried to do just that. Diminishing them, while implying vaguely that you have some yet stronger claim.'

'I do not belittle patriotism or duty, believe me. They are both of them admirable values, and we have sore need of them. Nor' – he shifted – 'before you exercise your reasoning at my expense again, do I imply that you are not patriotic or dutiful. But patriotism and duty should be felt, not appealed to.' The old man watched Flora Hathaway's eyes carefully; they had the habit, when thinking, of hardening. 'They might, moreover, seem insufficient cause to send a young person – a particular young person, chosen rather than innumerable others – on a journey that will certainly expose them to loneliness, anxiety and doubt, and conceivably to hostility and to danger.' Still she stared back at him. 'It is a journey for which one must discover one's own motives.'

Still the eyes, unblinking, reasoning.

The old man shifted again, and took in a long breath. The words came faster: 'Because we may be involved in a national fight for survival. And in such a fight, we must use our every capacity to its uttermost. We can't afford to exclude people on the basis of irrelevant aspects of their background or physiology. As individuals, by extension, we must use our strongest talents to the fullest. Success will depend on each of us being all that he – she – can be. I don't put a thoroughbred to pulling a cart. I don't put a scholar to checking a grocery bill.'

Flora Hathaway stared into the shadow. She felt oddly alive in the conversation. 'Sir, I loathe you for the cynicism with which you exploit the point. But I give you credit for being perhaps the first man I've met to understand it.'

'You're most kind, Miss Hathaway. But I'm not playing a game. Our every last capacity. To its uttermost.'

<hr />

'Someone already thinks I'm working for you!' Ballentyne had hoped for more impact. This Mayhew just raised his eyebrows in polite interest.

'They attacked me because of it.'

'Ah. Yes, rough business, sometimes. Foreigners get the funniest ideas about the British. Chap in your line – research and so forth – not the first time you've been accused of spying, perhaps.'

'The first time I've been cut up and shot at.'

Mayhew watched him for a moment. 'Look here, Ballentyne: I can't pretend there's not an element of... risk here. No, that's a foolish British understatement. Danger, is the word. We think you're the chap for this sort of work; but... you need to be aware of that. Consider it; earnestly. Reflect. No reason why you should be known. We take all precautions. But still. Europe is a tinderbox. The highest tension; mutual suspicion. That's before you even start on what the Germans are doing in Turkey, and what the Russians are doing in Persia. Everyone looking at everyone else. Particularly in the rougher parts, where you've tended to—'

'They – this German said I was working for a particular department. The – something... General-Co-'

'Yes, it's a bit of muddle here. Different departments. New outfits starting up. The Admiralty, the War Office; everyone's getting their own little intelligencing shop and no one's talking to anyone else. Quite properly but, well, the Sub-Committee sometimes... Look: quite understand if, on reflection, you feel...'

A knock, and a head thrust into the room. 'Ah, Ballentyne, isn't it?' Ballentyne couldn't quite make out the face; the bearing and voice seemed old. 'Good man. Tylor, at Oxford, speaks very highly of you.'

Ballentyne had half risen. 'He's a great man, truly.' The sun was in his eyes. 'I'm not sure our anthropology and ethnography are much use to your espionage; European politics—'

'On the contrary, Mr Ballentyne. European politics is all anthropology. I'm not interested in political philosophers and diplomatic flim-flam. You're a man who thinks about human animals. About tribes. And that will serve you in Paris and Vienna and Berlin, at least as well as in your Albanian hamlets. Don't let the frock-coats and feathers fool you, Mr Ballentyne. Modern Europe is essentially primitive.'

In the shadows that attended on the Kaiser, the honoured visitor settled himself in a chair and began to investigate the cigarette box in front of him. 'Now, Colonel: you're a soldier as well as a chief of espionage. What – in discretion, of course – can you tell me of your dispositions?' A finger still hovering, he looked up. *Come now: a little Prussian boastfulness...* 'How is our battlefield?' A pout, and he closed the cigarette box untouched.

Nicolai sat stiff-backed across the desk. He looked up over his shoulder to a large map of Europe, and with an extended palm began to divide the Continent. 'As you will I'm sure know, Herr Krug' – a glance at the visitor, who gave a little smile – 'St Petersburg: good; Constantinople: excellent, the spies are thieves and of little consequence, but we are well-placed in the Turkish government and this more than compensates; Rome: not bad, would be better if I knew to count them for ally or enemy' – another little smile from the visitor; *and that, my dear Colonel, is why you do not understand espionage* – 'Paris: not as good as I would wish; London: excellent.' The palm came down and settled flat on the desk. 'We have an excellent network in Britain.' He looked up. 'And you will have your own private sources there, Herr Krug.'

'Together, a most potent force.' He leaned forwards a fraction. 'Which must be protected.'

'The British are nowhere.'

'Distracted, Colonel. I told you.' He pulled a cigarette case from inside his coat. 'They are more worried by Dublin and Calcutta than they are by Europe.'

'And old-fashioned. An empire that has passed its time.'

'Yes.' A connoisseur's breath, a whimsy of memory. 'They used Latin for secret communication in southern Africa. Charming! Quite charming.' A slender, dark cigarette tapped precisely against the case twice. 'Now they are making new efforts; new bureaux, with new men.'

'Indeed. We watch them coming off the boats at Calais and Hamburg.' The visitor smiled; *why Colonel, that was almost witty.* Nicolai's gloved palm floated over the desk a moment, then slapped softly down. 'We will gather them when we choose.'

'Yes. Yes, I suspect that we will.' The cigarette glowed and sagged between two straight fingers. 'And yet. And yet I think you have never heard, Colonel, of the Comptroller-General for Scrutiny and Survey.'

<hr />

British Intelligence adrift. The threats unseen and everywhere. One threat – the threat – somewhere.

When the four had gone, their faces lingered in the old man's mind. Ronald Ballentyne: straight and perplexed. James Cade: confident, calculating. David Duval, watched from a window: challenging and sure, until he thought there was no one watching. Flora Hathaway – Flora Hathaway...

And then they faded, stepped back to the corners of the office, silent observers. The old man looked down at the desktop, at the cloud of papers. In them, he glimpsed a shape, the shape he had been trying to define for more than a decade.

He is one of three men.

He is the Spider.

The Web

B urim Balaj was not a lucky man.

    He felt this himself. And he knew that the village felt it.

It happens that every village has one or two families – one or two men – who are simply... unlucky.

It was surely not his fault.

It was probably his father's fault. His father had been a big man physically – bigger than either of his sons – and he should have made more of a success of himself. Then he would have left his sons a more fitting inheritance. But he had been rather stupid, and quick to anger. This made other villagers reluctant to do business with him. His mother had been lovely once – so his father had said. Now she was a shrew, always nagging Burim and his brother. Sick, wrinkled like an old quince, and criticizing.

The other villagers didn't like someone who was careful. Who asked questions before doing business. Not one of the handsome, smooth men.

He tried to get by, but it never seemed to work out. The other villagers said he was unlucky, him and his brother. Said they were cursed.

A man has to get by as best he can. Sometimes do things he wouldn't if he wasn't desperate. Sometimes life is a fight to survive. A little trade with other villages. An unlucky man can't afford to be choosy about his friends. If the Kelmendi want to do business, why not? And once, when he was visiting them, the terrifying foreigner. So quiet. Whispered threats and whispered promises. Everyone else in his village so friendly to their own foreigner, the Englishman. Why shouldn't Burim help the other foreigner, in the Kelmendi village? Get something in return for once. Just another stupid village skirmish. Only this time Burim knew what was happening. This time he came out on top.

But nothing really changed. Same life in the village. Same whispering faces. Same mother. The money didn't seem to stick.

Then, from nowhere, from out of the ground, the idea of marriage. Old Adem in the doorway, a nod to his mother, settling himself by the hearth, first time ever. And would Burim consider taking Besa? Not much of a family, no men left since her brother was killed. Not much money, and no one to speak for her. But for looks, now, surely a healthy fellow like Burim might be interested. Keep it all in the village, or no?

Burim had asked for time to think. Typical superior smile from the old man. But he really did need to think. To him, Besa always seemed... so haughty. Didn't want to think anything of him. Well, bottom rail on top now, maybe. Surely there'd be a bit of money left to come over with her. And... what might that body be like? He'd get to touch it. He'd have to. And with a woman supposed to look after him, maybe he'd have more chance to be the man he could be.

So Besa moved in, and brought one of the two cows with her as dowry, and the village had another wedding ceremony, and Burim danced when he had to and sat on the edge when he didn't, and wondered uneasily about his luck.

⊶⊷

Hidden in the thickest shadow of the deck, the light from the bridge spilling out above his head and illuminating the gangplank and the dockside, the passenger watched the bustle.

Now this, he thought, *is the proper way to start a civil war.*

He had to keep suppressing the urge for a cigarette.

No fooling around with the odd suitcase or mislabelled crate, a pound to a customs man and half a dozen pistols smuggled in. No, for one hour of one night, these people had arranged their own private dock and were bringing in a whole shipload. Sort of thing you could do in South America, but to do it here, in Western Europe! Not twenty miles from Belfast – he'd seen the lights over the water as they'd approached land.

His hand flexed, and he told himself it was because of the cold, and stuffed it into his pocket.

Another crate was carried down the gangplank to the reception committee. Like all the others, it was opened, the contents were methodically checked, and then they were loaded into a waiting car. A word of order, and the car sputtered away into the darkness, and another was waved into its place. The whole business as if they were unloading potatoes on a sunny afternoon, not bringing in an army's worth of rifles in the middle of the night.

Another crate, again the checking – *the Anglo-Saxon way to run a war* – and another car of trouble rattled out of sight. Over his shoulder, from the other side of the ship, he could hear the clank of the crane as it lowered more rifles into a waiting motorboat, to be transported farther down the Irish coast. The clank was muted; they'd thought to grease the chain.

He'd once been down a coal-mine in Saxony – a small problem of labour activism – and the image of the men beneath the earth had stuck with him. He saw it again now, in these earnest men bent over their work, lantern-lit faces shining orange in the blackness.

And these were the ones called loyalists. *Wonderfully confused, the British Empire.*

The next car had stopped, engine still thumping and shaking. The driver got out to watch the proceedings. 'All aboard the Tiger's Bay omnibus,' he called cheerfully. 'No standing on top.'

The passenger stiffened.

A typical British witticism; swallowed chuckles from the dockside. The one thing he'd not been able to practise, and he'd have to work to adopt the habit again.

He pulled himself out of the shadow as the next crate approached the gangway, made as if to steady the rearward bearer, and then followed down to the dockside.

At the bottom – *British soil* – he glanced at the crate, at the reception committee, and then back towards the boat, all in apparent satisfaction, then moved over to the driver so he was out of the way.

'Just think what we could do if we went straight,' he said. The English accent felt awkward in his mouth, and he tried to swallow the self-consciousness while remembering the precise phrase.

The driver glanced towards him, then quickly away. 'Next week, ladies' fashions.'

'Hah. Good opportunities for promising young men.'

The driver half turned, again avoiding his eyes, and nodded slightly.

The passenger stepped away, walked around the car, and got into the passenger seat. Behind the car, the line of waiting headlamps stretched up the slope into the night.

+≈≈+

Over mountain passes that carried no more than man or goat, a question travelled the Balkan highlands; along field edges; across rivers; in the frowsty council rooms of villages; creeping through alleys into the fringes of the towns.

A question; and a name: Ronald Ballentyne.

+≈≈+

James Cade came out of the shadow of the steamer awning and a world of fantasy blazed over him.

Jimmy Baba and the forty thieves.

More people than he'd ever seen, more movement, more colour, more life. Constantinople waterfront was an explosion of activity, ten thousand people – it seemed like ten thousand – in sharp suits and exotic uniforms and mostly in bright dirty rags – pantomime costumes, big trousers, strange slippers, reds and yellows and a dozen other colours never worn in western Europe – seething around each other, everyone waving something or carrying something or... or trading something. Fruit, fish, cloth, chickens, goats, carpets, crates of every size. Gangs of men swarmed onto ships and seemed to strip them of their cargoes in seconds, maggots on a corpse, carrying away their prizes to join the mob on the quayside. The noise came at him like a wall, a madness of shouting as if every one of the ten thousand were trying to catch his attention. Beyond, above, the old city rose in waves to the palace, the skyline pricked with the towers of the mosques. It was mediaeval; it was fantastical.

James Cade found himself in the greatest marketplace on earth and, amid the warmth and the luxurious smells and the waterfall of shrill noise, he felt his heart quickening.

On the quayside, a man squeezing through between a uniform and an enormous sack apparently with legs of its own, an anxious face scanning those coming down the gangway. Eventually he focused on Cade, as if unable to find anything better. 'Mr James Cade?' Cade accepted the offer. 'Burley. With the embassy. Welcome. I'll get your stuff sent on.'

'Do you always—' but the man was off up the gangway; thirty seconds later he was back again, hurrying and hotter. 'Do you always meet businessmen off the boat?'

Burley was looking into the mayhem. 'The carriage—' They were buffeted backwards by a surge of porters, and regathered. 'Not always. Got a message. Get you settled.' This shouted over his shoulder as he pushed into the mob. They weaved a clumsy path, Cade following Burley's suit as it disappeared and reappeared through the shoving of backs and bags and creamy faces. Once he saw another kind of uniform – grey, less embellished than others – and realized it must be German.

A clearing, a moment's breath, Burley checking and pointing a change of course; a jostle at his shoulder and a basket in his face and Cade stepped back and looked in time to catch an apricot as it fell. The man beneath the basket adjusted it on his head with one hand and reached for the rogue apricot with the other and, on a whim, Cade decided he wanted it. The colour shone against his suit and the flesh spoke of moisture and life. He grinned at the man, trying to signal that he wanted it; reached for his waistcoat pocket – 'Burley!' – no useful coin, of course. 'Burley! Ask him' – Burley was back now, worried and wary – 'ask him where he gets them, can you?' Burley more worried, floundering. 'Well, give me a – no, look: here you go, laddie. All right?' And he thrust a sixpence into the clutching hand. The basket man looked at it, glanced suspiciously at Cade, then held the coin up to his eye as if wanting to confirm that it was a fair likeness of King George. Then he grinned back, and turned away into the crowd, the swaying basket marking his wake long after he had been swallowed up.

SECRET M.O.5

VOLUNTEER MANOEUVRES, BELFAST DISTRICT, 24TH-25TH APRIL 1914 '

(A statement on activities by one familiar with the context and many of those involved. See also MO5/14/IRE/27 and MO5/14/IRE/28.)

As was widely reported, the Command of the Ulster Volunteer Force ordered an exercise for the night of 24th-25th April in the Belfast area. A range of routine manoeuvres was practised: inspections, motor vehicle movements, sentry-points etcetera. These activities incorporated the arrival of supplies for the Volunteers by ship, including weapons. Part of the drill did indeed involve landing, checking and transporting the weapons under close discipline.

The proceedings were widely reported in local and national papers, reflecting the public and civic spirit behind many of these activities.

The volume of weapons, predominantly rifles, was not small, so the logistical challenge was significant. In military terms they are second-order at best, being old Mannlichers and Mausers and inferior Italian designs. But it is hoped that it stands as a worthy demonstration of the strength of feeling against any interference to the Union between this island and the rest of the Kingdom.

The Command of the U.V.F, with the backing of the Unionist Council, declared themselves pleased with the performance of their personnel, who shall be ready to play their part in the defence of the established order in the event of any disturbances.

[PUBLIC RECORDS OFFICE, CO 904]

A uniform like a Leven Street commissionaire – *and what kind of cloth do you call that?* – a minute and exquisite moustache, and a woolly fez to top it all off.

Cade insisted that the official sit. The official refused. Cade repeated the offer. Again the refusal, and for a moment he wondered if there was indeed some point of protocol or custom he was missing. Surely the host shouldn't sit first. Or was the fellow worried the cloth in his trouser-seat wouldn't take the strain? He tried a third time, lowering himself towards his own chair, and this time the man sat.

So far so good.

Such a hat he definitely wanted for himself. The rest: at least a photo to show the lads at the Leith custom house. Show them what they were missing.

The official sat upright, and looked around the office. It was Cade's first acquisition. Burley at the embassy had spoken vaguely of helping him to find a house, and horses, and servants, and then in a week or two perhaps an office. Cade had insisted on finding the office that afternoon. After the fraught experience of one joint viewing with the Scotsman, Burley had excused himself and left behind one of the embassy servants. Cade was shown a series of wildly inappropriate places, presumably as the man worked through his property-renting relatives, until Cade took him by the shoulder, gave him a gold coin, and explained with simple words and simpler miming that one more cousin would lead to a punch on the nose. He showed a second coin, and described what he wanted.

The office overlooked the docks. Big windows that let in the light and the noise and the smell of spices and animals and salt and men; the main room for himself, and two smaller rooms that he'd no doubt find a use for; plaster and dark wood throughout. The austerity of the style was good for his discipline; standing with his hands spread on the window sill each morning gazing out across the seething waterway to Asia was good for his spirit.

Cade's second acquisition was Ali. Ali had turned up on the steps to the office within minutes of Cade moving in, alerted by some telegraph of the streets. Surname unknown, exact age unknown but somewhere in his teens, he had stood himself in the doorway and refused to budge. Cade had bought him a pair of shoes, which Ali never wore, and taken him on as doorman and general hanger-on, which function he had clearly been going to perform anyway.

Ali brought coffee. The uniformed official smiled, revealing a battleground of a mouth. Cade had restrained himself from asking anything until the coffee had come, and it was followed by fully ten minutes of pleasantry.

Eventually the man placed the coffee cup, between fingers and thumbs, on the desk in front of him, and looked up sombrely. 'Mr James Cade, I am required by law – please excuse these most important procedures – to take your documentation for verification.'

'You mean – what, my passport? That's already been checked.'

'Your documentation.'

'Yes – and I'm delighted to help, old son – but what documentation?'

The official didn't really know, and Cade didn't really have anything meaningful to offer him. In the end he remembered the greasy receipt he'd been given for the first three months' rent on the office and, seeing it lying on the desk, a letter signed by the ambassador describing the embassy's limited responsibility for Cade as a British subject resident in Constantinople. The official saw another paper underneath, and glanced at it hopefully, so Cade gave him the list of forthcoming services in the British church. The cumulative effect was so positive on the fellow that, casting around, Cade threw in the Army & Navy catalogue and a letter from his golf club that had somehow got caught up in his papers when he left.

Delighted, the official put them all in a leather wallet. Then he sat back down, and beamed.

Cade eyed him. 'Look, old lad, I'm delighted to have met you. But I probably shouldn't be keeping you from your duties.'

'Not at all, Mr Cade. I am looking forward to long and mutually rewarding acquaintance.' And he beamed some more.

Oh, aye. That's how we dance here, is it? He tried to look businesslike. *Bad as the Clydebank constable.* 'My friend, I'd be delighted to... begin a...

co-operative relationship with you. But the fact is that until I get to the, er...' He'd nothing against a bit of grease on the wheels, once he knew the right wheels, but he really didn't have any spare cash to hand.

In the end he found a packet of shortbread in a half-unpacked bag, and the man went away holding it, uncertain but mollified.

The papers came back the following morning. They had each – including the copy of the Army & Navy catalogue and the letter from the Bruntsfield Links Golfing Society – been stamped with an elaborate swirling shape, which he took to be some Ottoman mark, and a seal showing an eagle – splayed and crowned – which definitely was not.

+>==<+

MOST SECRET

FACTORS PERTINENT TO THE BELFAST GUN-RUNNING: AN
APPRECIATION

Sir, the following collation of reports and deductions
is in answer to your request, and tends I would suggest to
support the concerns you expressed. While trying to avoid
subjective remarks about the reporting from other (Military)
departments, the following of necessity draws attention to
differences of fact or interpretation.

1. The affair was widely reported in the press, as far back
as when the weapons were being loaded on board ship. The
two reports from Military Operations sources emphasize
the informality and amateurishness of the business,
compounding the impression of an escapade that was bold
and eccentric but essentially harmless. In this context
it is worth rehearsing the complexity and skill of the
arrangements, and the elements of deception that were
required to bring off the operation. The original shipment
as it was loaded in Denmark was substantial in size as well
as cost. (The very roughest estimate suggests a weight not

less than 150 tons.) The original vessel was obliged to flee the Danish authorities to make open sea. Off Ireland, the shipment was transferred wholesale to a second vessel, purchased for the purpose. This second vessel was disguised with a new name while en route. A third vessel was acquired and directed into Belfast harbour with deliberately erratic and suspicious movements, functioning successfully as a decoy from the real landing occurring at Larne farther up the coast. Meanwhile a large number of personnel was deployed and co-ordinated to provide both a security perimeter or cordon around the landing and to transport the rifles. Some may present it as an idiosyncratic 'show' by enthusiasts. It was also what amounts to a substantial military operation, involving the choreographed movements of personnel, motor vehicles and maritime vessels, a high degree of logistical and organizational skill, and a careful and deliberate campaign of deception.

2. As has been reported on Military channels, there were at least three different makes of rifle in the shipment, none of them the most modern type, and this materially weakens the capability and flexibility of the shipment. Yet more than twenty thousand rifles of any vintage, and several millions of rounds of ammunition, must be reckoned mischief enough, and it is surely specious to try to diminish the severity of the affair on this ground.

3. It is not within the purview of this appreciation to comment on the perception that the shipment, while illegal, was essentially benign because designed only to increase the defensive capacities of elements whose avowed aim is the preservation of the current constitutional settlement as it pertains in Ireland. It must though be observed that, however loyal the intention and however passive the action, it will serve significantly to inflame sensitivities in

this already volatile place, particularly among the Irish nationalist 'Volunteers'. The risk of armed unrest in this corner of the Kingdom is sensibly greater than before the shipment and greater than if it had never happened.

4. Several factors suggest that the sophisticated organization behind the operation involved powers outwith Ulster, specifically German official elements and most probably related intelligence actors:

i. That the weapons were purchased and originated in Hamburg is not conclusive of official complicity, but the involvement of the dealer Benjamin 'Benny' SPIRO comes near so being. He is routinely used as a factor or cover by German government departments. (You may also remember his role as agent for KRUG in the Mexican machine-gun scandal last year.) It is very unlikely that he would contemplate so substantial and so political a trade without the acquiescence of his patrons in Berlin;

ii. The complexity of the arrangements on land is arguably within the capability of the 'Ulster Unionist Council' and their U.V.F.. We have indeed tracked and reported the activities of CRAWFORD and ADAIR in this direction. The shipment itself is consistent with our estimates of their financial resources. However, the sophistication and scope of the maritime element is on or beyond the margins of the capability that we would have expected of the U.U.C./U.V.F. We are still unable to identify the HELLER named as one of the parties to the transfer of ownership of the second vessel in 1912 and then earlier this year;

iii. A Danish source reports that when the weapons were loaded aboard ship in Langeland, a passenger joined too. No link may be confirmed, but it is possible that this is connected to and corroborates the suggestion that an unknown passenger disembarked with the rifles at Larne;

iv. That the destabilization resultant from the affair
    suits German interests does not logically imply German
    official complicity. Yet it is consistent with it.

                                                    6th May, 1914

                                                    [SS I/17/35]

⊢⊣

A couple of weeks after his arrival in Constantinople, Cade discovered
a warehouse packed with silk on the Asian side of the Bosphorus,
the residue of a merchant who'd died leaving some spectacular debts,
pressing creditors, a tribe of daughters and a rather panicked younger
brother. He bought the whole stock for cash, and sent a telegram home
re. the opportunities for a combination of wholesale brokering and
direct retail.

So he was feeling pretty spruce when he arrived in the evening at the
British ambassador's residence – an enormous Italian-looking thing. The
ambassador was an ideal: tall, in good enough shape at fifty-odd to make
the splendid blue tail-coat look elegant rather than silly, monocled, and
topped off by a bicorne hat and feathers. Courtesies; the ambassador shook
hands, held the glance politely, then turned to his next guest.

Then back. 'Cade... You're the businessman, I think.'

'I am, Sir Louis.' A flicker of doubt.

'A little more trade and a little less diplomacy, and we'd all be better
off, I fancy.' Cade felt uncomfortable for the first time, as if he were
somehow betraying both his roots and the task that had brought him
here. 'Edinburgh, I think.' Cade nodded. 'Seem to remember my father
mentioning your family once. Something to do with his consultations on
tariffs. Your father, perhaps, or grandfather.'

Cade & Cade part of the establishment at last. 'The old man's always
pretty free with his opinions on tariffs, sir.' *But he never thought his name
would be heard from an eye-glass and feathers.* Now Cade escaped.

He'd felt rather pompous putting on his own tail-coat and the white
bow tie – at home rarely more than an annual bit of pantomime for some

guild dinner or other – but as he looked out across the expanse of the salon he found himself about the plainest man in the room.

'Try the sherbet punch.' Burley, the Embassy man, taking a drink from a roaming waiter and pushing it into Cade's hand. 'Come along; I'll get you started.'

The room was a fancy dress parade: an *Arabian Nights* fantasy of Asian get-up – silks and brocades in hats and scarves and sashes and even jackets or pantaloons – mixed with every kind of uniform, from relatively restrained get-ups like the ambassador's to arrangements that wouldn't have looked out of place on a pirate captain.

He was introduced to a Frenchman – joke from Burley about the Auld Alliance before he disappeared again – and Cade managed two lines of small talk then asked about French interests in Constantinople. 'Oh, we have none,' Monsieur Andrassy replied. 'But everyone else is here pursuing this interest or that interest, and so we feel we must be here so that we do not miss out.'

'Everyone I speak to goes on about how weak the Ottoman Empire is. Always good stuff going cheap when a business goes bust.'

Then there was one of the ubiquitous Germans, and Cade was wary. But Herr Hessler, large and over-pink and straining his old-fashioned tail-coat at every seam, was an archaeologist and ignorant – insensitive, indeed – on all aspects of diplomacy, and they had a cheerful few minutes on the cultural influences competing within the empire.

And then there was a Russian, demanding to know what Cade as an Englishman knew of English intentions regarding Russia's rightful claim on the straits dominated by Constantinople. Cade explained that since he was neither English nor a diplomat and knew nothing of what the man was talking about, damn all was the answer. The Russian recoiled, but then he was back on the offensive, goatee beard and bad breath thrust up into Cade's face, more unhappy than before: a Scotsman who claimed not to know what was planned for the straits was even more sinister than an Englishman who did. Was Mr Cade aware of the geography of Russia? Was Mr Cade aware of Russia's tolerance, her sacrifices for peace, during a series of European crises over the last decade? Did he know the proportion of Russia's exports and imports that went through the straits, and how many billions of roubles per month had been lost when Turkey had unilaterally closed the straits in 1912?

Cade could honestly answer 'no' to all of these. But, feeling that he didn't know enough about the possibilities arising from Russian traffic through Constantinople, he tried to make a conversation out of it. The Russian wasn't having it: beyond a couple of statistics he understood little about trade. Eventually Cade took advantage of him choking on his own excitement, and the providential arrival of a waiter with more sherbet punch, to step away.

The uniforms and costumes, for all their extravagance, tended to make the men more similar rather than less. They all seemed constricted, and somehow inadequate against the pretensions of their outfits. The women, on the other hand... all shapes and sizes were on show, monstrous bloated wives and pretty petite daughters, and a spectrum of complexions. All the subtleties of shading from Europe and the Near East were here, harmonized or accentuated with their silks and lace, and to James Cade it all screamed of market.

Near him now: a man he'd been introduced to before... Visited before. Ministry of Finance. Deputy something-or-other. Name something like Otto-... Otman. Osman. Surname rhymed with Caesar. The number two chap, the man who had some idea what he was talking about and kept the place ticking over and tried to prevent the number one chap from doing anything too stupid.

Such had been Cade's deduction, anyway. The same phenomenon in public institutions the world over. Nothing said by the fellow himself. Merely polite and rather worried observations about the effect of European tensions on price stability, the unreliability of supply routes through the Balkans, and the complexity of administration given the strong German presence.

'Why, it's Mr Cade, I think.'

Had he mentioned a wife? Children?

A careful, contained chap.

'Mr Riza, isn't it? A pleasure to see you.' Polite smiles. 'Glad to see a friendly face. How's your son?'

'Thank you, Mr Cade.' This smile was genuine. 'He's doing well enough.

Fit and strong. Needs to concentrate on his mathematics more.'

'Quite right, sir. Trains the brain, maths. Discipline.'

'I thought that, for English gentlemen' – Cade suppressed the wince – 'your Latin and Greek came first.'

'Oh, I did my share. My mother wouldn't let me off. But my old father, Mr Riza, he's a businessman through and through. Bleeds in pounds sterling. He bred me to numbers; had me doing accounts and interest before I could recite any of my Herodotus.' The Turk nodded pleasantly, and captured new drinks for them both. 'But tell me: your son – will he follow you into the ministry or, I don't know... politics, or the army?'

Osman Riza considered this soberly. 'It has always been our tradition, Mr Cade – over centuries – that the most worthy and rewarding career is in public administration. It has enabled the humblest men to rise to the greatest power through ability alone. Now, I'm afraid...' – he shook his head slightly – 'some of these certainties are changing.'

'Fellows on the make? Wanting short cuts to success?'

'As you have surely been warned, there are no short cuts in the empire's administration.' His little moustache wrinkled at the humour, and Cade tried to produce a smile of comparable restraint. 'But since the instability of a few years ago, our politics is a good deal more boisterous and it infests the administration more extensively.'

'Must make life complicated for a professional like you.'

'I am a servant of the regime, Mr Cade. I do my duty as well as I may. But Europe – your government and others like it – sees us as enfeebled, and obsolescent. Like greedy relatives – pardon me – around a dying man, they come with advice and hectoring and trying to get us to sign papers which we but half understand.'

'Perhaps that explains – I mean, I'm sure we're all as bad as each other – but I've seen a surprising number of German uniforms around the city.'

Again the smile, grave and delicate. 'The Germans are here to train our army, Mr Cade, as the British have been here to train our navy.' He settled his glass on an adjacent table. 'But...' – the eyes flicked down, and up again – 'the style is rather different.'

'Ah, Cade.' Burley out of nowhere, touching his elbow. 'Just the chap. Would you excuse us?' They were duly excused with a half bow, and

Burley guided him away. Cade looked over his shoulder as he went, catching Osman Riza's prolonged glance. 'Didn't want you trapped in some tiresome Turkish pontificating. Look, here's another sherbet for you.' Burley introduced him to a hearty gaggle of three British residents whom Cade knew for truly tiresome. Cricket. Corruption. The price and unreliability of servants. He escaped.

Across the room, two pairs of eyes watching James Cade. 'Him, do you see?' A nod. 'Smiling to the waiter. With the strong jaw and chest.' A firmer nod. 'Him.'

Cade stepped out of the pantomime reception room and looked over the garden, an acre or more of trees and winding paths. The evening was warm, lanterns had been arranged among the paths, and the air smelled of fruit – an oasis of citrus amid the city's reek. He was drawn out into it.

As he reached the bottom step and crunched into gravel, a man turned and saw him.

'Good evening, sir.' A little bow. There was a woman with him. 'We met, I think. At the bank. I am Varujan.' Cade reintroduced himself. With one poised palm Varujan indicated the woman beside him. 'Please allow me to introduce my sister, Mrs Charkassian. Ani, this is Mr James Cade, a businessman lately come to Constantinople.'

Not his wife, then; Cade took a second look. She was a beauty, right enough. She offered her hand, and he took it, contriving the little head-nod that he was developing in lieu of a proper bow. 'Ma'am.' She dropped her eyes.

The large, dark, almond eyes under a high forehead; firm jaw and full lips. *A Lauriston lad could go far astray here.* Her eyes had come up again and she was holding the glance, actually looking at him.

He smiled, and pulled his focus round to the man. 'We weren't properly introduced at the bank, Mr Varujan. You are... Turkish, presumably?'

Varujan's lips twitched. 'Armenian, Mr Cade. My family is Armenian.'

'Oh, you must excuse me. I do apologize; haven't got the hang of these—'

'Not at all.' A smile was managed. 'The price of the benefits of being part of the Ottoman Empire. We are a subject people, and must accept it.' He raised a gaunt finger. 'While remembering our own culture and identity.'

A voice at his shoulder and he turned away, and Cade was left with the woman.

'And your husband?' he said, partly as a reminder to himself. 'Mr Charkassian works...?'

'He is dead.' It was said soft.

'Oh, forgive me.'

'How could you have known?' She was still watching him squarely. A glance to the side, a demure smile, and her voice dropped. 'Please excuse my brother's... heat. He is most passionate on the subject of our identity.'

'Not at all. Myself, I'm a Scottish subject of the British Empire. And everyone here calls me English. I sympathize completely.'

Her lips opened slightly, apparently struck by the comparison. Her eyes wandered in thought a moment. 'It is becoming the defining question of our city, and all of the empires should heed it. Of our city, of our world, and of our time.' She looked at Cade again. 'Who one is, and who one is not.'

+⇒══⇐+

Perhaps two hours after Rheims the train had slowed, and then clanked and hissed to a stop. Down to one side, dawdling around islets, the Moselle was overtaking them. Looking out of the window at an angle, along the train, Flora Hathaway could see the grey suggestion of a town ahead. Metz, would it be? The Baedeker would have it, but she wanted to see if she'd remember it first.

The landscape surged in waves around the train, long slopes stretched with vines and sudden crests, thickly wooded. This was one of the great borderlands of the world. The French and Germans had been ebbing and flowing back and forth through these valleys since... since before Germany and France had existed. Metz, and the Lorraine around it – Lotharingia, of course; she tried to remember the mediaeval politics – were German now; for the forty years since the last war, and for the time being.

From along the corridor, the rumble and slam of the compartment doors being slid open.

A strange habit. Britain was usually busy with her colonial aggressions instead. When had we last...? The Crimea, of course; which had been a madness of geo-political logic, barely explicable even while it was being fought. Before that Napoleon.

The rumble and slam, now from the adjacent compartment.

We liked to steer clear of the Continent's troubles, didn't we? Much easier to send an over-ambitious young woman, craving... something. Visions of her previous visit: a magnificent bookcase; carved wood; tea and cheese that looked familiar but tasted different; handsome courteous young men; refreshingly serious girls; an extraordinary cake, which her host's child refused to touch.

The door rumbled and slammed open, and she looked up into the face of a policeman. *"Ten tag. Papiere bitte.'* He saw that the compartment was all female and saluted, forefinger to cap. The strange caps, of course, with the crushed peak. She unfolded the sheet of paper and handed it up.

The little girl opposite was staring up at the policeman. Eventually she spun back to her mother. *'Mutti, was macht er?'*

'He's a policeman, dearest. We're back in Germany now. He is keeping us safe.' The girl spun back to reconsider the policeman in this light, and Hathaway replayed the German to herself, noting the accusative, remembering the idioms.

The policeman was methodically copying details from her passport sheet into a little book. *He is keeping you safe from me.*

The sheet was passed back to her, a nod from the policeman and her over-pale photograph thrust towards its original. A glance at the mother's papers, another salute and he was gone, rumble and slam.

His presence lingered between them. After a moment, the mother said 'He is... very formal, I think.' Pretty woman; about her own age.

'Oh. Very – efficient. Highly impressive.' A moment of private pleasure at remembering the adjectives. She wished she could tell what part of Germany the woman's accent represented.

The mother and daughter were her only companions in the compartment. Somewhere around Rheims she'd had a stilted conversation with the child. Then the mother had commented on her copy of Schiller, lying on top of the Baedeker and getting equally little attention. A souvenir of her first visit, carried this time in theory as a refresher for her language, in practice as some kind of memento of self. Her German wasn't good enough for

Schiller at the best of times, and he was damned tedious going even when she could make him out.

'You have visited your brother, I think you said.'

'Yes. In Paris; he works in the German Embassy.'

'He is a diplomat?'

'No – no, he is a soldier.' There was discomfort in the answer. Was she not supposed to say? It could hardly be a secret.

'Has he a very smart uniform? Such an impressive life, I'm sure.'

'Oh yes! We are very proud, yes.'

'That's nice. We must hope that... that there is no fighting.'

Shock, the suspicion that Hathaway was privy to some terrible secret of war. 'Oh no! No, we must hope. Karl is not...' She looked to where the policeman had been. 'That is not who we are. Who he is.'

Poor girl; trapped on one of mankind's frontiers.

'Your husband could not be with you?'

'His work.' A shrug. 'And sometimes, I think: husbands and brothers, they are not always the best friends, perhaps.' Hathaway smiled, and tried to recapture an occasion when Ralph and Tim had been together. 'You – have you family?'

'Parents. One brother.'

'Not a husband yet?'

'No.' Matter-of-fact smile, well worn. 'No; it was planned. But he died.'

'Oh!' An instinctive glance at her daughter, cheerfully occupied with one of the curtains. 'I am very sorry.'

The shrug, likewise well worn. 'Who knows? The paths of life. Is Karl happy in Paris?'

'Yes. Yes, really. So beautiful a city; we have nothing to compare.' She hesitated, and Hathaway stopped herself interrupting. 'I think Karl is... is uncomfortable. He tries to be gay, but there are always suspicions and tensions with the French people. And his superiors. Always talk of war. "When the war comes." Like that.'

'Oh, but everyone talks like that, I'm sure. In London, too. Perhaps the French Embassy in Berlin is the same.'

The young woman looked at her sadly. 'But always... with us...'

'You think that they want a war, these superiors of Karl?'

'No.' A shrug. 'No, I'm sure...' She retreated into the seat.

Hathaway nodded, tried a sympathetic smile. Then she looked out onto the river and the trees. *Is this what I have come for?* Family anxieties and public speculations. Everyone really did talk like that. *Am I supposed to report on such things? 'Belligerent attitudes in the German Embassy in Paris'?* The speculations of worried humans.

The confidences of women. *Which I do not, anyway, wish to share.*

The clanking of machinery, the quickening drumbeat of the steam as the train began to move and gather momentum, and they were across the border and into Germany proper.

—◆—

If Cade had had one sherbet punch fewer, he might have been able to avoid the incident, or have reacted less impetuously.

After the reception: as he strolled down one of the cobbled streets towards his house, jacket slung over his shoulder, the warmth in head and spirit had him gazing around at the lanterns and the glistening cobbles and the beautiful wooden verandas and the decay, and not at the shadows and how they moved.

A voice hissing at his elbow, English with an accent: 'Into the alley, now!' And a hand coming towards him and a knife, forcing him to the side of the street and a black opening.

Affront and economy and the vague calculation that an alley could be even worse than the street and Cade's jacket came down smothering and deflecting the knife and he lashed out with his other hand, and sent the attacker staggering back. He was shaping for a proper punch when his collar was grabbed and he was wrenched backwards, feet scrabbling for purchase on the stones and stumbling as the alley swallowed him. The stumble surprised the man at his collar too, and Cade used the momentum to push him off, and he pulled himself up and set himself for the brawl, then his head was stunned and he collapsed.

Dimly, a roaring and throbbing instead of his head and, somewhere far away, hands scuffling through his jacket.

Then alone, a broken animal lying in the mud of an alley, on the farthest edge of the Continent from his home, unhuman and utterly abandoned.

He lurched to his feet, steadied himself against the wall, nauseous and slumped. Then staggering into the street, weaving home, hammering on the door and the steward Abdullah's face shocked and being helped up the stairs and collapsing onto his bed. The sheets were cool. Moisture against his head, where he'd been hit, and he brushed Abdullah away and, clutching like a trophy the watch that still hung from his waistcoat, he slept.

Cade woke to a dockyard hammering away in his head. He ate as much as he could keep down, some vestige of maternal wisdom to rebuild his strength, and headed for the office where he planned to prove a point to the day by turning up, and then sleep as much as he could. But Abdullah had been urging him to go to the police, and Ali at the office took one look at the bruise purpling his head and babbled the same, and then somehow Burley had heard about the incident and come from the embassy to insist that he went to report it.

They were an hour on chairs in a humid waiting room, which improved neither Cade's head nor his willingness. Burley piped up intermittently with fretting at Cade's recklessness in being out in the streets at night, indistinctly affronted at the offence to British dignity and wondering if it was his fault. A series of increasingly elaborate uniforms led the way to a fat man in shirtsleeves and an enormous moustache who insisted on meticulousness and smiled enthusiastically at every detail, and eventually signed off his work with a slow flourish, before discovering that he was missing the necessary stamp and refusing to let them go before it was found. He gave his guests coffee while they waited.

The whole performance had taken nearly two hours, and Cade emerged into the warmth of the morning feeling groggy, faintly foolish and very cross. Burley was saying, 'Of course, the chances are it really was, after all, just a robbery.'

Cade stopped. 'As opposed to?'

Burley looked grave, and leaned in. 'Well, one doesn't like—'

'They took money – a few greasy banknotes – but they didn't take a watch worth twenty times as much.'

Burley licked his lips. 'Quite. It doesn't necessarily... But there have been

61

incidents – Sometimes just to check the papers a man's carrying, see if he is who he claims to be. Sometimes to rattle you. Push you a bit.'

'They may consider me pushed.'

Cade strode on into the babbling of the Constantinople morning.

Ali was sitting on the steps to the office, looking worried, when he arrived. Taking advantage of Cade's prolonged absence, an official and another man – a foreigner, Ali claimed, wiping his cheek to mime a paler face – had visited and, waving some legal paper, insisted on searching the office.

+≒≒+

The Sub-Committee of the Committee for Imperial Defence: The echoes of Whitehall from somewhere beyond the panelling – corridor footsteps and, faintly, a military band.

'You actually saw Hearne take the wicket?'

'Own eyes. These very ones. What a summer.'

'Ain't it? Reminds a fellow what life is for.'

'Quite. I must say, I find some of the talk about the Belfast incident a bit melodramatic.'

'A boatload of guns is melodramatic enough.'

'The threat has been overstated. The motives have been misrepresented. The activities of these loyalists stabilize the situation.'

'The reverse. They anger; they provoke.'

'You'll pardon me, gentlemen.' The old man, a voice from the margins. 'It will not serve us to reconstitute the divisions in Ulster around this table.' Uncomfortable shifting in chairs. 'Should we not ask who else benefits from our discord? Should we not seek the hand that puts weight on our fault-lines?'

'German spies again? Surely that's a bit melod—'

'M.O.5's information is clear; you've seen our assessment, gentl—'

'But if I could remind you of the information that Special Branch is starting to acquire on the Continent—'

'Within the limits, I trust, established by the Secret Intelligence Bureau.'

The old man observed the routine; discreetly, a sigh.

James Cade sat at his desk, back to the window, glaring at the photograph of his parents.

Neither the interests of Cade & Cade, nor the interests of the British government, had been well served in the preceding eighteen hours. And he had taken a knock on the head to be reminded of the point. He reviewed the events of the evening and morning. His ease, his unfocused drifting at the reception. The attack. The morning's tiresome bureaucracy. He couldn't, of course, be sure that there was any co-ordination behind the attack and the search of his office. And yet they had happened; all of it had happened, and he liked none of it. He felt naive, clumsy, taken advantage of, and very angry.

Ali sat on a stool in the corner of the room, watching Cade's grim face and the coffee going cold, and not daring to speak or move.

Cade took a long breath – wincing as his head moved involuntarily – and a decision. The old 'un: *if you fall, pick something up*. Five minutes later Ali was trotting through the city with two invitations in his hand. To Mr Osman Riza, of the Ministry of Finance, for lunch. To Mr Ruben Varujan, of the Imperial Ottoman Bank, for tea; also invited to the latter were a Dutch lady ethnographer – and of course Mr Varujan's sister, Mrs Ani Charkassian.

Paris was everything that David Duval had been led to expect, and had grown to dream of. A circus of grand buildings touched with unnecessary beauties, of cafés where it was expected that one might pass an hour or a day over a drink, of women who dressed as women first of all and would look a man in the eye.

There'd been a previous visit, of course, and that had been lovely in its way: romantic – erotic, even – and pleasantly sordid. The earthiness of a back-street pension, of a café room, and of a woman's body. But nicer to do the thing in style, and on someone else's account.

Like this now. Arranged meetings with a couple of big names tomorrow.

Decent hotel, all the facilities, deferential flunkies, good food, a view from his window that he wanted immediately to sketch and then couldn't sketch because he wanted immediately to enter it. And Angelique Lapierre downstairs in the bar – a woman, alone in a bar – waiting for a man who never came; which meant, of course, just the opposite.

David Duval tended not to unpack his suitcase – perhaps the next day's shirt on the back of a chair – because... well, because you never knew; bit of a hurry sometimes. So when he returned briefly to his room to spruce himself up for the evening out, he was quicker than he might have been to reach the unlikely conclusion that his belongings had been discreetly searched. He'd left his sketchbook on top of the clothes in the case – more an admonition to himself to work – distinctly remembered how one corner of it had been caught between the two halves of the case, and he'd left it so deliberately: fixity of resolution.

Except now it was lying in the middle – on top of the clothes, but away from the edge of the case. A chambermaid? Except the case was still in exactly the same spot, askew near the window.

David Duval tended to leave a few banknotes between the pages of a book at the bottom of his bag, because you never knew; bit of a jam sometimes. So when he found them still in place, he was quicker than he might have been to doubt that it had been a thief who had been interested in him.

+≡—≡+

Cade had insisted that Osman Riza choose the venue for their lunch. The Ministry of Finance man seemed nervous when Cade arrived. 'I took you at your word, Mr Cade, when you said you wanted a restaurant that was not too international.'

It was international. Cade's vision – some vague confection of Roman couches and Egyptian belly dancers and clouds of sweet smoke – faded before the reality of dark wood booths and white tablecloths and waiters in the penguin outfits he could have seen at the Old Waverley. 'I'm sure it's ideal.'

They were escorted to a booth; the layout of the restaurant, the high partitions, made it hard to see other diners. 'I admire your wish to sample the local style,' Riza said once they'd sat. 'This is most discreet, and the food is considered excellent.' There was the implication that this was what distinguished it from international haunts.

A glimpse of someone with pale skin and a goatee beard passing their booth, accompanied by a German officer. Riza gazed after them, looked down, and then up a little primly.

'Well,' he said after considering Cade's face a moment, 'you could hardly expect me to choose a pilav cart.' And they both smiled.

'Will you take some wine, Mr Riza? This is all at my invitation, of course.'

'I wouldn't dream of letting you pay, Mr Cade; a guest—'

'The invitation was on that basis. I don't invite myself.'

'But our first—'

'If you wish to honour me as a guest, and if you wish to honour me by making this the first of many pleasant meals together, you can best do so by letting me try to be as courteous as you. Now, will you take some wine?'

'What is your normal habit, Mr Cade?'

'I don't touch the stuff when I'm working. Glass of water; keep the nut clear. But today, you'd oblige me by sharing something.'

They settled on a glass of sherry each. Another glimmer of the oriental dream faded.

'I'm afraid, Mr Cade, that there is now nothing so Turkish as a Paris-style restaurant.'

'Long as it's not Glasgow-style. It would be grotesque of me to expect you all to sit around in turbans, smoking those long pipes.' A sip of sherry: immediate image of his Aunt Rhoda. 'Sophisticated city, this, of course. Cosmopolitan.'

Food was ordered, and arrived.

'Forgive me for asking, Mr Riza – inquisitive sort of fellow, and the old 'un told me never to talk shop over the entree – but you seem... well, sort of uncomfortable with Turkey's situation with the other powers. All these damned foreigners.' He jerked a thumb over his shoulder. 'Including me.'

Riza dabbed at his mouth with a napkin; its starched folds seemed more substantial than his face behind. 'Our great sin is thought to be pride. But it is hard to be proud, when we depend on foreigners for everything.' A smile. 'Few of us have had illusions about the reality of our empire, not for a hundred years or more, but...'

Cade smiled sympathy: 'Bad taste to remind you of it, eh?'

'If I might draw a distinction, Mr Cade. Please believe that it is not mere flattery. A man who comes here to trade is welcome.' A nod towards Cade. 'As you would have been these many centuries. A man who comes as a diplomat, to represent his country here, is likewise our guest and welcome. But it is hard to warm to those who come to tell us what to do.'

'Would they claim they were helping?'

'A physician who comes to cure may be welcomed; a physician who comes merely to diagnose, loudly, a complaint that you know well, and to criticize you for your style of living, is tiresome; a physician who comes to empty your cupboards while you ail is objectionable.'

'Is it so bad?'

'It is a question of motive. Does any of these people care for my people, or my country? The Germans send us generals to run our army, because they want to protect their own communications through south-eastern Europe to Mesopotamia. The Russians police our commerce and complain at our every action because we have set our tent across their front gate and they want the Bosphorus for themselves.' He looked down, discreetly; the voice dropped. 'The British tell us what to do with our navy, because it is a cheap way to swing the balance of power in the Mediterranean and protect their routes through Suez to the east.'

'And in the ministries? Telling you what to do?'

'Again, it is that foolish pride, Mr Cade. I – whose ancestors one thousand years ago tended a beacon for the world in medicine, in mathematics, in poetry – may I be excused an occasional unworthy irritation when I am lectured by a man whose ancestors knew nothing but animal furs and attacking the adjacent tribe with clubs?'

Cade laughed, and Osman smiled ruefully. 'I am in a weak position to argue, I know it. In less than ten years we have had three – four? – new systems of government; last year with rebellion and murder; constitutions come and go; we have been beaten in war by the tiny nations we used to treat as servants and slaves. Of course you all look at us and know we are obsolete; of course you want to protect your own interests – perhaps exploit the situation.'

'I hope that the British – some of the British – aren't all that—'

'Oh, Mr Cade' – the hand, little, moved towards his wrist – 'do not let me be unfair. Your government is protecting your interests like any other, but you at least are trying to protect and stabilize my country, and I believe that your great parliament believes truly in the moral rights of my people.'

'Well, I wouldn't over—'

'But... Well, this very week we are drafting the plan for our finances for the next year, like any good businessman' – shared smile – 'and I have to tolerate a most unattractive gentleman handing to me without a word a copy of my draft which he has annotated as if I were a schoolboy who has done inadequate homework. Really, Mr Cade, these people...' A little shake of the head, soured lips. 'An additional three hundred thousand tons of steel, that is what we are to import. What are we supposed to do: armour-plate every fig warehouse from here to Izmir?'

'I wish there was some way in which I could help...'

'But you may, Mr Cade! Forgive me if I sound a little emotional, but in this situation true friendship and true business dealing, without regard for national interest, are the best that Turkey can hope for.' A smile, faintly embarrassed. 'I have been doing some reading. I understand that the Scottish people have always been known for sound businessmen.'

'Oh, we've been beggars and brigands since the year dot. When the market dropped out of cattle-stealing, we found that honesty was all that was left to us. Plain-dealing; nothing more, nothing less.'

'Mr Cade, I will drink to that. Could we even tempt ourselves to a second glass of sherry, do you think?'

<hr />

Paris, 13. May 1914

Sir,

as requested, I today gave lunch and a little tour to M. David DUVAL.

My impressions: Duval is in his way a charming

man – to the ladies no doubt, but also to anyone with whom he conducts a conversation that interests him. A certain insolence – no doubt arising from the obvious psychological factors and from his cultivated persona of the rogue – was succeeded by sincerity, politeness, and even deference when we became immersed in the cultural matters. His interest, I must say, in architecture and art more widely is quite genuine. He has adequate knowledge, real perspicacity and the eye of an artist. I am less certain of his academic credentials; he seemed ignorant of some of the faculty of the South Kensington Schools.

You wished, in addition, to hear anything of his encounters or acquaintances here. Your concerns, if such they be, would appear not without some justification. One of my interlocutors had noted him yesterday evening in the company of Angelique Lapierre, also known as Angelique Ritter, Angelique Rizzi, L'Ange, or, I fear, whatever name a gentleman of means might desire. Her affiliations are as uncertain as her name, but she is known for a highly intelligent and resourceful woman habitually used by the Service de Surveillance du Territoire and the Deuxième Bureau. I may hazard no speculation as to whether your Duval might be target or associate.

Separately, M. Duval remarked that Edouard Massenard had sent his card round to arrange a meeting. You know Massenard and his links well enough, I think, for any comment or speculation from me to be unnecessary.

I hope that I may have been some service to you. Please allow me the opportunity to repeat my gratitude for your

*observations on the activities of certain officials in the
'goose's nest' and your insights on the incident in Kildare
County.*

   I remain, sir, yours faithfully,

   P.

(by hand, care of Embassy of Switzerland)

[SS G/1/893/7]

❧ ❧

Cade was feeling breezy as his tea party neared. Osman's titbit about the
steel was a little something to offer London, and there might be more to
come there. Cades didn't get kicked twice; he was getting back on top of
the market.

The sight of the tea table – prepared with all the proper fuss by Abdullah
the steward, who had acquired from somewhere an encyclopaedic concern
for the strictures of what he insisted on calling English decorum – sparked
flickers of nerves.

A moment's examination of his attitude to Mrs Ani Charkassian. Then
the sense of his mother at his shoulder again, a force for teatime decorum
more powerful than anything Abdullah could contemplate.

Like the lunch, it went as well as he could have hoped. Ruben Varujan
was clearly pleased to have had the invitation – 'this is your first "at-home",
we understand': a new sense for Cade of the way news travelled, of how a
man might be watched – and relaxed into pomposity about the history of
his people. This enthralled the Dutch lady ethnographer, who overlooked
what Cade suspected was the occasional folk myth masquerading as fact
in her delight at having the chance to talk to a real Armenian.

This left his equally real sister to Cade.

Ani Charkassian had on a long frock, tight-bodiced, and full in the
skirt. Cade, mostly ignorant of such things, guessed it more formal than
would have been usual, or perhaps older in style; but then Varujan was

affecting a large blue cravat and he himself a rather natty waistcoat. She was careful, and watchful; mostly she was careful and watchful of James Cade. Her brother's flow of insight and passion – 'it is of course acknowledged, dear lady, that Nuh himself, Noah, was essentially Armenian, and by "essentially" I mean also and deliberately in his essence' – allowed her to slip fondly into the background of conversation, where her host was waiting. Occasional glances of shared amusement at the main conversation; attentivenesses of manners. She treated the tea – the institution, and its corporeal manifestation in fine if not entirely matching china – with the respect she would have afforded a foreign religion. She took cup and saucer as if accepting communion and, when the atmosphere had relaxed later on and she ventured to pour tea herself, she reached for the teapot like a grail.

She was... sensuous. A woman tasting and touching the world around her, a woman to be appreciated by every sense. But also a reserve; a calculation. Not one of her movements, so poised, so graceful, so flowing, was not considered and controlled. Cade, conscious enough still to be able to look at himself a little askance, was entranced.

+==+

The cabriolet swung round and bounced through a gate into a driveway and Hathaway thought: *Alice in Wonderland*. Bushes flanked the drive, spaced at exact intervals and pruned to spheres. Even the darkness of their leaves, uniform against the paler green of the lawn, seemed unnatural. An illustration from a picture-book *Alice*. The drive was too short for its breadth and grandeur, the house at the end – stripes of brick and stripes of stone, white in red and all crowned with a truncated dome – too small for the pretensions of its design. Unnatural; the fantasy of a suburban villa-dweller on opium.

She had the letter of introduction ready in a pocket, but surely it wouldn't be necessary. Explaining herself would be a challenge, otherwise. *I am a passing Englishwoman, curious to meet August Niemann, who foretold the destruction of my country*. The invitation, the carriage at the station, suggested he was as curious as she – or polite, at least.

Her host in Frankfurt: *Theoretically, of course, it is impossible to understand Germany's concerns today unless you understand Niemann.* His wife, as immediately shocked as if he'd broken wind or lunged at the maid; a hurrying of crockery and twitters.

Her own voice: *Niemann? Who wrote the book on the conquest of England?*

He. Except in the original – there was a certainty about her host, and she liked it more than all his previous courtesies and generosities – *it was called* German Dream. And he had smiled, challenging her.

Silence in the room for a moment; the wife the other side of a closed door and a crossed line.

I should like to meet him.

And so an exchange of letters, an invitation, a carriage at the station with a uniformed driver and a horse with a plume that wouldn't stay upright, the picture-book house and now she was walking up the steps and following a black coat and a beckoning hand, over a mosaic floor and between potted palm trees that framed a doorway, rosewood gleaming everywhere, a knock and Flora Hathaway was left to enter yet another male sanctum.

In 1904 a minor actor and author of pseudonymous novels had published a romance describing the combined victory of Germany, Russia and France over Britain, and the division of her empire between them, resulting in the greater happiness of all concerned.

The dark wood overwhelming her on every side, and the scent of lilies. Behind a desk, a thatch of white hair bent over a paper, the point of a beard following the motions of the pen. Hathaway put up with this performance for ten seconds, and then turned and began to skim the bookshelves.

After sixty-five years and nearly fifty books, August Niemann had at last made himself famous. And rich enough to build the gingerbread house of his dreams. She'd seen the book, surely; skimmed it, at least. The English translation had been notorious, but more mentioned than read.

She turned back just as he looked up. Pale, rheumy eyes, the skin hanging loose beneath them; a moustache that appeared to have been hung on top of the beard. He stood, and bowed his head suddenly in greeting. Then he was round the desk, waddling on legs that did not seem to bend, and clutching her fingers briefly.

'Fräulein...'

'Hatha—'

'It is my honour to bid you hearty welcome.' He dropped her fingers. 'Tonight, at house Niemann, we are speaking English.'

For a moment she thought she was going to curtsey. 'It's my honour to be here, sir,' she said in German. 'I should be practising my German, but I'm sure your English is better.' *My German is better.*

'Well, for your practice then.' German. The eyes looked at her but seemed not to see. He turned, tottered away, then swung round. 'So! You are come to see the monster of Gotha in his lair. To see what they are all afraid of. The man who dared to challenge the hegemony of Britain. A geographic hegemony' – the last syllable came out longer in the German – 'and a hegemony in the preoccupations of the other nations.'

How to engage with such a man? 'Well, I had heard a lot about you, Herr—'

'I'm sure you did!' The chest filled up and the shoulders went back, supporting sagging arms. 'Your politicians raged against me, I'm sure; and your nurse would scare you with the threat of the evil Niemann, is it not so?'

He was so wildly wrong about British intellectual culture, as well as the domestic circumstances of the Hathaways, that it was hard to know where to begin. 'I would hope that, if we could strive to understand each other better—'

'Understand? Ah yes, we must understand!' His voice was shrill generally, and the last word was stretched out into a squeak. He began to wave one finger at her, a frenzy of scolding. 'Always the British ask us to understand. Why it is necessary for you to dominate the seas, to restrain our trade, to bottle us up between the mountains and the marshes.' He came up on tiptoes, peered up into the thatch of hair, trying to remember the line. 'To understand why you make alliances to encircle us, why you incite these allies – these tools, these puppets of a strong-armed and vindictive master – to serve your ends, as you incited the Japanese against Russia.' The voice had lost a lot of its energy; it sounded as if he were reading from notes.

'Russia is lucky to face no comparable threat from her western neighbours.'

'Dinner is at eight. You are most welcome.' He began to usher her towards the door; he was slightly shorter than she. 'I'm an artist, yes. But also a philosopher. To the intellectual mind, every opinion is stimulation, however little or muddle-headed. I have correspondents in every country of note in Europe. Tonight you will meet some of them. I hold no prejudice for country or belief. Of all people, it satisfies me that I should have an Englishwoman in my house.' The door open, a hand on her elbow, the door closed, and Flora Hathaway was out in the hall again, enveloped in palm fronds.

Golly.

Another lunch, Osman Riza quick to reciprocate Cade's hospitality. Small talk: Cade had met a pair of Egyptians representing a consortium that wanted to import cotton. Perhaps it would be appropriate to introduce Mr Riza to them; no doubt they'd need to get square with the ministry, and perhaps Mr Riza would be interested to cast an eye over them. Mr Riza nodded; he would certainly be interested.

No doubt it would do Riza no harm to be seen as intermediary for this kind of affair, and that was why he'd mentioned it. Cade wondered how corrupt he was. On the surface a most moral man; but they said everyone in authority here was more or less treacly. Perhaps one of those fellows who accept a commission here and there and see it as standard administrative procedure; then find the nearest Scotchman to complain to about how terrible it all was. But Riza was sharper than that: a worrier, too, and somehow truly sad about the state of his world. A bruised pride, but also a bruised sense of propriety.

Cade was starting sincerely to like the fellow. There was a prudence to him, a restraint and – ironically, given Cade's interest – a discretion. They'd not have made bad partners. A whimsy: pulling Riza out of the ministry and setting him up as Cade & Cade's man in the Ottoman Empire when Cade went back.

When am I going back? Development of the whimsy: sending Riza back for a spell, while he stayed on here. 'And how are – I think this was how you put it – how are the doctors behaving themselves?' Take to it rather well, he would. The old 'un would like him; always liked a quiet one.

'The – please?'

'The doctors. The interfering foreigners: all these British and Russians and Germans and what-not kicking the patient when he's down.'

'Ah yes, ah yes!' Nodding eagerly now he'd caught up. 'Yes, very good.' Then a shake of the head, heavy and sour. 'Really, it's...' He hesitated. An uncomfortable shifting in his seat; uncomfortable smile. 'You must think me terribly indiscreet, Mr Cade.'

'No. No, not at all.'

'We seem to share a way of looking at the world.'

'Aye. That we do.'

Riza released a long breath; a release of tension. 'Really, Mr Cade: it is... well, it is most tiresome. The Germans are intending to increase their presence here substantially – fully 30 per cent; military mostly. And we are to share some of the costs. A new facility in Kadıköy, and a new office over here, both of which we will provide and fit out; as usual, such imports as are needed for construction and supply are to be purchased by us from Germany.'

'The doctor's prices are pretty steep too, eh?'

Riza nodded, then looked uncertain again. 'Perhaps it is natural that – that men of the same quality may be... just a little indiscreet.'

'Indiscreet... Call it: a harmless private revenge – a joke, almost – on those we cannot otherwise harm.'

And another tea: a quiet street halfway down the hill between the palace and the teeming of the waterfront, a door opening onto a courtyard of individual residences, leaves and shade and old wood. Mrs Charkassian hosted; her brother very much presided. Along with Cade and the Dutch lady, he'd made the mistake of inviting two acquaintances from the Armenian community, who competed to offer their own – sometimes conflicting – versions of their people's history. Ruben Varujan veered between disdain for these lesser enthusiasts and angry repudiations of their more outrageous errors. It left the Dutch lady bewildered and faintly alarmed, on top of her unease at the unfamiliar sweets she was being offered.

It left James Cade and Ani Charkassian to murmurs, to polite interest in each other's doings, to shared silent amusement whenever the anger rose elsewhere, to an easy compatibility in their movements around the table and the conversation. When he left, Cade took her fingers in his, and half bent towards them as if delivering a formal kiss.

A pair of wives from the British Embassy had expressed wide-eyed interest in visiting one of the markets on the Asian side, and Cade had been the obvious escort: respectable businessman enough to seem appropriate, with just enough of the disreputability of trade and bachelorhood to seem interesting. It was a natural addition – indeed, it enhanced the sense of propriety for everyone – to invite Mrs Charkassian as well.

The Englishwomen squealed and gasped at the vividness and swollen bounty of aubergines and peppers and tomatoes, at the obscene wounds of figs broken open for their consideration by the stall-boys, at the mountains of bright spices, at the bustling of humanity through the marketplace, and they apparently the only pale faces in the whole of Asia. Cade kept an eye on them, shooing away the most persistent of the beggars and doing the haggling for their trophy purchases; he had discreet conversations with sellers of fabrics and sellers of spices; and he watched Ani Charkassian as she moved through the swarm, a swan in the eddies gliding untouched.

When they shepherded the Englishwomen ahead of them, she slipped her arm through his. When they all took the ferry – the faces, fat moustaches, blank-faced women, the occasional watchful eye – back from Haydarpaşa to the European side she stood in the prow, figurehead, tragic princess come out of the East and unwilling to look back, glancing sidewards now and then to find Cade watching her. And when he handed her down from the carriage, she suggested that if Mr Cade was so interested in Ottoman culture he must visit the deserted house of her late aunt, which was reckoned typical and most charming.

＝＝＝＝

'I am a man of peace.'

August Niemann said it as if it were grace. 'I say that, most particularly, for our young guest here. The most junior in age and achievement perhaps,

75

but perhaps the most significant as a member of the race whose defeat I perceived.'

The whole table waited for her.

She had the uncomfortable sense that she was speaking on behalf of the British Empire. 'That I have the honour to be here, sir, is the best demonstration of that aspiration to peace, which I'm sure we all share.'

'Well' – his eyes screwed up, and opened again – 'we might debate that last bit; but that was prettily said.' He surveyed the table, like a conductor picking up his baton. 'Well, dear Baroness, dear young lady, Doctor, Eckhardt, my dear' – a bow to each, the last to his wife at the other end – 'I bid you welcome.' And they started on the soup.

Hathaway had come downstairs as they were about to go into dinner, and the introductions had been brief. Niemann had presented the Baroness von Suttner as 'a fellow novelist, and an enthusiast for peace', and something had died in the baroness's face, sad and fleshy and powdered – as if one of these occupations was an unseemly secret, or as if the experience of finding seventy years of life so briefly summarized had caused a sudden and complete acknowledgement of failure. Sitting to Niemann's right and opposite Hathaway, she stared down now, a crown of high-piled hair slipping forwards and threatening to overbalance her into the soup.

'I am curious, Fräulein.' She turned away gratefully from the two models of age. To her left was the doctor – Müller – a sanatorium had been mentioned. 'You do not seem either a relative or an acolyte of our host. Has his notoriety won him a place in the Baedeker guide for Germany? One of the country's... what shall we say?'

'Monuments?'

A laugh boomed in his chest, and was swallowed. 'Treasures, surely.'

'Cultural artefacts.'

'Very good. On the list of any intelligent English tourist.'

Niemann's voice came high above their conversation, and they all turned obediently. 'The young lady has come here, of course, to hear my views on European culture.' The baroness stared across the table at her, appalled. 'In truth, the culture that I represent, it is not some narrow artistic conception. It is the spirit of Germany herself. And this spirit has too long been imprisoned by domestic mediocrity and timidity, and by foreign arrogance and aggression.' He stared at Hathaway as if she were a dreadnought. 'But these foreign spirits – I know the young lady has her Shakespeare, and the French have their, their... – these are archaic, dead spirits, whose time has passed. I create – as Wagner creates – as the emanation of a completely realized national spirit, strong and just, entitled to be free of the chains imposed by the old corrupted empires, and to surpass them.'

Silence. Flora Hathaway said quietly, 'Wagner demanded the subjection of the spirit to some superior myth. More recent composers – Debu— Herr Strauss, for example – give a voice to the individual spirit.'

Dr Müller said, 'You think the twentieth century will be the age of the individual spirit?' And then a door opened and a maid hurried in with a rush of air and pork cutlets.

Niemann switched to English and offered a faltering toast to 'the liberation of the spirit', and they laughed politely and began to eat, and Frau Niemann said, 'Of course, French culture is so beautiful. Really, such civilization. We went to Paris once, and – I'm sure the baroness will agree – you've never seen such wonders!'

'You'll pardon an indelicacy at your table, dear lady,' Müller said in a heavy whisper, 'but I saw Fuller dance Salomé in Paris in 1900, and that is the wonder that has stayed with me.'

Frau Niemann giggled. 'The doctor was a great sportsman. He compe—'

Eckhardt, a young man with everything about him precise – face, tailoring, enunciation – was on a different track: 'Paris has the grandeur of her long history, and it is fading. Germany's economy is now stronger, and Berlin will—'

'Paris has suffered revolutions and bombardments in our lifetime.' It was the baroness, voice low but strong, and it came like the last tolling of a bell. 'That is why she fades.'

'France has a choice' – Niemann chirruping while the baroness still reverberated – 'if she will abandon her pathetic dependence on the empire that has done most to cripple her – I mean of course the British, who destroyed France one century ago in their ambition for world economic supremacy – if she will turn to Germany, she may yet have protection and peace. The world thrilled to hear the emperor's words of support for the 'unfortunate Boers, knowing that justice had a new champion. The great European war will—'

'To speak it,' the baroness said stolidly, 'is to will it.'

'The war will establish a proper preponderance of power in Europe. The new – the naturally strong – with airships now, and electric guns. A new harmony will grow out of the primitive age.'

Eckhardt said quickly to Hathaway, 'You English must worry that the tide of your greatness is ebbing.'

'What worries me, Herr Eckhardt, is that you assume because I am English that I must be taken as a representative of the English and placed in the conversation accordingly, like a... like a flag on a map. Treating this Continent like a child's building blocks betrays the crude mentality of the child.' Opposite her, the baroness was nodding ponderously. 'When we look for someone against whom to compare our progress; when we seek someone to justify our bravado; when we seek someone to blame for our problems: we will know them too easily by those flags.'

Dr Müller's knife rattled heavily on his plate, and it emphasized the silence around her. 'When you visit our town today,' he said, 'do you do so as a... an unattached person, independent of country? If you had the chance to do some great good for England – what shall we say? To learn some great secret, or to win some great economic advantage – should you not do it?'

He was turning to look at her, head on one side, the nose starting to corkscrew into her, and she flinched at this precise identification of her vulnerability, as if his finger had touched her naked thigh.

'There are things that make me proud to be English.' *I had not expected myself to answer that way.* And for a moment she glimpsed her parents, and the old man. 'But because of the value of those things themselves, not because they are English. If I were to do something worthy for England, it would be because I considered it worthy, not because it was for England.'

Müller was pressing on: 'And if I should find some deed you considered worthy, that was for Germany?'

'Was this not the very theme of my book?' Niemann. 'The Englishwoman who sacrificed country for love of the better man!'

Müller again: 'There, Fräulein Hathaway: love – would you consider that justification enough to do something for Germany?'

And immediately two sour emotions were colliding in her. A sick doubt about whether she would have sacrificed herself for Ralph. A distinct memory of Niemann's ridiculous book. 'If I should criticize such a woman' – she heard her voice sharp – 'it would not be for loving too much, but for being too little a woman.'

Niemann: 'It is the role of the German male to embody Germany, to fight as Germany, and to conquer. It is the role of German woman to sustain him.'

Hathaway felt her anger hot in her chest. *If I were an Englishman at this table, we would not be discussing love.* And she looked coldly at the faces – their pretensions, their stupidities, their games, their prejudices – at a place where it was important to polish wood until it shone, to cover it with lace, to present war as a logical outcome of musical theory.

You will find that I can be more than you can imagine.

✦

'I beg your pardon, sir.' The old man looked up, neutral. 'But you asked particularly for any reports in response to flags on the J list.'

The single sheet into his hand. Always so flimsy; like kitchen paper that had wrapped something greasy. 'But this has yesterday's date.'

Mild, but the eyes were up and cold.

'Yes, sir. I'm afraid we didn't expect – It's from the police, sir. The Metropolitan. We'd assumed only foreign—'

'The police?' The voice had drifted away, leaves swirling in the park; the eyes were in the paper. The secretary slipped out.

MP 8/G/X/122

Metropolitan Police
Foreign Liaison Section
To: General (Mr Hill-Padget)
To: Museums & Antiquities (Dr Brodie)
  Following persons identified by Rome, present and of
potential interest, during the trial of Peruggia (Florence)
– day 3, 15th May 1914.

```
Ackermann, H.
Boulay, P.
Du Bois, P.
Duval, D.
Fossi, F. (see Naples)
Grant, Hon. L.
Halle, I.
Meuzot, B.
Moriset, Miss T.
Nijinsky, Y.
Perez, V. (known as Peresa/ and as de Paresa/ and as
    Valfierno/ and as di Bollino), travelling as Valfierno
Ter Borch, Mrs Sophia (see also Mackensen)
Ackermann and Nijinsky in company. Ter Borch seen
    with Boulay and, briefly, Grant and several others.
    Perez spoke to Ackermann, Duval, Ter Borch. Moriset
    accompanied by 1 unknown male.
End
```

[SS G/1/893/10 AND SS L/7/8/G/X/122]

Three names had been underlined, emphatic but askew. For a moment the old man saw the effort, the clerk's doggedness through the hours and acres of paper.

Ter Borch's presence was surely coincidental and, more importantly, irrelevant in the current case. The name had been put on the J list in reference to a different affair.

But Valfierno?

A cypher. A front for other names and other activities. Once or twice an agent for the Spider, surely.

Had the Spider been involved in this coup of the Leonardo? Some game of politics between France and Italy? Or just money? Surely it was too melodramatic.

And Duval, speaking to Perez-Valfierno. What had Duval been doing there?

Duval's destination was Rome; Florence was supposed to be a stop-off, an obvious attraction for a student of architecture.

He saw the face, saw him standing outside an Italian courthouse, saw an intrigued smile. Saw him inside, looking around the courtroom, uneasy, watchful.

A vague instinct to be where there had been transgression – healthy enough in his new role. An interest in art, of course; and the theft of the Leonardo was the grandest art story going.

The old eyes stared into the page, seeing Duval's eyes looking across the courtroom.

Unconsciously, a faint nod. Above all, Duval had wanted to see the figure in the dock. The insignificant man who had carried out the crime of the age; the man who had captured beauty herself.

And it had brought him face to face with one of the Spider's minions. Valfierno would suck up new acquaintances like a sponge. Duval was probably similar; the eye for the chance. And the meeting had only been registered by chance; some plodding co-operation of police bureaux, the original report already dropping down a pile in Scotland Yard.

The old man gripped the two parts of the telephone. 'Colonel Mayhew, please.' Sitting upright; never could relax with the thing. 'Yes, now. To be located at once.'

⊹══⊱⊰══⊹

After dinner, Niemann's was a house of shadows and echoes, the strange shapes of plants reaching out of the darkness, everywhere a hollowness resonating from panelling and tiles.

Hathaway murmured, 'Frau Niemann started to say that you competed in something.'

Müller grunted. 'The enthusiasms of a younger man. I participated for Germany in the games of 1900, in the Exposition Universelle. That! Such a circus of... of competitive harmony. Our host would have been quite an exhibit himself. I rode, and shot. I did not win.' She sensed him shifting in the gloom. 'The important thing is... *de s'être bien battu?*'

'Or to have seen a beautiful woman dance, and been so alive that you remember it fourteen years later?'

He chuckled.

Hathaway found the baroness in the conservatory, staring out into the darkness of the garden. At first she thought her asleep, so still and slumped was the body. Then a hand flickered on the arm of the wicker chair, and the baroness blinked.

'Baroness? Do I disturb you?' The eyes came slowly round, and then the head half turned to follow. A heavy head, on a heavy body corseted tight. 'I hoped to learn more about your work. Such a great—'

'I have little enough time left, girl. If you wish to simper inconsequentially, go and find a husband who needs your services.'

Reflexes: of grief, of loyalty, of defiance. Then she realized that they were habitual, not deep-felt. She felt her intellect released.

'Why are you here, Baroness?'

'I do homage at the shrine of mediocrity and vindictiveness, because they are powerful.' The eyes scrutinized Hathaway harder. 'You know that only half of the Austrian Empire is Catholic? That less than one-quarter speaks German? But now we are the junior partner – the... the inbred younger brother – of an upstart Germany. I have spent the fifty years of my adult life as a world citizen, in debate with the world about what might unite us. And at the end, fate has declared that Niemann alone is my ally. Perhaps I must find a reason to like him. Why are you here?'

Hathaway pulled her chair closer and turned it so that she was beside the baroness, facing the same way. 'Fate has declared that he is my enemy. Perhaps I will learn why I am supposed to hate him.'

She didn't look round. 'That's wit, my dear. We must strive for a little more, I think. Intelligence is an opportunity, not an achievement. Like a weapon.' *Waffe*: she spat it softly. 'Your exchange was most amusing with Müller; beware that one, by the way. I suspect the world has little to fear from fools like Niemann. But there is no power on earth as terrible as a reasonable German.'

The substantial bust swelled up, and the baroness breathed out slowly. 'Most of all, I am here because I will not let them think that I fear them.' An owl called out of the night, and they both glanced up. 'There is an instinct that war is for the brave, and therefore that peace is for cowards. When the street is full of your friends going to the war, where is courage?

Is it out there with the songs and flowers, or is it standing at the window, returning the scornful glances of those who thought they knew you? Will it then be heroism to march, or not to march?'

She glared at the night. 'Their war will come. Europe has lost the habit of talking. There will be war because they cannot imagine how to do anything else. Always easier to make war than to make peace. To find a pretext; to find a hatred... so easy. And in war, everyone is right.'

Out of the solemnity her whole face wrinkled up, seeming to catch a stench. 'If they followed a Siegfried, one could... but this schoolboy fantasist!' Sombre again: 'Perhaps this is Niemann's triumph: no one has written romances in celebration of peace.'

'We have books in English that are just as belligerent; just as ridiculous. Your cause is—'

'The Swedish even gave me a prize for it. Each day I may say: today there is peace; and today, and today. But tomorrow there will be war.' She turned to Hathaway, and stayed looking at her. 'All that there is, is to be.'

The conservatory, the conversation, felt stifled; the over-decorated comforts of Niemann's world. 'Baroness, your cause – you are right.'

But the baroness had turned away into the darkness.

'What use will it be... to have been right?'

⊰──⊱

Duval had spent a blissful day in Florence. The trial in the morning: irresistible. Little Peruggia so insignificant to look at, but the sangfroid to do what he had done, and then the stamina to live two years with a priceless painting under his bed; and his interruptions – hysterical, patriotic, angry, weeping – every one of them played to the gallery. Duval didn't speak a word of Italian but he'd got enough of the gossip to know the speculations of international conspiracy, of shadowy rings of master criminals. They needed to believe such things, because they couldn't believe that the little Italian handyman had transfixed the world on his own.

Duval had watched Vincenzo Peruggia for a morning, watched his eyes as they scrutinized their audience and made their calculations, and Duval believed it.

He'd wandered the streets for the afternoon; and he spent two hours sketching in the Santo Spirito, losing himself in its lines and spaces.

Florence was glutted with its own beauties; bored of them. The magnificent *palazzi* spoke of money as much as art. It was the city of the Albizzi and the Medici more than of Michelangelo. Perhaps you had to be an artist, or just an outsider, to see the details of beauty, the hidden unnecessary joy in an embellishment that would always be in shadow, the mastery of architectural perspective that played with the minds of those who thought they were in control.

Twice he'd caught himself studying a gallery chamber and making amateur calculations about a robbery. Not his game; never would be. But it took a rare combination of skill, didn't it? Cheek as well as cunning.

And the Italian women, so elegant and so alive. Even the average ones dressed smartly. And every eye a game. He'd sat on a café terrace for two hours this evening, sipping at white wine and merely watching in the warmth, senses somehow sharper. The percussion of metal furniture and cutlery and plates and glasses. The elaborate melody of voices. The smell of flowers and drains. Flowing through the square, humanity at ease with itself. In Paris they were smart, sophisticated, yet it was brittle. And London... But here everyone, not just the lovers but the shopkeepers going home and the gang of boys on a spree and even the derelict selling matches – a derelict who'd found an old blue suit and slicked his hair down and would mutter snatches of music when he got a sale – they all belonged, they all seemed to contribute fitly to one complete place. Not a word with anyone, but such an embrace of people.

Then back to his hotel, the river whispering its goodnight behind him. The desk clerk was pompous and genuinely stupid, which combination always offered possibilities. Duval made up a query about the Uffizi as an excuse to slip him a tip, and tap-tapped up the marble stairs, feeling very much in the swim.

He was into his room briskly and almost missed the paper at his feet.

Not hotel stationery. Scrawled in pencil, a single word: *Valfierno*.

Major Valentine Knox, locked in a box, the darkness complete.

Testing the darkness. *Night vision.* Ten minutes into his confinement, guessing at cracks of light under the lid.

Couple of feet wide? He can't be more than two feet broad at the shoulders, and the slightest shift has his shoulders rubbing the sides. Length: more than six feet. Stretch leg, point toe, still his boot doesn't touch the end. He tilts his head back; the suggestion of sensation in his hair. Reaches his hand across the opposite shoulder and above his head and immediately his fingers stub against wood. At least six foot six long. Depth: *not much.* He raises his head – feels the muscles in chest and stomach – can't be more than an inch or two and his forehead touches the lid.

Coffin. Hamel's joke. Funny.

He exercises his muscles, tensing and relaxing them, limb by limb. *P.T.* One complete circuit, count to one hundred, repeat.

Supposed to be a common fear: buried alive. Go off your rocker. He wonders how he would escape; fingers brushing the interior of the crate, feeling the grain. *Punch through that? Kick through? Fill up with earth then.* A pause; ears checking for sound. *Pressure of earth helps crack weakened lid. But then crushed by lid and earth.* No sound. *Ears like bloody great gramophone horns now, ears like a bat.* He had to trust Hamel, of course. Had to trust him to send the box where it was supposed to go.

Hell of a prank. Breaking out of the box to find it's on top of the Arc de Triomphe. Leave it on a beach; tide rising. His imagination fires for a moment. Knox bobbing out to sea. He turns it off. Pranks. Memories of school. Petty; vicious. Fighting back until he couldn't stand and couldn't feel. Little Val; sneers and giggles. Made him what he is. Adult Knox justifies the child Knox and all his experiences.

Roll over. Rolling over would mean back protects you – arm round to finish pulling at the lid – also creates pocket of air under face. *Hunch up, woodlouse* – little Val again – *then start to push up.* How long would you have to hold your breath? *How you'd survive. How you'd win.*

Time passes. He walks the South Downs in his head. Straining for the pattern of fields, the number of stiles.

He remembers Alfriston High Street. The shops, one by one. Start on the Square, at the Smugglers, round the cross and up.

The box has ceased to inhabit the world. Major Valentine Knox has ceased to inhabit a box. He floats in a void.

He remembers the men of his first company. Axley to Young.

Some time in the second hour he notices the Knox-box gag. His mind wanders for a moment: *Knox in a box*; *Knox in a box that locks*; *Knox wearing s*— And he catches himself about to murmur aloud.

Steady, old chap.

He visualizes the map of Europe. Focus on each country, one by one. Capital city is. Capital's main stations are. Embassy contact is. Communication by. Emergency plan. *Begin.*

The whisper roars into his head, followed by a tap that hammers through him. 'Knox!' Heart thumping. *Steady.*

The padlock rattling in Hamel's haste, and at the last instant Knox thought to close his eyes.

A single lamp, screaming over his head. Arm up, head twisted aside, he sat up clumsily.

'Are you all right?'

'Good shape.' He matched the whisper.

'Here.' Hamel pushed a flask into his hand, checked that his fingers gripped it properly. 'Sneaking you out should be a damn' sight easier than sneaking you in, anyway.'

Knox took a swig, and handed it back. 'Not a bad billet after all.'

As his eyes began to allow, he looked around the hangar. First the brick floor flickered into view, then the timber walls, a workbench with its tools, and as his arm came down and his vision opened he saw Hamel's monoplane looming over him.

'Can you move all right?'

'Soon find out.'

He scrambled up and out of the box. The propellor with which he had shared it gleamed in the straw, varnished and polished to bright stratified amber. He brushed himself down.

Hamel's hand on his shoulder, mouth close to his ear. 'I'll tinker on the bird here for an hour, till we're sure the rest of the aerodrome's quiet. Froggies should all be at their dinner. Both doors are locked, but you'd better duck into that cupboard if anyone comes because I'll want to look welcoming. Show 'em I'm doing the Lord's work.'

'Give you a hand if you like.'

'Best not, old chap.' It was elegant, Hamel's gift to make everything sound pleasant, even if delivered in a whisper in an aeroplane hangar at night. 'Less risk of something out of place if someone does stop by, less talk, and less chance of you putting your bloody foot through the kite.' A form of apology from a British hero for having a Franco-German name.

So Knox sat on a box and watched Hamel fiddling in his aircraft, an outsize canvas cigar supported on what looked like pram wheels. After a few minutes, he began to list the counties of England in his head.

An hour later, and with a copy of a key that Hamel had borrowed during his week's residence on the aerodrome, they were fifty yards away inside another hangar. Hamel's mouth to Knox's ear again. 'Secretive so-and-so's have got the window well covered, but we'll stick with the torch.' It began to glow in his hand, creating a weak pool of vision around their boots and across the bricks. On the edge of the pool, between the world of light and the world of darkness, was the gloomy skeleton of a biplane. Hamel locked the door, and came in close again. 'You speak any German?'

'Some.'

'Enough to tell the watchman to poke off if he comes calling?' Knox nodded. 'If someone actually starts opening the door, it's the competition rather than the watchman, and we'll have to knock 'em on the head.' Another nod. Hamel pulled away, but then leaned in again. 'I say: would you mind doing the knocking? My face is a bit too well known.'

Knox looked at him. 'Perils of working with a celebrity, I suppose.' Hamel carrying a sack and the torch, Knox a toolbox and a can, they made for the aeroplane. As the pool of light loomed up the fuselage, it revealed a black cross.

+≈+

Duval sat in his room, sipping steadily from a brandy and picking at the braiding around the chair-arm and wondering who or what in hell Valfierno was. Smoked a cigarette.

Was this how London did their business? Hush-hush and hat brim pulled low.

The braid on the chair was starting to come away. He stood, poured another splash, and drank as he paced.

'Valfierno.'

To say it was to hear it, and Valfierno became a face and a voice and Duval was across the room pulling visiting cards from his jacket pocket, and there he was. Hector, M. de Valfierno. The courtroom. Some sort of dago, dapper in a grey three-piece, beautifully cut; in his forties, maybe well-oiled fifties; had he mentioned a daughter? The 'Marquis de' was a subtle touch, wasn't it?

A mouthful of brandy. So what? What did the London greyhairs want? Follow the chap?

Another mouthful. In years of scrapes and dodges, this was something new.

He was picking at the braiding again. *Keep moving.* Either way, he'd have to find him first.

The clerk was persuaded to jot down the half-dozen hotels in the city where a foreigner of means would stay. Duval scanned the visitors' register, and fiddled with the heavy fountain pen that lay in its crease. He slept uneasily.

At eight thirty – coffee gulped and he'd only shaved because the impression would count – Duval was stepping over suitcases to the first hotel reception desk on his list. New collar, handkerchief square, hunt-breakfast accent, and terribly sorry to trouble them but he'd been introduced to a chappie at lunch yesterday and during a bit of business with the bill the chappie had left behind this very smart pen and it seemed the decent thing to try to get it back to the Marquis de – Valfierno, is that how one pronounces it? Here, have a look at the card; and the marquis had mentioned this hotel at one point; think it was this hotel, anyway.

At about the same time the clerk in Duval's hotel was receiving his first guests, sour and impatient from the night train, and missing the fountain pen from the visitors' book.

Duval drew four blanks in four hotels – and one irate Frog who had a name similar to Valfierno but wasn't missing a pen and hadn't wanted his breakfast interrupted.

The Marquis de Valfierno had been staying at the fifth hotel, the Porta Rossa. But the marquis had checked out earlier this morning.

No, he had left no forwarding address. The marquis had come to Firenze for three days to indulge his enthusiasm for ceramics; he was not a regular guest. No, they could not give any information from a cheque, and, besides, the marquis had paid cash. If the *signore* was such an acquaintance of the marquis, perhaps he would be able to oblige him in the matter of certain oversights: a number of additional items and external purchases that the marquis had charged to the hotel but... forgotten to pay.

Another hurried exit, another silent curse. Then on the pavement outside the Porta Rossa, a flash of a smile. Pays cash; puts on a high front, visiting cards and a good hotel; and uses it for a spree on credit. The marquis was a bit of a lad, wasn't he?

Whoever he was. *And why in hell do I care anyway?* He was chasing a shadow, on behalf of a shadow, and it was all a bust. He couldn't just wait all week and hope to bump into the fellow. And so what if he did? Clap him on the shoulder and say, 'You are the Marquis de Valfierno and I claim my ten shillings'?

The midday sky opened white above him. The birds wheeling and gathering between the belfries reflected the people scudding across the square. He was hungry.

Tiles.

Twenty minutes later Duval was in the office of the curator of the Bargello Museum, dwarfed by floor-to-ceiling shelves of papers and unplaced treasures.

'But of course, Signor...' – the curator leaned forward to check the card set squarely in front of him – 'Duval, I should be delighted to accommodate you. To sketch the Brunelleschi designs as well as the Ghiberti, you say?'

'Comparative, you see?'

'And in the same medium. Yes, that's good. There was a rumour a few years ago that the designs of *i Jacopo furioso* had been rediscovered but, alas, it was not true.'

Duval looked up around the encroaching shelves. 'You inhabit your own paradise here, Signor Direttore.' Sober. 'I met a chap the other day – ceramic enthusiast – said he was spending a lot of time here. Valfierno, I think it was. The Marquis of Valfierno.'

The face opened in interest. 'Ah yes! The Marquis de Valfierno. Yes, the marquis did me the honour to pay his respects when he visited.' A flat smile. Duval had the sense of a secret about which he wasn't in the know.

Careful. On the shelf behind the curator there was a Roman vase, the handles two spindly swan necks.

'The marquis is a... an acquaintance of yours, Signor' – a glance again at the card – 'Duval?'

Not the time for flannel. Not the time for charm. The conversation, the sentence, each word seemed fragile.

'I'd never met him before.' Drop it and it smashes. 'Is he well known?'

The curator pursed his lips. 'The marquis expressed great passion for the ceramics; but, to be sincere, I suspected the passion to be...' – a little smile – 'glaze and not clay.'

Duval managed a chuckle. 'You must become adept at spotting such men.'

'I regret that some men who style themselves connoisseurs are mere dilettantes, and some are much worse.'

Breathing. 'Making quite the tour, was he?' Heartbeats.

'He said so. He had been in Paris. He was dismissive about Rome.' The curator considered this, torn between loyalties Florentine and Italian. 'He was going on to Germany.'

Germany. 'Can't think he'd find much in Germany, surely. Not compared to here.'

'Oh, Signore...' A burst of tutting. 'We must be fair.' A flirtatious smile, between men of taste. 'There are charming collections in some of their provincial cities. The fruits of warfare and greed rather than native genius, perhaps, but they are there, and may a people not learn taste? Do I not invite the schools to bring their children here – one afternoon only, of course – you must tell me if there is any derangement... Perhaps he was only trying to impress me, but the marquis made use of the name of the Director of the Museum of Decorative Arts, in Berlin.'

Mayhew standing in the office doorway, olive against dust. 'Duval was staying at something called the Lucchesi.'

'Is that pleasant?'

'For him, very, given that we're paying for it.'

'I trust he made the most of the amenities.'

'Well, I say we're paying for it; actually he absconded without getting his bill, so technically I suppose we're not.'

'Well, that's all right, then.' The fingers flexed over the blotter. 'Colonel, was there something more pertinent?'

Mayhew straightened. 'Of course. Duval was observed catching the night train to Berlin.'

'Not Rome? Mm.' The fingers drummed once on the blotter. *Valfierno?* 'It's a little soon for him to try to do a bunk, and I doubt he'd go northwards. So we must assume he thinks he's pursuing some line of interest.'

Colonel Mayhew seemed to be assuming it grudgingly.

The old eyes blinked, pale. 'Colonel, one of my little suggestions, if I may. Get your man Knox to Berlin; immediately.'

Mayhew digested it. 'May I ask why you think Duval should be following this chap?'

'Of course, Colonel. Forgive me. The man is small fry in himself, but potentially the link to a bigger fish.'

'I see.' What was there to see? 'Well, while Duval's nothing more particular to do. What... what sort of bigger fish?'

Hermes, Krug and Morgenthal. One of three men.

And not a fish. A spider.

'A bit of unfinished business, Colonel. A bit of history.'

Krug at his desk in Vienna, looking into Europe, peering through the babel of faces and voices; considering individual faces; seeking the hand of one man at work.

There were hints, and possibilities. Whispers from a distance, tremors at the edge of his network. A telegraph channel reactivated in London. A message to the British Embassy in Berlin. An enquiry in Constantinople.

Where are you, old fox?

A cautious, elusive prey. One never seen full face. A blurred photograph.

One who might be glimpsed from a tangent. He pressed the buzzer, and a secretary was in front of him.

'A request to Colonel Nicolai, please: have German Intelligence had recent word or contact with Duquesne, the Boer?'

+≈≈+

Night train: a heartbeat rattling steadily on an unquestioned path, the blackness erasing ugliness and muffling threat, a womb of light in the dark, of warmth in the cold, companionship and mystery, the breaking of borders and the breaking of habits, no one sleeping in their own bed, always the sensation of possibility, of escape from old constraints, of somewhere new, of tomorrow.

Duval loved the things.

He caught his reflection in the window, weird and pale, and turned away into the carriage. *Not too much reflection, eh? Best press on.* The carriage was cheery enough, warm light and faces that didn't scowl; all shuddering and swaying in unison when the train went over points. A pleasant company in which to drift off.

Duval stood – a mime to the man opposite to watch his seat and case – timid smile to the matrons by the door, matronly beams in return – and stumbled into the corridor.

The marquis would no doubt be travelling first class – Duval hadn't wanted to draw attention to himself that way; a name on too many lists – and dinner should be finishing around now.

Bull by the horns. No point just following the fellow across Europe. He checked that his suit was neat; being over-dressed for second class did no harm with the matrons, but being under-dressed for first would get trouble from the stewards. He lurked until he could see desserts being cleared, then slipped into the dining carriage, head high and focused on an apparent appointment at the far end.

'Why, surely it's the marquis – do beg your pardon – we met in the, er, the courtroom – Duval – no, please don't get—' Clumsy shaking of hands, Valfierno's tanned sleek face pleasant and careful; a glance and a nod at the woman between him and the window – *worth a second look surely, but not now* – and a nod to the man sitting across the table, don't mean to interrupt. A steward's white coat hovering on the edge of his vision. 'You'd suggested I call' – surely he wouldn't remember whether he had or hadn't – 'but I really didn't want to interfere; can be so tiresome when a fellow's trying to escape society, don't you find?' Quality but humility. 'Anyway, it was pleasant to meet a fellow sportsman, and I found what you were talking about most intriguing.' And pray he's feeling bonhomous not busy.

The steward in front of him now, waiting for instructions, or just a hint that this was an unwanted guest.

'It was my pleasure; won't you join us for a drink?' The English was as punctilious as the dress; the words sounded heavenly to Duval.

Don't get carried away. 'Oh, I wouldn't dream of interrupting...' But the steward was pulling out the fourth chair, opposite the marquis, and Duval was settling into it. Brandies and reassurances, an introduction to the chap next to him – Swiss, banking, dull – and now at last it was time for the second look at the woman. Valfierno presented his 'dear daughter, Maria', placing his hand on hers and keeping it there, and Duval kept his courtesy brief, his nod formal, and his glance as long as possible.

She kept silent; watched him. *Handsome face and kissable lips and everything swelling where it should.* She was perhaps thirty. The eyes, considering him, were amused, knowing. *This one's lived.* She pulled her hand away from her father's.

'Mr Duval, you said – "sportsman"?'

'Indeed, sir. No one particular sport' – he considered a bit of flattery, but dropped it – 'more... an attitude to life, let's say.'

The chap might or might not be a marquis, but he enjoyed the lifestyle and wasn't too particular about paying for it. Duval didn't know how much of a fraud he was, nor why he was supposed to be interested in him, but it all meant hidden depths and the need for care. He turned off the deference as well as the flattery. Now he'd got his seat, he needed to be interesting rather than merely nice.

Valfierno had considered the comment, smiled, wondering what it was supposed to say about him and what it said about Duval. He held Duval's eyes and he didn't speak; *a cool bird; a man who's gambled big and gambled clever.* There was age at the temples, around the eyes, but otherwise the face was ageless, a carefully maintained mask. 'Quite right, Mr Duval. Life is only a balance of risks and pleasures, don't you find?' The conversation was a game now, which Valfierno would enjoy, and Duval knew he'd played it right.

He smiled. 'And the question is only whether you find the pleasures riskier than the risks are pleasurable.'

'What takes you to Berlin, Mr Duval?' Valfierno was enjoying himself, but he wasn't relaxing. 'What was it you said you did?'

Careful. A moment of unease as Duval wondered if he'd used some different line to him in Florence, then he repeated the amateur architect line, which had elements of truth after all; been due to press on to Rome; got a message from a friend inviting him to Berlin and thought, Why not? *This is me: rough-genteel, world-weary but game.*

They fenced a little: impressions of Florence; Valfierno's interests. He mentioned – as he had to the Bargello curator – his contact at the Museum of Decorative Arts in Berlin. Duval sorely wanted to push, to find the fraud, but was halfway through a question about Renaissance pottery when he realized that what he least wanted was a man on the defensive or a man suspecting scrutiny. The question became a statement and they moved on to architecture. Had Duval planned to visit nowhere else in northern Italy? Had he any expectations of Berlin?

Duval had the sense that the marquis was testing his knowledge now. *Bad luck, old lad. You could catch me in nine kinds of lie, but not on this ground.*

They shifted onto politics, and Duval was happy to play bluff and ignorant. The Swiss joined in now, and gave the impression that he was itching to get back behind his mountains and stay there. Then the daughter announced that she was tired, and would retire to her compartment. The men stood, and the lovely Maria gave her father a kiss on the cheek and her hand to the two others – a squeeze of the fingers from Duval – and swayed away down the compartment.

'All these flare-ups between the powers must be a bit of a bind for you, Marquis; travelling man, I mean.'

Valfierno dismissed the thought serenely: 'I glide above these things, Mr Duval. I like to think I have as many acquaintances in Paris and London as I do in Berlin and Vienna.' Behind the accent, his English was fluent. 'The trick is not to be too tied to *patria*.' A smile. 'Different for you, perhaps. Are you man first, or Englishman?'

'It's a good question.' It was a good question. *Never really thought of myself as loyal to much.* 'Like to think I deal fair with any man, wherever he's from. But people on the Continent do seem to take against one sometimes, for being English. Find myself getting blamed for other fellows' success.'

'Oh, I don't think they begrudge the success, Mr Duval. But they'd be grateful if you shared the spoils; and if you weren't too hard on a dago just because he's a dago, eh? We can't all be Anglo-Saxon, much as we'd like it.'

'What is needed,' said the Swiss, 'is a stronger discipline with regard to currency.'

Cigars, and chat: what their respective plans were in Berlin; games of chance.

Duval declined another brandy. He'd the contact well established now, and wanted to demonstrate that he would always under- rather than over-stay his welcome. Before they next met, someone might even tell him why he was supposed to have latched onto the fellow. Civil farewells, mutual hopes of contact in the future – *though no specifics, and no address* – and he left them to it.

The grandest game. No idea what he was supposed to be doing, not really, but what he was doing was fine. *Pursue contacts as given, report any points of interest regarding European politics, be alert to suspicion or the suspicious, keep in touch via consulates and embassies, be ready for further instructions.* That was all very well, but it didn't really mean anything, did it? Nothing concrete.

Just keep moving, like always. The train rattled and swayed, and he enjoyed the cheerful instability of his walk and his shoulders knocking between windows and corridor wall and the warmth and the smell of tobacco and the memory of brandy on his tongue.

He checked the name card, and tapped on the compartment door.

It slid open, and two big brown eyes looked up at him. A moment, and then they smiled at him. Her lips opened, and her tongue pushed through between her teeth as if testing the air. 'Signor Duval,' she said evenly, eyes steady on him. 'You appear to be lost.'

'All my life, until this moment.'

The mouth opened in silent laughter; he had the uneasy sense it was at his expense. 'Your father is having another drink with his Swiss friend.'

She slid the door open, and his eyes followed down her throat towards her breasts, loose-held in a silk dressing gown edged with fur; the fur whispered of infinite softness to her dark skin. With an effort, he pulled his focus up again, to that mouth, to the smiling eyes.

'That's the wonderful thing about these European trains,' he said low; 'you never know where you're going to end up.'

A quick glance down the corridor, and then she kissed him on the lips, her own lips parted, the biting of a peach. 'He is not a marquis. And...' – the eyes dropped for a second, then came up to look at him square – 'he is not my father. And for both of those reasons... the train does not stop here.' She pressed a finger to his lips and pushed him out of the compartment.

So Duval drowsed in his second-class seat, glad enough of the company there, a reverie of a world of uncertainties in which he somehow belonged, and a particular vision of gorgeous eyes and a fur-fringed throat.

Eventually awake again, sour-mouthed and gazing at the plains as they rumbled past under empty sky. Then Berlin station, late in the morning, alert now and quickly off the train onto a platform that echoed with bootsteps and whistles, over-warm and bustling with people. It seemed as though half of them were in uniform – soldiers, sailors, policemen, customs officials, porters – he was only guessing at most of them, in their greys and blues and browns and greens – everyone bulky, bright-buttoned, leather-strapped, glistening with metal; and there were guns everywhere. He'd seen soldiers in England, of course, some with rifles; but they'd always seemed embarrassed by them, uncomfortable, as if carrying pitchforks or broomsticks. Here the uniforms seemed to strut more; the little deferences to the civilians, nods and salutes and after-yous, were heavy with implied power; and the rifles were lively, part of the man and part of the movement.

Duval lurked behind a pillar while the marquis got off the train with the girl, gathered bags and directed stewards and porters. 'Here, see these get to the Adlon.' Back to the girl. 'I must send a telegram. Wait here.' The usual suavity was missing. Duval didn't wait for the reply. A glance over his shoulder as he went, at the girl standing alone among the streams of people and the cases and the billows of steam. Did she catch his eye?

Duval booked into the Monopol, had a wash and a shave, put on a clean shirt and went down to the bar. He was on top of his man, now. And the non-daughter would be a game of her own. He ordered a half-bottle of wine with his lunch, and smoked a cigarette on the terrace, wondering about the best approach to the marquis, and wondering if he was supposed to be reporting his activities. Later, perhaps, when he had a little more to swank about.

But later, when he visited the Hotel Adlon to present his card preparatory to an eventual invitation to lunch, the Hotel Adlon had not heard of the Marquis de Valfierno. No such man was booked to arrive; no such man had arrived.

Duval took a taxi to the Museum of Decorative Arts, didn't bother with charades about sketching and casual acquaintance; the Museum of Decorative Arts had never heard of the marquis either.

For all practical purposes, the Marquis de Valfierno had disappeared.

✢══✣

Durrës was busy, and uneasy. Ballentyne had got to know the new Albanian capital when it had been just another town on the outskirts of the Ottoman Empire: lethargic, its bureaucracy a mix of the relaxed and the ridiculously pedantic, its rhythms set by the weather and the prevailing business – in this case fishing and a bit of trade – its style local rather than Turkish. In Durrës – *Durazzo* – Italian architecture had reached across the narrowest bit of the Adriatic along with Italian merchants and officials, and produced a handful of elegant three-storey villas. As the summer warmed up, the street dogs would seek the shade of the villa gardens, and the local officials would contrive to bump into each other near the villa doorways, against the backdrop of a more refined society.

Now there were Austrian and Italian warships in the bay, and the streets were a hurrying of European costumes – diplomat and traveller – diverse detachments of soldiers, and bewildered locals. Whatever they thought of the new monarchy, the arrival of Prince Wilhelm as Albania's king meant opportunity for merchants and mercenaries and fortune-hunters from across the country and the Continent. And presumably, Ballentyne thought with unease, for spies. There was a bustle around each of the big houses in the town – the new royal palace, and the government offices and the headquarters of each of the European powers – from dawn until late into the evening. Ballentyne woke late on his first morning and set off immediately around the streets; as he strolled, every doorway and street corner seemed to be an intent conversation, and a glance in his direction.

At the Clementi the waiter pretended to remember him – a new affectation. The Greek trader from whom as usual he bought tobacco really did remember him, but was too busy for their habitual exchange about heroic travellers. He called unannounced on Rossi, an acquaintance at the Italian Legation, and found him demoted to a smaller office. Ah yes, he had heard that Ballentyne was in town again. He had been seen – Ballentyne wondered at this – at breakfast. Yes, Durazzo was changed. Greater profile for diplomats of talent? Ah no, Ballentyne was a flatterer, a seducer. Poor Rossi would rot here, unrecognized and unrewarded.

The pleasantries were strained; Rossi looked tired.

Ballentyne said he'd heard there was trouble already; resistance against the king.

Rossi unfolded an elaborate shrug. 'The Epirotes in the south, of course.' He gave each syllable of the Greek word its full value and added an Italian melody to it. 'I fear the Greeks are not to be trusted in this matter. Nearer at hand' – a smaller version of the shrug – 'well, my friend, the king should not take for granted the love of his people. Not an antipathy to the man himself, I think.' He shook his head at this disrespectful idea. 'But each has his grievance, and now finds an occasion to express it.'

The door opened without a knock, and someone stepped in. Rossi was halfway to his feet while Ballentyne was still swivelling in his chair. The new arrival was a man in European dress – another Italian, by the face. Sleek, but running to fat. Rossi waited for instruction, and then saw that the new arrival was staring warily at Ballentyne. 'This is Signor Ballentyne,' he said in Italian, repeating 'Mr Ballentyne' in English for Mr Ballentyne's benefit. 'An Englishman,' he added, as he might have said 'a house-breaker'.

The new arrival stepped forwards and unrolled a hand as if doing a card trick. 'Castoldi,' he said, obscuring Rossi's effort to murmur the same information. Ballentyne rose and shook hands.

'Count Castoldi is the senior diplomatic representative on the king's council,' Rossi said reverentially.

Ballentyne wondered what the Austrian representative on the council would say to this. 'Welcome to Albania,' he said. 'How do you find it so far?'

Castoldi ignored the question. Still gripping Ballentyne's hand, he continued to look at him. 'What function do you have here, Mr Ballentyne?'

The Italian rendition of the English surname had a very different tone to the German, but for Ballentyne it immediately recalled the interrogation on the mountain path, and something of his fear. He smiled pleasantly. 'I'm an anthropologist. Been coming here for years.'

Castoldi's mouth opened in a grin, as if Ballentyne had made a witticism of brilliance, and then the lips formed a silent 'ah'. At last he dropped the hand, then studied Ballentyne from face to feet and back again.

Holiness and pollution not differentiated. *This is how it is to be.* Ballentyne remembered the conversation in London. *They will assume me a spy whatever I say.* He remembered again the terrifying interrogation by the man Hildebrandt. *And now, somehow, it has become true.*

Castoldi turned away. 'Rossi: as soon as you have a moment.'

Even without Rossi's hasty assurances, Ballentyne knew that the moment was expected to be immediate; he excused himself and left. Castoldi watched him all the way out of the door.

+≻═≺+

Duval stamped out of the Museum of Decorative Arts, sick and angry and embarrassed. His whole glorious vision of Berlin, elegant encounters and intrigue and a little flirtation, had burst like a farting bladder. He spat the instruction to the taximan. For some reason the bloody dago had decided to hook it. He could have gone anywhere in Berlin, or sent his telegram and hopped on a train to anywhere else.

Duval leaned forwards and, over the whine of the engine, yelled the change of direction.

The clerk at the station telegraph office was a puff of importance behind half-moon specs. Duval could hear two soldiers arguing behind him in the queue; hear the rattle as they shifted their rifles on their shoulders.

In response to a burbled mess of a story about an irate employer and a failed errand, the clerk revealed that in the ten minutes either side of 10.30 telegrams had been sent to Frankfurt, London, Geneva, Kiel and Dresden and multiply within Berlin. He was scornful of Duval the incompetent.

The murmuring from behind him was rising. *I don't want to be noticed.* Duval stared past the clerk, trying to absorb the layout of the room. The pile of sent telegraph forms was just out of reach. Another question? The name? Someone jostled him, and the half-moons were saying no and Duval hurried away.

He walked for fifteen minutes before he went into a café. He had to leave a gap; couldn't trust himself not to hurry it. The beer was the fizzy German stuff. Wouldn't smoke until he'd finished the beer. Finished the beer. Had the smoke. Another beer – but better not – a bit of courage, but it wouldn't do to go in with gas coming out of every orifice. He ordered a schnapps. Forced himself to sip it. As he was washing his hands he saw a shapeless blue cap, hanging on one of a row of pegs.

He found another café opposite the station building. He sat on a stool in the window, pretending to read a newspaper. The café name had been painted across the window; its thick gothic 'u' cradled a solitary door in the side of the station.

A nightmare vision of a maze of offices behind it, startled officials in every one. The waiter had to ask him three times; Duval, unthinking, ordered another schnapps.

Twice in ten minutes the door in the 'u' opened and someone came out, disappearing into the other letters of the café name. Once someone went in. They didn't seem to use a key.

Duval ordered another schnapps. *Steady, old lad.*

A telegram sent by a phantom. He knocked back the schnapps and stood and strode out of the café.

Two steps, and he stopped and returned and threw a coin down next to the empty glasses. Then across the road, twenty yards, ten yards, five, a thud and he went stumbling and someone was swearing and he made a noise of regret and he had to press on, two yards and one and he felt his hand clenching unwilling and he turned the brass knob and stepped inside.

Not an office but a corridor.

I was sent here by the luggage office. I want to report a loss.

Two or three doors on each side. He started to walk down the corridor. A sign on each door, painted gothic script. What the hell was the German for 'telegraph'?

He kept walking. Wanting to slow to scan the signs, wanting to hurry to get this over with.

The second door on the right opened and a man loomed out in front of him. Some kind of uniform, but dirty; flicking his hands dry. He frowned at Duval and started to speak, but Duval just pushed past him.

He'd hoped for a space to breathe and maybe take his jacket and tie off, make himself look a bit more menial. But this German railway lavatory offered two items as beautiful as anything he'd seen in Florence. A minute later he was in the corridor again, a boiler suit over his clothes and a bin in his arms, with the purloined cap pulled down low on his forehead. *Things I have acquired in German privies.*

The third door on the left was labelled '*Telegrafsamt*'. A breath, and he opened the door a crack.

The clerk was enormous in front of him, just two feet away, sitting at the transmitter. As Duval watched, his hand lifted from the transmitter key and he pulled off the earphones and placed the sent message in the tray. *How can I be sure that's the same pile?* The clerk moved to the counter, where a lady was waiting. *No choice.* Duval braced himself.

But the lady had only asked a question and now she was gone and the clerk was looking around his room again. Surely he would see the crack in the door. A beard appeared over the counter and the clerk turned towards it: '*Bitte sehr?*' The sound of a door opening behind Duval, no choice at all any more, and he pushed forwards into the telegraph office, head low and bin high and he was at the desk; his bin went down in his right hand, with his left he picked up the other bin, and with it obscuring the action he grabbed the middle of the sheaf of telegram forms and he was turning away and pushing the forms into the bin and then he was out and into the corridor. The lavatory door again, the bin, the forms into his boiler suit, a vision of the half-moon specs ballooning enormous and the mouth opening in a yell, and he was in the street.

The taxi rank was twenty yards away. Mustn't run. He realized how silent the corridor had felt now that Berlin was roaring with life around him. Hooters and hooves and wheels and voices and people moving everywhere. Mustn't run. He'd worked this bit out. Mustn't run.

Twenty yards, and the crowd seemed to go silent and drift apart and he was alone in a narrowing corridor of cobbles, peering towards a taxi distant on the horizon. *I am about to be shot.*

<hr>

Sir,

my vainglorious acquaintance with the vainglorious son has shared with me certain confidences regarding the latest discussions between the general staffs of Great Britain and France. Full details have been agreed for the deployment of British Army Corps in France in the event of hostilities; my acquaintance brags that the details extend to the railway transport: how many men in how many cars on which line, where the British troops will stop to drink how much tea, where their horses will find how much forage &c &c; codes and cyphers have been shared. There is a calculated vagueness regarding the command arrangements, and the French will not push the point until British troops are safely across the Channel. The French are delighted, *judging the British fingers trapped firmly in the mangle.*

As we had hoped, the release of Caillaux's letters to the newspapers has ensured that his soothing voice will not be heard at the French ministerial table. This will help to temper the pacifism of the new radical administration here. In truth, French calculations remain subtle; another acquaintance, lately retired from military service, told me just recently of a memorandum prepared by the general staff as far back as 1912 calculating that war in the Balkans would serve French interests by weakening Austria-Hungary and thus freeing Russia to fight Germany. Of such brilliant couplings of logical links are strategy and optimism engendered! It is rumoured that the government's Cabinet Noir is breaking the codes of Britain as well as Germany, who are too free with their use of the telegraph.

Permit me to drop one additional word into your ear. I have lately discovered that a long-standing acquaintance has among his many duties that of secretary to the committee responsible for the Carnet B – the list of suspected persons automatically to be arrested in the event of mobilization. It occurs to me that discreet intimations or suggestive disclosures could cause additional names to be added to this list, of a type calculated to increase confusion in Paris at a critical juncture.

'Metz'

Read twice through, in an office in Vienna of great discretion outside and great elegance inside. Read among other such letters, from Veracruz talking of American naval dispositions, from Calcutta talking of British Army gossip. Read with a connoisseur's smile.

Duval was back at the telegraph office two hours later, by which time it had become a brandy-seared nightmare of a quest. Ma reading *King Arthur* to him. And *Beowulf*. Taxi halfway to the Monopol, walk a bit, the borrowed clothes pushed into a bin, walk the rest of the way. An hour in his room, bent over the table with the telegraph forms and a dictionary and a bottle. Never could stomach desk work. Exams. Sitting still. Couldn't possibly translate... The bottle draining steadily.

He could identify the time Valfierno must have been at the office more closely, and that gave him – what? – say a ten-minute window; half a dozen message forms. None of the names familiar. Most sent within Berlin. The dago might have stayed in the city. Disappeared. Easy enough. He skimmed the Berlin messages, wrote down the addresses, hotels and houses. *So what?* So what if Valfierno went to one of these? In one of the messages someone's plans had changed. One message, to 'Mendel GmbH' – seen that on a few signs; some sort of company – said that because of a competitor the timetable would have to be shorter. He noted that down, this time concentrating on his handwriting more particularly. What was he supposed to do anyway? Frankfurt was probably too early. London? Surely Valfierno couldn't have been heading to London. But was it suspicious? *Oh, for God's sake...* Someone called Carter would be arriving on the 18th. He copied it down. Kiel was more likely. Someone called Becker telling someone called Niedermayer that... he got the gist of it, wrote it down. Someone in Geneva was told that someone in Berlin had... ignition? Infection. The pen scratching on the paper. A company in Dresden being asked to keep a complete something of somethings – set of... couldn't be... swans?

David Duval wrote it all down, and the bottle drained, and each time the chair creaked it was the door knocking and the telegraph clerk and the police.

And what was making him unhappy was the growing knowledge that the forms had to go back. Surely. If they hadn't been missed yet, they would be eventually; probably notice at shut-up shop that the pile was half its size – the quickest flick would show a block of hours missing, and that would be when the clerk would remember the Englishman who... when would the office close, anyway? There'd been some kerfuffle in England about the police monitoring telegraph forms; guarantee the Germans would do that sort of thing. The brandy glass rattled hollow on the tabletop.

The old romances, Ma's mouth in the lamplight, had become first embarrassing to him, then nostalgic. Now he was eight again, wide-eyed and white-knuckled and a dragon waiting under the bed. *Get a grip, old lad.* Put Grendel in a telegraph uniform and glasses and – the taxi pulled up at the station.

Meant to pay it off earlier; now the driver could link the hotel and the station and the police could... Make the taxi wait? More memorable; no. Into the station and wait for a crowd. Steam under the vault of the roof, the evening somehow humid. A fat smell, grease and meat. Noise rising, footsteps and more footsteps and a night train was getting ready and Duval took a breath and pushed through a press of people and headed for the telegraph office. Bought a newspaper, idled against the side of the telegraph office, the crowd still high and someone talking at the counter and behind the newspaper he pushed the telegraph forms through the vent above the transmitter and turned and hurried away. *Mustn't run.* A tentacle of people moving away from the platforms – and had the customer seen anything and what was he saying to the clerk just yards behind him? – and Duval pushed through the crowd and joined it and was carried away out of the station. Like a long sigh.

In the taxi, straining to look over his shoulder, but no running men in uniforms, arms waving guns, and for the first time in a day he felt himself breathing, felt the air reaching all the parts of his chest.

The damnfool business was over. Brisk report to London, done all he could. What the hell were they expecting, anyway? He sat back in the seat, arms outstretched.

The evening was coming alive. Shopfronts were still lit, a business Berlin of dresses and hats and confectionery, of frock-coats in first-floor windows pacing and dictating. And the twinkles of night were firing up, the Berlin of theatre porticos and grand glazed restaurants and glimmers of invitation down side streets. He deserved a night on the town. The taxi swung through... Potsdamer Platz, a glimpse of the gothic sign, an amphitheatre of haughty façades watching a circus of life, horse-drawn buses rattling among the crowd and trams cutting through all. Was there anything more continental than a mansard roof? The avenues rather fine, as an idea – perspective, a sense of proportion and place to everything – but the general building style uninspired. The last fifty years hadn't been kind to the frontages of Europe, had they? And Berlin had suffered more than most. Too much fussing over cornices and pediments, affectations of Renaissance styling on long slabs of barracks. Like a fat man considering himself cultured with half a dozen words of French and a gay bow tie.

Handsome women, the Germans; been told so. *Ye Gods, what's that?* Like an old tit sagging up into the sky. Church of some sort. *The crimes of the baroque.* All very pleasant to glide through. Again the strange whine of the taxi. Some innovation of the engine – always rather enjoyed engineering drawing, but never got the hang of how automobile cylinders – no, different; and a memory... Berlin's taxis were all electric. Whatever that meant. Now, this was more like it: roof was a witch's hat stolen from some fairytale castle on the Rhine, unfortunately, but the frontage now, elegant windows and the surround restrained; good proportions... Leipzigerstraße. A walk tomorrow. And so back to his hotel, the promise of hot water and a change of clothes and then out into the lights.

In his hotel room, a shadow was sitting in the corner and Duval's heart stopped.

And started again, hard: 'Who the hell are— Look! I've had about enough,' and sickly he knew he should have turned and run.

'Hallo, Duval.' Steady, quiet.

'Who—' but he knew. His shoulders dropped. 'Knox.'

A table lamp clicked on. Major Valentine Knox watched him for a moment, then stood and came forwards and reached out his hand.

London pub or Berlin shadow, always bloody watching like a block of bloody wood with a private joke. 'Look, you bastard,' – an angry finger up into Knox's face and then Duval growled and turned and checked the door was locked – 'I've had e-bloody-nough of...' He subsided again, and shook hands.

Then he brushed past Knox and strode to the desk, picked up the brandy bottle, found it empty, thrust it down towards the bin, and was already searching vainly among the glasses and mineral water as the bottle bounced from bin-rim to desk-leg and so under a chair.

Knox said: 'You all right, old chap?'

Duval spun and glared at him. 'You know, for about ten minutes I actually was? Then you showed up. You and your bloody secret messages, Knox, messages and run here and bloody there. Have you any idea—'

'Brought you a present.' Knox held up a bottle. 'Seem to remember...' Duval was on it in two strides and gripping the neck. 'If you're sure you haven't had...'

'Don't get funny, General. Doesn't suit the pose of military stolidity.' Knox let go of the bottle and Duval stepped away with his prize. 'Armagnac indeed. That is, quite literally, the spirit.'

They sat, Knox back on his chair and Duval on the bed, a cigarette in his hand. Knox sipped at the brandy.

Duval took a gulp of his. 'I lost him, Knox. I tried, I... He gave me the slip at the station here.'

'Gave you the slip? He knew you were following him?'

'Must have – I don't know. I assumed—'

'Best not, eh?'

Duval took a deep breath. 'It's just possible he changed his plans at the last minute, but... sending his bags to the hotel and not showing, that looked like a deliberate wheeze. Maybe he's just super-cautious; habits of a man in your business. You'd know better.' Knox considered this. 'Maybe it was nothing to do with me. I don't know. But he's a wrong 'un, certainly. The business with the – he sent a telegram, from the station – except he didn't, not in his name—'

'Valfierno isn't his only name. Apparently. Also goes by Perez and Bollino and a couple of varieties of the same.'

Duval pulled a folded sheet of paper from inside his jacket, and scanned it.

'Didn't use any of those names.'

'How do you know?'

Duval fluttered the paper at him. 'I, er, broke into the station telegraph office. Pinched the forms from—'

Knox's voice was flat as ever, but the eyes were a fraction wider. 'You broke into the telegraph office? A German, official, telegraph office?'

'Only way to find out where he was going. But none of the messages at that time is obviously him. Some kind of code, clearly. But which?' Knox was watching him with interest. 'Oh, don't worry: I went back and replaced them.'

Emphasis in the voice now: 'You broke into a telegraph office twice?'

'It has been, my dear Knox, quite a day.' He described the messages. Knox stretched out his hand for the paper. Duval watched his eyes moving slowly down it.

Eventually the eyes came up, as if something in Duval's face would give away the answer, and then down into the page again. 'Don't see how flu in Berlin could change plans in Geneva,' he said conversationally.

'That's what I thought. But I checked; there's no train to Geneva; nothing like.' Duval was up off the bed and pacing. 'He can't have gone on there.'

'Mm. Maybe Kiel then. A date set. Don't remember the German, do you?'

'No, Knox, I don't remember the German. The Berlin one seemed more promising.' Knox glanced down, grunted. 'And "swans"?'

'Yes, that does seem unlikely, doesn't it?'

'And what's that London one about, then?'

'Mm. Need checking, that one.' Knox folded the paper, and slipped it into his jacket. Duval watched it go with a vague sense of loss. 'They want you in St Petersburg in a week or two. For now, since you're in Berlin rather than Rome, there's a different set of people for you to rootle out, of course; different questions. Kiel too.' Knox stood, and passed a single sheet to him.

'Of cou— But – well, hang on, what about Valfierno?'

'What about him?'

'That's it?'

'Put out a lonely heart if you like. But keep an eye out for these birds now. The first in particular, apparently. Same drill.' Duval glanced at the page: half a dozen names, short notes after each; as many questions. 'Lots of interest in Kiel: naval construction, ship movements, that sort of thing. Let yourself go: break into the new submarine dock, why don't you?' He smiled maliciously, and then was serious again. 'It's all on there. Get that lot into your head and then burn the page, obviously.'

'Oh, obviously.' Duval looked at the face, impassive and waiting. 'Is that what it's all about? Little piss-drops of information on odd-bods and unknowns?' Knox reached for a coat from the back of the chair. 'You off somewhere?'

'That's about it. And yes, I am off.' Knox checked around himself, adjusted the cushion on the chair.

Duval watched, faintly dazed. 'Who was he, anyway? The dago.'

A little shrug from Knox. 'No idea.'

'That's it? I've hared across Europe – you've done the same—'

'It's not a coconut shy, Duval. You don't get a prize every time.'

'It's all a bust, then.'

'Usually is.'

Duval splashed more of the Armagnac into his glass. 'I had high hopes for this evening, Knox. Don't suppose you fancy a night on the tiles? Horse Guards let you do that, would they? Fraternize with the Hun in the interests of the cloak and dagger stuff?'

The smile came unexpected, as usual. 'Oh, fraternizing with the Hun is half the reason I'm here. That's quite all right.' His hand was on the door handle. 'But not fraternizing with you.'

Becalmed on the other side of the room, one of however many rooms in the hotel, in the city of uniforms and telegraph clerks and electric taxis and grand buildings, Duval suddenly felt the lack of a decent meal, felt somehow thinner with the brandy rather than warm.

Knox's fingers drummed on the handle. 'Duval,' he said; 'I confess it: I took you for a fop and a poseur; didn't know why the great men were bothering with you.'

'Thank you very much.'

Knox stood there, appraising him.

He didn't speak. 'Well? Sounded like you were going to deign to modify your opinion.'

Knox's mouth twisted into discomfort, and then into a smile, and he was gone.

HIGHEST SECRECY

Sir, further to telegram, with greatest urgency I report the destruction of air machine Ex.7 in a fire in our hangar at the Paris aerofield. The MERCURIUS device was destroyed in the machine.

The cause of the fire cannot be determined. Investigation by the French police was not conclusive, and I have not wished to allow the police to extend their presence. The unavoidable combination, in the wooden hangar, of electricity, machinery, fuel and combustible material (both the framework of the machine and its covering) offers many possibilities.

Although there is no indication of it, I do not exclude the possibility of sabotage by our enemies. This section of the field is fenced and guarded, and the hangar was locked, yet these obstacles are not insurmountable. The building and the machine, an ALBATROS of B.1 type, was completely burned, and of the Milewski apparatus, which had been installed for experimental flights, only fragments of metal and wire remain. (No hint of its design or purpose may be seen from the residue, but nevertheless I have prevented all further inspection by outsiders.) This has cost us one ALBATROS, and it will no doubt take 1-2 weeks for a replacement MERCURIUS to be assembled and installed in a replacement air-machine. Berlin will know the true cost of this delay better than I.

The embassy, at my direction, are pressing the police to put extra guards around the field, and improve arrangements at the gate. The companion air-machine was in a separate hangar, and is undamaged. We may continue unrelated testing and our other activities. I shall remain in Paris, pending your further orders.

v. C.

[DEUTSCHE BUNDESARCHIV (AUTHOR TRANSLATION)]

ALBANIA: A 'REBEL' VILLAGE; POSSIBLE AUSTRIAN INFLUENCE
Italian Legation acquaintance ROSSI raised concerns of
Austrian attempts to exacerbate unrest of rebel Muslims in
villages of central Albania. Also made loose claims about
international collusion against Italian interests.

Rossi dropping into the seat in front of him at breakfast. The eyes; the hands never stopping; the anger. Trying to calm him; trying to find clarity in the fog of words.

Ballentyne wasn't sure about the style of the report. There had been no guidance in London. He was allowed a bit of analysis, presumably. But he had the sense that a more telegraphic style would be appropriate – more military. He'd tried to imagine Mayhew reading the report.

Superficially, the circumstances of the rising are clear.
Men mobilized and armed by Minister of War ESSAD to go
south to fight rebels there have themselves rebelled. That
they are Muslim is a factor of identity, and perhaps a reason
for some concern about what they hear of Durrës politics,
but not a strong motive. Real grievances are likely to be
simpler, and neither political nor religious. Nevertheless,
their religion remains potentially fertile ground should
any external actor wish to stir mischief.

Salted milk, and the bread had been warm, and there'd been coffee of course. The men drifting in, each arrival marked by the clatter of a rifle being laid against the wall just inside the door; some known to his host, some not. The usual exchanges – their health, their families' health, whether married or not, sons – and then what Ballentyne referred to as 'the difficulties'. It turned out there were lots of difficulties. The government; corruption; the minister of war, who was corrupt; prices; rotten grain; the weather. It was a rising, perhaps: the rifles, the sentries, the trouble he'd heard about in half a dozen places. But it was age-old.

For now the 'rising' is essentially passive. Those involved
– often the inhabitants – are claiming to hold selected
villages. They control and restrict access, and the royal
gendarmerie have not the inclination to test the point.

Passing an idling handful of troops by the road, uncomfortable
and uneasy in their new uniforms. The dirt road rising out of the dry
swampland around Durrës – acres of scrub littering the ground – and
across a line of hills. The heights and valleys of central Albania in front of
him, purple and vague in the haze. The mountains ghosts in the distance.
A mile farther on the challenge, two men in village dress acting as sentries;
waiting although there was no suggestion of threat. And then the escort; a
man who for a moment seemed to think he recognized Ballentyne.

As he remembered it, he reviewed it. *I am now so alert to who people
think I am.* Discomfort. *Who I am is now a subject for uncertainty as well
as interest.* The escort's questions. Where was he from? He was English;
always better to be foreign among the Albanians, even if he could have
pretended otherwise. What was he doing? Just riding; he'd been travelling
here for many years. What was he – diplomat? soldier? He was a scientist
– insects and such like.

It was a line he'd often used in the villages of the north; less obnoxious
than saying straight out that you studied the habits of the people
themselves. *Have I always been dissembling about myself?*

A 'rebel' village shows little sign of disturbance from its
routine. Such places would not know regular visits from the
authorities even in normal times.

Scattered lath-and-mud houses, the occasional threadbare donkey; a
mangy dog, which might or might not have been dead, slumped on the
verge; a chicken, tattered and berserk, bursting out of a shed and weaving
across their path; in a yard, half a dozen healthy-looking horses.

And yet there were signs of unfamiliar activity, and
activity that was to be kept secret.

The horses. The house where they were going to have coffee, a line of
shoes outside and among the broken dusty specimens of village cobbling a
pair of good-quality western-style boots, and a guard who muttered to the
escort and it seemed they would have to get their coffee elsewhere. Then,
when they were riding out again, looking back to see men coming out of
that forbidden house, and the boots being pulled on by a large Albanian;
a man with elaborate straggling moustaches and a pistol tucked in at the
base of his spine.

Moreover, as the Italians had suggested, there has been
at least one foreigner in the village. His motives and
activities are not entirely clear.

His punt. Had they seen a friend of his in the district, just recently?
A *frengji*, a foreigner, like him? Yes, they had. And at last the escort had
understood why Ballentyne had seemed familiar: another fair-haired man,
and not unlike Ballentyne. The villagers arguing about the foreigner. He
was a priest; he wasn't a priest. He was Muslim; he wasn't Muslim. Had he,
Ballentyne had asked, been trying to preach to them – to give them ideas?
No, they'd said. Just visiting.

Like you, they'd said.

Something about the dry landscape and the empty sky, the plod of
the horse through the dust, had reconjured a childhood illustration of
Don Quixote. With each step, the strength of the idea of the Austrian,
or whoever this foreigner was, dwindled. As, lurking alongside, did his
clarity about his own role.

Why had he ridden out? A chance to get out of the city. A chance to
seem to take Rossi seriously – and perhaps to prove to Rossi that... what?
That he wasn't a spy? But, demonstrably, he now was.

It is not clear why Catholic Austria should be interested in
fomenting Muslim unrest. But so many truisms of European

[SS G/1/891/3]

He'd not been sure about that last bit. A bit too pat, a bit too wise, for Mayhew? But he refused to give up all habits of style and argument.

What would they think in London, reading it? Ballentyne on target, or Ballentyne missing the point completely? Mayhew's requirements: to maintain an understanding of the forces in play in Albania and Serbia; to note the activities of other European powers; to communicate anything that seemed unusual, of concern, or in flux.

Forgetting Rossi's empty alarms about what people were or weren't telling him, there was something: an Austrian active among the rebels. That, at least, had been the solid fact behind Rossi's concerns.

Or that, at least, was what Rossi wanted him to think was fact.

And so the madness begins.

+=—=+

'My dear Hildebrandt.'

Hildebrandt's eyes came up fast, watchful, measuring. The lips merely smiled pleasantly.

'My dear Hildebrandt, I recall your description of the death of the Englishman Ballentyne.'

'Indeed, sir. And I gave my explanation. Even if I had not time to get the information we wanted, he were better—'

'My dear fellow' – the voice was subtly sharper – 'you gave me the explanation, and I accepted it. No need to repeat; no need.'

And yet here the subject was again. Hildebrandt's eyes watchful, measuring.

'No, what is perhaps worthier of explanation... is this.' The hand turned outwards, revealing a slip of paper.

After a moment, Hildebrandt reached for it. Its meaning was obvious and instant.

'He seems rather less dead than you had thought, or no?'

Hildebrandt's lips wrinkled. 'A second chance is a rare treat.' He handed the paper back.

'I hoped you would see it that way. This time, let us see if Mr Ballentyne can have a while to explain some matters before he dies. Eh?'

The older man turned, and left. Hildebrandt watched his back, watched the slip of paper protruding from the fingers. *But not a very long while, Mr Ballentyne.*

<hr/>

This is what Germany should be.

A cart weaving through a forest, sunlight dwindling through the canopy of pine branches and myth, sounds snatched from imagination's undergrowth: a river in spate, birdsong, wolves. Then a gate held up by ivy, the forest opening to meadow and distant mountains, and a castle out of a fairytale, towers and turrets. Inside it, dogs snuffling around her waist and a silent servant and every chamber a stone and tapestried tomb with hammer-beamed heavens.

The Germany of romantic fantasy. Ironically, the Germany behind Niemann's fantasy. And with modern plumbing. A Germany to take refuge in.

At the heart of this Germany, Freiherr Gerhard von Waldeck, sixty and six feet tall, straight as one of his turrets with only a fat Saxon moustache to break the line. The welcome seemed genuine – as first welcomes always are in fairytales.

He didn't remember much of her uncle at the university; a pity; but delighted to get his letter. Hathaway seemed to remember that Uncle Peter had only been at Heidelberg for a term; to be honest, really an old family friend rather than a relative. Lucky to have her, the Freiherr thought. No sons, Hathaway explained, and his male relatives more interested in money or hunting. Their loss, the Freiherr's gain. He understood they'd got women students at Heidelberg now – charming innovation – might have been the one thing to drag him out of the library. And mountain stream eyes stared down at her.

The baron's hair was white now, but she knew it had been blond and just as thick forty years ago. Men like this had prowled and hunted these forests for thousands of years, luring Roman legions to their doom, and no doubt the occasional Red Riding Hood.

Von Waldeck was showing her the library – which was magnificent, a leather forest of rarities – before she'd even been relieved of her coat. She managed to excuse herself once but, when she came back a little while later to give her host a rebinding of the Appendix to Carlyle's *Frederick the Great* and a pot of Oxford marmalade, she found him laying out manuscripts for her.

'Is it particularly the Council of Constance that your uncle is interested in?'

'Yes, though not only as an act of diplomacy and internationalism in itself; also as a turning point in the Church's relations with the national movements.'

'Of course; yes, a most interesting perspective. Because I've a little curiosity you might enjoy, here: a letter home from an English monk who attended the Council of Basel.'

'Well, I'm not supposed to get into Basel. I think my uncle finds the chaos rather unsettling —'

The clunk of the latch – a thing as big as her forearm – on the library door interrupted their re-examination of the Conciliar movement. 'Daddy, have – yes, I knew it!'

A young woman strode towards them, a crown of golden hair and a plain white dress. 'I pushed you to invite her, and you kidnap her before I've even said hallo.' She came level with them, and her fingers brushed Hathaway's shoulder. A flash of even teeth as she turned. 'I'm a visitor from the twentieth century. I liberate souls who are trapped in the Middle Ages.'

'Fräulein Hathaway might be a natural inhabitant of the Middle Ages, and stronger than you.'

The woman stepped back and studied Hathaway's face. 'She definitely looks twentieth century. And very handsome. Do all Englishwomen—'

'Fräulein Hathaway is researching the Council of Constance.'

'But why?' She seemed genuinely surprised. 'All those grim monks, talking for years and then burning poor Hus.'

'Conciliarism was a worthy attempt to bring together—'

'Rubbish, Daddy. A political game and it didn't work. The true progressives were in the individual courts: Burgundy; even Bohemia.'

'My daughter wants to become an engineer, and is only interested in things that move forwards or preferably explode.'

'Like her introductions?' Hathaway said. She'd always found German women rather frustrating – the promise of common sense overwhelmed by deference or the urge to bake something – but the vitality of von Waldeck's daughter was appealing. Again, the teeth as she laughed.

A graceful taking of the hand. 'I'm Gerta.' She was suddenly more formal. 'It's my pleasure to welcome you to our house – Father probably forgot that. I insist that you be my friend and wake me from my sleep of a thousand years.'

Hathaway saw a woman of around her own age and height. Blonde where she was dark, an old-fashioned hour-glass of a figure where she was more slender; ironically, it was a nineteenth-century figure. Full lips in a full face, eyes the crystal of the father. Gerta von Waldeck was luxuriant. Hathaway said: 'The consensus has always been that I'm unfriendly. But it seems I've incentive enough to pretend like mad.' Von Waldeck's wife had died early, she'd been told in London – the absent mother didn't seem a strong presence in the house or in her daughter – and there was the impression that Gerta had had responsibility too young to be spoiled. 'Engineering?'

Some of the poise dropped away to be replaced by earnestness. 'When I went to Heidelberg I was still foolish enough to be listening to my father, and he wouldn't let me study anything more practical than logic. I'm ten years older now and it's about time I did something useful.'

Von Waldeck was still standing close, smiling from his height. 'If you must discuss these obscenities, could you go to the boiler room?'

'I love this library, but we mustn't tell him – Did he show you his Locke? I'm sure to an Englishwoman I seem very – what would you say? Unladylike?'

'If it's any of my business, I think it's admirable.'

'You are a mediaevalist?'

'Not really; only enough to help this uncle of mine with his research.'

'But you were at university?' *A question a woman would never think to ask a woman in England.*

Hathaway glanced sadly at the old man. 'Mathematics, I'm afraid.'

A groan. 'A spy!' von Waldeck said, waving his fist. 'An intruder from the sciences in the citadel of the arts.' He smiled, but Hathaway caught a flicker of genuine disappointment. 'What I thought a well-exercised classical brain turns out to be a soulless juggler of equations. You'll want to measure everything, I presume, or mechanize it.'

Gerta was holding her arm now. 'Father, who is coming to dinner?'

'Bierhoff has some people staying. All bankers like him, I fear. And Löwenthal to keep me company.' He turned to Hathaway, straight and polished and weathered as the spines lined up behind him. 'Tonight, Fräulein Hathaway, this old ruin will once again host the men who truly rule Germany.'

⊹═══⊹

A knock, and Hildebrandt was standing in Krug's doorway. 'You made an enquiry of Nicolai, Mein Herr. About a Boer named Duquesne.' Krug waited. 'He was in America. Now he is in Brazil.'

'Brazil? Why should he be there?'

'Perhaps the Americans wanted rid of him.'

'Well they might. Or perhaps he was sent there, eh, Hildebrandt?' Hildebrandt smiled innocence.

The British were more active – more diplomats, more economic interests – in South America than in many places, certainly than in south-eastern Europe. And so more of a target for German Intelligence.

'Hildebrandt, before you go.' A newspaper, sharp folds, opened out on the desk. 'My friends in Berlin seem to be having a little difficulty.'

Hildebrandt came forwards, and glanced down. 'Yes, Herr Krug.'

At the bottom of the page was a brief report of the destruction of a German biplane in a fire at Issy-les-Moulineaux aerodrome. 'This was the machine with the experimental wireless equipment?' Silence, and an insolent stare. 'Oh come, my friend. The invention of the Jew from Krakow, no?'

'Indeed.'

'Presumably visiting Paris to consult Coquelin. I'm afraid I never understand the technical details.'

'As always, your information is exceptional, Mein Herr.'

A tut. 'We must see if my connections can be of service to your superiors. This is what friends are for, surely.'

A smile, lifeless. 'I am sure that would be most generous.'

'Not at all. This alliance must be made to mean something. Who is the man on the spot?'

'Your newspaper says that the pilot is von Cramm. He will be in charge of this phase of the project. He is... highly trusted in Berlin.'

'We must try to help him regain that trust.' Krug nodded to himself, another item on the agenda approved.

From his hotel window the previous evening, Duval had watched Knox crossing the street and disappearing into the night. Other eyes had watched the same movement. Shortly afterwards those eyes had been scanning the hotel register.

It was late in the morning when Duval set out into Berlin for a stroll. There'd been rain, and the air felt fresh. He'd got fifty yards when his inattentive vision filled with policemen. One looming in front, two close beside him. An instant of shock, and panic and the necessity of making a run for it, and one of the bayonets brushed his sleeve as he stood there.

'Papiere, Mein Herr.'

He reached very carefully into his jacket.

The policeman's eyes kept moving between Duval's face and the paper, as if the name on it was also stencilled on his forehead – in not very clear letters.

He handed the paper back, and withdrew. They were disappointed.

Duval forced himself to take a roundabout route back to the hotel, but he was still there inside five minutes. And out again, with his kit, inside another five. Time to lie low.

Later – 'You're next to me. When you've finished dressing you must come to my room and we can talk properly' – Hathaway found herself perched on the edge of Gerta von Waldeck's bed, watching her finish rearranging her hair.

There was only one chair, wooden, and it had Gerta's day dress thrown over it. Hathaway had expected a princess's boudoir, and found a plain practical room, old rugs at bedside and dressing table. There were half a dozen elaborate dresses in the open wardrobe, and her immediate impression had been how old-fashioned they were – *really, do German women know no age between adolescence and matronhood?* – and then she realized they were hand-me-downs from a dead mother.

Gerta had offered her a cigarette – accepted – and sat on a stool facing her dressing table, smoking as she deployed pins and glanced occasionally at Hathaway's reflection in the mirror.

'You must forgive me asking personal questions, Flora. But I was so pleased when your uncle wrote to ask if you could visit the library. I think it's wonderful, a woman travelling on her own. Though I worried that you would be fifty and dull. You've no idea how pleased I was to see you standing in the library, and my father with his chest out like one of his young heroes.'

'You must come to visit England.' And then alarm that she might actually accept; Gerta von Waldeck having to bed down in the boxroom at home.

Gerta twisted round on the stool. 'I'd – oh, but I couldn't. These days, it wouldn't seem—'

'These days?'

Gerta turned back to the mirror. 'The way everyone talks. When he got your uncle's letter, Daddy was very earnest about English scholarship and English schools. But really, well...'

'We don't feel like enemies, Gerta.'

'I know. Would you...' She was stretching for a box of pins on the bed; and there was a rip and a curse.

A fussy exchange, before Hathaway was on her knees with needle and thread working at the tear. 'I thought I was going to be Rotkäppchen; turns out I'm Aschenputtel's king.'

'Flora, I'm so ashamed. If I had a maid, you wouldn't have to—'

'If I had a maid, I wouldn't know how to.'

'I was worried you'd be disappointed if you found out.' Gentle laughter from Hathaway. 'Oh, I wouldn't say it, except you seem so sensible. We've really no – Daddy has sold most of my mother's pictures, and it's so expensive for Rudi in the army. Really, we're like vagrants who've broken into a palace when the owners are away.'

'Sit still, will you?'

'I'm sure it's different in the castles in England.'

'Dear Gerta, I've never been in a castle in England, except when I paid sixpence for a tour. My father is a doctor and his whole house would fit into your hall. There. It's clumsy, but I've turned it in so it won't show.'

Gerta glanced at the repair, and placed a kiss on Hathaway's forehead. 'I thought all English girls rode around in carriages and went to balls. You're such a rich country, and so aristocratic.'

'Where do you read such stuff?' She sat back on the bed.

'It's – it's what we know about England.' She turned away to the mirror. 'It's why you're such a... such a superior country.' She giggled, self-scorn. 'When we got your uncle's letter, I assumed he was a rich lord who didn't know that Daddy was poor, and that you moved around Europe from palace to palace and had never even seen a public library.'

'I'm here because the true civilization – of the intellect, of humanity – crosses borders more easily than it crosses social barriers.'

Gerta spun round on the stool. 'Oh!' A little excitement. 'Are you a radical, Flora?'

'I – I don't think so.'

'You mustn't say anything too revolutionary at dinner. All these bankers are always terribly worried about social unrest. Daddy is really the most – well, almost liberal of men, more than any of them. But he's quite old-fashioned about dinner conversation.'

'Will you at least let me put time-bombs under their carriages?'

'I – I don't know...'

'I'm sorry. English humour.'

'Oh.' A shy conspiratorial smile, and Gerta von Waldeck returned to her crown of hair.

⊹═══⊹

'What else vexes the worthy Nicolai, Hildebrandt? How else may we be of service?'

'You are in most obliging mood, Herr Krug.'

Deliberately, with focus, Krug lit a cigarette and waited for it to glow to his satisfaction. 'This is the age of mass, Count Paul. Of machinery. Of millions. In every sphere of human endeavour, even one as subtle as my own, it is essential to be at one with the age. I recognize that the approach that served me twenty years ago, and ten years ago, may become as obsolete as the fashions and technologies of those years.'

'And Nicolai's structures – his resources, his networks in Britain – you think that joining them will serve this purpose.'

A smile through the smoke. 'Joining? Adopting them, Hildebrandt.'

Hildebrandt watched the face as it paled and clarified through the drifting smoke.

Krug enjoyed it. 'The age of mass does not mean the defeat of the individual; it means the triumph of the individual who can control the mass.' Another puff of smoke. 'A time when we find out which German counts have the brains, eh?'

Hildebrandt ignored it; lit a cigarette. Eventually he said, 'Nicolai has been set a... a problem of intelligence.' Krug stifled a smile theatrically. 'German Intelligence have an agent...' – hesitation; Krug looking away – 'in the Russian Embassy in London.'

'Oh, my compliments!' It sounded genuine. 'That is smart work indeed. Surely not – if I guess rightly, I considered the fellow, but there seemed little chance...'

'A matter of German ancestry, I think.'

'Ah, truly German blood is thicker than anything.'

'The agent reports preliminary naval conversations between Britain and Russia.'

Krug nodded. 'It was inevitable, I suppose; truly the British are rattled if they are moving so fast.'

'The Russians are keener than the British. In Berlin, the Admiralty and the Stadtschloss are worried, and at the same wondering what to do with this information.'

'They should not worry too much. The Russians are as mischievous to Britain in Persia as they are conciliatory in Europe; neither trusts the other. And as to using the information... Such a fascinating snippet deserves a wider public airing, I think.'

'Risk exposing a spy over information that by definition Moscow and London know?'

'Half of Britain's politicians will be alarmed by this development, and this will cause their government to hesitate; that's good. The Russians will think the British irresponsible or double-dealing; that's good. The German public will be angered; and that's very good. As to your spy, I can contrive adequate cover. Perhaps this information could appear to leak from Paris to one of your newspapers. Would that satisfy, would you say?'

Continental deceptions as if he were trading potatoes. Hildebrandt smiled, nodded: 'More than adequately, I would say.'

'Good. *Bon voyage*, my friend. And good hunting.'

Dinner with Freiherr von Waldeck in his castle was surprisingly similar to going to supper with the Pattisons at the Rectory. Despite efforts at sense, Hathaway had not avoided an expectation of a picture-book banquet, a pig on a spit and flagons and women with pointed hats. The setting was mediaeval enough, and one could have ridden into battle wielding the cutlery, but electric lighting supplemented the candles and the three-course meal would have been no more than normal on the table of any solicitor or businessman – or doctor – in Britain. The men had dressed with the professional's concern for acquired propriety, the women with money and caution.

Something else common to the equivalent table in Britain: it was a gathering of men, with their wives. The conversation was between the men, careful talk of the situation in Berlin, of prices, of what one had read in the newspaper, of what another had heard from a neighbour's gamekeeper. The wives listened, or were occasionally given the chance to offer a descant to the conversation drawn from domestic or cultural spheres. In the archaic setting, Hathaway had a momentary picture of the men as knights, solid and cumbersome and supported by their squires.

Löwenthal turned out to be a retired lawyer, who was briefly persuaded to talk about his real passion, which was ornithology, and otherwise chattered to von Waldeck about books; the other men joined in that conversation intelligently and respectfully. And Von Waldeck, for all his pose of romanticism, was shrewd enough about their commerce. Discussion of banking. A current concern about pressure on the Mark's relationship to the gold standard as a result of developments in the United States. Someone had seen a pamphlet from the Social Democratic Party identifying the three ills of the age as imperialism, militarism and capitalism, and felt that these were only negative labels for the necessary expansion of economic productivity, which was hard enough in these times; general agreement. Hathaway had shifted in her seat, and started to wonder what she thought of this, when she'd caught a look of such alarm from Gerta that she'd stayed silent.

Hathaway had been briefly explained when they were gathering for dinner, and attracted little attention. At one point Bierhoff, the banker, observed that she was presumably travelling because of the persistent strength of sterling, which turned out to be the comedic high-point of the evening. The man next to her – of her own generation, with a fine profile and rather alarming teeth – had the courtesy to flirt with her, over-attentive with the condiments and asking politely about her home, but they both felt it wrong to ignore the main conversation.

Otherwise she felt like an observer, watching mannequins through a window.

At the end of the meal, Gerta – who made a poised and stately hostess – invited the ladies to withdraw, a practice Hathaway had loathed on the few occasions she'd been at dinners smart enough for it to happen. A glance over her shoulder as she went showed the men silent and waiting for the last dress to glide away, and she wondered whether with the ladies' departure conversation would suddenly veer into the most boisterous lewdness or ossify completely.

The sitting room into which she followed the other women was the one over-furnished room in the building. With creaks and sighs the frothy dresses settled into sofas, and Hathaway had the impression of a troupe of dancers returning to the dressing room.

'That was most pleasant, dear Gerta.'

'I do hope so, Frau Kuhn. We do try to make the best of the place when we have special guests.'

'How is Helga, Sonja?'

'Much rested, my dear. Thank you for asking. Just two weeks – it's not cheap, you know – but the peace helps as much as the air.'

'You'll pardon me, dear, but I thought Kuhn is looking rather tired. A very difficult time, I'm sure.'

'My dear, he's working all the hours. I had to fight to get him away even for these four days.'

'Otto was saying the markets are flat.'

'I don't know how these things relate, quite, but in the overseas department Hans is frantic.'

A glance at Hathaway, representative of all overseas problems. 'The newspapers are so alarming.'

'Some nights it's nine or ten. Then so early in the morning. All these foreign currencies he's in charge of, and now he's ordered to convert them to gold. Such a strain. It's not healthy.'

'Lena, dearest, how is young Stegemann?'

'Thank you, Frau Kuhn. He's well. Away with his regiment, of course, but he's very good at writing to me.' Frau Stegemann was the only other young woman in the room, a plain and constantly worried face on an athletic body.

'He didn't think of going into his father's bank?'

'No, Frau Edler. No, he thought it his duty to—'

'The army is invincible, we understand. We need the respectable young men to apply their brains to their real interest: maintaining financial stability and thus keeping order in the country.'

Hathaway found herself scrutinized as if she were an immediate threat to financial and political order, and started to ask about the destabilizing effects of capitalism, but Gerta hastily invited Frau Stegemann to play some Schubert.

When Gerta closed the door behind the last of the guests and turned to scold and then broke into laughter, Hathaway joined in – and then went upstairs to write a letter.

✦

The Sub-Committee of the Committee for Imperial Defence:

'What news from Paris? Your delivery.'

'Still closed in. Three days now. Weather, mechanical trouble, then weather again.'

'War Office getting very fidgety, old chap.'

'My compliments to them, but they're not half as fidgety as poor Hamel. Stuck out in Paris, sitting on the goods, gendarmes and German spies breathing down his neck. The German Embassy have got the Frogs in a rare fluster. Extra guards at the aerodrome; checks on entry and departure. Thirty seconds of clear sky and he'll be up like a firework and on his way home.'

'That's all very well, but it only underlines the need to find a solution quickly. I don't need to remind—'

'No, you really don't. Not unless you want... That's my man out there, and a good one. Hamel'll pull it off. Always has.'

'We should start thinking about alternative transport.'

'We've finished thinking about alternative transport. You know damn well you can't put this thing in your coat or take it to the post office.'

'There are still options by road and sea.'

'With guards on the gate and the Hun no doubt watching every harbour?'

'Nonetheless. I'll make some enquiries. Ports and so forth.'

'You'll pardon me, gentlemen.' A grey voice, from beyond the edge of the conversation: the old man. 'A word of interference from an old warhorse.' Tight-lipped reassurances. 'I presume we don't want to rattle the cage too much. If Hamel and his shipment are still intact, then it looks like our opponents don't suspect – not enough to act, anyway. In which case, we don't want to draw attention to him, do we?'

<hr />

For their next lunch, it was Cade's turn to host Riza again. The opening glass of sherry had become routine.

The newspapers had reported rumours about the signing of the Protocol of Corfu; Riza was interested in Cade's interpretation. Cade had heard of a new edict issued by the Grand Vizier specifying which ethnic groups in the empire were permitted to trade, and wondered what was behind it.

By the time they were finishing their lamb, Riza was winding himself up at the latest affront to his dignity and independence committed by German advisers in the ministry.

Cade's heart began to pound; it wasn't the richness of the food.

Now, surely.

'... a humble man, Mr Cade, but I think I may fairly say that I know something of the basic precepts of financial...'

Make the pitch.

'... not as if Germany was without economic challenges or social divisions...'

'What eats at me, Mr Riza' – it came out a little loud, and he moderated it – 'and please forgive me butting in, but it does as I say eat at me, is the destructiveness of it all.' Riza wanted to agree, but waited. 'I mean to say: as a friend I naturally sympathize with you over these rudenesses, but to me as a businessman – and I suspect to you as a professional official – the worst is the impact on good and prudent administration.'

'Quite right, Mr Cade.'

'I like to think I know you a little, Mr Riza, and I think you're probably the sort of fellow who's experienced enough and sturdy enough to put up with these personal irritations, but that it's the damage to principle and to good practice from these come-and-go, fly-by-night fellows that's what really niggles you.'

'That's absolutely— Ah... "niggles"?'

'Bothers you. Angers you. Gets on your what-not.'

'Thank you. Mr Cade, you are absolutely right.' He waved a last piece of meat on his fork, then laid it down. 'In fifteen years in the imperial administration I have, I am sad to say it, got used to superiors who are ignorant, incompetent, or inconsiderate, or all three. Stupidity, alas, does not recognize national borders.'

'Quite right. You should see the Glasgow Chamber of Commerce, especially after lunch.'

'One sighs, one does what one can to avoid disaster, and then one goes home; a glass of wine, a conversation with my son, a book of verses... the irritations are past.'

'Hear, hear.' *Don't rush him, Jimmy.*

'But when the interests of the Sultan, and of the people – basic principles of good administration – are set aside...'

'You mustn't feel you have to tell me details, but is it... is it really as destructive as that?'

The fork had come up, and now went down again with a rattle. 'It is, Mr Cade. It is thought that the empire has always been ruled by whim, by the caprices of the Sultan; but this has always been balanced by the prudence and the long-term perspective of the administrators. This was true in the time of Suleiman the Magnificent, and it has remained true. These great buildings you see around the city, their impetus was the inspiration of one man, but they each represented decades of proper financial management. A foreigner – a stranger to our systems, to our habits, a stranger with no concern for the financial stability of the empire – he knows none of this. You cannot simply rule that we will purchase new rifles for every soldier in our army without the most desperate effects on the finances.'

'That sort of thing should be part of a strategy. Matter of years.'

'Quite so. But these decisions are being driven through with one stroke of a pen. A calculation in a foreign capital, to their own ends, and years of prudence go out of the window.'

Cade shook his head.

'I fear for where it will leave us, Mr Cade.'

'Is there no way to – to moderate these irrational urges? Counter-balance them a little?'

'I do not see it.'

'I mean to say, if every time one of these daft ideas came up, there was an alternative voice. Voice of sense. Longer-term thinking.'

'Such voices are rare, it seems.'

'These other powers – the French, the British – you'd think they'd be doing it. They don't want the Germans running unchecked. And you know that they want to preserve the empire.'

'That's true.'

'They should be the ones – just sometimes, you know, when there's something particularly destructive? – the ones putting a word in with the Sultan and the Grand Vizier. Bit of common sense. Proper planning.'

'It is a pleasant idea, but it seems unlikely.'

Heart pounding.

'Mr Riza, I've learned to trust your judgement. You're realistic. You're restrained. When you say something's so, it is so. I'd like to think you could trust me equally.'

Riza was frowning; nodding slowly.

'If you felt you wanted – just sometimes, when you judged it necessary – if you felt you wanted to share some of these details with me, I could then drop a hint or two – nothing specific, just the shape of things – into the right ear. The embassy, perhaps.'

Riza's eyes were wide. Cautiously, the tip of his tongue made one circuit of his lips. He dabbed his mouth with the napkin.

'Enable just a bit of sensible balance to be offered. A bit of prudence against these excesses. Give you a chance to do your job properly.'

Riza just gazing at him, and surely every waiter in the room was standing watching, and the silence stretching out for years.

The words came with a rush. 'I think that would be too much, Mr Cade. I fear I have said too much.' He examined the remains of their lunch, then looked up. 'You must please excuse me now.' And he was gone.

Damnit.

Damnit to hell and back on the rail, steam-powered and over-stoked and screaming.

Cade's fist was thumping softly on the tablecloth, as he stared at the empty chair opposite.

Shelagh Macrae, the tea-shop in Penicuik, wide-eyed. *It's just a little too fast, Jimmy.*

Deliberately over-tipping the waiter, just like the last time; trying to put a bit of grace back into his world.

As he was leaving, before the door, there was a man suddenly at his elbow. 'Mr James Cade?'

'What?' *What further nonsense...?* 'I mean... yes.' Another forgotten face from another reception. Scrawny sort of chap. Clothes a bit flash.

'Radek, Mr Cade. Of the Russian Trade Legation in Constantinople.'

'Of course. I'm sorry; I didn't—'

'Oh, we've not been introduced, Mr Cade. But I'm an admirer, sir. Aware of your reputation. Will you permit me to send you a gift, sir? A token?'

There were times it felt he'd never understand how they did business. 'That's... most kind. Surely not necessary.'

'Thank you, Mr Cade. I wish you good day.'

And the fellow was gone, slipping through when the doorman opened the door for two German officers.

⊱—≈—⊰

The Balkan night; shadows and noises from the edge of civilization, the edge of dreams. Ballentyne woke and did not know why, waited to remember where he was, waited for the shapes in the room to resolve themselves and their relation to each other. The sound of the river was rushing beneath him. Or perhaps the sewer channel in the alley. Or perhaps it was behind him, in sleep. From far off, shouting. He stood, and padded naked over the floorboards, feeling the shape of his feet on the wood.

From the window, nothing. The crumbling brick of the building opposite, two blank yards away; the alley beneath him ink. He pulled on his clothes in the darkness, a habit of camps and mountain villages, and slipped out.

The hotel was asleep, but he could hear the noises of its slumber. Water in pipes; wood creaking; somewhere, someone cried out into the night; a door was banging, irregularly, softly.

He stood in the shadow of the veranda, watching, adjusting to the night. From one end of the street, there came the shouting again. It was briefly comforting; confirmation that the sounds of his half-sleep had reality. A moment of self-awareness – *why am I doing this? Is this the rebellion? If I can't get back to the hotel, do I have what I need?* – and then he set off into the gloom, hands to pockets – wallet, penknife, pipe – and mind remapping the town.

Didn't fancy being alone in the main street if it was some kind of mob. He turned down an alley and then onto a side street running parallel. Durrës at night was grey-yellow, shadows swallowing lamplight, the whisper of water in the gutters, stench, the yelp of a stray dog in sleep, something rustling. From ahead, like a rushing river, the voices.

Eyes fixed on the light of the street ahead, his chest slammed into something solid, which shuddered and sighed and shifted. His hands found flesh, hair – a mule. He muttered an apology and walked on.

Around a townhouse on the main street, a crowd had gathered. Not a mob, not a riot: a crowd, spectators, singly and in clumps, watching the house. A few wore coats over nightshirts. Those who were dressed were dressed poorly: dirty clothes, torn, unmatched; broken shoes or bare feet; beggars, vagrants and thieves distracted from their normal pursuits. The faces were greasy and rough, staring wilder in the hand-held lantern light. The inhabitants of night, gathering around a strange intrusion of day to their domain.

From the front of the crowd, a raised voice: measured, but the words straining in the attempt at volume. From the shadows, Ballentyne could glimpse a uniform hat. Looking more closely through the waving shining faces: there was a line of the king's gendarmerie at the front, bayonets golden stabs in the light, and their officer was calling up at the house.

On the first-floor balcony of the house – it was a grand affair, three storeys in the Italian style, ground-floor windows protected with grilles – a shutter opened and a head appeared. Cries of appreciation and merriment from some of the idlers. The head peered around at the street, and then focused on the officer. He shouted down something Ballentyne couldn't hear – petulant, dismissive – and there were more yells of amusement. The head looked at the crowd again, and in more colloquial Albanian called out: 'Long live the King! Long live Albania! Now bugger off!' Cheers and boisterous laughter from the crowd, and scattered applause, and the head disappeared and the shutter slammed closed.

In shadow, from where his complexion couldn't reinforce any doubts about his accent, Ballentyne muttered a question at a man slouched nearby.

The man didn't take his eyes from the house. 'Essad is being arrested.' He was enjoying it, but it wasn't clear if it was Essad's predicament or the entertainment on offer.

Essad: the king's minister of war, and the king's rival; the man who'd armed troops to go south and then apparently lost control of them. 'Doesn't sound like he wants to be arrested.'

The man cackled happily. He was looking forward to some indiscriminate shooting and shouting; it was a night for boys, for irresponsibility. Ballentyne drifted away in the shadows.

He followed a rough loop of streets and alleys, all asleep, that brought him out on the other side of Essad's house. The crowd was still there and, fifty yards off, he watched for a few minutes more. The sky was starting to pale at the suggestion of morning, and the faces were looking colder and more wretched.

A little behind Ballentyne, back where it was still night, a hand pulled a knife from a belt, and held it up. A face considered it, and looked at the Englishman outlined against the street ahead, and then back at the owner of the knife. And shook his head. The knife disappeared into the depths.

Ballentyne's erratic tour of the gloom, of the sins and decay behind the scenery of the capital, took him through the diplomatic quarter. The royal palace was all lights; presumably they'd ordered the arrest and were waiting for news of their gendarmerie. Ballentyne wondered if the officer was still pacing under the balcony, between the crowd and his bayonets and the mighty front gate of the minister of war. The British Legation was silent; the others much the same, just an occasional light peeking through a shutter to show someone who, for some reason or other, did not sleep. Finally the Italian Legation, and as he approached its outline the shadow of a balcony suddenly lit up, as a door opened and two figures stepped out onto it. The light revealed a staircase down from the balcony and, as he watched, one of the figures dropped from sight and then reappeared as legs lengthening on the steps. The figure on the balcony, staring out and then turning away into the building, looked like the man Castoldi, the new man, the self-declared senior diplomat on the king's council. The figure now reaching the bottom of the staircase, looking around himself and then dwindling into the gloom, had distinctive moustaches and a pistol tucked in against his spine.

With dawn, the pop and chatter of rifle fire. Ballentyne listened from the hotel balcony; common sense said half-trained men with guns were poor companions for another foray through the streets. Then, as if ignited by the sun coming over the mountains, the single thump of a cannon.

Then silence; morning and the end of dreams, and everyone went to breakfast.

⎯⎯⟩⟨⎯⎯

Another slip of paper; the old man set it on the table in front of him.

There had been a time of action; of hard riding across African early mornings, of meetings in shadows across Europe. Now he seemed to live only through paper.

This time it was Major Valentine Knox's report of his meeting in Berlin with David Duval; received via Mayhew.

The old man tried to imagine the conversation between the soldier and the student of architecture. But it wouldn't crystallize quite; they weren't natural companions. Knox and Ballentyne might find things to respect in each other; both were restless, questing sorts of fellow. There was a competence about James Cade that might appeal. Even, strangely, Knox and Miss Hathaway: so utterly unalike that they could be imagined to form a wary *modus vivendi*. But Knox with poor rootless mercurial Duval...

The report was brisk about Duval's tracking and losing of Valfierno, the sham marquis. Then the story of the telegraph office, and the old man knew that that would have surprised Knox. He wondered if he could read in the words a readjustment of the major's tone, smiled faintly; *good for you, lad*. The summary of the messages that Valfierno might have sent – credit to the major here, for thoroughness; most men would not have passed on the messages they themselves discounted.

But not thorough, implacable Valentine Knox. Which turned out to be a good thing, because the major's thoroughness was stronger than were his deductions.

Three hypotheses. First, and most likely: Valfierno's telegram had nothing to do with Duval or the Spider; second, it was addressed to the Spider, some routine maintenance of contact, but not to do with Duval; third, it was a reference to Duval.

Any of the messages could be made to mean something; and most of the destinations.

He doubted that the Spider would allow a telegraph address to reveal his true location. Most likely messages were routed through intermediate offices in his network, allowing him to travel and dramatically limiting the number of people who knew where he was.

Any of the Berlin or German addresses could... but somehow that seemed too partial. As his interests aligned ever more closely with those of Germany, the Spider would be the more careful about distancing himself. Could still be intermediates. London would be bold, and the address would have to be checked, but surely it was too much of a risk to run a front there. The Dresden swans were presumably porcelain, of course.

Geneva. The old man felt something glowing in his chest; then scolded himself for the indiscipline of responding to such a set of contingent hypotheses. But just supposing that the message was to the Spider, and just supposing that it was referring to the appearance of Duval in Valfierno's life, then the message to Geneva about infection was plausible. And Geneva... Good place for a façade: in Switzerland but close to France and Italy; cosmopolitan, commercial, and discreet. And if by chance it was Geneva, then Hermes was immediately less likely, and the Spider would be one of two men: Krug or Morgenthal. And the restless spirit of David Duval would have happened upon something of real value.

＋⟫══⟪＋

Sir, I have now made discreet contact with diverse members
Irish nationalist movement. Our successful import of rifles
to so-called loyalists as expected caused great alarm. With
my support, plans now advancing for similar purchase of
weapons by nationalists. Expect enquiries by CASEMENT,
CHILDERS, FIGGIS to usual representatives in Brussels and/
or Hamburg. Codewords FITZGERALD and/or BORNA.

[SS I/3/102 AND SS X/72/150 (APPARENTLY A DECRYPTION AND TRANSLATION,
PROBABLY OF AN INTERCEPTED WIRELESS COMMUNICATION)]

—✦—

With impressive reflexes, the owner of the Hotel Roma had turned his
lobby into a café within a week of the arrival in Durrës of the king and
his entourage. This he had achieved with nothing more than a few pots
of whitewash, a pair of folding screens, and the transformation of the
reception desk into a bar. Against all odds the result had a kind of tatty
elegance, although the occasional appearance of one of the hotel's guests
– a merchant in from Shkodra or Tirana, or a prostitute, emerging from
behind one of the screens and looking around and retreating in alarm –
betrayed the transition.

Sitting in the far left corner of the café, from where he could watch the
bar and both entrances, was Major Valentine Knox.

He was wearing European travelling clothes, and the white felt hat of
the Albanians. He looked at Ballentyne as the latter entered, and didn't
break the look.

Ballentyne took this to mean that he could approach without subterfuge.
He sat. 'I got a message to meet a Monsieur Ali here.' He ordered coffees
from the orbiting waiter.

'No such chap.'

A silent 'ah' from Ballentyne, and then he winced. 'Knox: the hat, for
God's sake.'

'Local style, I understand.'

'In the villages more than the towns, especially for men of status.'

135

'Blend in a bit.'

'You look like an Englishman wearing a villager's hat. And like an idiot.'

Knox's mouth twisted, and with two hands he removed the hat and placed it on the chair next to him. 'Present for the old girl, perhaps. Likes these mementoes of my doings.'

Ballentyne looked at him. 'There's a... a Mrs Major Knox?'

Knox looked even more stuffed. 'My mother. Since you ask.'

'Of course.'

Two coffees arrived, small and black and presented with flourishes.

'How is the town, Ballentyne? Changes? Tensions?'

'I'm no expert on the pol—'

'I don't want political expertise. I want a man who has been here before and who understands something of the rhythms of the place and the people to tell me if he notices anything different.' He sipped at the coffee. 'God, that's foul stuff. It's barely liquid.'

'Acquired taste. Give yourself a week.' Ballentyne sat back in his chair, which creaked dangerously, and his gaze wandered emptily around the room. 'The arrival of the king has changed it, but not as I'd have expected.'

Knox's eyebrows rose. He tried another sip of the coffee.

'I'd assumed that – at least in the beginning – it would have settled things a bit. United people; for a while, anyway, until they found that nothing had changed in their lives.'

'And yet...'

'The opposite. It's as if the tensions – the divisions – had been held in check by the anticipation of his arrival. And the reality has released them.' He turned to Knox. 'And that means the foreigners as well as the Albanians.'

Knox frowned. 'I thought all the Powers created Albania together.'

'The Albanians were lucky for once. When they declared their independence from the Ottoman Empire, it suited the European Powers to indulge them. Chance for a bit of stability in the middle of the chaos. Not favouring any of the countries that had fought the Balkan wars. For Austria, an independent Albania was a way of blocking Serbia's access to the sea. And the Italians didn't mind a new statelet they reckoned they could control. All decided between the Powers, over afternoon tea in

London. Botched the job, of course, by leaving some Albanians outside the new borders, but otherwise all very cosy.' He sipped at the coffee, enjoyed the sweetness and the scald. 'The Powers aren't so easy, one year on. In London, and in Berlin, they've forgotten about this funny little place they created. And that's left the Austrians and the Italians room to get back to playing against each other. They've each got a man in the king's entourage – I've bumped into the Italian a couple of times – and with no one else giving the poor chap a second's thought, he's completely dependent on them. You've seen their ships in the harbour.'

Knox grunted. 'Hard to miss. But this needn't mean trouble.'

'Unfortunately, the new king got here just in time for the place to start falling apart. The Albanians are united by blood and nothing else. They all waited to see whether independence would give them what they wanted, and now they're pushing it or complaining because they haven't got it. Albania is a line on a map and a fine idea. Inside the line, a series of local squabbles. Most of the participants like the idea, but only because they see it in terms that suit them. The king isn't really king of anything beyond this town. And the Austrians and the Italians are exploiting the fighting.'

'Fighting?'

'Oh yes, Major. Your war's started already; didn't you know?'

Knox took a long sip at the coffee, and set the cup carefully in the saucer.

'Fighting in the south, probably stirred up by the Greek government. Remember Miss Durham and the villages? They armed some of the tribesmen in the centre of the country ready to pacify the unrest, except they wouldn't go, and took the chance to let off some steam. The Minister of War became a kind of scapegoat for the fact that everyone was rattled, and now he's been sent into exile in Italy. Austrians complain he's Italy's man, Italians complain he was kicked out under Austrian pressure. Whoever is behind whomever else, and whatever they're really doing, Italy and Austria are already fighting their war for control of the western Balkans, and they're fighting it through these peasants.'

'Mm.' Knox absorbed it all, face set. The fingers of one hand drummed once. 'Have you checked your hotel register yet?'

'Have I what?'

'See if anyone interesting's in town.'

'Knox, do you tend to find that you don't get second invitations to people's houses? You've checked yours, I gather.'

'Heard of – couple of Italians, I presume – Catania? Belcredi?'

'I don't think so.'

'Rakick?'

'Rak— No. Oh, Rakić.' Knox took the correction as neutrally as he'd taken the sarcasm. 'Think I met a journalist Rakić here once. It's quite a common name.'

'Those three were here but have left. McKenna?'

'American mining engineer.' Something was nagging in Ballentyne's head, something that wouldn't settle.

'Right. He's still here. Anyone taken any... unusual interest in you?'

'Not until the non-existent Monsieur Ali turned up looking like Grock the clown.'

A kind of growl from Knox. 'A faintly serious question, Ballentyne, if your physical safety is of interest to you.'

Ballentyne saw his hand starting up towards his cheek, and pushed it down onto the table. 'Nothing... Difficult to tell; everyone makes a fuss of a foreigner, and I'm known by enough people from previous visits.' He looked up. 'No, there was one thing. Might appeal to you. On my first morning I called on an Italian acquaintance; he'd heard I was here because a colleague of his had seen me at breakfast.'

'But...?'

'But I hadn't taken breakfast.'

'Spotted you coming through Trieste, perhaps, or at one of the Italian borders before that. Passed the word on. Or just a shilling to the hotel boy.'

'But why? If it even was that way. Why is Ballentyne's arrival news?'

Knox nodded at him, somehow combining gravity and mischief. 'Why indeed?'

<hr />

The house of Ani Charkassian's late aunt was high in the old city, in the warren of elegant and crumbling wooden buildings crammed between the mosques, the palace and the sea. The directions to it had been based not on street names but on features – a cobbler's, a sudden view of the Asian side down a vertiginous side street, a cripple on a blanket selling mint leaves – and Cade reached it through veils of transience: dust, rubble, glimpses of faces that stared at him then disappeared. A woman opened the door to him, unspeaking, pointed him up a flight of stairs, then disappeared again into the shadows. He climbed through a gloom of sackcloth, of timbers that creaked and slumped beside him, of rooms that had lost all but the faintest of their memories – a portrait mildewed and cracked and askew; a chair.

Into a breeze. The top floor of the building was light, and airy, and discreetly furnished. A net curtain billowed in from a terrace, ghostly-luminous and teasing. He brushed it, and it danced away from his fingers.

She was sitting on a divan, upright, back against the wall – where she would be shaded, he realized, and less visible; more curtains protected the side of the terrace. She stood to greet him. 'It is my pleasure that you see this place, who are so interested in the secrets of our culture.'

'You've come to know me fast.'

'As a man of affairs you are efficient and dispassionate, it is clear. But you have an enthusiasm for the world wherever you are. An... appetite.' She gestured inside. 'There will be tea.'

'I didn't see—'

But there was tea. In the moments since he had walked through the room, a spindly table had appeared on the rug, a teapot as gaunt and unlikely as the house, glasses and crystals of sugar.

Cade jerked his thumb towards the stairs. 'She is...'

'Trusted. Her family has served my family many generations. We have forgotten who depends on whom.'

Ani Charkassian served the tea herself, carried it out onto the terrace. It made her seem more of a physical being, more real.

'For a man of this duality,' she said when they were sitting, she back on the divan and he in a wicker chair that he shared with too many cushions, 'Constantinople is the ideal place.'

'Two worlds. I was thinking it when I looked at those two beauties up the hill.' He waved a finger over his shoulder. 'The old Christian church

– before it was a mosque, anyway; great barn of a thing, ain't it? – and the newer mosque opposite. Sort of looking at each other. Different styles. Different approaches to life. Where Europe and Asia meet, that's what I'm supposed to say, no?' She went on watching him; he wondered if she was listening. 'Me, I'm half and half myself. The old 'un came out of the docks. The mam from the croft – you know, a rural, peasant life.'

She described her genealogy with an exactness of which her brother would no doubt have approved. Cade described what his family knew of theirs, with the suspicion that he had lapsed into myth more quickly than she.

The terrace looked out over other houses in the same style, fine but decaying, different floors built by different generations, many topped by the same veiled summer rooms. In front of them the houses dropped away down the hillside, and beyond them was the sea: *did they call it marble for the colour, or for the trade?*

'Aye, it's a grand place,' he said. 'Endless possibilities. A place to be going places.'

She watched him; frowned. 'This is Constantinople, Mr Cade. It is not a matter of where one is going but how one lives.'

'Is it getting time that I asked you to start calling me James?'

'No.' Gracious; pleasant.

'Righto. Life is what you make it, Mrs Charkassian. My family were peasants and scoundrels. What we are is what we've done.'

'And what you've done must be most impressive.' Long look at him, languid eyes. *Oh, damn this slantendicular spooning.* 'But more than one emperor has come to this place, knowing himself the most powerful man on earth and determined to shape Constantinople to his purpose, and all have been swallowed.'

'It's the triers who give it its life, maybe. Few succeed, but their drive is what makes the place. Vitality, you know? Otherwise, everyone would be like those fellows down at the station, and the dockside: just idle beggars slumped on blankets hoping someone'll throw them a penny.'

'Or perhaps they were the men with the biggest dreams, the most handsome, who have fallen farthest, and whose despair is greatest.'

There was no rousing her; always the same even, pleasant, melodious voice, somehow both earnest and faintly mocking. 'There's a new wind going to blow,' he said. 'The British already run the navy; the Germans have the army and the railways. Might shake things up a bit here.' He grinned. 'Good thing, maybe.'

'A new wind, perhaps. But perhaps not the one you think.'

'Have you had a look at Europe lately? Warships; and empires. It's a new century; a new world.'

'Oh, Europe has always been warships and empires. Shall I ring for some more hot water?'

━━◆━━

On the 21st of May, rebellion flared nearer Durrës. When Ballentyne woke he could hear louder voices, more movement, outside in the corridor.

Knox was waiting for him in what passed for the hotel's restaurant. 'The boy looked rattled,' Knox said without preamble; 'no hot water; signs of a couple of hasty departures. What's the ruckus?'

Ballentyne gestured for coffees. 'I've heard three different versions in as many minutes. Unrest. In Kavaja – on the road south, say five miles out – the locals have chucked out the gendarmerie and declared for Turkey.'

'Declared for Turkey? Thought they'd only just got independence from Turkey.'

'I said they were unhappy; didn't say they were coherent.'

Knox studied him. 'Prudence is our watchword, yes, old chap? We're not here to be heroes. Discreet observation, right?'

Ballentyne hadn't been feeling imprudent or indiscreet. 'Right.'

Knox was a looser man out of uniform. Open shirt, kerchief around neck, a coat that had travelled far: it made him seem fitter, more flexible, more willing to have a go at what life was offering, whether an uprising or a cup of coffee. 'Danger to us here?' he said mildly. A liveliness in him that Ballentyne hadn't seen before.

'None. Not today. By tomorrow it could have—'

'And what danger if we have a little wander out to the front line?'

The town was bustling. A handful of houses and shops – mostly those owned by non-Albanians – were being closed up. But much of the activity was what Knox referred to as 'unco-ordinated civilian scampering'. On the road south they passed an unhappy-looking squad of royal gendarmes and, shortly afterwards, a pair of rebel sentries willing to let two friendly Englishmen pass without even bothering to stand up from the roadside dust. In the village beyond they found a café, and in it an ageing idiot ready to swear loyalty to Allah, to Turkey, and to the king, in as many sentences.

The only threat to them came on the return journey, a motor car – rarity in the region – that coughed and shuddered up behind them at speed, lost in its own dust and sending their horses wheeling and bucking into the scrub by the road. They both peered hard at the inhabitants of the vehicle as it passed, Knox with the instinct to be able to recognize his enemies for the future, Ballentyne because the pair of moustaches fluttering in the back seat was familiar.

'This is a tourist war,' Knox said as they resumed their ride. 'A picnic, some inoffensive shellfire and home for cocktails.'

Ballentyne watched the cloud of dust shrinking ahead of them. 'I'm not sure,' he said. 'Rather reinforces a suspicion.'

He described Rossi's phantom Austrian, and his own visit to the rebels a few days earlier, and the moustaches that had been busy in a house that was not to be entered, and that had reappeared on the balcony of the senior Italian in Albania, and now in a car in a rebel town.

'Stirring it up a bit, you'd say?' Ballentyne shrugged. 'Or reporting back to the Italians on what the rebels are up to. With the rivalry, I presume they and the Austrians would both of them be keeping a close eye on things.'

Ballentyne looked round. 'Which is what we're doing too, surely.' Knox glanced at him, thought for a moment, and grunted agreement. 'Except the British government doesn't run to a motor car.'

'The exercise is good for you. You know, of course, that we're hoping to make the Italians our allies?' Only when he'd said it did he turn to look at Ballentyne.

'I'm sorry, Knox, would you rather I turned a blind eye when your hoped-for friends are up to no good?'

'They're all foreign, aren't they, the lot of them? Mean to say, it's all a cookhouse shambles. But if war comes in Europe it's likely to be all the various breeds of Hun, including the Austrians, against the rest. Italians on the fence waiting for the sun to come out, and we're hoping to tempt them into the right camp when the time comes. That, I mean, is what Sir Edward Grey would say.'

'Sir Edward Grey isn't here.'

Back in Durrës, they found the car parked within fifty yards of the Italian Legation. Which made it also, as Knox pointed out, within fifty yards of most of the other legations. Knox called in at the British office on the pretext of awaiting a telegram, and Ballentyne found a café nearby, and from these vantage points they watched. The man with the moustaches and the pistol neither entered nor left the Italian Legation; nor did he go near the car.

But a steady flow of unmoustached, unpistolled people did enter and leave the Italian Legation, and the other legations. And Ballentyne wondered at the international urge to bustle, to know and to control, more energetic than the sleepy feuding that was its focus.

They had agreed to maintain their watch for an hour, after which they would be drawing attention themselves. Knox waited his hour in the British Legation, and then a further quarter-hour for luck and because working to strict hours was a dangerous habit. He left by a side door and back streets.

It was a turn in one of these that brought him face to face with a pair of moustaches like those Ballentyne had described. Knox did nothing, looked nowhere, and walked on. At his next turn, a glance showed the man approaching the car – from the opposite direction to the diplomatic offices – and climbing in to the back. Knox walked on, chewing a hunter's dissatisfaction at a blown stalking, and heard faintly the coughing of the engine as it started.

Ballentyne smoked a pipe, and waited a further quarter-hour for stubbornness, for frustration that a day of possibility and activity and open fields was dwindling in a café with weak coffee and a fire that wouldn't take. He left, trying to find pleasure in the stretching of his legs and the prospect of hot water, and saw no one.

From the window of the German Legation, a pair of field glasses watched him go, trying to measure the man and the mood by the stride.

'Herr Hildebrandt?' A voice from behind, efficient and eager. 'Is there anything else you will need?'

'No, thank you,' Hildebrandt said without turning, and tapped on the window. The tapping was unnecessary, for the man loafing down in the street was waiting for the signal. Hildebrandt jerked his head in the direction Ballentyne had taken, and the man set off. 'No, that's excellent.' He lowered the field glasses, and turned away from the window.

The tapping – and the immediate movement of the man in the street – had been noticed by other eyes. In a room across the street from the German Legation, in a place of honour beside the stove, was an old villager. His clothes were from a place of tougher routines and no European influence; his face was worn by weather unknown in the lowlands.

Despite the warmth of the hospitality, the circle of faces around him, the old man was always uneasy in town. Too many walls to see the world properly; too many people to know the world properly. His eyes strayed constantly to the doorway and the window, and they had caught movement in the upper window of the grand building opposite, and they had seen the man in the street move off immediately and with purpose; and they had returned to the face in the upper window, and immediately they had hardened.

A command, ignoring whoever was speaking, and two young men who had been crouching nearer the door were at his side. The old villager murmured fast.

'In the building opposite is a *frengji*, with black hair and the eyes of the crow. From this minute, you become his shadows. And you stay with him until you are freed by me, or by death.'

The two glanced at each other, and back at him, and his ominousness was not felt without apprehension. Two nods, and they left.

He settled back against the cushion, held his hands closer to the stove, straightened his spine. His host said nothing. 'Pardon me, my friend,' the old villager said quietly. 'It is a matter of blood.'

The host, and the men nearest who had heard, nodded slightly; and they said nothing.

Dear Uncle Peter,

perhaps you've forgotten your envoy – who has been gone as long as a fifteenth-century Council-goer, with as little to show for it so far; any impatience from your royal court would be excusable.

Goodness knows I couldn't – no chance – think of wretched England – the village, its limited minds with no ideals, gloomy, rainy, dormant – and not give you your due: I'm loving it. Duty has excluded the possibility of too much detouring and gallivanting, but I am remembering why I enjoy travel and why I enjoy Germany. The atmosphere is sometimes a little queer: a few things said about the tensions with Britain and an odd sense of inferiority; many more things clearly unsaid. But the country and culture are magnificent, and the hospitality most generous. The Papins in Paris were very kind; the Burkhardts in Frankfurt introduced me to a very interesting lawyer called Lehne, and the historian Messel. Then a rare dinner with August Niemann – Baroness von Sutter, a young official called Eckhardt and a friendly doctor, Müller, who runs a sanatorium.

I've now reached the eighteenth century and Freiherr von Waldeck's castle. He's a fine man, his daughter most friendly, and we had a charming supper with friends of his, including a former lawyer named Löwenthal and some bankers named Bierhoff and Kuhn. Even if I was tempted to neglect my duty, the Freiherr will not allow it, and I've already been introduced to the library. At first glance I could not immediately see any new records on Constance, but there may be some interesting perspectives from those attending or commenting. The Freiherr says he has some relevant original manuscripts, which I shall aim to copy.

Once again, my thanks for stirring me out of my torpor. I'll be sure keep in touch as and when the research bears fruit. Meantime I remain, with fond affection, yours,

Flora

[SS G/1/894/13]

The letter reached the old man quickly, but by strange detours: clerks who did not know its destination, trays whose fillers never saw their emptiers. Only the old man's secretary, who understood that names are easy-worn garments, knew the desk on which the letter should at last be placed.

The old man didn't recognize the handwriting, but noted its neatness and strength. The name on the envelope only confirmed his instinct. He surprised himself with the edge of a smile. In this envelope he would be Uncle Peter, and in it he would find the first clear reckoning of one of the four choices he had made.

Almost too reflective when they'd met; perhaps too hasty through Paris. Naturally someone who wanted to hurry along? Naturally someone more comfortable in Germany? No set frequency of reporting was required. Flora Hathaway would want to test a system, but not waste effort. The envelope flicked over between dry stick fingers.

The wording of the salutation: the indication that the letter contained an encyphered message. He forced himself to read it through first; the encyphering was a restraint – less so for a mind like Hathaway's, which was partly why she'd been told to use this method – but hints about underlying feelings always showed through. The sentiment about England was formulaic – she was too steady for that much emotion – though some of the language interesting; then... Again the possibility of a smile: Miss

Hathaway was genuinely enjoying herself. Then appropriate gossip and reporting. The names in clear – if intercepted, it would only seem the habit of a pedantic diarist – would be checked.

And so to the encyphered message. Seven letters in the first word; then the first 'x'; then...

Well, Miss Hathaway. Let us see what you're made of.

⊹══⊱⊰══⊹

Two days after his failure over lunch, Cade was one of a group of businessmen invited to the Ministry of Finance and therefore meeting, among others, Deputy Chief Accountant Osman Riza.

He hung back as they filed through a secretary's office, where they were relieved of sticks and coats and a diversity of hats, and in to see Riza himself. He was the last to shake hands and sit, had to force himself to meet Riza's eyes. They showed nothing, and Riza looked away quickly.

He's even more uncomfortable than I am. Again the frustration burned. Almost certainly destroyed a promising business relationship as well as the ridiculous possibility of Riza ever giving him any useful secrets.

Riza listened politely to the observations of the delegation – or at least their self-appointed spokesman, the representative of a German engineering firm – regarding tariffs and customs procedures, and then delivered a description of ministry procedures. He was more than bored by it, Cade saw. Distracted somehow; nervous. *Damnit.* A wonder he hadn't had the police waiting for Cade when he arrived.

Soon, and mercifully, the meeting was over. Polite emptinesses from both sides, and Riza was escorting his guests out. He insisted on helping redistribute the hats and coats and sticks; it was a charming courtliness, and Cade felt a pang of loss for their pleasant relationship.

'No coat, Mr Cade? But this last hat must be yours, I think.'

'Thank you.' He took it, managed a nod of thanks, and started to put on the hat.

But stopped. Something... There was a paper tucked into the lining. Instinctively his fingers were reaching for it, then he pulled them back, stuffed the hat onto his head, glanced up and round. The others were drifting into the corridor. Riza was already back in his office, door closed.

+>===<+

'Dalton, I beg your pardon. Could I delay you for one moment?'

The old man; never quite gathered which department he represented on the Sub-Committee. Never seemed to say anything. Dalton smiled pleasantly.

'I assume that you have people who can monitor German international financial transactions; conversion of assets, that sort of thing.'

'Well, we don't like—'

'I said that I assume.' There was a coldness in the face. 'Don't expect you to comment on it one way or t'other.' Dalton smiled again, while he re-evaluated the old man. Bankers and spies; nice to do business with discreet men. 'Chum of mine – don't want to say who, exactly; embarrass the chap – got a titbit the other day. Thought it might mean something. There's a banker in Germany, name of Kuhn, K-u-h-n; I assume he has at least semi-official status. Thing is, his department are calling in gold.'

The politeness dropped out of Dalton's face. 'Are they now?'

+>===<+

The paper tucked into his hat was the most up-to-date draft of the headline items for the next year's state budget, including the various new military additions. Office door locked, the paper unfolded on his desk, Cade had let out a long whistle: at the usefulness of it, and at his luck, and at the strange ways of humans.

But where did it leave him and Riza? Had this been a one-off, an attempt to placate, to make him go away?

He was wondering at it as he strolled through his appointments the following day, wondering what he was supposed to do next with the relationship. He was still wondering as he trotted down the steps of the Imperial Customs Department – struck, as he was every time, by the transition from the cool grandeur of a state office to the bustle and smells of the street outside – and bumped into someone coming up them.

'Mr Cade, surely. Good day to you.'

'Mr – Mr Riza! That's... a surprise.'

They stood there. *What does one say? 'Thanks for betraying your country; we must play golf some time'?*

'I was... most grateful for your time yesterday. To meet our delegation.'

'It was my pleasure.' Nothing in the eyes.

'Really. You were... you were very generous.'

'I am happy to help, Mr Cade.' Nothing in the eyes.

The deal is there on the table! 'You – yours is a – a relationship that I value very much, Mr Riza.'

Was there the suggestion of a smile there? 'Likewise, Mr Cade.'

Close the deal. Make the trade. 'I do hope that we can continue it.'

All his instincts screaming at him: *offer him something!*

'That would be most agreeable, Mr Cade.'

Close the deal. Make the offer. 'Let's lunch together again soon.'

'Let us.'

Offer him something.

Very slowly, Cade extended his hand. Riza took it and gave it one heavy shake.

When Cade got back to the office there was an envelope on his desk. Inside, a compliments slip: 'With deepest respect, J. R.' printed in anonymous capitals. Cade didn't know a J. R. Pinned to the compliments slip, three or four pages of typing – not original type, but carbon-paper copies. He dropped them onto the desk for later.

⁘

By the 23rd of May, there were rebels within sight of the Albanian capital. It had come to seem natural, as if according to some law of physics, that Major Valentine Knox should be at that part of the line closest to them. Ballentyne found him settled comfortably against a hummock, rifle alongside and scanning the ground ahead. He scrambled over to him.

Knox continued to look ahead through field glasses. 'How's the town?' he asked.

'Chaos.' Ballentyne stretched out beside him. 'Bumped into a chap I vaguely know at the palace, running for the docks.' Knox snorted, still not looking round.

Ballentyne pulled the field glasses down, forcing Knox's attention. 'It's not good, Knox. They're evacuating the king. Onto an Italian ship. On Italian advice. Unless the situation changes very quickly, he's an Italian puppet for good – if he ever comes back, that is. In the worst case he never returns, and this place is left to anarchy.' He shook his head, and looked out over the terrain, bumpy and dusty and sprinkled with scrub, rising with the Tirana road to the heights. 'How is the anarchy?'

'Rather sedate, actually. Got a match?' Ballentyne pulled a box from his jacket, and Knox lit a cigarette. Holding it with the glow cupped in his hand, he defined the battlefield. 'Rebels on the heights: there, there and... there. King's forces out to our left here – see, towards the huts? – and more advanced to the right here. Under a German tearaway called Baron Gumppenberg; chap after my own heart. Now they've got the artillery working from the town, it's keeping the rebel heads down tidily. Who's manning the guns?'

'A scratch team of enthusiasts. A handful of European travellers – the sportsmen and layabouts from the hotels – who think it's fun.'

As if to prove his point, two thumps barked out behind them; Knox lay his cigarette down and snatched up the field glasses. A few seconds later, part of the slope ahead exploded in dust. 'That's the stuff,' he said, and puffed the cigarette into action again.

'Doesn't make a damn bit of difference, if they're guarding an empty capital. Rossi, my Italian, was full of doom. All be murdered in our beds. The sort of guff they've been spreading to scare the king. The Italians have their way, the king'll lose without the rebels ever reaching the town.' Ballentyne gazed out over the slopes. 'If only the palace could see it wasn't so bad.'

'Mm.' Knox puffed at the cigarette. 'Trouble is, it might yet get bad. The rebels aren't in a hurry, but they're pushing forwards right enough. Show you.' He rolled over, and picked up the rifle. He loaded it, settled himself comfortably against the crest – 'Watch now; but head low, eh?' – and fired. There was a clang from out in front, and seconds later a sputtering of rifle fire. What had seemed like an empty stretch of ground three hundred yards in front was now movement and puffs of smoke from the rifles. 'Water can,' Knox said happily. 'Get 'em thirsty as well as surprised. See? There's a dip there, and an advance detachment of the rebels in it. Can't be sure how many, but they've been filtering in during the day. Guns aren't shifting them, and tonight if not sooner they're going to get bored enough or bold enough to make a dash for the bridge. And I don't know if my Hun friend over on the right there will be able to stop them.'

'The king has to be persuaded that it's worth sitting tight in Durrës.'

Knox considered this. 'Better if there was a bit of good news to take back.'

Half an hour later, a rush of horses burst into the slumbering afternoon. Silence and stillness became thunder and a fist of cavalry that swung out from the right of the royal lines and charged for the rebels. The landscape came alive, the rebels in their forward position firing off a few panicked rifle shots and those on the heights firing at random; then the king's gendarmerie, first stunned by the idea that their side was attacking, were joining in the indiscriminate fire, and finally the cannon were roaring out as well. It took only seconds for the attackers to cover the two hundred yards, blood up and yelling and horses wild, a monocled German aristocrat out in front yelling snatches of Heine, an Englishman beside him silent and smiling and willing himself on the enemy. The rebel detachment was routed before the charge even reached them.

⊹═══⊹

A village marking the end of the old, rural France of the eighteenth century and the beginning of metropolitan modern Paris was also the place where that Paris – the nineteenth-century city of grey townhouses with an artist in the attic and a barricade on the doorstep – was meeting the twentieth century. When a venue was sought for the first flight trials in Paris, those gentlemen used to making their weekend excursions to the forest around Clamart and Meudon, or beyond them to Versailles – to pursue one sport or other – remembered the large flat meadow on the left bank of the Seine, where the barns became terraces, thatch turned to tiles, and the roads sprouted cobbles. Issy-les-Moulineaux was the capital's first aerodrome – fateful start-point of the 1911 Madrid air-race when 300,000 people watched an aeroplane crash into the spectating French cabinet – and nursery of the French aviation industry.

A take-off could still draw a crowd. On the 23rd of May 1914, a few hundred had gathered to watch the English pioneer, M. Gustav Hamel, fly his new Morane-Saulnier for the first time. A chance to share the world of the most advanced technology, without expense and without risk. French engineering, of course, from the frail bird-like fuselage to the angry black ring of cylinders behind the propeller. A chance for fresh air and a picnic, after days of cloud and rain, and the crowds came out dressed for Sunday, and milled around the field with muddy boots and jostling parasols, and felt rather fine as they smoked cheroots and flirted and pointed, and it was all the gendarmes could do to keep a bit of space around the aircraft itself.

Two men were watching the crowd from a short distance off. Behind them was a hangar, closed, and twenty yards to the side of it a scorched skeleton that had once been a hangar.

'It must be him. It must be in the machine.' A tall man, very blue eyes, which did not blink as they stared at the day-trippers and over their heads to the sweep of the aircraft's wings.

An overcoat accentuated his height, and covered knee-length boots. The man next to him, conventional, wore a suit and a hat. 'We have no proof, Mein Herr.'

'Proof...' It came out as a growl. 'The British have little interest in destroying an apparatus that can be replaced in a week, and every interest in stealing it. We learn th—'

'There were traces of the Mercurius after the fire, Mein Herr.'

'A few remnants of metal and wire; they mean nothing. No interest in starting a fire to destroy it, and every interest in using a fire to conceal its theft. Now we learn that Hamel and his flight to England are the concern of their Military Intelligence. Almost impossible to get the apparatus out through the airfield perimeter unobserved, but easy to hide it, and easiest to hide it in a machine like that one. It is no surprise that Hamel is so anxious to leave.'

An open-topped car turned in at the airfield gate, and began to lumber over the grass towards the crowd.

He watched it for an instant, and then turned and took two strides into the hangar, buttoning his overcoat as he went. He was out as quickly, and he slowed only to snatch the hat from his companion's head and pull it onto his own, brim low.

'Mein Herr, we should not—'

'Nothing that cannot be achieved with this' – with an effort he brandished a camera in his left hand – 'and this.' From his pocket he pulled a pair of pliers, then replaced them and hurried towards the crowd.

Hamel stood at the centre of the ring of faces; a chattering, calling, pointing wall constantly murmuring and shifting as he watched. His back was to the aircraft; the leading edge of the wing hung over his head, a shelter. The week of waiting had numbed him. Each morning of rain or of mechanical difficulty flared in his gut as disappointment and – say it – fear. He spent too much time pottering around the plane: extra checks, routines; little gestures of superstition, which he'd never succumbed to before. Long walks. Supper with a pretty girl, trying to lose himself. He'd not been eating enough; he'd found himself – just a glass or two over – drinking too much. Every face had its accusation.

Now there was a mob of them, so many he couldn't distinguish any one face, an encirclement, black and brown and white, gesturing and restless, hats and moustaches and parasols and the bicycles that some idiots would try to chase him with – if he ever broke free, that is – and always the noise, the buzzing of angry insects.

A stirring in the crowd, new jostling, and he heard a horn, honking windily. At last the nose of the car pushed through the bodies, and Morane was clambering over the side, hopping down and striding over the turf towards him. Hamel didn't like to move away from the shelter of his plane. Morane's greeting was as enthusiastic as ever, handshake like he was pumping fuel, grin, hair perfectly combed and all terribly elegant. Good chap; very French. Then three or four photographers were stepping out of the mass, bent over cameras cradled like babies, waltzing tripods forwards clumsily, calling instructions and requests, and the crowd was newly unsettled and noisier and Morane was turning to face the cameras, handshake gripped and the grin for the newspapers and Hamel stepped forwards and did his bit. Then the young Frenchman was speaking to the fluttering notebooks – *proud, honoured, British pioneer, best of French engineering, eighty horsepower, development of the Garros model* – and more noise from the cameras and Morane had unclipped and opened the engine casing and the photographers were gathered around and more smiles and more pictures, and Hamel was fretting about his routines and making sure he should be the last person to touch the engine, and smiling at Morane, and it was all like school again and everyone crowding round him when he won the mile and all he wanted was to be let loose to run.

At last: the engine resealed, his hand pressed on the casing like a thoroughbred's neck, his feet gliding up the side of the aircraft, and the engine exploded in noise and smoke and the sweet reek of fuel, and the beast was roaring and straining to be moving, and he was in the cockpit and free.

⊱══⊰

Ballentyne and Knox rode back into Durrës together, the ghost of the smile still on the soldier's face.

As they came level with the cannon, Knox called out his compliments, and there were answering enthusiasms. He turned back. 'If we can get this lot settled for more than ten minutes, Ballentyne, might be time for you to push on. Me too, but we're on different roads.' Ballentyne was silent. His road ought to head into the hills, to the villages, to his real work. He could pretend Durrës was merely prelude to that. But it wasn't. 'Serbia; that's where the great men want you. You know it, I think.'

'A few visits.'

'Speak Serbian?'

'A little.'

'Rather similar to Albanian, is it?'

'Utterly different.'

Knox had a cigarette in his mouth and was frisking his pockets for matches. 'What – rather like English and German, that sort of thing?'

'Rather like English and Chinese.' He passed Knox the matches.

'Oh well, sure you'll muddle through.' The words blurred around the cigarette.

'Have to, won't I?' He had unfinished business in a village, and he wanted it righted. That was what had made him accept; the scar that still burned. But it was to be by the longer road. 'Should be able to arrange a boat up the coast in town.' Evil comes quickly, as the Albanians said; good comes slowly-slowly.

'Odd business,' Knox murmured through his cigarette as they passed the Venetian tower that marked the edge of the town. 'Riding out with that Hun back there. Good chap, that. They say the Germans are rather like the British, don't they? More your bailiwick, that sort of thing.' Ballentyne watched the walls rising around them, whitewash and yellow mud brick, and didn't want to debate European anthropology. 'Place is a bit topsy-turvy. We've put this king in place—'

'Who's a "Hun" himself, of course, if that means—'

'Well, quite. We've put him here, and until we receive orders to the contrary I suppose we must assume our masters want him kept in place. And right now it's the Austrians – our likely enemy – who are doing their best to support him, and the Italians – hopefully our allies – who seem to be undermining him.'

'You're worrying about Sir Edward Grey again, aren't you?'

'Constantly.'

'Knox... you're enjoying this, aren't you?'

At the royal palace, an Albanian face yelled down from a window that the king had gone, and all the Europeans with him, and no, there was no one they could speak to and no, he certainly wouldn't open the door. They cantered through boarded-up streets to the dockside, where the quiet of the city was immediately overwhelmed by a crowd that filled the quay, moving with no purpose and chattering with no real facts. They nudged their horses through to the water's edge, where a gendarme pointed to an Italian warship a few hundred yards across the water. There Europe's foothold in Albania wavered, waited.

'A boat?'

'And stand in the prow yelling up at a warship and demanding to speak to the king?' Knox was stolid again, and it took the edge off the words. 'The British Legation?'

'Might give us tea, but we need someone who'll get a message onto that ship, and be believed.'

'Sounds like the Austrians or your Italians, then.'

Ballentyne nodded, and they pushed their way back through the crowd, knees nudging past shoulders and the horses' heads high and wary.

As they came clear of the crowd, Ballentyne put his hand to Knox's bridle. 'Austrians or Italians,' he said. Knox waited. 'Been nagging at me. Chap in your hotel register: Belcredi, right?' A grunt. 'No reason to believe he was Italian?'

'None. Just sounded—'

'You see' – he kicked his horse forwards again – 'there is an *Austrian* called Belcredi. Anthropologist. So he calls himself. Don't know much about him, but the consensus has always been that he's as mad as a hatter. Something of a charlatan, and in his way a lunatic.'

'Well, it's your field, old chap. And your neck of the woods.'

'Thanks. Thing is, one of his pet theories, based on the most dubious racial anthropology – Gobineau, Blavatsky – really the' – he saw Knox's impatience – 'the theory is that Muslims and Germans are natural allies. And, therefore and conveniently, that German dominance in the Near East should be welcomed by the inhabitants.'

'And he's been in Albania.'

'Makes one think.'

'Mm.' Knox took in a deep breath, and flicked at the reins. 'But not too much, eh?'

There was sporadic life in the city – an open shop, a house with washed linen hanging from the windows, a huddle of men in conversation – apparently oblivious to the possibility of rebels being in the city within hours, or perhaps happy. Then cobbled streets again, and the villas. The German Legation, pink and squat, was closed up. There were lights on in the British, and the Union flag still flew, but they rode on past before dismounting.

'Try the Austrians first, I think,' Ballentyne said, 'and then—'

He stopped, and Knox said 'Hallo...' Ahead, protruding from the side

156

street where they'd twice seen it before, was the nose of a motor car.

They strode over to it, no thought of concealment, and Knox put his hand against the bonnet. 'Warm. Just got here.'

A shout, and they looked round. From a doorway a man – Albanian clothes but with leather gloves, and goggles around his neck – gestured them away from the car. 'Where's your friend?' Ballentyne asked in Albanian. A shrug, again the gesture, and the man turned away into the shack.

'There!' Knox pointed up the side street. Fifty yards away a back was disappearing into a doorway, something in the sash tucked against the spine, and Ballentyne was striding towards it. Knox came alongside him. 'Legation's t'other way. We haven't—'

'I've an idea. Perhaps more credible than me just bleating to Rossi and appealing to his good nature.' He stopped. 'We don't know if that's a meeting place or a café, do we? Even a – Anyway. D'you have that hat with you?'

'No, Ballentyne, I don't have that hat.'

'Have to buy one off... Got your pistol, though?' A nod. 'Well, come along, then.' And they continued up the cobbles, close to the wall, boots stepping carefully through the weeds and slime of the verge.

Twenty minutes later: a murmuring, the animal sounds of men chuckling and playing at affection, a purse passed, a back slapped; a set of moustaches walked into the afternoon. He checked instinctively the pistol tucked into his sash, snug against his spine, and turned his face to the centre of town and the sea rising over the roofs. The car was ahead, and his destination just beyond it.

An alley blinked beside him and passed behind. The memory of movement, steps, something sharp against his back. 'Don't turn!' hissed at him in his own language. Somehow the suggestion of two men, a glimpse of a face, dusty-dark and hatted, his own pistol pulled out of the sash. A puff of smoke, and a voice distorted by a cigarette. 'You don't know me, my friend.' Breathe. *If I am to die, I would be dead.* Then more words, murmured, earnest, and his eyes widened.

Silence. A sharp prod against his spine and he flinched, feared. But it was his pistol returning to its accustomed nest. 'Don't look back. Don't remember me. Now go safe, my friend.' A slap on his shoulder, then nothing. Had they vanished? The world of the shadows. The risks, the routines. He started to walk forwards, shoulders tensed, but they felt nothing and he began to walk more freely. He did not look back, and his stride quickened as he came closer to the foreign legations.

In the alley, Knox said, 'What did you tell him?'

'That I was a friend – from the village where I first saw him a couple of days back – and I'd just seen him coincidentally. That there'd been other visitors to the village.' Ballentyne pulled off the hat and pushed it at Knox. 'Thanks; a shilling well spent. That I'd just heard that the Austrians were taking the opportunity of today's chaos to put a detachment of marines ashore and pick their own stooge to negotiate with the rebels and take power. Warning him to trim his sails.'

'That should shake up the Italians a bit.'

'We hope.'

Knox looked at the crumpled felt in his hands. 'Now I've got two of these damned hats.'

<hr/>

The Sub-Committee of the Committee for Imperial Defence:

'The foreign sec. is livid.'

'Grey livid? That must be worth seeing.'

'Not as funny for those of us in the room, old chap.'

'Quite. I had a Latin teacher used to look at me that way. Seems the foreign sec. saves the nature-loving for the weekends.'

'He was windy enough about having secret conversations with Russia. Now the German press have got hold of them and it's proved his point. He's livid about the leak, and self-righteous about the inadvisability of conducting them in the first place. Not a pretty sight.'

The old man, listening, thought of yet another calculated damaging leak; thought of three men; perhaps two men.

'He'll get over it, surely. Sort of serves as a warning to Germany, don't it?'

A sucking of teeth. 'The foreign sec. has a point. Parliament'll be up in arms about secret diplomacy with the Russians at the same time as they're playing silly asses in Persia. The Germans will be more fired up than ever about encirclement. And the Russians will cry foul because they'll suspect we're trying to wriggle out. We're three ways weakened.'

'Gentlemen, now that we're all here perhaps we can get started.' A scraping of chairs; a straightening of papers. 'You've all seen the appreciation of the Turkey situation circulated by the FO. The India Office take this very seriously. They're insistent that Turkey must be kept out of the war at all costs, otherwise we risk losing every Muslim subject in the empire.'

'The foreign sec. makes the same point.'

'Same from the War Office: Kitchener himself.'

'Kitchener? Ah, was it necessary to—'

'I should report, Chairman, that Sir Louis Mallet at Constantinople has been instructed to give a clear message to the Sublime Porte: in their neutrality is their security as an empire; but should they weigh in, there would be no limit to the territorial losses that they might suffer.'

'Short and sw—'

The knock, rare, rang loud across the room. All turned.

The door opened, and a young official slipped in. A deferential nod to the chairman, and then he was bending over the ear of one of the men seated around the hollow square.

A frown of inconvenience from the man, then his face opened, paled, and he turned to look at the messenger. A nod only, and the man turned back to the room.

'Gentlemen, I regret to have to report – and, ah, various of you will be aware of the different implications of the news – that young Gustav Hamel is, ah... well, he's dead. His flying machine crashed into the Channel.'

Noises of regret from around the table. On three faces, the expressions were grimmer. Shock. Anger. Wonder.

The face of the old man: stone; cold; far-off.

＊＝＝＝＊

The document sent by the unknown J. R. stayed on Cade's desk, unconsidered, until Ali announced a late afternoon visitor, and Cade said to send him up and filled the ensuing ten seconds by flicking at the pages.

He flicked at them with indifference, then surprise, and then interest. Russian shipments... To—

'You are Cade.'

He took against the man from the start, from his tone alone; took against him without even seeing him.

He finished scanning the last page. *Russian supplies to her representatives in Persia.* Then he looked up.

The man standing on the centre of the rug was local, by the look of him. Taller than the average; a heavy build that was turning to fat at neck and gut; large-lipped, large-nosed and large-eyed; improbably, the combination was handsome, in a decadent sort of way.

'You're absolutely right,' Cade said. He stood; slowly.

His visitor seemed to have taken against him already too. 'I am Muhtar.'

'I'm delighted to meet you, Mr Muhtar. Won't you sit, please?'

'I choose to stand.'

'Righto. I'll sit, if that's all right. I paid dear for these chairs; like to make the most of them.'

'You know who I am, presumably.'

'I know the name Muhtar; banking and... mainly insurance, isn't it?'

'It is. I am here on the subject of your association with Mrs Ani Charkassian.'

Cade sat up straighter. 'Oh, aye? Are you indeed?'

'I wish to discuss it.'

'You'll find it a pretty one-sided discussion.'

'The association is of concern to me.'

'The association, as you call it, is none of your damned business.'

'Mr Cade, we are discussing a lady; one who deserves to have her interests protected.'

'We are certainly not discussing her, sir.'

'Your association with Mrs Charkassian, whether it is innocent or whether it is not innocent, could be misinterpreted.' Muhtar leaned forwards, and smiled in what he presumably thought was encouragement. 'That is why it were better that you ended it.'

'That I what?'

'You do not know our ways, Mr Cade. If you... respect the lady as you seem to, you will understand that she should be left to associate within the domestic community here. Among those to whom she is more naturally suited. A rash association with a foreigner...'

Now Cade stood. Muhtar watched him come.

'I'll say it once, Muhtar, and I'll say it good and clear. I decide with whom I "associate". Mrs Charkassian, presumably, can decide with whom she associates. You don't come into either calculation.' He held out his hand. 'Good day.'

Muhtar breathed him in, and didn't seem to like it. 'You're a foreigner here, Cade. Another fortune-hunter come to take the maximum of advantage for the minimum of responsibility. Just another tourist in the Orient, seeking souvenirs and trophies.'

The outstretched hand became a pointing finger. 'Good day.'

'If you won't take it as advice, you must take it as warning.'

'Get out.'

Now Muhtar got out.

Cade stared after him for half a minute, feeling his blood settle, waiting for anger to turn to calculation.

He found he'd picked up the pages from J. R. again. The Russians had representatives in Persia; they were a well-known source of anger for the British there. The document showed a recent shipment of supplies to those representatives. Written in English, which meant it had to be some kind of manifest that would be going through non-Russian officials. No doubt a useful indication to London of the Russian strength and posture.

His attention wouldn't stick. *Damn the man.*

⊰══⊱

The Sub-Committee of the Committee for Imperial Defence:

'One very unpromising sign that I should report' – the heads shifted round – 'acting on, ah, information received' – he couldn't stop himself glancing at the old man, but the old man was lost in a paper and the glance went unregistered around the table – 'we've been checking up on German foreign exchange transactions.' Frowns, on faces that understood the power of a battleship or a spy, but not the insidious workings of international finance; hardly the sort of thing for the Sub-Committee, surely. 'The Germans...' – a pause for effect – 'are calling in gold.'

There wasn't much effect. A few pens wrote down 'Germans calling in gold', glancing at neighbours to check they'd got the phrase right; check with the office what it meant later. Why the hell were the Treasury even on the Sub-Committee, anyway?

'Ah... if you could give us... a little more specificity, Dalton.'

'Of course, Secretary. Like any other country of economic significance – like us, indeed – Germany has gold reserves deposited in selected banks around the world, for convenience of her trading and her national expenditures, against which she holds sums of the local currencies. Now it seems that the relevant offices in Berlin are calling it all in, converting everything back into gold, to be held locally or back in Berlin. Once we knew to look out for it, we've logged dozens of transactions.'

'And the... the implications of this, Dalton?'

'It's the act of a country that doesn't expect to be able to trade normally for much longer, but which still needs to buy essential supplies from other countries. It's the act of a country preparing for war.'

Leaning forwards, nodding, grunting. They understood that bit.

'Flora, offer me a fantasy.' They were walking in the grounds, and the formality of the words and the unfamiliar prettinesses of the setting – the freshness of the green, the sound of running water, the peaks on the horizon – made the moment theatrical. 'I'd like you to tell me that when the war comes we will still be friends.'

Hathaway pulled her cape tighter around herself. 'Everyone says "when the war comes". I met a woman a couple of weeks ago: Bertha von Sutter, the Austrian; very remarkable. She said "to speak it is to will it". When even someone like you takes it for granted, what—'

'We've not talked about it because we're too polite.' When unhappy, Gerta could look very girlish. 'And because we don't want to think that there could be a difference between us.' Hathaway nodded. 'I think that is not typical of you. You say you are always too honest.'

'But you want to dream still. You don't want the honest answer about how we will feel if our countries are fighting. We both have brothers, don't we? We know what that means.' Hathaway felt herself chewing her lip. 'My friendship with you – intelligent, equal, civilized – is the most special gift I have received in a long time. But if war comes, I will think the war stupid and curse the politicians and generals and worry about you and your father, and then I will watch Tim marching away and I will love him and want him to kill Germans.'

Gerta turned away and walked on. 'You are ruthless!' she said, without looking back.

Hathaway strode after her, stretching her thighs and hearing the path crunching under her boots. 'Gerta, this honesty is precious to me,' she said as she caught up, surprised by her vehemence. 'All of my life I – I compromise in every relationship; every conversation. When I don't, they look at me as a freak; an unnatural woman. To be honest and yet be respected – liked – this is rare, and... and precious.'

Gerta nodded as she walked, still not turning.

'I've had dreams of better worlds,' Hathaway went on. 'And I've shouted and argued for them. And still I find myself in this one. In it, I am told that there will be war, told by people who have more power than me to control it. The men I've met in Germany these last weeks – they're no different from the men in England. Same conversation. Same weaknesses; same needs. What you feel when you endure those evenings over dinner – the boredom, the futility, the... the distance, the feeling that you're acting in a play but you haven't been given any lines – you'd feel it in England too.'

Gerta was watching her, considering her, and nodded again. 'And when the war comes...'

Hathaway took a deep breath, feeling the cold in her nostrils. 'I shall knit socks for soldiers. Or escape to Switzerland.' She slowed, and then recovered her pace. 'I shall be glad I don't have sons. Be glad that Ralph is dead.'

Gerta put a hand on her arm, squeezed; smiled. 'Those intentions are all passive, aren't they?'

'Except the socks. I'll make damned good socks.' Their laughter sounded subdued, world-wise. 'When I was in Paris everyone was talking about a woman who'd shot a newspaper editor. I think the trial was still going on. She did it to save her husband's honour, somehow; the sort of nonsense August Niemann would appreciate. But the idea – taking a gun, taking control – the kind of... of ruthlessness' – she glanced at Gerta – 'ruthlessness of calculation; I liked the sound of that.'

'Perhaps we should both have been French. Charlotte Corday.'

'Ah, my childhood heroine. But in the end she was just another part of the chaos. That's the problem with the movement in Britain: too many of the women think they want to be men. I want to be a woman, without restraint; to be me.'

'And it is a restraint that I am German and you are English.' Gerta stopped, glanced around the landscape, took in a breath. 'In the war, we shall both know of the possibility of a friendship with a woman on the other side of that restraint. Perhaps that will have to be enough.'

<hr />

By nightfall on the 23rd of May, King Wilhelm was back in his palace in Durrës, and Ronald Ballentyne had booked a bunk on a Greek steamer for his journey north up the coast to Split the next day. After breakfast, Knox walked with him to the quay to see him off. It was a warm morning, the sky clear over the sea, as if trying to compensate for the previous day's political tumult. Out in the bay, among the fishing boats and merchant tramps, a yacht was skimming over the waves. The clarity of her colours, white sails and polished hull sharp against the misty warships beyond, a swan sleek among the crows, was beauty.

The *Poseidon* was not. Ballentyne's transport was a fifty-foot steamer, rusty and ill-maintained. As he stepped onto her, exchanging his few words of Greek with her captain, even his limited experience as a leisure sailor was enough to notice the greasy deck timbers, the clutter, the splaying and unmatched ropes.

Knox, discreet against a lamppost and occasionally glancing at a sentry slumped against a wall with rifle propped against his shoulder, was not the only man watching Ballentyne's departure. Fifty yards farther along the quay, obscured inside a café entrance, a man lowered a pair of field glasses. A private smile, as the steamer's engine growled and the water behind it churned whiter.

From a similar distance beyond him, the man with field glasses was himself being watched, by a young man in the clothes of a villager.

On the *Poseidon*, Ballentyne took a last look at the morning and the sea, a wistful glance at the yacht gliding near but unattainable, and then squeezed down the ladder to reach the only internal deck.

The passenger accommodation was a curtained-off space in the bow, and he dropped his kitbag on a mattress, against a pillow and blanket; the second mattress didn't even have those luxuries. Back in the main space, the captain was squatting over a hatch in the floor, yelling something into the clanking and coughing of the engine space.

A fixed desk doubled as chart table and eating area; two tin bowls, stained with the remains of a stew, were starting to leave their own brown notations on a chart. The captain looked up, then pointed towards the passenger berths. 'Other,' he said, hoarse, 'no come. Agent say: we go.' Ballentyne nodded and the engine throbbed and the boat swung and moved away from the quay.

There were perhaps six charts splayed under the bowls; no locker or drawer to keep them in – they were stored where they lay. Instinctively he moved one of the bowls aside and looked at the uppermost sheet: Durrës. He pulled up the corners of the sheets beneath: the southern Adriatic, though the captain would be hugging the coastline rather than taking any more elaborate course; Bari; Vlora and Saranda farther south in Albania; a chart in Greek. The regular destinations of a boat carrying cargoes licit and illicit up and down the Albanian coast and occasionally across to Italy.

What there was not was any chart showing Split, or indeed any destination farther north in the Adriatic than the Durrës quay from which the boat was now departing.

Ballentyne turned away, absorbing the point and uneasy, as the captain stood from beside the hatch.

A second passenger for whom no preparations had been made; a destination for which there was no chart. Perhaps Ballentyne gave the suggestion of a frown, saw the captain registering what he'd been looking at, the captain's immediate discomfort. He didn't know it was saving his life, just heard his own words instinctive, pleasant: 'Know where we're going, Capt—'; and then the captain's face hardening and his hand reaching for his pocket, and Ballentyne knew that something, somehow, was badly wrong.

Two men over-reading each other and over-reacting. Ballentyne took a step back, knocked into the desk. The captain's hand came out of his pocket holding a knife. He stepped forwards, knife first, and Ballentyne twisted his way around the desk and scrambled up the ladder. Something brushed at his foot and he kicked out and pushed himself up through the trapdoor into the wheelhouse, hands and knees, turned and slammed down the door, no bolt, just two useless rings to take a long-lost padlock and he pressed down with shoulders straining as the captain thumped against it from below. 'Knox!' he yelled into the madness. The door juddered under him and Ballentyne knew he couldn't move and knew he couldn't hold the door for ever and wasn't there another— 'Knox!' A screwdriver! On the deck, a yard or two off, and he reached out a foot and his toes stretched and the boat shifted and his boot kicked the screwdriver two fatal feet across the wheelhouse.

A massive thump through the trapdoor and he pressed down, stiff arms and knees. Then the deck tipped again and the screwdriver rolled a smooth swift arc to knock against his wrist. He snatched it, jammed it through the two rings, and edged his weight off the trapdoor.

The quay was fifty yards away and shrinking. Turn the boat? He reached for the wheel, and knew it was nonsense, heard the trapdoor thumping, stumbled out of the wheelhouse and gazed at the distant figures on the quay; swim? Must deci— and his collar jerked back and he was thrown to the deck.

The other crewman soared into his vision. Dirty torn shirt and face angry and a knife held high; a crack and a slam as the trapdoor gave way. Ballentyne saw a shift in the hand and the eyes widen in the last instant of anticipation of the leap, and then the shirt burst scarlet and the man dropped.

Ballentyne scrambled up and for one stupid moment he and the captain were staring towards the quay. A strange tableau: the sentry sprawled on the stones, and a figure standing rigid beside him, the primitive rifle still level and rock steady in the hands, the eyes set in the moment of the shot that had found its man on a rolling boat eighty yards off.

The rifle stayed level and the eyes stayed set as Knox wrenched the bolt back, slipped in a cartridge and snapped the breech shut, a blink, a breath, and the wheelhouse window beside the captain's head exploded.

The captain lunged into the wheelhouse, and an instant later was back into the sunshine with a pistol. One hasty shot towards the quay and he turned. The pistol was a yard from Ballentyne and enormous, and he pushed backwards and there was a shot and his arm was burning. A cry, high and unplaced in his head: 'Jump!' He had to jump, but where was the quay? Where was Knox? Only the open sea ahead of him, his arm burning and his shoulders flinching at the thought of the shot that was about to split them and he leaped for the rail and kicked off it and dived clumsily into the swell.

He came out of the wave coughing and disoriented: waves and sky and salt stinging his eyes and he rolled; now the *Poseidon* turned into his vision, ten yards away with the captain crouched over the rail with his pistol arm steadied on it. Again a cry, and Ballentyne turned again and gaped and jerked his head back and dropped under the surface as the hull of a boat soared over him.

The hull shouldered him aside and down and his legs fought for traction in the water and tried to kick him away and his head was exploding airless and he burst out of a wave and turned and his whole vision was the timbers gliding past him. Splashing and coughing, and somewhere there was the cry again. He couldn't place it, couldn't understand it. Where was the *Poseidon*? Where was the pistol? 'Catch 'old!' A husky scream: 'Wake up, damn you!' A rope dropping across the vision of the hull and at last he understood: the hull was protecting him from the *Poseidon*, the hull was – the rope moving past him and he lunged out of the water and clutched at it, a straining and a shrieking in his wrecked arm and then someone clutching at his jacket, a body reaching over him, clutching at his belt and rolling him over the rail and he tumbled into the boat.

Above him the snapping of a sail loose in the wind, around him his limbs, aches. 'I must go about! Keep your 'ead down!' Ballentyne's head came up, and he saw the *Poseidon* and the captain rising and the pistol arm lifting. 'Get the sheet!' And the boat lurched around, the boom rushed at him and he ducked away; he saw the rope, wrapped it round his good hand and pulled it through hard and locked it in the cleat, and the boat settled on her new course, at a racing angle in the water with the sail full of wind and the water rushing along the hull.

Slumped in the cockpit, the sheet rope still wrapped around his fist, Ballentyne spat out the last of the Adriatic and blinked his eyes clear of salt and looked up. Sitting low in the stern with a slender forearm on the tiller, glancing between the mainsail and the *Poseidon* disappearing fast behind, a headscarf and an open shirt and a cigarette poised at the lips, was a woman.

━━━━ ❈ ━━━━

Cade managed to get out through the dancing wisp of curtain to the terrace and down into the wicker chair before he spoke.

'I had a visitor. Man named Muhtar.' Immediately she was concerned: straighter, eyes worried. 'You know him, presumably.'

She said nothing.

He took a deep breath. 'I'll do nothing for bluster or threats. But if I'm interfering in another... association; if I'm—'

'You are not.' The eyes were wider, angrier.

He breathed out more quickly. 'Well, that's all right then. He tried to warn me off.'

'To—'

'To suggest I should not see you.'

The anger was still there, hot in her lovely face. But she was thinking hard too. She said nothing.

'Who is he?'

'The bank has existed a generation or two. I understand that its decisions are sometimes... very speculative. So it has not always prospered. They also offer insurance; there is a suspicion of... of unscrupulousness. My brother can tell you.'

'And – pardon me – he's just a concerned citizen, or does he have a reason for making himself your protector?'

It was all anger again. 'I need no—'

'I know. I told him as much.'

She subsided. 'Time by time the Muhtars have been our competitors in business. Also, he has sometimes... pressed his attentions on me.' She folded her arms. 'He has had no encouragement. Perhaps he thinks he can absorb or neutralize my brother's interests through me.'

'Aye, I could see he was a romantic.'

'James, please be careful.'

'I'm careful to a fault; but he's the one who'd better watch himself.'

'You are fine and brave. But you do not know this place, and you do not know these people.' There was a passion in her he'd not seen before. *And it's 'James' now, is it?* 'It were better that I... moderate my behaviour; be a little less selfish with my attentions.'

'What the hell's that supposed to mean? I'm damned if I'm going to be hustled off by that pudding. And I'll be damned if I'll let you show him anything more than a closed door.'

'You speak of "letting me"?'

'Easy, lass; I'm not for melodrama – duelling pistols and such nonsense. But I'm a stubborn so-and-so, and I'm not for pushing.'

She had to leave first and, as she was leaving, he took her hand and bent to give it the suggestion of a kiss that had become their habit, half affection and half joke. But now her finger was under his chin, pulling his face up again. A moment as she stared into him, and he tried to read the look but couldn't, and then she was kissing him hungrily.

A moment later she was gone.

<hr />

Dear Uncle P.,

 I'm still enjoying both life and library with the too-generous von Waldecks. A privately printed selection of correspondence includes several documents relating to the dispute with the Teutonic Knights – the Freiherr is really most uncomplimentary about them! – which I know is only of marginal interest to your work; but there are two addresses by representatives of the Knights which, in passing, assume significant pretensions to omnipotence by the Council and then rebut them on grounds of both theory and prevailing reality. Anyway, I shall transcribe them, and you may judge. The Freiherr also has a beautiful original proclamation by the Council, posted in towns in this region, combining observations on the Easter festival and tetchiness about shortfalls in the supplies being provided – free, of course – to the Council; transcript, with some attempt at the layout and style, attached.

When discipline has failed me I have been enjoying the countryside, usually with Gerta von Waldeck. We had one visit to Leipzig; one is obliged to see the new monument to Napoleon's defeat, and the station building, while older baroque Germany fusses around one. Gerta wanted us to attend a lecture at the university – all most earnest and impressive, a hunger for scholarship and for experiment – on the Central American canal; proceedings ended with three cheers for the Kaiser, at which point someone pointed out that they had an English guest as well, and the convenor led the group in three cheers for the king too. My little bit for European amity.

Gerta is insisting that I should accompany her on a forthcoming visit to a man called Auerstein, farther east. He apparently is another of these splendid country gentlemen like the Freiherr, but rather better off, with a famous estate. I am promised a library – which might *compensate for the ghastly country pursuits that are apparently the principal attraction of the place – and many interesting guests. If I can finish my researches here satisfactorily, I am minded to go. I think the journey includes a night in Berlin, which might be fun.*

I am, with best wishes and respects to you, yours sincerely,

Flora

[SS G/1/894/15]

The old man scanned the letter with interest. The salutation told him that there was no cypher, but the young lady's insights on Germany were of interest, and he found himself curious how she was faring. *Sentiment.* Miss Hathaway herself would not approve.

A knock, and Colonel Mayhew appeared in the doorway.

'Yes, Mayhew; I'll be along directly.' He half lifted the papers off the desk. 'One of our pigeons.' Mayhew slipped into the office. 'The young lady.'

'Getting along all right, is she?'

'Bearing up well enough, and putting herself in the way of interesting people, which is what we wanted.' He glanced up again. 'Come across a chap called Auerstein? I know him by reputation, I suppose; but has he cropped up in any of your doings?'

'Don't know the name off-hand. I'll check.'

'Mm.' The grey head dropped towards the desk. 'Careful with those checks, eh, Colonel?' He refolded the papers and slipped them back into the envelope. The head came up. 'We worry about telling people what we know; telling them what we don't know can be just as damaging, can't it?'

❧ ❧

She was the Contessa Isabella di Lascara, and in the madness of the preceding five minutes this new exoticism barely registered in Ballentyne's battered mind. Slumped against the side of the boat, beginning to get a grip of where he was and what had happened, he'd introduced himself with something like embarrassment. She'd replied with formality and a suppressed smile.

'Brandy,' she said. 'On a shelf in the cabin. Get it now.' He did what he was told, with a vague sense of seamanship and the vestiges of crisis. 'Now, your jacket off. 'old the tiller.' Again he obeyed; the jacket was sodden and fought back. Crouching over him, she glanced for a second at his upper arm, then took the torn material in two hands and ripped it open. Then she poured brandy over the wound – Ballentyne's pride managed to restrict him to a gasp – and pulled off her headscarf and wrapped it around his bicep with deliberate ferocity.

She patted him on the cheek. 'Brave boy. Now move over.' He surrendered the tiller and – another check of the sail and the sea around them – she took over. 'First we get clear away, then we do fancy nursing.'

Ballentyne didn't reply, didn't challenge. He felt light-headed, took a swig of the brandy, slumped down in the floor of the cockpit again and began to get a hold of himself. The boat was a yacht; thirty-five foot, perhaps; not new, but well-kept. In his hunt for the brandy he'd vaguely registered the cabin, compact and neat. Probably a motor as well – then he saw the lever next to his arm which presumably regulated it. But for now she was under sail, and being sailed well. Jib and mainsail were swollen with wind and the boat was heeled over and racing above the water. The sun and the purity of the sail and the speed all seemed one.

The woman doing the sailing he'd saved until last. She fitted the sun and the sail and the speed too. With her scarf now doing service as bandage, her hair streaked away behind her, and this and the set of her face and the elegant line of her arm on the tiller all flowed with the momentum of her boat.

And she was, of course, really rather beautiful. In her thirties, surely. More strong than delicate, more handsome than pretty. Ballentyne caught himself looking for too long, and turned away and began to coil the main sheet where it straggled loose under his boot.

'You are English?'

He turned back. 'How could you tell? How did you know to shout in English?'

She was keeping her eye on the sea ahead. 'You didn't look Italian, and I only know to speak English otherwise. Now I know you are. Only an Englishman would make a priority to introduce 'imself while 'e's bleeding and the bandits are still shooting. Don't you 'ave no visiting card?'

'Of course. But they got wet. Pardon me... did you say you're a countess?'

'You disappointed? I know a duchess; she 'as a twenty-metre boat – crew, everything. Pity she's always in Amalfi this time of year.'

'And you're out here alone?'

'You were out 'ere alone too. At least I 'ave a boat.'

'I mean – I mean that you sail the boat very well. To her limit. Well, I mean... Most impressive.'

Now she looked at him. First as if to check something, and then the face opened, big eyes and bright teeth, a face for life. She turned away to the sea, took a cigarette from her breast pocket and stuck it between her lips. 'And they say the English are not passionate,' she said to the waves. 'I should watch myself, I think.'

<hr>

Another sheet laid precisely in the centre of a desk in Vienna, and plucked at like a vine for fruit. The letterhead advertised a sanatorium in southern Germany.

My Dear Sir,

I should first thank you for yet another generous testimonial on my behalf. The prince, apparently on your recommendation alone, spent a week as our guest. I hope and believe he left a little better in mind as well as body; he certainly enriched our community here. If there is one thing more pleasurable for our visitors than indulging their ailments, it is indulging their ailments in good society.

I offer you this month no grand illumination, but the usual selection of what I hope might be enlightening details. The public reports of Ryczynski's condition are overstated; he has a good chance of lasting a year or more, and his staff are relaxed about the Bank's prospects accordingly. Entelmann I give three months at the most. Speyer, a lawyer known to be familiar with Minister von Jagow, made two visits to the town when staying in the district in March, at the same time as we had with us Tommasi, who as you will know is on San Giuliano's staff in Rome. Stefania, the wife of Kupfer, the banker, is here again with her younger companion, Miss Divisi. That the lady is an invert is mere speculation based on certain signs and habits, but it is certain that she spends freely on the young person and on their joint amusement, and more than would seem prudent if her comments about Kupfer's condition are to be taken as truth. Trott of the Naval Staff takes his annual cure; his casual remarks to me about the grand admiral no more than reinforce common gossip about the latter's lack of influence, but of perhaps greater interest are two urgent and apparently unhappy visits to him by more junior officers involved with engineering or design. James Rice, of whom I have previously written, was here again two weeks past. This time one of my staff made sure to see him quite definitely enjoying the company of one of the waiters down in the town. A single goldmark would buy the boy's testimony, though in truth I think Rice's nerves would need no more than a threat to be quite compliant. Zu Herford arrived last week in the grand style — in a carriage hired by the day in town — and asked for a cheaper room, while his one servant lodges in an inn; naturally I have given him his usual room, at the cheaper price.

Believe me, Sir, most respectfully yours,
Müller

P.S. You are always emphasizing your interest in the most trivial, and I know how you like to cultivate the rarer fruits. I mention, accordingly, an Englishwoman visiting Germany on some errand of mediaeval scholarship. We dined together at Niemann's. Miss Flora Hathaway is, I judge, highly intelligent — with the suggestion of a coldness of rationality unusual in the English — and indeed most charming. I offered to recommend her to Bartels and Wundt.

P.P.S. Remembering that you were kind enough to suggest that they had offered you some amenity, I take the liberty of enclosing a box of your usual prescription.

<hr/>

They'd sailed north-west from Durrës. After an hour, they brought down the mainsail and anchored, and the contessa had a proper look at Ballentyne's arm. She declared it not serious – which was easy for her to say – too wide for a stitch – which he was grateful for – and she covered it in a foul-smelling salve, bandaged it up tight again, and improvised a sling.

'You didn't ask what happened. Thank you.'

She shrugged. 'Men. Guns. 'ot day.' She leaned forwards and adjusted the sling on his shoulder. 'And in the Balkans, too. Fight over a girl, or a game?'

'I don't know.' This amused her. 'I mean to say: neither of those, certainly.

I'm working... I'm helping – I'm an anthropologist, originally.'

'Anthro–?'

'I study different human societies; tribes. Their customs, their cultures.'

'And sometimes these 'umans don't like this?'

'It seems not.' He looked into her eyes. 'I've been... helping my government.'

'Oh, you are spy.' She said it without emotion, and fetched the brandy bottle and two glasses.

'You sound unexcited.'

She sat beside him on the banquette that ran the length of the cabin, and smiled. 'I should scream a little, maybe. Faint? I'm a woman, Mr Ballentyne. An Italian woman; a married woman. Of all the things that men do and do to each other, spying is the least surprising, and perhaps the least 'armful.' She handed him a glass. 'Just don't get my boat shot up.'

He considered this. 'I'm a bit embarrassed about the whole thing, to be honest.'

'Why? Anyone in your position would be doing it. I've carried messages across the Adriatic myself. If I meet government friends in Bari or Pescara they ask what is 'appening across the sea and I tell them. Anyway, isn't it supposed to be your... patriotic duty?'

He settled back against a cushion in the corner of the cabin, and tried to shift his shoulder. 'Honestly? I spend my life trying to get people to trust me, to be open with me about themselves. Now I'm doing the same thing, except it's the mirror opposite; like – like saying the Lord's Prayer backwards.' He took a shot of brandy, felt it washing through him.

'And now you start to worry that you 'ave always been un'oly.'

He nodded. 'And people keep trying to kill me. That's the second time. I don't like it.'

She smiled sadly. 'Pride, and doubt. Ah, so 'ard to be a man.' She watched him take another mouthful of brandy. 'You should change.'

'I dried well enough in the sun. Anyway...' He glanced at her blouse, at the tight slacks. 'I'm not sure we're the, er, same size.'

'There are some of my 'usband's clothes 'ere.'

'Ah, yes.' Ballentyne examined his brandy glass. 'There's a... a Count di

Lascara, presumably.'

'Presumably. 'e is no longer a concern of mine. Nor I am of 'is.' She poured them both more brandy. ''e continues the same amusements 'e always did.'

'Ah.'

She shrugged. 'I 'ave compensations. And now I travel the sea, like a... like a lonely witch. But I am free 'ere at least.'

'Surely you can—'

'You are not an Italian, Mr Ballentyne. And you are not a woman.' She smiled without warmth. 'In love as in war, men do what men must do, and the lives of women change accordingly.'

'In the Albanian highlands, when all of the men in a family die, sometimes a woman chooses to take on the role of man. The clothes, the status in the family and the village. So that the family has a head. They call themselves sworn – pardon me – sworn virgins.'

He could see her imagining it. 'They take control. They have the status. I like that.'

'It's terrifying. A renunciation. A loss of... of femininity, of self.'

She was almost pitying. 'Femininity 'as its limitations. Especially for a woman who 'as failed to 'old her 'usband.' She sat forwards on the cushion. 'But this is becoming tiresome for us both. I'll get you those clothes. Where are you supposed to be going, anyway?'

'I'm reluctant to risk land immediately, to be honest. I wanted to go to Split.'

'If you want to, you can still. We can stop at the island on the way.'

'You have an island?'

'Not all. A house; estate a little. You don't think I could have an island?'

'Why not? I'm pulled miraculously from the sea by a beautiful woman who turns out to be a countess. I'd be disappointed if you didn't have an island.'

Burim Balaj, the unlucky man with the surprisingly beautiful wife, began to realize with frustration that her beauty had not changed his luck, but that his luck seemed over the weeks to have tarnished her beauty.

The other men, when they spoke to him, would only speak of her, and how beautiful she was. Sly look and prod him in the arm. They still would not seek business with poor Burim. Obviously, they were saying that she was too good for him. Good enough for them to leer at, he could see that. But too good for him. Probably he should suspect her of adulteries.

And his brother now. Just stare at her. Agron was simple, of course, but even so.

To Burim, her silence was complaint and accusation. Her passive, open-eyed acceptance of him when he rolled on top of her in the darkness was a statement of his inferiority. He wanted to hear her moan. Hear her scream.

Sometimes he hit her. That made her moan a bit. But she still didn't scream, not even then.

He noticed her imperfections. The dark spot on her upper lip. The nose, too straight for a girl. Sometimes, her animal smell.

Probably he had been unlucky in his wife too, after all. Somehow he could have done better. His father had said that his mother had been lovely once. His father had done better.

Every week, Burim would walk for three hours down the valley to the next village, to sell the tools he made or repaired. They didn't know him as well there. Normally he went on his own. He didn't want Besa's eyes following him. He didn't want more men staring at her. This time he had to take her with him. The flooding river had blocked him the previous week, and he felt he deserved to sell twice as much this time. Also, a man there was offering to sell him a goat at a good price. So he might be bringing that back too. He'd have taken Agron, but Agron had twisted his ankle and still walked with difficulty.

He told Besa that morning, and saw her eyes light with interest. That's right, my heart, bit more concern for your husband would do no harm. So they set off together in the dawn, unlucky Burim and his surprisingly beautiful wife, down the track beside the ravine.

Three hours later Besa came running back into the village, wailing about Burim's accident. The curiosity; the slip; the fall. They pulled him out of the ravine on a rope, his head smashed and disfigured by the impact of rocks.

Burim Balaj, who had betrayed his wife's brother to death, was dead.

+=====+

Another Adriatic port: they were blending into one now, these harbours, on the Italian coast or the Balkan. Whitewashed houses rising into the hills behind. The landscape beyond them arid. In the foreground, most of the quays were ancient: limestone or sandstone, blended with the sun and the dust and the drowsy whisper of a slower age. A few touches of elegance left behind by the Venetians. Wooden boats alongside, colours, fruit, fish, archaic rigging. The little pottering trade of millennia.

But today the peasants, whether Italian or Albanian or Slav, would hurry out of their stupors and gape at the sea. Today the infinite pearly distance had gone dark; the glistening light had turned grey; the softness of sea and scrub and sky had become steel: 22,000 tons of it, between 1 and 14 inches thick, propelled by turbines producing more than 50,000 horsepower. Sliding across the horizon, or perhaps discovered in the morning like some awful monolith over the town, was the imperial battlecruiser S.M.S. *Goeben*.

And from an office in Rome, or Trieste, or Sarajevo, another message would go to London announcing a visit by the *Goeben*. And in London, another mark would be added to a map, and certain calculations would be repeated. The size of the German Navy. The projected size of the German Navy. Plus of course the Austrian Navy. Even if the French could be relied upon in the Mediterranean. Again and again the arithmetic and, on the other side of the equals sign, doubts and fears and angry headlines.

+=====+

Kiel Opera House was like an overgrown Board School. Duval was forcing himself to spend an hour sketching it, but gave up after forty minutes. Muddle of conflicting styles, none of them understood; every borrowed detail swollen with the self-importance of the whole; bloody great mountain of brick.

In Kiel they seemed very proud of it. A policeman at the station, a waiter, and an old lady who stopped as he sat there all told him it was what he should be sketching. He smiled politely, chewed on lumps of dry sausage as he worked, mentally reworking the building as he felt it should have been designed.

On his way to the opera he'd found the Niedermayer to whom the telegram had been sent from Berlin. A toy manufacturer; a message commenting on a product and changing an appointment was credible.

A week of Knox's schoolboy errands around Berlin. A conversation here and there; some clearly in his role as architecture connoisseur, some more obviously hole-and-corner ferreting. Reports dutifully passed through the embassy, for what they were worth. Dresden, and back again.

Feeling a bit seedy. And the women on the stout side and damned unfriendly.

A letter of recommendation from Berlin had won him the hospitality of Professor Markus for the evening, most of which the professor spent sorrowfully offering advice about the shortcomings of the British Navy, in eccentric pop-gun English. Assertions of doctrine – 'Your boys need less Nelson, more engineer training'; 'big guns and oil engines, Rule Britannia, but ship design is lazy' – were interspersed with exhortations to have more stew.

Duval had generally spent his time denying other people's impressions of him. Never thought much about being British, anyway. But Germany was beginning to twist him. The game he was playing was surely all about being not what you were, quite; he could do that. And it was easy enough to agree with the professor – wasn't like he knew or cared about the navy, was it? – polite repetition of whatever had been said, comment about class system; distancing himself from what was being criticized came easily to him. But intermittently, something stubborn would flare in him; *that is me, and that is mine* – and he would offer a question instead of acceptance.

He walked, drank a brandy in a dead café, walked on, needing air. The street lamps glowed weak on the cobbles. He was feeling hungry already; he needed a girl.

Hot meal when you could get it, and keep moving. For now that meant Knox and his superiors, damnfool games and no expense spared. *Well enough.*

He'd impressed Knox; could see that. He wanted to move on. Never did to linger.

Ahead a checkpoint: uniforms with guns, lamps, a striped barrier. He reconsidered his surroundings, saw big faceless buildings, tasted salt. Kiel's dock district was supposed to be vast. He walked on, into the shadow of a wall, ten or fifteen feet high, endless and featureless; presumably part of the perimeter.

Twenty feet ahead of him the wall broke open and two figures stepped into the street, laughing about something and slamming a door closed behind them. Duval hesitated, as if he was the unexpected one, feeling his foreignness and his mission. The two figures, uniforms of some kind, strolled off in the other direction. Slowly, Duval began to walk again.

The door, he saw when he reached it, was wood, iron-studded, with no external handle.

The door had not closed properly.

Possibility; a scheme; defiance... And Duval was checking the street around him and the emptiness was his friend and his fingertips pulled at the door and he was in, closing it properly behind him. *This is me, Mr suave bloody Knox, and I may surprise you some.*

After the second shed he started to note the signs over the doorways. Vorarbeiter; Administration; Sicherheit. Voices somewhere, and he pressed himself into the brickwork of a wall, feeling its rasp under his palms. He couldn't place the voices among the maze of buildings, until two shadows launched themselves at him down the gap between sheds and two black figures crossed from the end of his to the next.

On the scrounge at school. A woman and her brother trying to find him in a fairground: *Polly Atterbury; Lord, what a fiasco that was.* Somewhere, a dog barked.

Duval continued to chart the sheds in his pocket sketchbook. Finally, the last shed in the row: Kran-Betreiber. Then away round the end of it.

It was monstrous and it roared up over him and he gasped.

Duval had never seen a battleship, not outside the newspapers, and hadn't begun to appreciate their size. Ships, yes: ferries, the boat-train to France, a father telling his son how big the funnel was and how many minutes it took to walk a circuit of the deck. Never really thought about it; never seen anything more than a gangplank, a bit of a deck, a view, a bar. Nothing like this; and this was just one slender end of it – *the bow, would it be?* – an elegant line swooping up over him. An Olympian axe-blade, mighty out of the night.

This... this was... St Paul's Cathedral; looking up at the dome of St Paul's, wondering at its beauty and wondering at the mighty engineering that held it up.

Again, a dog barking somewhere. Another moment gazing up. Then he retreated from the shed to the wall, and followed its shadows as it turned sharply. It was wood now, vertical slats twice his height dividing off a separate part of the docks. Brick and wood; primitive materials in the shadow of the steel titan.

The dog appeared first around the shed, then behind it a man pulling at the leash. They wandered towards the timber wall, and the sentry was reaching for a ring of keys at his waist when the dog began lurching and straining and the man was only holding it with difficulty.

The dog was straining for Duval. He shrank away, panicked at the possibility of protrusion beyond the line of shadow, tried to retreat into the wall. The dog was a screaming sinewy outline; the sentry was swearing at it and pulling at the leash two-handed, but the dog wasn't having it and continued to heave the man on towards Duval's shadows. Snapping and snarling and lunging, the sentry shouting, shifting a rifle slung over his shoulder as he tried to wrestle the dog, and still the noise and teeth straining forwards.

Can't distract scent. His jacket snagged up against the wall and the teeth lunged out and in a moment of clarity he remembered the uneaten sausage in his pocket and fumbled it out and dropped it and continued to back away in the darkness. The dog went madder, heaving and whining in the leash and the sentry was yelling and straining at it and a second later man and beast were at the wall and the dog was tearing and shaking at the meat in its wrapper. At last the sentry saw what the dog had got and kicked its rump and managed to drag it away. The dog went with a swagger, gulping at the fragment of sausage, wrapper hanging from its teeth, and Duval let out one silent breath.

His blood was up now, and when the sentry took his keys again and opened a gate in the timbers and pulled the dog through, he didn't even think; seconds later he was at the gate, listening to the dwindling sound of the dog and the sentry cursing at it. He pushed tentatively at the gate, it swung, and he slipped through into the next part of the dockyard.

Buildings – the end of the dock – off to his right. In front... the suggestion of water, the sound of its clucking against the dockside, flickering suggestions of the surface, patches of blackness; the smell of oil thick in his nostrils.

Gradually he worked out the other side of the dock, a hundred yards or more away, another wall. Nothing showed on the water in between.

The sentry and the dog had gone to the right; he moved left. For the first time, Duval was aware of the coldness of the night. He buttoned his jacket, envied the dog for the last of the sausage.

Part of the darkness on the water didn't move as it should.

He stopped; took a step back, and then forwards again. He'd got a sense of the water, its grey, the faint sheen. Now some section of it stayed matt, stayed black, gave no suggestion of depth or life. There was something there, in the water. Low, dark, and up against the dock. He moved closer, and it caught a trace of light and gleamed metallic, and the shapes reordered themselves in his mind and he understood the curves.

This is how David Duval saw his first submarine.

<hr/>

A townhouse in Prague; among the soot-black, lantern-yellow mediaeval alleys, a drawing room of taste and gentility. The city was, Krug thought, a most unlikely place in which to find Colonel Walter Nicolai; its refinements too elegant, its history of superstition and revolt too unsettling, for his stolid Germanic person. Whereas he himself fitted in rather nicely. A moment's intellectual fancy: himself as Rabbi Loew, his network the rabbi's *Golem*, loose in the shadows of Europe.

Yet here was Nicolai, stiff and watchful on the edge of the room.

'My dear Colonel; I am honoured, humbled that you found time to meet.'

'Germany owes you no little gratitude, sir. Your intervention in the matter of the British attempt to steal our apparatus in Paris was vital. You have saved a secret of great value. I am empowered to pass on to you the thanks of... of the highest levels.'

Krug frowned, covered it with a smile. 'I trust my name is not too much mentioned, Colonel.' Nicolai's face grasping for the point; getting it. 'Your own respect – that of a fellow professional – is what matters to me.' A nod. 'Sincerely, Colonel, I see no difference between our interests, and no difference between our activities. If there is to be war, your Military Intelligence and my own net of influence and information must be more than partners. Won't you sit, please?'

They sat, Nicolai trying to arrange himself with adequate dignity on a plum-coloured chaise-longue. Krug lit a cigarette; Nicolai, he knew, did not indulge. 'I regret that I have no information on the name your office passed to mine – this man Pinsent. Nothing in my records.'

'Nothing of significance, I suspect. An Irishman picked up in a routine check by our police in Berlin. We had no record of him either. I would not have troubled your office except – this new spirit of co-operation...'

'Quite so, Colonel. A good habit for us both. In that spirit, let me try a little harder for you. Time by time it is possible for me to... to explore certain of the records in London.' Nicolai's eyes widened in the otherwise blank face. 'Let me make an enquiry there regarding this man Pinsent. As you say, it is a triviality, but I want you to feel able to benefit from my little network.'

'Following the success over the spy Hamel, Herr Krug, there is increasing support in Berlin for this partnership. If you are able to accompany me back to Berlin, we may make substantial progress.'

'I should be delighted, Colonel.'

'Your own work does not detain you?'

'*Our* work, Colonel. I find myself... intrigued, let us say, by certain activities by British Intelligence agents. But this will not stop me travelling with you.'

Nicolai shifted on the upholstery, and a spring twanged under him. 'You speak of this... Con- Comp—'

'The Comptrollerate-General. Perhaps. Its strength is in its vagueness. It is rarely seen, and more rarely recognized.'

'A phantom.' Confusion becoming mistrust becoming scorn.

'If you like, Colonel, yes. And not to be underestimated. The Comptrollerate-General is older than most nations. It was a power in Europe when Germany was still a gaggle of barons slaughtering each other over their superstitions.'

Nicolai didn't look convinced. *History is not something from which we escape, Colonel.*

'You have some... great respect for this piece of history.'

'I do not wish to join the list of men who have made the mistake of not respecting it. Do you know of Fouché, Colonel? Joseph Fouché, the Duke of Otranto.'

Nicolai losing the thread. 'He is...'

'He was, Colonel. He was Napoleon's master of espionage. A very ruthless and clear-sighted man. After our forebears defeated the emperor at Leipzig in 1813, Fouché turned against him. He switched back again for Napoleon's final campaign, and once more against him after the final defeat. After the restoration he held the same post under the monarchy that he had under the emperor.'

'A disgraceful renegade.'

Krug could not restrain a chuckle, grinning sleek through the cigarette smoke. 'You must forgive me, Colonel, but I find him most impressive. As part of my – your words – my respect for pieces of history I have acquired Fouché's papers. Rather a coup, for they were closely guarded even a century later; I'll describe it to you some time. Fouché is most illuminating on his contest with the Comptrollerate-General for Scrutiny and Survey.'

Nicolai still didn't look convinced. A pause. 'You have heard the news of Ireland? The British parliament's decision?'

Krug nodded, and lit another cigarette. 'So-called "Home Rule". It is the least the British could do to stop Ireland exploding. Rather similar to what Vienna had to do with our Hungarians. Give them enough autonomy to hold the empire together.'

'This means that Ireland will be quieter. The patriots there will not distract London as we had hoped. They will not seek their rifles now.'

A smile. 'I remain optimistic, Colonel. The Irish nationalists will not trust a decision of the British parliament until they see it enforced; they have been tricked too often. They will want their rifles still. My operations require only a small elaboration.' Nicolai's eyebrows came up. 'I will allow news of the forthcoming shipment to become public.'

The eyebrows came down hard. 'But—'

Again the smile. 'You must think me terribly cynical, Colonel, but I little care how many Irish, of whichever persuasion, slaughter each other. What matters is that there is unrest. What matters is that Britain is divided and distracted.'

+≈+

Duval spent two hours in the submarine dock, pacing its dimensions, understanding the arrangement of the dry dock, counting not only the number of submarines, but also the cranes, the gantries, the workshops, the fuel tanks. He didn't really acknowledge the new calm he'd achieved, the certainty with which he acted; but sometimes faces came at him out of the past and for once he smiled at them. Knox's face, too. *This'll shake you, you smug so-and-so.* At first he'd reached for the sketchbook, but he couldn't see to write or draw a line or a figure. So he visualized the dock from above, and its pools became nave and side chapels, the cranes became pillars, the control-tower a pulpit, and in his mind he mapped the cathedral of the submarines.

He hadn't thought through the question of how he was to get out. But he got lucky: the sentry did make more than one tour, and when he unlocked the gate and let the dog in to check the submarine dock, Duval gave them thirty seconds and moved to the gate and slipped through, widening the opening as little as he could.

'*Wer is da?*'

The shout stabbed out from behind him. He had been stealthy, but the light from the area of the battleships had turned his stealth into a shadow that loomed back through the gateway. Again a shout, and the dog was barking, and then a whistle shrieked cold across the yard.

Duval ran. The yard in front of the battleships was too open, the space and the light terrifying, and he hurried back along his wall, hands flapping at door handles as he passed. Locked. Locked. Where was the sentry? Locked. The barking roared out again; the sentry had been releasing the collar. Locked. Another whistle, a different direction. Surrounded now. Locked. And then a handle turned and his feet were scrabbling to stop his momentum and he pushed through the door with shoulder and knee and stumbled in and pushed it closed and dropped. A moment: relief; breath; hands steadying himself in the crouch. Then the shouts and the barking nearer outside. He flapped around himself, found a key in the lock and turned it.

He crouched, gasping and trying to keep it silent. Move from the door? More likely to be heard. Did they know he was in here? The dog. Could they open it? The key. Would they shoot?

Light reached over him. The door was solid but there was a window just above his shoulder. The beam of a torch swung pale around the room, uncovering ghosts and provoking shadows: a noticeboard, a drawing board, shelves, another drawing board, a table, a hatstand.

He could hear the dog snuffling somewhere outside, but it didn't seem to be close to his door; perhaps the trace of sausage had saved him again. A voice. Two voices, scowling at each other in German.

The rattling of the door smashed into his ears and his heart lurched again. Then the torch swung away and the room was night. The voices moved off, and he heard another door being rattled.

Twenty cramped minutes huddled there. Then he crawled forwards, and as the blood began to flow and his legs strengthened he pulled himself up into a wary crouch against the table. As far as he could see through the window, the dockyard was deserted; no sign or sound of sentries. Little light penetrated, and he risked a match and began to patrol the edge of the room where the torch beam hadn't reached earlier. A series of blueprints and designs pinned to the wall: a gun barrel; what looked like a turret. Didn't seem likely that they'd actually design things on the spot. Perhaps this was where they copied, or checked, or assessed what materials they needed. Something called the Foster sight; then something detailed and mechanical, a motor or some part of it.

More productively, his search revealed a window, shuttered – which suggested the public street beyond – and another door. A new hope bloomed; it might not be necessary to cross the cursed yard again. Keys hanging on pegs adjacent, and a moment later David Duval slipped back into a world where he was allowed to be. He found a bar half full of slumped sailors, put on his Irishman again and got a little drunk. A police patrol came in some time later, two men as bored and surly as the men they peered at; Duval produced papers, to indifference.

Lurching emotions in his head: a little triumph; the sense that if he'd had more nerve he'd have stayed to copy some of the designs.

In the grey cold of dawn, he got the first train back to Berlin.

———

A café in a Constantinople side street: smoke, reek, covens of old men peering at impenetrable card games; wheezing and back-slapping and muttered advice, and cackles of laughter. Cade had chosen it because he'd thought it would be discreet; a place he'd seen in passing, off the beaten track. Actually, he stuck out like a fart at a Morningside tea party. But at least there was no chance of another European seeing him here.

Jozef Radek, his generous new acquaintance from the Russian Trade Legation, was exactly on time. He was not impressed by the surroundings, sneering at each of the people he squeezed past and then wiping the chair with a handkerchief before sitting. For a junior clerk, and apparently not a flourishing one, he'd picked up some pretty snooty tastes somewhere; *which might do us no harm, eh?*

'Did you get it?' Radek said as he sat. There was something of the dandy about him; waistcoat and cravat patterned.

'What'll you drink?'

'Nothing, I thank you.' And the suggestion of scent?

'Drink some coffee; pep you up, or calm you down, whichever suits. Two coffees!' The waiter went away again, and Cade smiled at his man. 'Yes,' he said. 'I got it. Very civil of you.'

Jozef nodded, like an overexcited dog.

Another smile, to fill a space. 'Kind of you to think of me,' he said.

'But I'm – I'm not sure what you expect of me.' Could it be some sort of ploy to smoke him out? *Let 'em know you're a buyer, and the price goes up awful fast.*

Jozef sat up straighter, and smiled with what he clearly judged was shrewdness. 'Mr Cade, sir: you are known as the coming man; an up-and-at-them businessman, as they say in United States of America. It is known that you have employed two new clerks in the last week.' He smiled again, as if this success were down to him.

Their coffees arrived. It was interesting hearing, for Cade; nice that word was getting around – *nothing like the impression of success for bringing success*. And it increased his wariness of Radek. What did he want – a job?

'Also, sir, you are known as...' – the stirring of his coffee absorbed him, and suddenly he tapped the spoon twice on the cup – 'as a man of significant influence with your own embassy.'

Are you hinting what I think you're hinting? He kept quiet.

Cade badly wanted to ask where he was from. It seemed to mean so much to everyone hereabouts; subtle subdivisions of empire, everyone unhappy about something. He'd guessed he wasn't Russian; but that didn't mean he wasn't a subject of the Russian Empire. Or he was from one of the umpteen peoples of the Ottoman Empire. *Find what makes a man truly happy, or what makes him truly angry, and he's yours.* But Cade had held back: didn't want to label the fellow's motives too casually.

'Frankly, sir, I do not plan to be a junior official for ever.'

The not-so-subtle hint that Jozef thought he knew that Cade was doing a bit of snooping for the king, and all veiled in the business pitch of a young bull.

'Let me see if I understand you right, Mr Jozef.' Jozef nodding, eager again. Cade felt for his words, stepping stones in a moor-bog. 'You, like many businessmen in this new century, distinguish between economic activity and narrow national political interest.' The face opposite still pleasant, waiting; *one step at a time*. 'While continuing to serve your employer loyally as regards your political duty' – a nod; it wouldn't last, but perhaps he genuinely wanted to believe it – 'you are prepared to share information of potential business interest, on an informal and unofficial basis, with me, someone who has no interest in politics' – his own lie, for form's sake; *is it a lie? for what reasons am I enjoying this?* – 'so that perhaps it might… stimulate some healthy business activity.' Nodding and a smile. *Steady as you go, Jimmy.* 'Now, I'm sure you don't want to seem to be selling information.' Watchful now; *perhaps you don't care so much, eh?* 'But it would seem only fair that you would get some share of the return, if an investment was successful. Nothing wrong with a fellow speculating in his own time, on his own account, is there?'

Jozef shook his head, and smiled wide.

What now? 'Until then, perhaps you wouldn't be offended if I gave you a small token of my respect; businessman to businessman.' The smile widened. Cade set a box on the table, compact and ribboned. 'A gift for a wife or mother, perhaps.' Jozef's smile flinched; *or for you to sell on at the first corner, you kern.*

Cade raised his coffee cup, and released a breath. 'Here's to free trade,' he said.

Jozef vaguely got it, nodded, and took his box and left. *Could have given you a shopping list of questions and a bag of gold sovereigns, couldn't I?* Cade paid the bill, and wondered at the games people played with themselves.

❧⸺⸻⸺❧

On their second night at sea, Ballentyne was at the tiller at the dying of twilight, when the immense purple of sky and sea gave way to darkness. Isabella came up from the cabin with glasses of whisky. She handed him his glass silently, sat next to him, and pushed up against his shoulder cat-like.

Ballentyne glanced round; his whisky arm was now trapped. He transferred the glass out of the way, and shifted slightly so that her head fell more naturally against his, and they waited for the moon to rise.

Later, they lay on a blanket on the cabin roof, and Isabella told him to tell her a story about the stars, and Ballentyne began quietly to explain the composition of the Orion constellation and its usefulness in locating other stars.

Her head came round, and for a minute or so she watched this performance with something between amazement and amusement. Then she rolled up onto her elbows and kissed him. They made love there, naked under the moon, and the languid rocking of the boat on the sea became theirs.

Flora Hathaway had fallen asleep in the Germany of girlhood romance; she woke in the Germany of *Daily Express* hysteria. She mistrusted both models.

She had closed the compartment curtain on forest, the mystical empire of princesses and wolves and Saxon heroes with lovely libraries. She opened it onto a city of iron and stone, the Kaiser's empire of military power and global ambition. Through the window, as she adjusted her hat, she could see tramping people and a uniform with a rifle and a boy selling newspapers – he had a uniform, too – and she tried to catch the headline flapping in his hands.

Enough of fancy. Let us see what the breakfast tables of Britain are so afraid of.

The people in the torrent weren't all that different from those who tramped along the platforms at Euston; quieter, perhaps. The porters were certainly more efficient here; she thought of Purvis at the station at home, leering and lazy, knew he'd take to a uniform like this one, knew he'd look ridiculous. She watched how the passengers behaved with the conductor or the policeman: as if confronted by a butler who happened to have power of life and death over them. Everything smooth, respectful. It was rather pleasing to be part of the machine.

A café, a bookshop and a detour into a museum of clockwork later, she and Gerta were crossing onto Museum Island. A policeman had looked at them as if they might both be English spies, and given them detailed directions to the Schloßplatz and a salute. *One feels like an over-protected princess.* The river's expanse allowed even better views of the buildings, imposing and stately, everything with the space proper to its function and architectural requirement. It was managed grandeur.

As they neared the first crossroads on the island, they could see a line of people moving across in front of them; then they saw it wasn't a line, but a column – a march. From a distance the marchers all seemed to have the same black-brown clothing, and Hathaway had assumed uniform. Close to she saw it wasn't a uniform exactly, but a standard of working clothes – *for all the difference that makes* – trousers in boots, heavy coats, loose caps.

They marched in silence. It was the most unnerving part of it.

Instinctively, Hathaway took a few steps in parallel with the marchers.

Berlin seemed bigger, colder as Duval walked. He'd drowsed on the train, woken with a buzzing head and a sour mouth. He wanted a bath but wanted air more. Grey streets, brown buildings, white sky. Kiel had been... what? A spree, a series of alarms, a demonstration of something – *to whom?* Now this bland capital, with its smart citizens and uniforms everywhere. He tried coffee, tried brandy; still he needed to move.

Eventually, a square he hadn't visited before: yet another great building – they'd got the Italian a little more effectively this time, almost delicate around the windows, columns strong but not oppressive, balustrade along the roof rather fine. And in the middle of the square a fountain, sprays of water that reached out to him, four houris draped around the edge of the basin, strong-thighed, reclining most alluringly, *fancy a splash?*, and he wanted to know which sculptor had found himself marooned this far north of the Alps and created this oasis.

Across the square, at a corner: 'He comes: you see, Sergeant? The grey suit – near the Neptunbrunnen – putting his hand in the water now.'

'I see him.'

The water was cold, electric, and Duval splashed some on his face. Somehow it produced a shouting, and he turned.

If my will is unrestricted, Hathaway thought, *the outcome is predictable. If my will meets another will, the outcome is predictable competition. If three wills meet, the outcome is chaos.*

They had kept pace with the march and then, when by some unknown inclination it had paused, they'd entered the square slightly ahead. An impression of faces, some enthusiastic, some blank. Banners drooping between poles. Then the policemen marching forwards to intercept them, long coats and squashed caps, and the first jovial and scornful exchanges between the front lines. Glancing to her side, Hathaway saw Gerta's wide eyes, the open lips.

'Gerta, you're enjoying yourself.'

Gerta looked naughty. 'We can't hide in the forests for ever.' She looked across at the waiting crowd. 'This is our century. The power of people together. The collective unconsc—'

'Where did you read that? Crowds are unintelligent.' *I never felt as stupid; I never felt as excited.*

'It's rather exci—' Then a new shout, and a reply from one of the policemen, and then the shouting was general and the line between marchers and policemen was swallowed and the line of confrontation was all arms and fists and hats falling, a policeman was trying to hold two men back using his rifle as a barrier and something was thrown, and they heard a whistle, whistles, and then a shot.

They picked up their hems and began to hurry away across the square. As they went, there were hooves rattling on the cobbles somewhere behind them. 'There – the café!' Gerta called between gasps, and they altered direction. Hathaway was aware of her ankle boots slapping on the ground, of the jolting in her legs, of the foolishness of skirts, and of people around her: scattered figures hurrying away like them, some still oblivious, one man crossing the square in front of them.

'He's coming!'

'Sergeant! Look!' Across the Schloßplatz a crowd had become a mob and the mob had become a riot, and then a shout high above the rest and a whistle and a squad of mounted policemen was cantering over the cobbles like hailstones.

'Your orders—'

'I know my orders, mate. Arrest him we shall.'

'Sergeant, shouldn't we help—'

'He's still coming.'

'I can see him well enough.'

Duval was still coming, wary glances towards the crowd, a sense that he must not be where there was trouble, a perverse Englishness telling him to avoid a scene. Two women came towards him, and he stopped. Ears dulled to noise, eyes sharpened to beauty, he watched them come. Hell of a pair they made: one dark and slender, one blonde and curves, clothes smart but not showy, moving quickly but smooth. Just a little *dérangées*, hearts a little faster; Neptune's nymphs come to life. They passed within ten feet of him – a glance from the darker one; handsome she was, and the blonde was a beauty. On an instinct, legs leading before the head could ask any damnfool questions, Duval changed direction and followed them into a café.

+========+

Not a healthy sign: ogling a couple of girls; voyeur. Duval drank a coffee, and then a brandy, a steady and unthinking rhythm of hand to mouth. He considered the two women aesthetically, and then wondered about them. Found the ideal job for transience, hadn't he? For never settling.

For a quarter-hour the sound of the crowd reached into the café, a chaos of shouting and whistles and sporadic gunshots. And the customers in the café kept glancing towards the front of the building, flinching and guessing at the bursts of noise, waiting for the riot to swallow them. The waiters were tight-lipped; saucers rattled and sloshed. The gentility of the place – the costumes of the customers, the filigree ironwork, the delicate spoons, the forced politenesses – had become ridiculous, and a trap.

Eventually the noise dwindled. The waiters recovered their poise, and the customers leaned back in their chairs and the volume inside the café grew. Duval ordered another brandy, and savoured it this time. As he left, he made a point of walking past the table where the two women sat.

Each glanced up as he passed: the darker, handsome woman watchful, the blonde interested, and he had to stifle the urge to twirl his moustache. The suggestion of giggling from behind; *that's right, ladies, you're never as controlled as you think.*

And still he was alone in this great parade-ground of a city. In the distance he could see debris: hats, items of clothing, loose cobbles, banners straggling in the mud.

He hesitated on the step; a glimpse of a uniform to his left and he moved briskly right, *keep moving*, and as a tram hummed past he caught the handrail and hopped on, another man following him a second or two later, and they lurched around a corner and away.

A uniform appeared in front of him, and his stomach kicked. *Will I ever be able to look at brass buttons again?* He paid the conductor.

Surely he wasn't hunted. Couldn't be that easy, anyway; big city. He tried to work out which of the faces around him was the one who'd followed him onto the tram.

Duval the hunted. Duval and the submarines. Penny-dreadfuls; couldn't say he didn't enjoy them. The tram whined and swayed, the foreign faces around him shaking their disapproval back and forth. Except his was the foreign face, wasn't it?

Back at his hotel he spent three hours with pencil and paper, translating the products of his night's nerviness into the precise work of a draughtsman. *And how many men could do this?* The papers went into an envelope, the envelope into the hotel post box, and Duval out into the evening. A club, a steak and half a bottle of wine, and a chat with a couple of the girls, enough of the world in them for a chap to feel swell rather than desperate.

Precisely as he'd said to Ani, Cade was not a man for melodrama; nor for pushing around. He set to find all there was to be found on the subject of Mr Muhtar and his dealings. Discreet enquiries here and there; a perusal of certain records; casual questions.

Two days later, Ali did not appear at the office in the morning. He was still absent after lunch and, with an hour to spare, Cade tracked him down by means of the man who sold tea on the corner and various urchins. The trail led only a couple of hundred yards, but down alleys that neither Cade nor the sunlight had ever visited, to a cellar room obviously too close to the waterline.

There was no light, until Cade struck a match and turned the shadows into shapes. Two boys, vacant and scared, and a mewing woman were watching the twisted figure lying on a tangle of sacks. The place stank. As Cade's match travelled, it showed Ali's face bloody and battered with one eye flickering dull in the glare, a bruised body with something wrong with one of the arms, and then an obviously broken leg.

James Cade went silently berserk. Half an hour later Ali was in the Jewish hospital, over the protests of every official as well as the lad himself. Cade overrode it all, an implacable engine of gold coins and roaring Scottish fury that had doctors backing away and nurses hurrying out of earshot of words they did not understand and clearly should not want to.

The news of this new Scots eccentricity spread quickly. Ani Charkassian refused to meet him, until he threatened to come into the house and carry her out.

When she came through the curtain onto the roof terrace it was with obvious trepidation. But she found Cade pacing cheerfully, looking energized but not obviously homicidal. He strode to her, took her face in between his fingertips, and kissed her deeply.

He stood back, and watched her a moment. Her eyes were cautious, waiting. Her tongue was reviewing the taste of him on her lips.

He smiled, calmer. 'Because today this city seems hellish ugly, and so I badly needed to see your face. That's why. Remind myself there's something worth caring for.'

Silent still, she nodded. Then her hands came up and began to undo the buttons on her dress from throat to waist – as they came loose, her body swelled and came free – then the bows on a chemise as wispy as the curtain fluttering behind her, until she was naked to the waist. Her eyes never moved from his.

<hr/>

Mayhew was through the door with only the suggestion of a knock. The old man looked up, austere.

Mayhew fought for the words. 'Duval – Duval, he's a... a fraud. An impostor. A – an intriguer.' He stepped forwards, leaned in insistent: 'What have we done?'

'Sit down, would you, Colonel?' Mayhew sat, but failed to settle. 'Could you be more specific?'

Mayhew took a breath, stared at the ceiling. Suddenly the old man saw the boy Mayhew, trying to collect himself in exams that always seemed just beyond his understanding. 'I've had a flag on the names of our four bods; just in case – long shot – some other department gets interested and risks gumming up the works. Today I get a copy of a routine enquiry being made in police records.' He didn't notice it, but the old man's eyes were a fraction wider. 'Duval. Except his name's not Duval – well, it might be... The request was for information on a man named Pinsent, and police records from York showed that Pinsent was a name used by a man who also went by Duval. And it's clearly our Duval.' He brandished a slip of paper, and picked out words as it fluttered. 'Forging cheques. Goods and services on credit, then absconding' – he looked up a moment – 'that wasn't the first hotel bill he's skipped.' An uneasy breath. 'He's an adulterer, a – a philanderer, a – a seducer.' He shook his head. 'God's sake, he's—'

'All right, Colonel. May I?' The old man took the paper, skimmed it only briefly, and laid it on his desk. A flicker from Mayhew at the loss of it. 'This is critical, Mayhew; I'm sure of it. But—'

'You're dashed right. We're employing—'

'Not that!' Real asperity. 'Not his character. The fact that a search was being made in police records.'

'With good reason, it seems.'

'Colonel, doesn't it strike you as rather an extraordinary coincidence that we select a man for an extremely secret job of espionage work, and he is shortly afterwards the subject of a police enquiry?'

It did not seem to strike Mayhew thus.

'I urge you not to, Colonel, but I'll wager that if you did try to chase down the origin of this enquiry, you wouldn't find it. So many copies of so many trivial requests circulating in our systems.' He shook his head. 'Lord, in our own police records...'

Silence. Mayhew, cheated of an appropriate reaction, tried again. 'You don't seem... all that worried about this – this revelation.'

The flicker of a shrug across the shoulders. 'Candidly, Colonel, I'm not. Not about Duval. I confess I suspected there was a little more to him; one gets a knack for reading between the lines of the files; between the lines of a life.'

'You suspected – and still you chose him?'

The old man sat back in the chair, looking somewhere over Mayhew's shoulder. 'More than a hundred years ago, Colonel, there was a rather remarkable chap called Kinnaird. Sir Keith Kinnaird. A shrewd navigator of the currents of secret intelligence. At one point the holder of... a certain office in this...' His hand circled to suggest the world between him and Mayhew. 'A time of great national peril. Napoleon poised ready to invade, unrest at home, and London full of treacheries.' A wry smile at some private impression. 'I have thought a great deal of Sir Keith Kinnaird. Taken a certain inspiration from him.'

'I'm afraid I don't quite see the point...' Mayhew: restraint; discipline. *Lord, the plodding and the fancies of these old men.* 'Duval is—'

'Duval is not the point, Colonel. The point is the man whose shadow falls on him.'

'This would be...'

'I mentioned him before. A man who is himself shadow, but if I can manage...' He looked up at Mayhew. 'He is one of three men, Colonel. Or rather, he inhabits the persona of one of three men.'

Mayhew was lost. 'Duval,' he said, trying to regain solid ground. 'I realize that – this game – sometimes a rogue has certain – well, aptitudes...'

'That's true. But in certain quarters it also makes him more likely to attract attention. And that, Colonel, is precisely why I chose him.'

⊹═══⊹

Berlin mellowed in the evening: lamplight warmed the stone, and the city of shops and offices became a warren of cafés and clubs. The Germans took their business seriously, and it made them dull and forbidding; but they also took their pleasure seriously, and it made them sophisticated and enticing in the twilight. Was he hunted? He didn't care.

Duval took a taxi straight to the station. He'd done his duty with that envelope, and now for Russia – the instruction had been received, an envelope under the door on hotel stationery – and whatever came next.

The station was earnest Berlin again, crowds of suits defined by the clock that followed them around the concourse with its great gothic finger. And at every entrance and platform gate, a uniform or two, rifle barrels prickling the air. They were watching faces, checking papers.

He drifted through the main entrance in the middle of a knot of people, forcing himself to look at the policemen but not letting them catch his eye. Surely they weren't looking for him, though? Routines. Germans. He bought his ticket, and sat and had a brandy while he waited. Mostly he watched the sentries at the gates to the platforms.

Fifteen minutes to go. *But they're not looking for me.* Better to saunter because more relaxed? Or better to hurry because more troublesome to stop? They weren't stopping everyone, anyway. The drift of people on the concourse was funnelling itself into a loose stream moving through the gate to the Petersburg train, and he joined it.

They were stopping the single men. He was fifteen yards off when he realized. Was the whole of Berlin focused on him? Couples and the elderly were being waved through. Duval stooped, and adjusted his shoelace, glanced around himself.

And saw her. Coming level, looking around, somehow excited – or at least more lively than the rest. The face was alert; petite features, brown waves pulled back under a neat green hat; not beautiful, but... alive.

She noticed him as he stood, seemed to consider him, a frown and then interest, eyes widening a fraction – *and good evening to you too* – the combination repeated as he moved closer.

'May I say,' he said, a little closer than appropriate – *the hell with whether she understands; she'll get the idea* – 'that that hat suits you very well?' And he smiled.

She considered this – the language or the idea. 'Thank you,' she said brightly, in accented English. 'You may.'

They moved forwards a step, nearer the gate. 'Looks like we're going the same way,' he said.

'Yes,' she said. 'It does.' And she slipped her hand through his elbow.

Contact Report

M.G. 14/Ü/5/94, period 2

Subject: G738 – DUVAL/PINSENT

Contact with G738 was maintained during this day,
consistent with Headquarter Directive 14/Ü/G738.

Man fitting the description of G738 was observed at the
Hamburgerbahnhof arriving on the 1030 Kiel train, by the
same post who had observed his departure two days previously.
Consistent with procedure he was stopped. He produced papers
in name of PINSENT, British (Irish), and was allowed to pass.
Clarification was requested from Headquarters, and Headquarter
Directive 14/V/5/62(G738) was revalidated (amended) for DUVAL or
PINSENT. (Checks with Kiel show that PINSENT spent night of 24.5
in the Baltik Hotel in Kiel and was recorded in a café earlier
this morning.) Observation was maintained while preparations
were made. G738 visited two cafés.

By the time that the arrest was readied, G738 was near
Schloßplatz. At this time the situation in this district
was becoming restive as a result of the political protest.
As G738 was coming near the arresting squad he appeared to
change direction, and entered Café London. Consistent with
procedure, detachment first ensured observation of all exits,
before one officer entered. G738 was observed drinking alone.
He was not observed to make contact with any other customer,
although of necessity he was not under observation for every
minute. It was naturally impossible to verify the identities
of all other customers. It was possible to check the papers
of one: a Swede, PEHRSSON. Another was an Englishwoman,
accompanied by a German woman. Subsequent enquiries showed
her to be HATHAWAY, travelling with Fräulein von WALDECK and
staying with a WALDECK family member in Berlin. (For Freiherr
von WALDECK see also H 3/17/506.)

By now, other duties arising from the situation in the
streets forced the decision not to execute Headquarter
Directive 14/V/5/62(G738), and G738 therefore remained at

liberty. He moved by tram and on foot for a further one hour, looking at shops but not entering, and meeting no one, to his hotel. He stayed in his hotel three hours. Hotel staff report no visitors before his arrival, and he was observed to meet no one during this time. He had supper at the Club Nachtslilie. He spoke there to two women of the house, who are known. He went directly to the Stettinerbahnhof. Contact was lost here, despite many inspections of likely men. But timing suggests that G738 took the 2300 train to St Petersburg.

St Petersburg have been informed and will have him under surveillance pending further instructions.

Berlin, 26. May 1914

[Deutsche Bundesarchiv (Author translation)]

A gloved hand brushed once over the report, as if reading the lines through the fingertips.

'Merely routine business, Herr Krug; but you observe our procedures.'

'Most efficient, my dear Colonel. Most thorough.' The suavity was automatic. 'My networks can offer you choice details, but the effectiveness of your machine...'

'On this occasion, the partnership is stronger than you may know.' Nicolai was pleased with himself; Krug affected interest. 'This Pinsent, or Duval, is the name we passed you, and which your contacts researched in London.'

'Ah yes; the name seemed familiar.'

'But there was an unfortunate inefficiency here. The patrol were following the man as Duval, and it was only when they checked with headquarters that they found that we had investigated him as Pinsent and – thanks to you – made the connection. A low-level criminal, it seems. A deceiver. If he comes to Germany again he will be arrested, and we will see how many sets of papers he carries.'

'Again, I am pleased to have been of some small service.'

'At any one time we have between fifty and two hundred foreigners under observation; some at the lowest level – that is to say documentary observation – hotel records and so on; up to those at the highest, under twenty-four-hour observation.'

'Most impressive...' Still the glove hovered over the report.

'Something in the report... interests you, Mein Herr? The subject is known to you?'

'Not until you brought him to my attention. So obvious a rogue would be a poor choice of agent for that part of the British apparatus that most concerns me. But something...' The eyes blinked rapidly, and then swung up to face Nicolai. The hand was placed discreetly in a pocket. 'Nothing. Too many foreign names in my life.'

'Then we may continue the tour.'

'With pleasure.'

'While we walk, Mein Herr... I wish to ask you about your relationship with Hildebrandt.' The colonel's eyes were fixed on the corridor ahead as he spoke; his guest's glanced at him politely. 'You are accustomed to collaborate with him, I realize. He is a German, though, and has been employed by this department.'

'Indeed, Colonel. And I would not dream of trying to strain the loyalty Count Paul feels to his nation and his employers. It was his efficiency, and his reports of the growing efficiency of this department, that first convinced me of the potential of a closer co-operation between us.'

'A man can have but one loyalty.'

Oh, dear Colonel, you do not begin to understand... 'Quite. As an individual I find him most efficient, and I trust that he keeps you properly informed of our activities. Might we say that he is the ideal... liaison, between us, as we strengthen our bond?' A grumble from Nicolai's throat. 'Now, that I may be clear: your navy's two priorities are the latest British oil-fired engines and their new fifteen-inch guns, yes?'

Later, in the shadows of a Berlin ministry porch: 'Hildebrandt, your compatriot Nicolai worries that you forget your proper duties to your emperor.'

'I am a better judge than that potato of how I may best serve my emperor.'

'Indeed.'

'I trust you wish no change in our relationship.'

'Any change would... would displease me' – the verb was cold – 'greatly.

But if we are to get what we desire from this collaboration, Nicolai must be kept content.'

'Or removed. You have the influence.'

'Or removed. But for now: play the part of the loyal German, would you? Be busy; be Prussian in your efficiency. Report to him my activities and idiosyncrasies as your amusement dictates.' Hildebrandt nodded, bored. 'Your friend Ballentyne has eluded you again.'

Now Hildebrandt was more alert. 'He will be found. He was aiming for Split. He is watched for; awaited, in half a dozen places. Belcredi was in that region already; he can do some real work for once.' Krug was considering it all. 'Ballentyne will be found.'

'I do hope so. But if you cannot get me the one, perhaps you may do better with another. There is an Englishwoman called Hathaway. Nicolai's peasants observed her in Berlin. I have read her name within the last week. I don't approve of coincidences, and I want to know why Fräulein Hathaway has become one.'

❖

Contrary to the impression she'd given, Isabella di Lascara's island seemed to be largely hers. No more than a couple of miles in any direction, outcrops and ramparts of rock breaking up fertile stretches of fruit trees and vegetables and even vines. The two of them spent half a day riding it, and the people they met working in the fields, dark and gnarled like their olive trees, acknowledged the contessa with deference. Ballentyne they treated with respect and no curiosity. Ten years ago Isabella had come to the island a stranger, and been absorbed; later she had stayed alone, and this had been accepted without comment. Whatever the world brought to the island would be given its due, and no more. A little feudal Eden in the middle of the sea.

After their ride they swam, pale in the blue like the limestone, and walked and saw the lemons swelling on the branches, and ate bread and figs in the dusk. Later, dazed and slumped like a pair of armies that had clashed and wrestled and could not overcome, they lay in a tangle of sheets, and traced dreams on each other's flesh with gentle fingers, and watched the moonlight icing the balcony tiles.

Ballentyne said, 'I have to go, Isabella.'

She stopped tracing, and prodded him very deliberately with her finger. 'Yes,' she said. 'It seems to be the custom. Usually I get an island, or at least a boat.'

'Don't—' He sighed. 'No. Do. You're entitled to.'

She sat up and looked down at him, the sheet pulled tight around her breasts, the torrent of hair falling around her shoulders. 'I 'ave few illusions, Ronald. But... is there really nothing 'ere that would tempt you to stay?'

Delicately, he brushed the hair away from her shoulder with the back of his hand. 'You are a perfect Calypso. I can think of no greater magic than this place – and you. But, like Ulysses, my journey isn't over.'

'You 'ave your fight; and perhaps your – what was her name?'

'Penelope. No, there's no Penelope. But there is... there's an old man, in a village high in the Albanian mountains. I have unfinished business.'

'Always the men, they go off to the war. And always the reasons are stupid reasons: pride, duty, fear of shame, 'atred.' She dropped back onto the pillow. 'You know they are stupid reasons.'

'Yes.'

'But you go anyway.'

'Yes.'

'There is not one man in Europe who will break this 'abit.'

'Those people gave me hospitality. They offered me everything. In return I brought death to them, and I don't even understand how. I owe it to them to find out; to make it right, somehow, if I can.'

'You can't make death right. You can only make more death.'

'Someone's tried to kill me; twice. I can't just—'

'Of course you can! Men are always trying to kill other men. The reasons are irrelevant. Either you become like them, and do more killing, and continue the stupid game. Or you step away, because a life is more important than a death.' She stroked his arm. 'You could stay 'ere. Your slippers by the door and... your pipe by the fire. We could stay 'ere and the world would never know.'

'I'm not... I'm not finished with the world.'

'You don't like the world, Ronald.'

'If I chose to settle anywhere, Isabella, it would be here. But I wouldn't be choosing. I'd just be... hiding.'

'This place is out of the world. It belongs to a different element. Perfectly placed between the coasts; between west and east, between the Renaissance and barbarism.'

He smiled. 'Oh, I don't know. There was civilization on the Dalmatian coast when London was a swamp.'

'Brought there by Romans and Venetians.' Beautiful pride.

'Who also brought the politics, which led to the barbarism.' She snorted prettily. 'Truly, I've met more civility – a human respect for each other, and that's the only thing that can make a *civium* tolerable – in Balkan villages, than I ever have in London, or Berlin, or any of those places.' He pushed his hand through her hair where it bunched and splayed on the pillow, feeling it rolling over and round his fingers. 'And there seems to be wildness in Italy still.'

Her eyes widened, her mouth, and she brought up her hand and very deliberately scratched her fingernails over his cheek and down onto his chest. Over his heart, she squeezed a little and the nails bit.

He hissed softly. She glanced up at his face, down to his chest again, and bent and kissed the nipple. 'You 'ave something in there, then?'

'Yes. Though I'm not always sure what it's for.'

'I worry you are a scientist only. A brain. Who goes into these villages to examine and to experiment.' Her eyes were big, sad. 'That perhaps I am just another experiment.'

He considered, and shook his head. He pulled the sheet down, uncovering her torso, and bent and kissed her carefully on the stomach. 'Certainly a valuable specimen.' Then between her breasts. 'A journey of discovery, say.'

She clutched his hair and pulled his face up to hers.

'All right. I go to the villages because I...' – he watched her eyes flickering left and right as she tried to look into him – 'because I... I want to understand.' The eyes – brown gold, *like treacle* – narrowed. 'And don't ask what.'

'Dear stranger.' She stroked his hair.

'People. If I could understand—'

'Plenty of people in London. In Roma.'

'Too many. I have to start small.'

'Start with one.' And she pulled his lips down to hers.

＋══╤══＋

Her name was Anna, whispered to Duval as they came level with the sentries at the platform gate and were waved through. She was a sport, right enough. They amused each other with fictional domesticities for the benefit of the other inhabitants of their compartment, then went and smoked together in the corridor, while the last of Berlin's suburbs twinkled to nothing outside. She was from Alsace, visiting a younger cousin who was studying in St Petersburg. He was the wandering student of architecture, as ever.

'With a taste for hats too, I think,' and she looked at him with amusement.

'I'm going to be stuck for hours on this train. Rather do it with a pretty woman than without.' She dropped her eyelids prettily enough. 'You seemed... friendly.'

'Russian literature is as long and boring as the train journeys; especially when it's translated into German.'

Night and the friendly rattling of the train swallowed them, as they thundered eastwards into Russia.

＋══╤══＋

Some time around the 27th of May, two rumours began to circulate in Constantinople, around the diplomatic quarter, and the dock offices, and even at the gates of the palace itself, swirling and rising like leaves in a vortex until their strength quite obscured their origins, whatever those might have been. According to the first, the Egyptian government was considering impounding – or perhaps had impounded – certain foreign ships currently trading in Egyptian ports; according to the second, there had been protests – or if not protests, at least words of concern – from certain embassies about the activities and practices of one or two of the smaller private banks.

The stories were negligible, even if true, but taken together they had the unfortunate effect of causing doubt about the viability of one small banking and insurance firm in particular: the firm of Muhtar Bros. Customers went elsewhere, or hurried to withdraw their money; at one point there were even suggestions of a run on the bank.

James Cade watched the hullabaloo with grim satisfaction. Let Muhtar stew a little.

On the 28th, he had lunch with Osman Riza. Riza passed him a copy he had acquired of the accounts sent by General Liman von Sanders, the head of the German Military Mission, to Berlin.

And another envelope arrived from the man Radek, in the Russian Trade Legation: a copy of a request from the Russian consul in Isfahan, in Persia, for typewriting machines and other items to support their forthcoming tax-gathering activities in the region. That afternoon Jozef Radek learned that a bank account had been opened in his name, with money loaned to him by a friend, who also gave him two investment tips.

And James Cade spent the late afternoon with Ani Charkassian, feeling pretty spruce.

It was thirty hours from Berlin to St Petersburg, and the train compartment relaxed and developed its own regulations and domesticities. Snacks were shared among the six inhabitants, and experiences compared, and family histories presented. Duval and Anna joined in sporadically, or chatted to each other, or drowsed, his shin pressed against her boot. Everyone came and went for meals, to the lavatory – seats kept, bags watched – and the two of them had dinner together, fencing cheerfully. When she slept, Duval watched her suddenly younger face, and felt his sins.

Some time early in the pale blear of the second morning, he was aware of her moving, focused on the way her body twisted under luggage rack and over feet, and then focused on her face. Her eyes wide, considering him. 'You must excuse me,' she said quietly. 'This at least I must do alone.'

A smile, her fingers brushed the back of his hand, and she took her small bag and writhed her way into the corridor.

Soon there were houses sprouting outside, shadows through the condensation on the window, the slums of another city. Then the train was slowing, and the inhabitants of the compartment began to shake themselves out of hibernation, straightening and brushing and gathering and checking. Duval realized that he was looking forward to seeing Anna's face appearing in the doorway again. The woman just across from him saw his eyes travelling around the compartment; 'St Petersburg,' she said, and smiled encouragingly.

Then the woman beyond spat a word loud, and then more, rummaging in her handbag. Duval wondered at it vaguely, muffled by lack of language from the reality and the murmurs of his companions. Now the man next to him swore – something vicious, anyway – hand in jacket. The murmurs became a chatter, angry faces, glaring at each other and Duval and the empty seat opposite him. He stiffened in the confusion. Then a uniform in the corridor, the conductor, and the compartment was shouting at him and the woman was brandishing her open bag and he was saying something back to them, and again the glances swung to Duval and the empty seat.

The train had stopped, he realized, and there were whistles and bustling outside and the unique echo of a station.

Somehow an unhappy situation, which he'd be better off out of, but as he looked around at the faces he knew he wasn't going to be allowed to leave.

The conductor said something in Russian – Duval realized it was directed at him – then: 'Where has your wife gone, monsieur?'

'My wife? Oh, my w— just – just to the lavatory.'

A doubtful face in the doorway, and then another uniform beside it. Muttering between them, the conductor saying something down the corridor to someone else. Then, 'There will also be the small matter of her ticket, monsieur.'

The woman with the bag said something angrily.

'Her ticket?'

'While you slept; she assured me that you have both tickets.'

Cold, sick; 'But she's – she's not...'

The compartment glared at him.

Duval was two hours in the St Petersburg station police office. The woman called Anna had vanished into the city. Money and valuables were missing from a dozen compartments on the train. Some time during the second hour information arrived that a woman of the same description was sought by the German police, for confidence tricks and thefts at three Berlin hotels.

St Petersburg station was a beauty, vaults of elegant ironwork, but Duval had seen none of it. He walked head down between his police escort, half awake and stupefied and only starting to think. It brought nothing good. Understanding of his basic predicament was followed by a silly hollow hurt – the luxurious illusion of a night now showed foolish. And only after that, the embarrassment that the schoolboy glowing at his own stealth and importance had got himself pinched before he'd even got off the train. A ghastly vision of Knox and the grey men in London, scornful, outraged. *Alone again.*

Keep the lie simple; keep moving. He was plonked on a bench; bare room; vile green walls. Then another uniform appeared in front of him, sharp eyes, watchful, silent – and was there the hint of a sneer?

For one instinctive minute Duval found himself saying that the woman was indeed his wife. Then, fully awake, he gave that up – a perverse instant of shame at this betrayal – and by some unspoken agreement the policeman never mentioned it again either.

Out of the layers of pretence, Duval began telling what was almost the truth: that he'd wanted company on the train and picked up the girl, not realizing that she was picking him up. Never seen her before.

Inspiration: 'Have to be a hellish risky scheme – wouldn't it, Officer? – to have one of the confederates deliberately arrested.'

The uniform – those superior eyes – considered this, then nodded. 'For you, indeed. I had not imagined that you were an equal partner in the crime, nor the motivating brain.' The English was crisp, cultured; another aspect of St Petersburg's style that Duval was ill-placed to appreciate. But the sneering was fine, however much it rankled: better a dupe than a criminal.

'If you checked, I'm sure you'd see we'd been in different places. I could give you a list... I only met her at the station.' It was out before he realized his mistake.

If the Russians asked them, the German police could easily discover that this was not Duval the confederate of criminals; but they would as easily discover that this was Duval the breaker of telegraph offices and dockyards, and God alone knew how that would play. Could the Russians send him back?

The policeman watched him.

Duval tried to look innocent. Of what, he wasn't exactly sure.

'I hope a pretty face was worth it.'

The face alive; the face at rest. Fingertips. Duval made a show of looking around the dingy room, and produced a rueful shake of the head. The memory of their conversation at the edge of the compartment, the rest of the world muffled and unknowing. He'd thought himself quite the lad for breezing out of Germany on her arm. But she...

A glimmering of admiration; of confederacy; of loyalty. As part of his effort to demonstrate co-operation and humility, Duval paid for her ticket. Which, in a way, made her his wife after all.

+===+

Sir, NICOLAI Military Intelligence returned twenty-four-hour journey Prague. Travelled alone which unusual and with unknown purpose. Suspicion of high-profile visitor now. DUVAL left Berlin St Petersburg train. Monitored by German police German Military Intelligence plus suspected representative French Deuxième Bureau.

[SS D/2/98, SS G/1/893/16 AND SS X/72/153 (DECYPHERED)]

The old man watched the message slip; traced its edges with his two index fingers.

Poor Duval. Encircled by hounds, and still running.

And where is the Spider? His fingers hovered over the paper. In Prague? In Berlin?

Nicolai and the Spider. A triumph for the Spider, to get his hands on the

German network in Britain; a boost for the Germans. The discipline and structure of German Military Intelligence, and the subtlety and reach of the Spider's contacts. United in the service of a belligerent enemy.

A breath. For a moment he saw the faces of his four: Duval, Hathaway, Cade and Ballentyne.

Keep running.

Eventually Duval was walking out of the office and out of the station, breathing in the soaring architecture and no longer the focus of every eye in St Petersburg.

'Made a bit of an ass of yourself, I'm afraid.' He'd been uneasy about involving the British Embassy, but when the policeman had assumed he'd want to contact them he'd not wanted to raise new suspicion by refusing; besides, he really hadn't done anything wrong in Russia, not yet; and a friendly face couldn't hurt.

Giles Lisson wasn't a friendly face. This wasn't the first of his snooty remarks, and Duval's ability to maintain the pose of humble regret, on an empty stomach, was weakening fast. He'd been hating the Giles Lissons of the world since he was a boy.

'Parents always wanted me to make something of myself; beggars can't be choosers. And this beggar got a night with a pretty girl.' Not nearly as much as he'd wanted, but Lisson didn't need to know that. He glanced at Duval as they stepped down onto the cobbles, affronted. 'Anyway, thanks for hoicking me—'

'We're not done yet.'

Duval didn't care for the tone. 'No motor car?' he said as they set off through the bustle of a square. Might get a drink out of it, at least.

'Not for you.' Lisson turned to him, as the crowd washed around them. 'Can you remember Millionaya Ulitsa? Millionaya Street?' Duval nodded. 'Last door at the western end, by the canal. Be there in thirty minutes exactly.'

Duval was glad to be rid of him for that long, at least. As he walked, he became increasingly aware of St Petersburg around him, and he liked it.

The boulevards had been cut with an eye not for the houses but the spaces; there'd been someone in control, and he'd known about proportion. The buildings themselves were fine, often monumental but generally elegant with it. And canals: more space, more light, and a constant freshness as he walked. People pretty ugly, but they couldn't complain about their surroundings, at least.

The morning was overcast and none too warm, but he welcomed its crispness. With time to spare he followed one of the canals; changed some money, bought a piece of fruit, watched an argument between a man on a boat and a man on the bank for a few moments.

Millionaya Street was grand and quiet. The occasional carriage rattled past him, bouncing on the cobbles and slipping in the slime that coated them. The buildings were large, as he came near the end by the canal, but somehow faceless, and jumbled. Their frontages were the other side, against the river.

The last door was set into the wall, sheltered and shadowed. He waited, then knocked; waited some more. The street, the great buildings, were silent behind him. Eventually the door opened, and a rodent of a man looked at Duval, then past him at the street.

The rodent grinned, said, 'Owight sa?' and beckoned him inside. Pure cockney. Duval followed down dirty corridors and up three flights of stairs, until one further door opened to reveal the other side of the building, mosaic-floored and grand. They stepped across a corridor, the cockney knocked on a door and opened it and Duval found Lisson.

'Thank you, Harvey.'

'Sa.' The door closed.

'Look, Lisson, thank you again, but do I really need—'

'London told me to expect you. They probably hadn't imagined so public or ignominious an arrival, but...' – he looked up from a pretence of papers – 'as you say, beggars can't be choosers.'

Duval pulled a chair forwards from against the wall, and sat.

'Have you reported recently?' Lisson was brandishing a pen.

'Oh, is that what that's for?' Lisson lowered at him, then made ready to write. 'I sent some drawings from Berlin. For obvious reasons I didn't say what they were.'

'Which was?'

'They, er...' – he smiled pleasantly – 'they're a map – disguised, obviously – of the submarine dock at Kiel.'

Lisson's pen sagged, and he looked up doubtfully. Duval nodded.

'Perhaps you'd better tell me.'

So Duval told him: his other researches in Kiel; getting into the dockyard; the battleships; the submarine dock; the escape through the drawing office; the plans of the barrel, the Foster sight, the turret, the more complicated machinery.

Lisson interrupted occasionally; not, as Duval had first expected, to tell him to exclude the excitement, but instead to ask for more detail. Lisson was a prig, but he was methodical, which was presumably some benefit in this game.

'Get the name on the shop?'

'No, Lisson, I didn't get the name on the bloody shop.'

'Hmm. Pity.'

'If I'd only thought to ask one of the sentries.'

Lisson looked up; frowned. 'No need to get ratty, old chap.'

'I was hounded out of Germany – which, by the way, was why I picked up the girl – and got pinched before I'd even properly arrived in Russia, all in your service. I think I'm entitled to blow off steam.' He glanced around the office. 'Is it sensible for you to meet me here – me being such a desperado?'

Lisson looked distasteful again. 'Meaning you'd rather we were scurrying around the slums in disguise. You'd be better off with my – well, let's not call Lockhart my colleague; probably just your type, anyway. Melodramatic bloody Scotchman.' He leaned forwards and tapped the desk. 'Bit of common sense is a much better disguise than all the false beards and secret knocks. Better if we're not seen meeting around town. Embassy back door and a wary eye are good enough.'

'Such a disappointment.'

Lisson's face was austere. 'It is not the empire that is the servant of your fantasies of adventure, but you who are the servant of the empire.' Obviously a practised line. 'Grief, the trouble we've had from popular fiction.' He sounded genuinely affronted. 'North Germany is crawling with British officers using their holidays to thwart invasions while dressed as gypsies or bicycling clergymen. There's enough chaos in Russia as it is, without amateur enthusiasts getting involved.'

'You won't be needing me, then.'

'Up to you, old chap. You're happy to pay your own fare home, are you?' Lisson didn't wait for an answer. 'You're obviously able, Duval. You can make yourself useful here. Worthy contribution, I'm sure.' He pulled open a drawer, and counted out a handful of banknotes. 'Enough to be getting along with, I should think. Put up at the Angleterre. We'll send word. Any message including the word "yesterday" and the name of a Russian writer will also include a number somewhere; means meet here at that hour.'

Duval stood, collected the money, and made for the door.

'Duval.' He looked round. 'Odd thing, surely. In that office where you hid out; the drawing you saw.' Duval shrugged. 'Written in English, I mean.'

❖

Flora Hathaway in another mighty entrance hall, trying to swallow new surroundings and being scrutinized.

Heinrich Auerstein had the height and bearing of Gerhard von Waldeck but, lacking a moustache, the face seemed more austere.

'Gerta von Waldeck,' he said to her companion, Hathaway left to one side along with their baggage. The surname made it clear on whose behalf she was welcome.

'Lieber Herr,' Gerta began, *Dear Sir,* as if he were a business correspondent or a schoolmaster, 'my father sends you his respects.'

It was a different Gerta, cool and buttoned, and Hathaway felt a moment's ache.

There was a further pair of formal sentences of greeting, then Auerstein turned towards her. 'Fräulein,' he said with a little bow, like a willow creaking, 'I bid you welcome to my house. A friend of Waldeck is a friend of Auerstein, and you honour me by your visit.' It was charming, and cold. *I do not feel welcome, and yet I am being welcomed.* The hallway, chequerboard tiles and lots of wood, stank of ancient duties.

She said something formal and gracious, and Auerstein left them in the care of a housekeeper.

From the walls, stuffed animal heads stared down at Hathaway, extravagantly horned and haughty.

⊱━━⋆⋆━━⊰

Another reception at the British Embassy, the glittering from chandeliers and chests, colours and feathers and a hundred murmurs. The British ambassador was saying to the minister of finance, 'Now that's a name I keep hearing: Riza. He's one of yours, isn't he? Won't say he's been exactly helpful to us – been pretty strict with our people on some of the procedures, I understand – but he's certainly most impressive. Must be reassuring to you to have that sort of chap's loyalty.'

Cade had contrived to be nearby; he turned away with a smile. Might help.

The white tie and get-up was feeling a bit stiff; perhaps he was putting on weight. He wriggled inside the waistcoat, and gazed around the hall. He'd a list of half a dozen people he wanted to see. To two – including the minister – he wanted to give only a couple of words of acknowledgement and respect; keep himself in the picture. He wanted to nag Burley on a point of embassy procedure with his correspondence, he wanted to get a meeting with the Austrian deputy ambassador to get recommendations of possible commercial contacts, and he wanted to talk shop with a couple of foreign merchants.

He did not want to see Muhtar. Actually, he did, in a Leith dockshed with the police paid off and no limit of rules or rounds, so that they could go at it in the old style. 'Mr Cade!' But here he was. At least there had been a 'Mr'. Perhaps he was feeling a little humbler now.

Muhtar stood a few feet off. Their respective stances created a space, but also the first glances of interest.

'You have been most busy, have you not? You are trying to destroy the business of my family.'

'All business is risk, sir.' He said it quietly. 'You should not take on more than you can suffer.'

'And how much can you suffer?'

'Oh, I'll bear up. Try me. Next time, rather than sending your thugs to cripple a lad, you come and call on me, and we'll settle it ourselves.'

For a moment Muhtar seemed to be considering it. Then he pulled himself up into a kind of dignity. 'Hardly the behaviour of gentlemen.'

'I've no claim to be a gentleman, Muhtar. And you surely do not.'

Muhtar was heating up properly, but held himself in. 'And have you considered our little discussion about your attitude to other people's treasures, Mr Cade?'

The arrogance of it, and the crassness in this setting with so many people around, were staggering. *Oh, laddie, you've not a clue about the Scots, have you?*

He leaned forwards, pleasant. 'I have, Mr Muhtar. And I'll see you in hell; we could discuss it further at that point, but until then I'll mind my own affairs and I suggest you do the like.'

He'd meant it to be discreet; but the curse at least had travelled, and there were a couple of wide glances and what might have been a gasp.

Muhtar gaped at him, then turned away, looking rather stiff.

It took a few moments to focus on the faces around him again. The whirl of colours and chatter spun past, and his anger eased. There was a face in front of him: sort of solid – a moustache large but trim – fit-looking type of fellow. 'Mr Cade?'

Recapturing courtesy. 'I am.'

'I'm Major Valentine Knox. I've been hoping to catch up with you.'

In the world of Constantinople, the theatricals and the emotions, London seemed more than a continent away. It took Cade a moment. The man in front of him waited, silent.

'Of course. I was told to expect you. You're – you're out of uniform.'

'Sorry to disappoint you. Bit less conspicuous.' Knox glanced around the hall. 'How are you getting on?'

'Fine! Grand. Some... some promising stuff, I think. I've sent four reports.'

'This evening is us meeting for the first time, and you as a friendly sort of chap inviting me as a new boy in town to call on you tomorrow. We can talk shop then.'

'Fine.'

'What was up with that chap just now? Looked a bit fraught.'

Parts of his world colliding. 'That? Oh… he's nothing. Misunderstanding. Don't really know him.'

Major Knox considered this; considered Cade. 'I see.'

<hr>

'Herr Krug: Colonel Nicolai's reporting shows that the Englishwoman Hathaway is going on to stay at the Margaretenhof.'

'I know that name, surely.'

'It is the country estate of Auerstein, the—'

'Auerstein?'

'The old—'

'I know who he is, Hildebrandt. Auerstein… Why do I—' Krug darted to his desk with a speed that Hildebrandt had never seen in him, an arm stretching for a report. 'Just yesterday… Yes! The British were conducting a check on Auerstein. But why…?'

'He is quite well known for—'

'Think, man!' Hildebrandt flinched. 'Or be silent. Or go and enlist as one of Nicolai's policemen. An Englishwoman is travelling in Germany; it is nothing. Our reports show her to be unusual; it is trivial. German Military Intelligence mark her in the same café as a suspect Englishman; perhaps it is happenstance. But then Fräulein Hathaway decides to visit Auerstein, and within days British Intelligence are reviewing their records on Auerstein.' He turned, face alight. 'My friend, I think we will have a little gift for the worthy Nicolai.' Then he was away into his papers again. 'Oh, Fräulein Hathaway, you are altogether too much of a coincidence…'

<hr>

Seeing ourselves as others see us. Major Knox was sitting in Cade's guest chair in the office, and Major Knox was appraising Cade. In his own chair, Cade was wondering what he was seeing.

The council or the police come to check up on something. One of his own visits to a warehouse or a shop. Looking for the frayed edges. Listening for the false note. But nothing frayed or false in Cade & Cade. He felt a little surge of warmth at his father's traditions, and his own fitness to uphold them. His office, he knew, looked prosperous but not luxurious; prudence and success.

'I stopped into the embassy,' Knox said. 'Consensus seems to be you're making a good thing of it here. London are pleased with what you've sent.'

'Glad to hear it. Satisfied customer.'

'You've two particular sources, I understand.'

'A senior official in the Ministry of Finance and a – well, sort of a clerk – in the Russian Trade Legation. It's a... a commercial department of the embassy, really; oversees their trading activity; organizes supply to and fro particular Russian missions around the place. Constantinople's a particular centre for them, because—'

'What are these two bods doing it for?'

Cade smiled. 'You think like a merchant, Major Knox. Understanding the deal.' Knox's eyes narrowed. 'My pal in the ministry is offended by the Germans – and others – poking their noses in; pulling the strings. And... I don't want to sound sentimental, but he seems to find me a sympathetic ear. Friendly.'

'Good. Nothing wrong with that. Can be the best possible bond. Sometimes the hardest to maintain.'

'Gold sovereigns a bit less emotional, eh? That seems to be my appeal to the other lad.'

'How did you come across him?'

'Sort of threw himself at me. Spotted me as a likely source of spending money, I think.' Knox nodded, once, but it was acknowledgement only, no comment or approval. 'I've got a little puzzle with him at the moment, as it happens.'

Knox's eyebrows came up. Behind the moustache, nothing else.

'I told him I wanted to know more about what the Russians are up to in Persia. Intentions; strategy. Seemed to be the sort of thing London would care to know.' A nod. 'Well, turns out there is such a thing – a document – because he's heard his boss talking about it. But he's not seen it; he was away when it was received, and it's kept in a locked cupboard in the boss's office, along with other important papers.'

'Could he be persuaded to have a go?'

'I've tried. Pushed him; promised him all the money in London. Not a chance.' Jozef's face this morning, dappled and flickering as they walked under the trees on the waterfront, and alarmed. 'Got to the point I was scaring him, so I dropped it.' The game becoming real.

'Worth us having a go?'

Cade's face twisted. 'Like your spirit, Major. I've the layout of the place from him, exact. But... well, I'm reluctant myself, tell you the truth. I'm fool enough for most games, but if I was caught – even linked...' He shook his head. 'If you tell me there's something there that's worth burning my whole position for, I'd consider it, but...'

Knox grunted agreement. The suggestion of a smile under the moustache. 'Not you, then.'

'How's your Russian, Major?' Knox began to see the point. 'The documents so far have been in English, I suppose because they get seen by some people in the chain who aren't Russian. This document's more likely in Russian.'

Knox nodded. 'Couldn't pick it out easily. Could take the lot for translation, but then they'd know; probably end of story for that channel. We'd have to be damn sure it was worth it.'

'And I'm not.'

'Good man. Not good to lose your head on these things.'

'Pity, though.'

'We'll give it some thought, shall we? You've got me a day or so. There's a place I'm hoping to find; maybe you can help – or one of your bods here in the office.'

'If I can.' Cade smiled, magnanimous. The customer seemed pretty content with Cade & Cade.

⊰══⊱

CONFIDENTIAL M.O.5
28th May 1914
Reference your enquiry of 25 inst. No record in

```
our files of BELCREDI. Only one occurrence of
name, wireless intercept dated 28 April 1914,
relay from Berlin of message apparently origin
Constantinople. TO: HVE, CARE OF EMBASSY BRUSSELS,
FROM ATHENESINSTITUT. ORIGINAL MESSAGE BEGINS. WILL
DEPART FOR ALBANIA THIS WEEK. EXPECT GOOD PROSPECTS
DESPITE REPEAT DESPITE INTERFERENCE YOUR COMPATRIOTS.
EXCELLENT PROGRESS CONSTANTINOPLE. ONE DAY WE SHALL
CELEBRATE TOGETHER IN GARDEN OF ROSY HOURS. BELCREDI.
ENDS. (Translated)
```

[SS G/1/891/17]

✦

The Sub-Committee of the Committee for Imperial Defence:

'Ghastly news of Canada.'

'A thousand souls drowned? And the boat wasn't even in open sea?'

'Our reports say slightly over.'

'But how?'

'They're saying it was fog.'

'Not enough excuse. Not with navigation lights, whistles, all that engineering. This was a four-funnel liner, not a rowing-boat.'

'One source says there's a strong supposition – strong supposition, mind you – of deliberate action.'

'Germans involved, I heard.'

'The ship that hit her was Norwegian, not German.'

'Well...'

'We're not taking this seriously enough. I've said it before.' Shifting around the table. He had, often, said it before. 'The *Aquitania* sails today, gentlemen. Her first voyage. More than three thousand aboard—'

'Three thousand?'

'They're going ahead despite what happened in Quebec?'

'The point is that we have a wholesale failure of security in our yards. Look, my people have collated the police reports on this.' There had been collated reports before, too. 'In the Clydebank yard, in the three months before the *Aquitania* launched, ten incidents logged where trespassers were evicted, cautioned, or arrested; the Lord knows how many unlogged. Separately—'

'Gentlemen, I wonder if we—'

'If I may just finish this point, Chairman. Records of dockyard staff.' A finger tapping on another paper, a grimace. 'From a sample of two hundred personnel, fully 29 per cent had criminal records of some kind, and—'

'They're dockers; the dregs of—'

'And four per cent had some connection of family, history or professed interest in Germany.'

'Statistically—'

'Statistics be hanged. We know what we're talking about. The Germans have a net of agents in this country. A rash. Small fry, but inconspicuous. Shopkeepers, tradesmen, travellers. An eye on a barracks here; an ear in a council meeting there; a visit to a dockyard. All going back to Berlin.'

'That's the interesting point, surely? The communication.' The old man; they didn't think it was interesting.

'Are we talking about interfering with the mails again?'

'There's no other—'

'Whole thing's a mare's nest.'

'There's a question of the mails, and a question of wireless telegraphy.'

'We should be doing more to intercept German messages.'

'I doubt all these blasted German grocers have got wireless transmitters.'

'I was also referring to the security of our own communications.' The old man again; always obsessive about these technical points.

'I, ah, had a chap get into the German station outside Berlin – not an S.I.B. man, but a local we've trained up as a plumber – place called Nauen. I mean to say, it's vast. Absolutely vast. Our technical bods are doing some calculations based on antenna length; the Germans can transmit to the Pacific, and the distance at which they can intercept—'

'Even the Admiralty can't reach the Pacific.'

'So we should be sticking to cable.'

'We shouldn't be letting ourselves fall so behind in wireless.'

The conversation petered out, and the chairman drew their attention to the questions of funding requisitions from Ulster and the attaché network in South America.

The old man faded.

✦

Duval had spent his first night in St Petersburg drifting between worlds. Supper at the Astoria, everything glass and gold, every throat white-tied or sparkling, a bottle of excellent champagne to celebrate Lisson's banknotes, and a fussiness of service and ritual that irritated him into leaving before the second part of dessert. A drink in a tavern near the Fontanka, firewater vicious in his throat, a circle of faces, broken and dirty and staring blank out of the world, and a stench, and a consciousness of his clean face and comfortable unleaking shoes that shamed him into leaving before he could force the last mouthful down. The faces didn't move at all as he left. Between the Astoria and the pit, he wandered; in and out of clubs, in and out of constellations of candles and shadows that were slimy underfoot; past the Marinsky, ghostly and astonishing above the streetlights; past clumps of decrepit humanity who huddled around braziers and shivered and moaned and gaped, and who watched him as if they were rats and he a dog – or perhaps it was the other way around.

Then sleep, blissful white sheets and the promise of breakfast, and faces that watched him in the night.

'This doesn't look too good, Duval.'

Duval was learning to ignore Lisson's anxieties. 'My restaurant bill?'

'They intercepted a wireless telegraph message – addressed to an outfit here in St P., one we've had our eye on – from an outfit in Kiel calling itself the Baltic Design Bureau.'

He looked up at Duval; waited.

'I've never heard of it.'

Lisson smiled, heavy and satisfied. 'But they've heard of you. The only word in the message in plain text was your name. Now why should that be?'

Duval shrugged. 'It seems as though they're... some sort of front.'

'It seems as though they're on your well-polished heels.'

The point had not escaped Duval; it had started to fester immediately.

Lisson watched him a moment longer. 'The information about the Foster sight, that went down well. But this... You're getting a little too hot to handle, Duval.'

'Then let me go.'

'Might have to.' He smiled. 'No hard feelings. But not yet.' Then thoughtful: 'Don't mind the Hun so much, but if the Okhrana get interested...'

'The what?'

'Secret police. Brutes.'

'Why should they care about me?'

'Well, they're a tricky lot. Out of control, some would say. Bit of skullduggery's all right, but they've taken provocation to lunatic levels. Half the anarchists in the city are working for them to stir up the other half. At least two assassinations of public figures caused by this sort of nonsense. I mean to say, you can't have the police egging on revolutionaries to blow up the minister of police, can you?' He shook his head. 'We don't want to get dragged into that muddle. So keep your head down. London have something in mind for you.'

'Oh yes?'

'They gather you've a touch of the Irish.' He said it as though pointing out that Duval had excrement on his boot.

A flicker in his gut. *London not so slow after all?* 'Spent a bit of time there, that's all.'

'Mmm.' The smell lingered. 'London seem to think it might come in handy.'

⊹⟞⟝⊹

On the fringes of the Sub-Committee meeting. 'It wasn't going to help to say it in the meeting, sir, but I suspect you're right about our communications.'

A smile from the old man, rueful. 'Thank you, Thomson. And no, there's little point trying to get the committee to focus on the point.' Nods of farewell to two other departing officials. 'How's Special Branch getting on with the German net?'

'Badly. We can pick up the odd one here and there if he does something particularly stupid, but it achieves nothing except alerting the enemy to our procedures.' Thomson's voice never wavered from its monotone. 'We've no idea of the size and reach of the network.'

'There must be some co-ordinating contact.'

'Mm. German Embassy, of course. Funnily enough, we've an idea where the linkman might be; passes himself off as a barber on the Caledonian Road, of all places. But other than keeping a constant watch, there's little we can do about it.'

'And you don't want to... sweat this chap, of course.'

Thomson was wooden. 'Not that I've any scruples left, but we'd have no guarantee that anything he said was accurate, or more than a small proportion of the network.'

'And they've probably a way to warn off the network if anything odd happened.'

'Quite. They'll all have some agreed code; and no doubt there's a way to change it if they fear it broken.'

'They can't be communicating by wireless.'

'Lord no. Impossible to assemble the equipment discreetly, let alone keep it hidden. Probably something simple through the mails. Some commercial disguise.'

The old man nodded. 'So much for the Germans. A pretty puzzle for you. But the other...'

Thomson grunted his interest into the silence.

'Thomson, I must reflect on something. Would you be so good as to call, tomorrow? I may have a little suggestion for you.'

<hr />

That night, the offices of the Russian Trade Legation in Constantinople suffered a small fire. No one was present, mercifully, and it burned itself out quickly without damaging the building.

Difficult to say how these things start; the electric wiring in the city is not always of the highest quality.

Only one room was significantly affected. In it, papers and curtains and furniture – including one cupboard – were partly or completely destroyed.

The next day, as part of their clearing up – his boss was sitting in his charred office, mourning his favourite chair and a signed photograph of the ballerina Rodionova – clerk Jozef Radek took the initiative to request from St Petersburg and elsewhere replacement copies of certain strategic documents.

⊢≈≈⊣

The journey from the island to the port of Split took most of two days. As if to prove a point, on the second day the wind dropped almost to nothing and they had to motor against the tide. They'd developed, unspoken, routines and responsibilities on the boat. Their passion was tender, and rather sad.

On the second afternoon, the limestone ramparts of Diocletian's palace rose out of the sea to meet them. Isabella was grown petulant at Ballentyne's impending departure, and he was pedantic with checks of borrowed rucksack and maps. With the boat nuzzling against the quay, he kissed her – on the eyes, on the forehead; and then on the lips, with sudden hunger. Then he stepped ashore.

Split did not appeal. Its beautiful façade was obscured with market stalls, and concealed a mediaeval city; alleys of slime and commerce and sin. It murmured of all the things that men will do when they gather too closely together.

The engine chuckled hollow under the water. He gave a gesture of rueful farewell, half wave, half salute, and turned away.

'Dear stranger!' He turned back. 'You don't go into the villages because you want to understand. You go because you want to belong!' Her voice, high over the engine's throb, was almost sung. Then, quieter, sadder, hopeful: 'Ciao.'

She bent and shifted the motor into gear and the boat surged away. He watched her as she dwindled, standing tall, the edges of the blouse glowing against the sun, hair streaming out from under the scarf, then with a little growl he hefted the rucksack on his shoulder and turned and began to stride into the town.

In a cabin along the quayside, the harbour master lowered his binoculars and yelled; a boy stuck his head in, and the harbour master spat a message and immediately the boy was running hard, feet slapping on the warm stones.

◆━━◆━━◆

With Ali still out of action, Cade was inavariably first to his office, early for Constantinople business; get a head-start on the day. Half an hour or so later the clerks would appear, once he'd decided the priorities for the day.

This morning, Cade found the door unlocked when he arrived. Was Ali now mobile? If he was, he'd obviously left again pretty quickly.

It didn't take long to see why that might have been.

In the middle of Cade's office, sprawled out on the carpet which he'd been gently rather pleased with, was the body of Muhtar. There was an ugly wound in the temple, turning black.

Shock, then revulsion, and then the need to check, to test. The body was cold – and clearly dead.

Speculations, and understanding: Ali? Some revenge or scuffle, but it was inconceivable that the boy would dare, or have a gun, even if he could get about; and the body didn't seem recently dead – wasn't that the point about the temperature?

But if not Ali, then whom?

And the answer, very obviously, was himself.

Now James Cade felt cold, and a little sick.

It hardly improved his feelings about Muhtar. He suppressed an instinct to kick the body at his feet. The man had been a walking disaster from the beginning, and dying on Cade's carpet was only a development of his trouble-making. Some part of Cade's mind noticed that the wound hadn't stained the carpet much.

Had he killed himself? This much of an oaf surely had reason to. But why here? Some obscure revenge? Or had someone else...?

It made no sense. And it wasn't fair, not hardly. Everything had been going so well...

Sense glimmered again, and with it the fear. For it didn't matter what had really happened. What mattered was that the body was on Cade's carpet.

The telephone rang.

Major Knox. Parts of his world colliding.

The telephone was still ringing.

At the back of his mind, the vague sense that the worst of it would be having to explain to his parents.

Distracted, he picked up the earpiece and mouthpiece. 'Mr Cade?' The voice when it was connected was tinny and accented and could have been anyone from Sultan Mehmed to Greyfriars Bobby. 'It is Riza speaking to you.' Cade murmured a greeting. 'Do I disturb you?'

'No – no, I'm...'

'Mr Cade, are you quite well?'

'Fine! Yes, I'm fine. No problem.'

'You do not sound well, sir; pardon me.'

'I'm fine.'

'Some problem, perhaps. May I help you?'

And yet, could he though? 'No. No, it's nothing. Well, a difficulty, I don't—'

'Mr Cade, I will be at your premises within ten minutes.'

And he was. He had to show himself in. He found Cade sitting behind his desk, watching him with the greatest discomfort. Then he saw the body on the carpet.

'Great heavens!'

'You'll not believe it, but I swear to you this was not my doing.'

Riza stared into his face. Eventually he said, slowly, 'You're a man of passion, Mr Cade, but not of stupidity. I think this deed would have taken both.' Cade breathed out. 'And yet the fact remains: the fellow is on your carpet.'

'Ain't he, though?'

'This is something to do with your... your embassy work?'

Cade shook his head. 'He and I... We had... we had business, Mr Riza. A matter of, er...'

'Mr Cade, the whole bazaar knows what your business with Muhtar was. And whatever you may say, whatever you may prove, the bazaar will decide its own truth about this.'

James Cade folded his hands in front of him, and regarded the corpse on his carpet.

'I have wanted to play by the rules,' he said sourly.

'If you did not do this thing, then he or someone else wished to do you great ill by— but forgive me, you have considered all this, I am sure.' His lips twisted uncomfortably. 'And the Varujans will have been calculating their advantage—'

'The hell they...' He stopped, running out of certainties. 'Mr Riza, is there any way that I can... manage this?'

Again the trim little face gazed into his. At last: 'Mr Cade, you must put your trust in me.'

'You have long had it.'

A formal nod. 'There is a man... Not of this city, but with many contacts and much influence here. A man of business like you; but, if you permit me, of much greater scale. A man of affairs.' Cade found himself leaning forwards instinctively. 'Frankly, a man whom it would profit you to know in any case. If you will take my advice, you will let me entrust this matter to his agents.'

Another deep breath. Another long glance at the obscene heap on the carpet.

'Please do so, Mr Riza.'

<hr />

Muhtar disappeared. When Mr Cade's two clerks arrived, it was to a note on the door informing them that their employer was busy around town that morning and that they were accordingly free until the afternoon. An hour later, a cart appeared in the street next to the office, delivering a new carpet for Mr Cade; it was carried in and the old one, likewise loosely rolled, was carried out onto the cart. It rattled away into the back streets of the metropolis, destination unknown.

Cade watched it go, relief and unease. Without the body gaping up at him, the episode seemed less real. His office was purified. And since he hadn't killed Muhtar, and the remains had been dragged away in a carpet, there was nothing to link him to the business. The aberration had disappeared. Business as usual.

And yet... Two matters nagged at him. First and most dramatically: who on earth had killed Muhtar and wished Cade such mischief as to dump the corpse on him? It surely hadn't been Ali who'd shot the man. Could he really have killed himself over some small business setbacks, and decided to implicate Cade as a revenge? Knowing the man, he was surely more likely to have used a gun on his tormentor than himself. But if not Muhtar himself, who?

Uncomfortably, the role of the Varujans – and by extension Ani – worried at him. Muhtar had been a competitor of theirs and a nuisance, and now he was gone; and where did that leave their relationship with Cade? Cade realized that he badly wanted there to be no complication, nothing sordid, in his relationship with Ani Charkassian. Vulnerability. Damnit, though, couldn't a man...

Second, and more uncomfortably, he found himself dependent on others. Ali's silence would be cheaply bought. He was loyal, and had more to gain from staying so; and in any case perhaps few would believe a hysterical story of something he might claim to have seen. But Riza, now. Riza had been increasingly dependent upon Cade's protection of his indiscretions; the balance had shifted back a little. Not completely: Riza had genuinely been indiscreet; Cade had genuinely not killed Muhtar. But the relationship had just got more complicated. And then there was the mysterious man to whom Riza had entrusted the problem. A man named Silvas. What did he know, and what would that mean?

※━═━※

Thomson's knock on the old man's door was exact to time.

'Ah, Thomson; good man.' The eyes, the voice, seemed to come out of the years.

Thomson sat as bidden, and waited patiently. The old man liked his manner. He studied Thomson, still considering his decision. Eventually, resolution; palms flat on the desk. 'A little suggestion from me, if I may.'

Thomson just nodded.

'We were talking yesterday of the German network in this country. This is something quite different. A different element, reporting to a different man, with different ends.'

Still Thomson waited.

'I recommend a bit of digging. I have the strong suspicion that somewhere in our official records administration there is a spy.'

Thomson's eyes opened in faint interest, as if told that it might be about to rain.

⊷══⊶

James Cade's day was a dream, familiar things lurching with strangeness. The memory of Muhtar's body lurked on the edge of his world, while he wrote at his desk, while he talked with his clerks; as if the corpse had only been pushed to the corner of the room, as if, now and then, it smiled at him.

Jozef Radek reported that he had sent the messages as instructed, and that his suggestion of fresh copies of strategic documents had not provoked suspicion. A Greek shipping agent visited to offer, after reconsideration, a lower price if Cade would commit to a certain number of shipments. Even though the image of the man, looking pleased with himself in the visitor's chair, kept blurring into the image of the body on the same spot on the carpet, these fragments of his normal life began to make him think that the morning's upset was somehow less real. Strange place anyway, Constantinople; always somehow distorted, always the suggestion of the mysterious. He had been the victim of a rather distasteful, unsettling accident – and now it had passed and he had recovered and the city's version of normality had resumed.

Ali had identified the place that Knox had asked after – and told Cade only grudgingly, urging him not to go. 'Not place for English gentleman.' Cade trusted Ali, but he didn't want to seem ineffective in front of Knox, not today. So at nine that night the two men met in the Muslim city, at an entrance to the Grand Bazaar, small against the Nurosmaniye Mosque; and from there they set off, away from the public buildings and the classical façades, through the back streets into the old city. They were shadows in the gloom, between the grimy plaster walls, the shambling wooden frontages.

Then the derelict... church? surely it had been something since – striped brickwork, pink and white, crumbling at the edges; it looked like a half-sucked boiled sweet. Beside it there was an alley as promised, and after a mutual raising of eyebrows they followed it. Then there was an ornate wooden door, and a man opening it who did not blink; 'Welcome, dear gentlemen' – immediately spotted as foreigners – 'to the Garden of the Rosy Hours.' And they were in.

There was the suggestion of lights through veils, lights among leaves, and everywhere a sweet smoke. They were ushered to a booth in the garden, offered cigarettes, brought drinks. From somewhere there came music, the thump of drums and tambourines and the squeezed whine of some stringed instrument, and a voice that wailed.

The two men settled against cushions, inhaled the smoke, heard the wailing, and – quite independently – thought momentarily of their mothers.

Cade said, 'Very charming. Why are we here?'

'Chap we've a possible interest in was mentioned in connection with this place. Thought I'd come and see what sort of shop it is.'

'A pretty seedy one, by the looks. What are we supposed to do now?'

Knox couldn't bring himself to recline properly against the cushions. 'Nothing. Get a feel of the place. Make a judgement if possible about his activities. Find out anything more about it, if you get an opportunity in the future.'

'And until then?'

'Enjoy yourself, I suggest.' The music wailed louder, the singing with it, apparently coming nearer among the trees and veils. Still the pungency of spices burning in the evening.

'Right-o.'

Their drinks came, thick with herbs. 'You seem to be toddling along all right, Cade.'

Cade waited. Through one of the veils, there was the suggestion of a woman's body dancing.

'Confess I wasn't sure how you'd fit in. Man of business. Tendency to... well, look to the profits.'

'Oh, I do that. But perhaps I calculate profit differently to you.'

Knox seemed to be considering this, but gave no sign that he'd understood it. 'You said earlier that I'd make a good merchant because I try to understand the... the deal. That's all there is to this business, too. Understand the other chap's needs and wants. That's all you do, isn't it? Offer him enough – but no more. Recognize the possibility of the unexpected, and have contingencies.'

'That's about it.'

'Seems to make for a good contact man: focused on the result; thinking about what makes the other fellow tick.'

Cade nodded; reputation intact.

From nearby, there was the rattle of dice and the click of backgammon pieces. They finished their drinks; ordered more. Smoked a cigarette each. To Cade, the world – so distorted in this place of scents and glimpses – was starting to find a new equilibrium; one that accommodated the strangeness.

Ani was right. Constantinople was a place between worlds, and he was becoming used to it. And what was a borderland, but a place of exchange – a place of trade?

❦

Ballentyne's train journey from Split to Belgrade was a sour one. Duty was hurrying him from a city that might have been worth exploring, a city that had known half a dozen civilizations, to one he had never warmed to. The railway crawled through the Dalmatian hinterland, winding and feeling its way through impossible gorges and doubling back around mountain ranges; the Balkan determination to prove its resistance to the most modern engineering. Guilt was nagging at him, for almost a week of idleness; and something else, less familiar, left him out of sorts and snappish.

A station in the foothills. Ballentyne hadn't caught the name, if there was one. If there was a station there was presumably a town; but it couldn't be seen from the railway. He tried to picture the map.

Air. Leg-stretch. The train was still clanking and jolting to a stop as he stood in the open doorway and filled his lungs. The sky was vivid, a blue that shone, and the mountains cut up into it like diamonds. A forest of firs between him and the mountainside.

The station building was a shack, tucked against the front line of firs. He walked away from it, around the end of the train, and already a gaggle of half a dozen gypsy children was flocking to the carriages. He pushed through them – their pleas were lacklustre, unhopeful; he wondered if they slept out here, looked for signs of habitation in the first gloom of the trees ahead – and immediately the ground was rising.

Another great breath, and the fresh air burned his throat – touched with the reek of unwashed human. He lit his pipe, enjoyed the lengthening of his stride; within seconds he was among scattered trees, the train only a suggestion of voices and steam at the back of his mind.

The world did not reach this place. The train brought traces of it: a few coins, perhaps some scavenged food, whatever waste was left behind on the tracks. Shadows, echoes, of the wealth and power and energy of the Europe somewhere outside. These people past whom the trains rushed would be counted unfortunate, but the idea of an escape from the posturing and the insecurity, the belligerent headlines and the games that caught men up and thrust them into the machine, was seductive.

But it was not possible. Ballentyne had found himself with a duty; knew that the steep and rugged pathway had to be trod.

It wasn't about belonging; Isabella had been wrong. He followed where his intellectual curiosity led. Right now there was responsibility, too. All over Europe, men were recognizing that.

He was back at the train a few minutes later. As he walked down beside it towards his compartment, he caught a glimpse of the other side between the tender and the first carriage, a glimpse of a man, a face, looking around but not seeing him.

The face.

Ballentyne was a yard past before it registered, but it registered with bewilderment and unease. He knew it. Surely, he knew it, vaguely, but what area and period of his life? And why did it so lurch at him?

Where had they met? Nothing. They hadn't met; he was remembering a photograph. But why should a photograph – now—

Belcredi.

Belcredi, the eccentric Austrian anthropologist, the theorist of natural links between Germans and Muslims. Belcredi, who according to Knox's hotel register had been in Durrës a couple of weeks back.

Now Belcredi was on the same train as him.

⊣═══⊨

An inconspicuous townhouse in Berlin: solid, grey, in good repair, but with a front garden only dirt and one under-developed tree. The garden seemed to distance the house from the summer evening city beyond. Distinctions: a brass plaque on one of the porch columns, and a flag hanging above – but limp, so that only a few stars and one stripe showed, as if the Republic were shrivelling in winter rather than blossoming.

In the drawing room, two whiskey glasses clinked.

'Thank you, Ambassador.' A courtly condescending drawl to a younger man. 'Kind of your man to wait up for me.'

'That's our pleasure, Colonel.' They called him 'Colonel' in Texas, and they called him 'Colonel' in the White House; so 'Colonel' he had to be in Berlin. 'Wire get off alright?'

'And not sugar-coated, either. That's how I am, sir, and that's how the President likes it. "Militarism run stark mad." That's what I said. What do you think?'

'That's what it is, Colonel. Nice if Washington listen for once.'

A New York machine politician, this ambassador, with New York lawyer punch behind the eye-glasses. 'They listen to me, sir.' The 'sir' imposing rather than respectful.

'The Kaiser is quite a fellow in the face-to-face, ain't he?'

'I never saw such a deal of tinware on a chest. The gentleman looks like a Georgia sideboard. And do you know what, Mr Ambassador? Do you know the thing that scares me most?' A theatrical pause; a sip of whiskey. The ambassador waited obediently. 'He's the sharpest of the lot.' Now the interest became more than polite. 'His wits; the clarity of his thinking. He sees the thing cold and he sees it clear. Clever men in London, of course, all prosing in Latin and Greek and so forth, but their thinking's stuck with old Julius Caesar too. Trying to prove to me the logical impossibility of war, all the statistics and fancy tags a man could want, and outside the window that old navy of theirs just getting bigger and bigger. The French are cut up every which way: some want a war and some don't and no one's paying attention. They know that if it comes there's only one country they're going to be fighting. But I had to go back twice in the one day to check the same fellow was still prime minister.' Another sip of whiskey. 'Som-nam-bulism. That's the dandy phrase, isn't it?'

'Something you learned in London, Colonel?' Grim smile from the colonel, satisfied that the previous witticism had registered. 'Sleepwalking to war, you would say? And the Kaiser isn't sharp enough to stop it?'

'The damnedest fellow you ever saw. And high-strung like a debutante at her first dance. His pride's bigger than his brain, and he's using his brain to convince himself he's justified.'

The ambassador moved to a table by the window to fetch the whiskey decanter. The curtains were still open; the street was drowsy with strolls and goings-home.

'They're all justified, by their own lights. Each one's only got to look over the fence. Britain's ship programme is perfectly justified if you look at Germany. Germany's programme is perfectly justified by Britain's. France is justifiably worried by Germany and Russia's justifiably worried by the whole twentieth century, including Germany, and they've both got troop programmes that'll give a gun to everyone from grandpa to the kid who shines your shoe. And that's before you start trying to work out their cock-eyed calculations about the Austrian Empire and the Turkish Empire. Every offensive weapon makes someone else feel angry. Every defensive treaty makes someone else feel threatened.'

The colonel held out his glass for the refill. 'A fellow on the train tried to convince me that all these elaborate alliances meant that war was impossible – a phrase I keep hearing, usually from a man wearing a sword – because no one would go to war without their allies, and it was impossible to conceive of a crisis in which all the allies in the alliances would see their interests threatened enough for war to be justified and the alliance deals to be called in.'

The ambassador swirled his glass, looking into the eddy. 'And what would happen, Colonel, with all these fellows running around the powder store with lit matches, if they should happen across a crisis that actually affected no one's interests?'

⊹══⊹══⊹

'Where did you disappear to, Gerta von Waldeck?' It was childish, and Hathaway was annoyed she hadn't been able better to restrain herself.

Gerta's face snapped round; the pink was accentuated in her cheeks, the cold blue in her eyes. 'Don't be harsh,' she said. A finger came up and touched Hathaway's cheek. 'If you won't let me have a world, at least let me have a Germany.'

'Must it be this one?'

'We all have our duties.'

Hathaway nodded.

Von Waldeck's castle was three centuries old, and the money was long gone. Auerstein's Margaretenhof wasn't more than three decades old, and the money still hung thick. It was a grand statement of wealth and status, imposing in its size and its style, in the frontage that could be seen a mile off, in the fat stones that finished each corner, in the outsized proportions of every doorway.

The emperor had hunted from the Margaretenhof in '05 and again in '06 – one of the critical telegrams in the Moroccan crisis had been sent from here – and the fashion had not yet faded. Auerstein's son Otto had added intellect and discretion to name, and made himself indispensable in the Foreign Ministry; in a generation the family had bridged heritage and power. And not the quiet power of von Waldeck's bankers, but the busyness of government.

Every few days a morning's shooting or hunting would be proclaimed, and this by some phenomenon of social telegraphy would draw additional guests to the house, and the corridors and dining table would be busier. On Hathaway's second day another soldier arrived – a smart major called

Immelmann – and an Austrian count. The next morning brought a Swiss metal-trader and later, when Hathaway emerged from the library to get some air, there was a face in the hall that she recognized: Eckhardt, the young man at supper with Niemann.

Eckhardt was aggressively charming to her while they waited to go into dinner; she had a two-minute monopoly of his well-cut face and his intelligent observations on travelling in Europe. He introduced her to Major Immelmann – his height, his leanness, the close-cropped, close-skinned head, would all have said soldier whether he was in uniform or in the bath – and Otto Auerstein, red-headed, and stockier than his father. 'Eh, Eckhardt, are we surprised that you are already acquainted with the handsomest of the ladies?' She'd have appreciated the flattery more if Immelmann had given her more than a glance.

'Actually, Fräulein Hathaway and I met at Niemann's.'

'Oh, Niemann!' and a laugh, echoed by the others, a shared scorn.

Again dinner was the orchestra of male opinions, with only the occasional trill of feminine interest or distraction. Hathaway could feel the anger in her own face, despising the men and the women. Despising everyone. *I have spent my life spectating on a German dinner party.*

Major Immelmann, erect and emitting certainties: 'The emperor will have the respect that is due to his seniority in Europe.' The man opposite Hathaway murmured something to the woman beside him about Major Immelmann being aide to the Chief of General Staff, and the woman gazed at Immelmann, and Hathaway resisted the urge to throw a fork at her. 'As a German, sir' – this to the older Auerstein – 'you would be proud to hear him: wise, just, clear, decisive.'

'They treated him as the schoolboy of Europe; now he dominates.'

'I should say – forgive me if I do not say much – the emperor's great patience is all that stands between Europe and war.'

'Germany seeks the same freedom to pursue her natural economic interests that all nations have enjoyed. To develop, and not to be threatened.'

'But could we fight alone? The British whale as well as the Russian bear?'

A glance between Immelmann and Otto Auerstein, a private joke. 'Do not be sure that it would be necessary.'

'Austria is our eternal ally, of course.' A glance at the Austrian count.

The Austrian count, too late, said, 'The Austrian Empire has always been such a fragile balance.'

'Sir, Austria has been too balanced. Too tolerant.'

'But really, are these little peasant pretensions not better indul—'

'Indulgence can become too easily weakness.'

'And – your pardon, sir' – Immelmann – 'not all in Vienna share your tolerance.' Another glance at Otto Auerstein. 'Serbia is the mouse that will come to steal the cheese one time too many.'

Flora Hathaway watched it angry. *They will not notice me even to moderate their bombast.*

And watched in particular the major. *I did not take you for a braggart. So what is it that you really know?*

At one end of the table, Frau Auerstein – solid and spectacled – watched the discussion with uncomprehending satisfaction. At the other, old Auerstein watched it as from a great height, distant but not disapproving.

The following morning Hathaway was in the library, skimming a set of fifteenth- and sixteenth-century chronicles, when the door opened and Immelmann and Otto Auerstein entered, in conversation.

'Ah, we violate the Temple of Vesta,' Auerstein said, a flick of red hair.

Immelmann, somehow startled, was pushing a paper back into a leather document case.

He recovered. 'Good morning, Fräulein.'

'Good morning.'

Stalemate. They watched each other.

She glanced at Immelmann's document case – light brown, a zip in dull brass, his fingers clenched on the skin – and up.

He said, 'You seek some light reading?'

She smiled, a little pleased. 'It depends how light you find the *Albrechtschronik.*'

It hit, and he had the grace – and the insufferable suavity – to bow in acknowledgement. His eyes wandered over her face and upper body. 'Not many women...' he began; 'that is to say – most impressive.'

She contrived a little bow of her own, and he watched her a moment longer and followed Otto Auerstein out.

She looked at the door. *With one breath he condemns me and my nation to defeat; with the next he's getting hot and bothered because I read worthy books.* A rationality about women as well as war? Or a kind of pornography: his thrill at watching a foreign woman doing something he would forbid a German wife because she should be keeping house? *Oh, my poor Gerta.*

⊷══✦══⊷

The platform at Belgrade station was fifty metres long, and Heinz-Peter Belcredi walked it half a dozen times in increasing unhappiness.

Eventually, after another glance through every window, he walked to the end of the platform, gave up his ticket to the collector who'd been watching him with increasing curiosity, wandered onto the concourse and hesitated.

'*Sehr geehrter* Herr Belcredi? Do not turn.' Belcredi stiffened. 'Go to the newspaper stand, and again do not look for me.'

Licking his lips, Belcredi did as told. 'I am Kopp,' the voice, German accent, said through newspapers; 'we were told to expect—'

'The Englishman has disappeared! I had him—'

'He is in the café, watching, Mein Herr. He was off the train before it stopped, I think by the wrong side. Is it possible that he became aware of you, Mein Herr?'

'I – it's – I have been most discreet.'

'Of course. Now the Englishman thinks he has reversed the position. We will reverse it again. Proceed as you would normally; go where you choose. This Ballentyne will track you, and we will track him.'

'And what—'

'These are Herr Hildebrandt's instructions. We will all follow his instructions, Mein Herr.'

Belcredi's head flickered in a nod, and he set off across the concourse.

⊷══✦══⊷

'We have the Englishman, Herr Krug. Belcredi has Ballentyne watched, and Ballentyne thinks he is watching Belcredi, so they are most comfortable. But one takes one's shot when one has it.'

Krug only raised his eyebrows. 'What news of the Margaretenhof?'

'Nothing yet. Colonel Nicolai has sent one of his officers to join the party, to observe this Englishwoman.'

'One of his officers?'

'Another colonel.'

'What an extraordinary disguise.'

Hildebrandt smiled. 'He will at least send more data on the Englishwoman. Nicolai is passionate about data.'

'Mm. The passion that will carry your army to Paris and St Petersburg, no doubt. Fortunately, I too have a man at the Margaretenhof.'

⊰⊱

Hathaway returned to the fifteenth century. She picked at the pages, recognizing it as a kind of refuge, and suspicious accordingly. Would it have been better if the cover for her snooping had been photography? At least she'd have got outdoors more. Music might not have required so many hours of plodding. But she liked cerebral places, where she could be alone, and the old man in London had known that. And once she was in the books, her instinct for analysis overcame doubt. *Funny old Flora.*

She walked out into the grounds again before supper. As she came down the steps a motor car was arriving, puttering steadily and swaying round the arc of the drive towards the house.

Even Auerstein's car was disproportionately tall. It stopped, and continued to shudder, while the back door opened and Auerstein's colonel friend, Bauer, got out. He had a leather document case like Immelmann's under his arm, and stood and waited – courteous or suspicious – for Hathaway to walk past.

She heard the car coughing away behind her and Colonel Bauer's boot tips clipping up the steps as she walked on. First an avenue of plane trees along the front of the house, their fat shadows stretching across the gravel and mottling the stone, and then a path that meandered down towards a grove of trees by a lake.

On the other side of the grove, standing against a stone bench beside the lake, she found Gerta and Major Immelmann.

Her mind had been drifting across the sweep of the grass and the water; otherwise she might have registered the voices, the suggestion of a giggle and a chuckle. She certainly wasn't seeking company or intrusion. Mercifully there was no hasty dropping of hands, no flustered rearrangements. The soldier looked like a rock; Gerta looked rather lovely.

'Bother; it's like a cheap play.' Genuine irritation in her voice. 'I do beg your pardon, Major. I seem forever to be interrupting you.'

'Merely that we seem to share the same enthusiasms, Fräulein.' A bow to them both, and he strode away past Flora and up towards the house.

They both watched him go, and then Gerta was watching her, trying to maintain poise.

'Flora, you're not... you're not cross, are you?'

'Why on earth should I be cross? Lord, you don't think I interrupted deliberately, do you?'

'You've seemed a little—'

'He's a splendid-looking man, and it's natural that he'd be attracted to you. If Germany was a lot of Immelmanns and Gertas the rest of us would be in real trouble.'

'Meaning I am your enemy also, now?'

'Is Immelmann my enemy?'

Gerta's face didn't move, didn't relax. 'Not "enemy", perhaps. Object. You have that look when you watch him: as if he were a mathematical problem, or a page in a book.' Now something changed in the face, something around the eyes, and she was sadder. 'You wouldn't have an enemy, and you wouldn't fight a war, because to have an enemy and a war you must first have a passion. But if you are presented with a puzzle, or a challenge, you will be remorseless. Your brain is stronger than any army, because it does not have muscles to weaken or a heart to soften.' Her boots shifted on the gravel. 'If I became a problem for Flora Hathaway, I would be very fearful.'

'He's my... competitor, perhaps.' She offered it as a compromise with the too-accurate picture of herself.

Gerta looked a little pink. 'It's nothing serious, Flora. It's just... well, it's the done thing. The Waldecks are known as a good family, but it would be awful if we were thought snooty or fuddy-duddy about – well, especially around men like...' Hathaway was watching her, a kind of ill fascination. 'We both know we're playing.'

'That you should be attracted to a man who is handsome, intelligent and able would be understandable. To be dallying with him because you feel obliged to... that's grotesque.'

'Why shouldn't a woman dally as a man might?'

She winced. Words she had used herself. 'A proud argument used in a sorry cause.'

Gerta flushed, and turned to look out into the dusk.

Hathaway gazed at her a moment longer, and then walked away.

More than she had in all the weeks of travel, Hathaway felt alone. She tried scolding herself for weakness, for nostalgia. She had been, surely, as emotionally isolated at times in Britain: sometimes in London, a solitary woman in a male world, somehow the subject of suspicion as well as scorn; sometimes even at home, strange Flora whom none of the young men could relax with.

But not like this. Her fellow humans – intelligent people, impressive people, for once people whose company she should enjoy; one of them a woman of rare insight and sympathy – had made themselves alien to her. The German nation had become a crowd of students on the other side of the lecture hall, sharing a story she alone was not fitted to enjoy.

As usual, it made her first vulnerable-sick, and she felt the tremor of a sob from childhood, expanding like a bubble in her chest. And then, as usual, it made her angry. First she felt desperate at being Flora Hathaway. And then she felt determined to be Flora Hathaway.

She walked faster, harder, towards the house. It glowed out of the evening with the promise of dinner and society. As she came past the ante-hall, many of the guests were already gathered for drinks. She saw Immelmann tall among them, immaculate, and for once without his damned document case.

That would be upstairs in his room, presumably.

She took the staircase one step, one heartbeat, at a time. The top of the stairs, and on towards the guest wings, the carpet stretching out ahead of her towards the moment of decision.

The junction: the female guest rooms, including hers, to the right; the male guest rooms, including Immelmann's, to the left.

All my life I have braved the world of men.

Thoughtfully, every room had a card on the door naming the guest in long scratched handwriting. Another glance around her. As soon as she'd turned she was transgressing. *As soon as I was born I was transgressing.*

Immelmann's door was the second along on the right. The 'I' and the 'l' were particularly stretched on the name card. Her hand reached for the handle, the handle was turning under it, and then nothing.

'Flora!'

Her heart staggered, and she spun round. Only a hiss, but it had roared down the corridor.

Gerta was standing half a dozen paces off, face showing the same shock that her voice had. 'What were you—'

Hathaway took a deep breath, collected her breathing, and strode towards her. 'Locked,' she said as she came level, and stopped a moment; 'your German purity is safe.' And she walked on.

When Hathaway came down for dinner five minutes later, Gerta was among the other guests chattering in the ante-hall. A neutral glance at Hathaway as she appeared, and nothing more. Immelmann, too, looked at her without unusual concern. Within a minute they were all invited in to eat, and by some great mercy Hathaway found herself between a deaf old neighbour and a doctor whose views on Strauss were actually interesting.

After dinner, the guests drifted apart and regathered in new groups and pairs, permutations of the same conversations. Hathaway's companion was determined to display an enthusiasm for Offenbach equal to that for Strauss, and she pleaded a headache and went and sat in one of the drawing rooms. Two or three other women appeared on the edge of her awareness; there was talk of music, and cards.

Another arrival, alone and standing still a moment; Hathaway glanced round. It was Frau Auerstein, who looked at her, hesitated, and then walked towards her and sat in an armchair opposite.

Hathaway said something polite about the meal, as if Frau Auerstein had had something to do with it.

Frau Auerstein removed her spectacles, blinked at Hathaway a few times, and replaced them. 'I do so admire you, Fräulein. Leaving your own home, your family, your people, and travelling over here, and living among strangers.'

It was so unlikely, and so precisely phrased, that Hathaway knew it to be the exact opposite of the truth. For a moment she felt rather sorry for her hostess, faced with a guest and a woman who did not fit. 'I'm afraid I have not always found it easy to settle, Frau Auerstein. My mother worries, I know.' Frau Auerstein nodded. 'But I've been very lucky in Germany. Everyone is very polite; very hospitable.'

'But of course. This is only correct.' It wasn't the warmest of endorsements, but again Hathaway felt for her, wondering if she actually enjoyed anything. It was her duty to be gracious to an English guest, just as it was the duty of her son and his friends to plot England's destruction.

'I must say that I admire you for running such a large house so efficiently.'

'Thank you.' No more than her due. 'Will you play some cards?'

'Perhaps I could watch.'

And she did, for a couple of hands; some variation on whist. Inconsequential twittering, and polite compliments. Eventually she drifted back to her armchair, and flicked at an illustrated magazine on the table beside her.

Some minutes later, the article on the tribes of south-west Africa went dim. Hathaway glanced up, to find a dress immediately in front of her. She followed it up, over a waist and a full and tight-wrapped bust, to a collar that frothed around a slender throat and led the way to Gerta von Waldeck.

Gerta looked down at her, some passion hardly restrained. Then she coughed, brought a handkerchief to her mouth to stifle another, and rested her hand on the table a moment.

The eyes were empty, and somehow deeply sad. They held Hathaway's for a moment, and then turned away.

Gerta had left her handkerchief on the table. Hathaway reached for it and made to call out and then her fingers brushed at it, and saw that something lay underneath it.

Gerta von Waldeck's tight-strung hourglass back had reached the door, and left without turning round.

On the table, she had left the key to Major Immelmann's room.

❧━━ ━━☙

Colonel John Mayhew didn't like uncertainty. It bred confusion, and indiscipline. Shifting sands. He'd knocked at the old man's door in that spirit. 'Think I saw the way your thoughts were going. Earlier, in the Sub-Committee.' Clear the air. Get things straight. 'If I may, sir, you seem rather... obsessed with this man.'

The old man considered this. Then nodded. 'You're right. I am. Not healthy, perhaps. King Charles's head, and so forth. And yet I fear...' He straightened in the chair. 'You may have gathered that I did a bit of work in the South African war. When I was more your age and fitness; not this old relic living off past glories.' Mayhew felt his shoulders straighten; tried to look reassuring. 'I became aware that there was a man active on the enemy side. Behind the scenes, if you know what I mean. A man to whom men in the field reported, without knowing who he was. A collector of information, and a spreader of misinformation. An investor who could create a scandal or an explosion and capitalize on it. Not a Boer. Perhaps—'

'A German?'

'I don't know. Possibly. But not a patriot. He was active on that side because it suited his interests.'

'What are his interests, if not country?'

This got a ghost's smile from the old man. 'Information. And thus influence. And thus great power. I believe that he has accumulated wealth, but I suspect that it is less important to him than the sheer joy of control; of manipulation.' He glanced at Mayhew. 'As you say, I became a little obsessed with him. We exchanged tactical victories in the Cape, and—'

'We won the war.'

'If you say so, Colonel. In any case, the Spider – you must excuse the rather childish moniker; over the years it has come to seem so right for

245

him – he emerged from the war with more money, more contacts, more information, more power. In the dozen years since I have felt his pull; fancied I've found traces of him. He has built and exploited and continued to build a network of influence across Europe.' An uncomfortable flicker at the mouth. 'His web, if you will. I have ideas of the identities of some of these men and women; no more than ideas. Sometimes I see them act, and I sense the controlling hand of the Spider behind them. I doubt he has pulled a trigger in his life, but at the tremble of a finger governments may shake.'

'Pardon me, but that seems – rather—'

'Fanciful? It does seem it, doesn't it? You will recall that in 1911 two French newspapers published the secret clauses of our 1904 agreement with France and Spain.' Mayhew nodded. 'I strongly suspect the identity of the conduit who passed the information and encouraged the publication: a man – Italian-French – I believe to act at the behest of the Spider.'

'He wanted to embarrass us.'

'Yes. And to stoke public anger in Germany against us. And to seem to vindicate Germany's aggressive posture in north-west Africa at that time. I suspect this was also his way of gaining influence in Berlin. That is the currency he craves. Again, earlier this year, *Figaro* published the indiscreet letters of the French minister of finance. I am more sure of the identity of the source in this case, because an acquaintance of mine was previously offered the letters for money. Again I feel the tremor of the Spider on his web. The minister resigned – and his wife shot the *Figaro*'s editor, indeed. Now the new minister is indebted to someone who is indebted to the Spider. France is weakened, and Germany is satisfied. He feeds on the chaos, Mayhew!' Rare emotion in the voice. 'You remember the explosion at the Nobel factory in Scotland – February? Thomson and Kell think they know who managed it: a suspected German agent – a Polish doctor from Glasgow. But how did he know his way around the factory, know the critical point? No one knows – except that one of the directors of the firm that built the plant is a man I've had my eye on for a while now; visits to a certain sanatorium in southern Germany; a name on some of the paperwork connected with arms dealing between Hamburg and Stockholm and Brussels.' He spread his hands slowly over the papers on the desk. 'This is the terrain where we fight, Colonel. These suggestions. These shadows.'

'So who is he then?'

The old man's mouth twisted; his voice dwindled. 'I believe him to be one of three men. A Swiss-French financier named Morgenthal. An Austrian businessman named Krug. A German scholar and collector named Hermes.'

'And you're trying to find out which.'

'And I have been for more than a decade. For now, he is the Spider.'

⌁

This time it was a more calculated act, and Hathaway felt correspondingly more uneasy.

But if Flora Hathaway is to succeed, it should surely be by a coldly considered deed.

Instinctively, she sought solitude and strength in the library. It was lit by table lamps only, and the upper tiers of books were only suggestions in the gloom. The leather of chairs and tabletops glowed warm.

On one table she saw a document case, like a grail.

Surely it wasn't...

It wasn't. Re-checking that she was alone, she pulled it open. A notebook, blank. A 'gentleman's' magazine, with a picture of a 'lady' on the cover. A train timetable. A pack of cigarettes. A stern-looking official pass. This wasn't Immelmann's case, but the colonel's.

She closed the case, smiled at it. *I am better than this colonel. Surely I can be better than the major.*

She went at it like a quadrilateral equation: sure but unhurrying, weighing the factors but driving through them to a solution.

She considered the size of her shawl. She left her clutch-bag beside a table leg in the library. She took the back stairs. She had an excuse in mind for each geographical stage of the journey – hall, servants' corridor, stairs, guest wing. Nagging at her, the certainty that it would be a trivial victory merely to look inside the case.

The corridor of the male guests was empty, its residents at cards or billiards or other games. She must not think of Gerta.

Should she think of Gerta as an ally? *Concentrate. Move. The world will not wait for you, girl.* Still the corridor empty. Immelmann two doors away, one door away, and then the long letters of the name card in front of her. She knocked. Nothing. A breath, a thrill of tremendous power, *now I will be...* and she unlocked the door and slipped in.

Immelmann was not there; his document case was.

Seconds later, another breath, opening the door and slipping out into the corridor, the door closed, locked, and turned, and Frau Auerstein was standing at the junction of the corridors, staring at her.

She took in the Englishwoman's flushed face, the shoulder of her dress awry, a bootlace trailing, the shawl clutched to her breasts.

Hathaway gazed back at her. Her glance flicked to the door she'd just closed, down in apparent discomfort, then up defiant. 'Some things even an Englishwoman may appreciate,' she said. And she strode past and away.

The spy moved through the shadows of the shipyard.

A key to a side-gate had been stolen, temporarily, by a riveter and copied; and now the spy would make regular night-time calls to monitor the progress of the new British ships.

He'd been given basic instructions: what to look for; the different types of ship. But the shipyard was an alien landscape, its shapes unfamiliar and distorted. Sheds of all sizes, brick and wood and metal corners that caught at his shoulders. Traction engines and cranes and gantries lurking and reaching over him. At his feet, railway tracks snaked through cobbles and glistened under the moon.

He turned a corner, and gaped; gaped upwards, and shrank.

The hull of a ship, and it was immense. It roared over him, an inconceivable size, impossible. It was bigger than the biggest house, he knew, because there was a house under the prow and it was tiny, a silly doll's house against the monster over it. A century ago they had built wooden ships here, and the house had been an engineer's or a yard director's and appropriate against the elegant vessels being built nearby. Now that world had shrivelled, and the iron giants ruled.

Just the hull. The superstructure had not been started. Its height would grow further – it might even double... He forced himself to note the state of progress. He would have to report every detail back to the contact in London. And then he allowed himself to contemplate the size again – as a man; a German man.

Usually his instructions arrived by letter – once there had been a visit, a man nervous yet somehow inspiring, somehow frightening – innocuous suggestions or words in a code that had been sent separately and sometimes changed – and how many letters could the police check, anyway? Once an envelope had contained a newspaper cutting: July 1913, a speech by the British First Lord of the Admiralty.

A promise to deliver one torpedo boat to the Royal Navy every week; one light cruiser every thirty days; one super-Dreadnought every forty-five days. Nothing else in the envelope; it did not need to be repeated that Germany could not match this.

⊢⇒⊣

Hathaway had thought thirty minutes would be ample to see what was in Major Immelmann's document case and then arrange its reappearance. A child's game; a stubborn dare.

First, a return down the back stairs, flitting through the shadows to the dining room, visualizing the table and dinner and dropping the key under Immelmann's chair, the tablecloth starch-stiff and scratching at her face. And up to her room again, unseen.

In her room, the door locked behind her, the document case on her dressing table. She let her hand stroke the leather once, saw the gilt initials – *Shakespeare's pun: oh guilt indeed* – K.-H. I.; then she unzipped it.

When she saw the number of documents in the case – a dozen sheets, *records of meetings?* neat hand, *Immelmann writes like a schoolboy* – she decided she could risk forty-five minutes to skim them and note any essential points.

An adult game of hide-and-seek. How long would he dally in the moonlight with Gerta?

Then she started looking at the titles, saw the density of the information on the first page. *'Visit of Italian General Staff; summary of their proposed contribution'*; *'Summary of the Emperor's remarks to Chief of Staff after his 26.5 meeting with the Arch-Duke Franz Ferdinand of Austria'*.

Sixty minutes would hardly make a difference. Then back down to the library, *realized I left my bag somewhere*, and Immelmann's case left where Colonel Bauer's had been.

'Chief of Staff audience with the Emperor: the strategic situation'.

Even assuming Immelmann did come back to his room before she'd finished, how likely was it that he'd look at his document case?

So: ninety minutes. *Oh, be charming, my Gerta*.

What could actually happen if they did catch her?

✦

Belgrade was as Ballentyne remembered it: the women with their strained beauty; the men too keen to demonstrate their manliness; a place eager to forget the Ottoman flavours in its past, but picking uncomfortably from the Austrian. It seemed excitable; the headlines and the hotel lobbies were full of fear and outrage and defiance against Vienna. But the same was probably true of London, and the other capitals. He met up with a couple of acquaintances from the small Albanian community, in the unnamed cafés where he knew they'd be found, and they were worried. A belligerent Serbia was an uncomfortable place for those who were not Serbs.

He didn't quite know what he was supposed to be doing. He could gather the mood of the place well enough, if perhaps not as deeply as he had in Albania. But what to do with Belcredi? That first afternoon he'd followed the Austrian to his hotel, and felt rather pleased with himself for doing so. But then what? Was he supposed to lurk there permanently until Belcredi came out again? Turn up every morning? And what did it achieve, beyond at best a list of places the man visited?

In any case, it all rather came down to Belcredi's game. It was neither surprising nor objectionable if an anthropologist went travelling in the Balkans, however much of a crank he was. Had he some additional motive that took him into the Albanian villages – Ballentyne felt a vague proprietorial jealousy – and now north? So what if he did? *And how different is this from me?*

Most of all, was it only coincidence that had put him in Durrës just before Ballentyne, and then on the same train at Split?

Ballentyne had decided that he wasn't going to be hiding in the shrubbery for the night. Belcredi would be staying at least until morning, and so Ballentyne got himself settled and had supper with an acquaintance from Belgrade University.

The next morning he followed Belcredi to the Austrian Embassy, and then to a private address which he noted. By lunchtime he'd had enough. It was a pretty shoddy sort of activity, and it didn't seem to be achieving anything. In a moment of inspiration he stopped at an hotel and got the concierge to telephone to Belcredi's hotel to find how long he was staying; the fact he had reserved for a week was reassuring, but didn't help with what to do with him.

The British Embassy? Mayhew in London had been cagey about embassies; *at your service but use with discretion*, whatever that meant. Ballentyne himself had never had much time for diplomats, but they might be able to check, or help, or get guidance. Frankly, Belcredi seemed like a waste of time he'd like to be rid of.

Contact any serving military officer on the embassy staff. It wasn't clear whether this was because of their inherently greater trustworthiness or efficiency, in Mayhew's world. Ballentyne sat and waited to see Major Bruce.

'Why, surely it's Mr Ballentyne!'

This, surely, was not Major Bruce. Admittedly his idea of majors was dominated by Knox, but none of them could be fifty-somethings with straggling grey hair, and a suit with a stripe and a sack-like quality that suggested Belgrade tailoring rather than wherever British officers had their suits made.

And who should know he was here?

'Ronald Ballentyne? Oxford, and London – anthropology? Heard you speak at Fitzroy Street once.'

'Yes. Yes, I'm he.' Ballentyne stood. 'You must forgive—'

'Don't think we were introduced at the time. Pickford. Charles Pickford.

I'm sort of senior prefect for the informal British community hereabouts; cultural evenings and picnics.'

'Have I read something of yours, sir? Artistic traditions in Serbia – something like that?'

'If you have you're a rare man, and I can't say a wise one.' The first suggestion of bluster had gone. Pickford's whole manner was quiet, civilized. *A pleasant expatriate with a hobby and an under-exercised brain.* 'Could I invite you to take some tea with me?'

'Well, I'm supposed to be meeting—'

Pickford came a step closer, his voice lower. 'Now, Mr Ballentyne? Away from this place?'

Ballentyne nodded, and followed the older man out of the embassy. 'You see we've quite a group of enthusiasts in the Anglophone community here,' Pickford was saying more loudly, 'and I'm secretly hoping I could dragoon you into giving us a little talk.'

He used the same story to the maître d' at the Royal Hotel. 'A discreet table please, Dragan!' Again it was louder than was natural to him. 'I am on a vital mission for the society, and I have a valuable victim.'

They sat; Pickford ordered for them both, with feigned fussiness; Ballentyne waited.

'The busybody enthusiast, Mr Ballentyne.' The voice was quieter again. 'Not a bad persona with which to snoop and meet people. One rather fears that it really is one's persona, and the snooping merely a convenient way one can make oneself useful.' The eyes were sharper as they looked up. 'Perhaps you have a similar sensation.'

Ballentyne nodded at the point, a faint smile. It felt like being in his tutor's room at Oxford again.

'I was asked to keep an eye out for you. You don't strike me as an embassy sort of fellow, so I assumed you had some special reason to call there.'

Their tea arrived. Ballentyne watched the older man for a moment longer, stirring his tea and not looking up until Ballentyne spoke. Ballentyne told him: Belcredi, Durrës, the train, here; he tried to be as concise and precise as possible in his facts and his speculations.

Pickford tapped his spoon against his cup, slowly, rhythmically. 'Interesting. You'll know the cultural possibilities better than I. Serbia doesn't have all that many Muslims; pockets in the south, and a few more civilized merchants and intellectuals in the city here. But they don't get much love from the government, and the government would worry they'd be fertile ground for trouble. I can arrange to have some questions asked; about the man himself, if nothing else. I don't like him popping up on the very same train as you.'

'Quite. Does he need to be followed? Feel it's a bit of a waste of time.'

'Well, perhaps there are local fellows who could do it more easily. Blend in. Free you up. Sure we can make use of you while you're here.'

'If I can. I assume the idea of me doing a lecture to your dashed society was part of the pretence.'

Pickford and his voice went rather stiff. 'No, Mr Ballentyne. It was not. I've been badly let down by my musicologist for tomorrow – Russian; damned high-strung brutes – and you're just the chap. Seven p.m. sharp at the Miša House. And nothing too... ah, outré, if you please, about highland village life; some of my flock are a little delicate.'

***

'Your friend Immelmann is quite the tiger, Otto, isn't he?'

'Mother, what can you – Oh, you mean the lovely Waldeckchen! A handsome couple, no? But they're both only trifling, I think.'

'I did not mean Fräulein von Waldeck. The English girl was also... paying him a call.'

***

'Immelmann, you're a goat and a monster!'

'What do you mean, Auerstein? Kindly—'

'The women are queueing up to polish your buttons, it seems!'

'Auerstein, this isn't an idiom that amuses me. Von Waldeck is a charming woman, but she is behaving with at least as much restraint as I.'

'Happily the English girl, *die Eisanmut*, is not so circumspect.'

A council of war in a cabin.

Heinrich Auerstein was surely the host, for it was his cabin, on his estate, for the benefit of him and his guests when hunting. But Colonel Walter Nicolai, Chief of Military Intelligence, was presiding.

Colonel Bauer: 'Major Immelmann reported his concerns to me, and based on your earlier direction I judged it appropriate to summon you directly, Herr Colonel.' Nicolai's position got him the 'Herr', and Immelmann's family got him the 'Major'. Auerstein watched the manoeuvring with irritation. Nicolai would be pleased to have someone on Moltke's staff at disadvantage; he was tense, wondering how to play the fish he'd hooked. *And this is my society.*

'Quite correct, Colonel.' Nicolai enjoying himself. 'Now, Major, it's not my habit to see mistakes where there are none. In our army, duty and honesty will always be respected.' Not a bad effort, Auerstein thought, at putting the young man politely in place; but Immelmann was sharp enough to see it and proud enough to resent it, and Nicolai would lose in the end.

'Herr Colonel. Thank you. As I reported to Colonel Bauer, I have only coincidences; but the possibility is grave enough that it was essential to bring them to your attention.' Immelmann wasn't talking about mistakes, and quietly starting to shift responsibility onto Military Intelligence. Immelmann described the coincidences: the dropped key, the switched document cases, and the Englishwoman outside his room.

Nicolai hesitated, the expectation now on him again. 'What you may not have been told, Major, is that we had prior suspicions of the woman Hathaway. Your conjectures reinforce them, and are reinforced.'

Auerstein spoke, cool and quiet. 'Colonel Bauer did inform me. I remain concerned that she has been left free to travel. I remain concerned that business properly of the Military Intelligence Department is conducted in a private house.'

Immelmann shifted on the bench, perhaps fractionally closer to Auerstein.

Nicolai said cautiously, 'Naturally the department is grateful for your support, Mein Herr.' More assured. 'Naturally there is no suggestion that her association with the Margaretenhof is anything more than accident.'

As if I am nothing more than their porter; as if I am somehow responsible for the foolish games they carry on under my roof.

Nicolai shifted to his fellow soldiers. Even out of uniform, the three of them had a likeness to one another, an exactness. 'And the papers she might have seen?'

Immelmann, after a glance at Bauer: 'Of the most serious, sir. The diplomatic secrets of the Chief of Staff.'

'If she has seen them, has she been able to pass on her information?'

Bauer: 'She has sent no letter since yesterday at least, and has no other means of communicating out.'

Nicolai spoke after a moment; magisterial thought: 'Normally we might let her run a little; keep her watched. On this occasion – the knowledge she has – that could be too much of a risk.' Immelmann nodded.

Bauer: 'We can arrest her? Interrogate her?'

Nicolai shook his head uncertainly. 'I doubt we have the evidence. Not an attractive measure.'

The tip of Bauer's tongue made one circuit of his lips. 'Then perhaps we must arrange an... accident, for the young woman.'

Immelmann frowned. Nicolai hesitated, again feeling the expectation, and then started to nod.

'There will be no outrage in this house.' Auerstein's voice had altered, and the soldiers turned to consider him. His head came up, sixty years of pride. 'English spy she may be; she is certainly a guest in this house.'

Major Immelmann shifted again on the bench, glancing between his host and his superior officers.

⊱ ✦ ⊰

Ballentyne had a solitary supper, stew and beer in a back-street tavern. Pickford had given him a couple of errands for tomorrow – *I think you might...* as if directing him to some reading on the folk customs of the Berbers – but he felt out of place, as usual. If his mother were still alive she'd be fretting about him not settling down.

Fat chance. For when he strolled out into the night, through the cobbled streets towards the Fortress, and was tempted into a café, sudden bright art nouveau elegance after the ancient gloom outside, the first face he saw was Belcredi.

Damn the man. It had to be coincidence, but... And a hatred for the whole stupid game swelled in his chest, a refusal to skulk around after other men.

If he's innocent then I will seem innocent; if he's not, then I have nothing to lose.

'It's Herr Belcredi, isn't it?' Ballentyne said pleasantly, dropping into a chair, and saw the shock. *You knew. You bastard, you guilty... You were after me.* 'Recognize you from a photograph. We've never met, but I've heard about you. Ronald Ballentyne. Thought I'd come and say hallo.' He smiled, with all the malice he could find. 'Do I disturb you?'

'Herr Ballentyne.' Calculating furiously. The sense that for once his enemies were on the back foot meant a great deal to Ballentyne; he held the smile. 'I've read, of course... Yes. Customs in the Albanian villages; property marking and property disputes, that was you, I think?'

Ballentyne nodded. Part of his brain maintained the fiction that this was a civilized conversation between scholars.

'That's me. I wondered if I might have seen you at one of the conferences – Lyons, or the Royal Anthropological last year – but I don't think you were there.'

Belcredi looked nettled. 'My theories do not always appeal to the old men.'

'We're a new science, Herr Belcredi. Our pioneers must be men of courage.'

And, insanely, they talked. Belcredi was open about his travels among the Muslims of different countries of the region, the residue of half a millennium of Turkish rule. Ballentyne ordered a whisky, and Belcredi even sought his opinion on the attitudes of the Christian villagers of the mountains.

A moment of earnestness, but as if by mutual embarrassment they moved on hurriedly.

'You're still chasing your thesis of the affinity of the Muslims and the German peoples?'

Belcredi smiled; proud, patronizing. 'The Muslims who live in the old empires – the Turkish Empire, and also others – they are unhappy, Ballentyne.' The smile, a little manic. 'I help them to... articulate their unhappiness. I try to understand it. You can appreciate that, I think.'

'You're exploiting their beliefs. Their simplicity.'

'If the great imperial powers make war on the Teutonic races, the people who have suffered in those empires must react as the instinct takes them.' Ballentyne considered this sourly. 'And what of you? You... You're a distance from your villages.'

He knew I was here, and he was trying to track me. Did he know that I knew he was here? If either of us was innocent, this approach would seem natural.

But neither of us is innocent any more.

<hr />

Late in the afternoon at the Margaretenhof, with the light cool on the hall's chequerboard tiles, a woman's hand – unwatched – had placed an envelope in the basket from which a servant would soon take letters to the post office. Even sooner, a man's hand – unwatched – took the envelope out again.

Later, elsewhere: 'Hildebrandt, I have had a telegram from my acquaintance at the Margaretenhof.'

Hildebrandt waited.

'Do I infer that German Military Intelligence has had some little difficulty there?'

Still he waited.

'Well, perhaps I may at least be able to help Colonel Nicolai, in my small way. Having guessed that she had aroused the concern of your colleagues, my man has intercepted a letter that Fräulein Hathaway was sending home.' Now Hildebrandt started to smile. 'Naturally I do not wish to—'

'The Englishwoman acquired the key of one of von Moltke's aides, broke into the man's room, exchanged his document case for a few hours, and has therefore gained sight of the most sensitive papers.'

Krug's control broke into a delighted smile, and then he tutted elaborately. 'This lone young woman? In the heart of Germany, with all those Military Intelligence experts around?' A deep breath. 'I confess a growing interest in Fräulein Flora Hathaway. My correspondent writes of her... in almost emotional terms.' The smile, and the affectations, switched off. 'His intervention – my network – has afforded you a small delay in the sending of the letter, but soon it must be allowed to be sent. I do not make my activities known. You leave for Belgrade at any moment, I think, and your Englishman?' Hildebrandt nodded, and Krug echoed the gesture. 'You have your hunter's eye. Before you go, kindly urge Colonel Nicolai to do promptly whatever he needs to with Miss Hathaway.'

+=≡=+

Days passed empty for Duval in St Petersburg. A city of great beauty, with ugly people forced into hiding by its grandeur. A city of refinement, where barbarism lurked in shadows and public offices. A city of all his pleasures, but he couldn't seem to care about any of them. The prospect of a woman, of a drink, of a ballet: trivial; fatuous.

He found Rüdiger Frosch as instructed and watched him in two cafés before approaching him in the bar of the Grand Hotel.

The German was a caricature of joviality, a gallery of smiles and nudges, and eyes that promised to keep on swelling until a joke was shared. He ignored Duval's claim to be an Irish nationalist sympathizer who'd been told by friends of his part in smuggling rifles to Ulster. 'Assertions of identity are so irrelevant, are they not?' Another smile. 'Come! Sit – sit!' They sat at a newly empty table. 'On which side of the Irish Sea are these friends?' Duval flinched, and Frosch laughed gaily. 'Oh, such a muddle in Britain in these days, or no?'

Duval tried to look grave. 'Accusations of treachery aren't something we take lightly. Either side of the Irish Sea.'

'Of course! Every luxury in the British Empire, including the luxury of principle. The rest of us cannot be so pedantic.' Duval's face still merited a giggle, it seemed. 'Come, my friend. One half of London and one half of the British Army supports the men who got those rifles. I should apply for a government pension.'

Duval managed to chuckle. 'You probably know better than I do how much support there was. It went so high?'

'My dear fellow, King George the Fifth gave me his personal blessing. No, you don't get no names from me. Most of them are known by the newspapers anyway. Just think about it: that whole shipment, and most of all the payment – how was that managed, without many blind eyes and deaf ears?'

'They must have been laughing in Berlin – seeing the British tearing at each other for once.'

'Who needs Tirpitz and his battleships, when they can start a civil war instead?'

Duval took a breath. 'Hence the, er, the extra cargo.'

Frosch's grin died, and then after a moment's consideration was reborn as a smile. 'Ah, you heard about him. Well, even the British might not start a civil war without a little help. But here's a free secret for you' – he leaned in, and so Duval did the same – 'he wasn't Berlin official. Our people didn't know him; their people didn't know about him. So, we ask ourselves' – a single finger waggled rhetorically – 'who was he then? And we answer— Ah! My dear friend! No, no, join us!' The newcomer was the image of a respectable clerk. Spectacles; neat moustache; cautious – especially at being yanked down into a chair by a drunk German smuggler. Frosch was oblivious. 'You will enjoy this, my friend. We were complimenting Berlin on provoking a civil war in Britain and so not having to fight a war themselves.'

A superior, lifeless smile emerged from under the moustache. 'It is not against Britain that Germany wants to fight her war, but against her own working men. Even if the lion gave up his empire tomorrow and all his warships, Germany would still find a pretext for war, against someone, because they would rather that the German proletarian was fighting in France or in Russia, and not in the streets of Berlin.'

Frosch leaned towards Duval and spoke in a stage whisper that could have been heard ten feet away. 'Afanasiev is a true revolutionary. A Menshevik. He comes to the Grand to slaughter the rich, or no? But not before pudding, heh?'

'First there is comedy,' Afanasiev said primly; 'then there is tragedy. I will meet with anyone, anywhere, who is ready to discuss a more equal society.'

Frosch spoke over the last words. 'So to say, here we are! What a crew! One, the shipper and smuggler' – he slapped his chest – 'whose companions must suspect he is a German spy.' The grin flashed. 'No? Two, the anarchist who has a good chance of being an Okhrana spy. And three, the Irish who could be spying for Russia, for Britain, or even for Germany.' Duval felt his empty stomach; Afanasiev looked like a respectable clerk who'd been told a dirty joke.

Frosch raised his hands in show of harmlessness. 'But don't worry, dear friends. We have nothing to fear! In the unlikely situation that we all speak the truth, God blesses us for our holiness and he keeps us safe. Or, as long as we are all three spies, we drink together very happily, yes?' Duval, caught between amusement and concern, waited for the punchline. Frosch leaned in, head low and leering up at them. 'But heaven protect the man who alone is telling the truth, for he's in real trouble!' And his head lurched back and burst into giggles. He'd thought that was very funny.

A smile crept over Afanasiev's face, dead. He excused himself.

The grin disappeared from Frosch's face like a light going out, and he watched the Russian's back weaving through the tables. 'Revolutionaries I don't mind; good tough businessmen. But why can't they none of them have a sense of humour?' His hand fell fat on Duval's wrist, while his eyes continued to watch Afanasiev out. 'Well, my friend, whatever you are. Have you got what you wanted? Can we share a little supper now?'

Together they put away a mountain of roast duck and apple, harassed the waiters and got more than half drunk. Frosch chattered of his activities, without once giving a name or a fact that could interest the police. His integrity was a professional asset rather than a scruple, and people were mentioned in the same dispassionate tone as shipping crates. And to be abandoned as easily; Duval got the impression that more than one had been lost in transit over the years. Duval accepted the role of apprentice, and amused the German with stories of his little schemes and exploits.

They'd got on to characters they'd met on their travels – without naming names – and in the middle of this comparison of rogues great and small Frosch started to describe a Latin who travelled Europe: 'Always a pretty woman, always some game – little game, yes? Deception, smuggling, fraud – always luxury; his father was a shopkeeper, but sometimes he calls himself a marquis even. I could not—'

And Duval had blurted 'Valfierno' before thinking.

Frosch's smile died, and the face and body sagged. 'You do business after all.' The eyes were cold again.

'No – honestly, no.'

'You have business with this man.'

'No. I have... I have unfinished business with a woman he called his daughter.'

Frosch watched, considered. He hadn't quite caught his breath after his cataloguing; he sighed twice. The second sigh caught in his throat, and became a chuckle, which rose into laughter, and then he was shaking and roaring and punching Duval on the arm. 'In all this! In this time, and this world, that is what you think of! Oh, my friend, I like you very much.' He put his arm round Duval's shoulder. 'We have another bottle, yes? Then I tell you proper secret, about Vienna.' He yelled for the waiter.

When Duval got back to the Angleterre, Lisson was waiting in the lobby, a policeman slumped on the sofa beside him. Duval's levity shrivelled immediately.

Lisson seemed uncomfortable, which was an improvement. 'Look, Duval: sordid business; you're one of the few who can identify her. Might do yourself a favour, too; and us. Regain some good odour with the Russians. Make up for the inconvenience you've caused us all, what?'

The body had been found in an attic room in the Sennaya; if the landlady had been less nosey, it might have lain there much longer. The policeman's lantern made ill shadows of the damp and the peeling paper as they climbed, flight after flight of stairs.

The room when they reached it was mean: a mattress without sheets, a shelf without books, a table without a chair, a small skylight without light. On the mattress, a pale thin underdress veiling a pale thin body – a hip bone, her breasts, pushed ghostly through the material – was the woman called Anna.

The police had found an empty bottle next to the body; they suspected an overdose of laudanum.

'So? This is woman? This is woman on train?' The policeman escorting him was barely five feet tall.

They'd found almost nothing in her bag. What she'd brought out of Germany and the night train she'd lost, given, or hidden; or the landlady had taken it, or the police.

'You recognize?'

Her young sleep face, white and transparent.

He thought of it alive, thought of her skipping out of Germany ahead of the police, lighting on him, her hand under his arm.

He took a breath; shook his head. 'This isn't her. She's still free somewhere.'

⊢══╾══⊣

The day after her liaison with the major's document case, Hathaway had woken surprised to find herself waking at all, and had wanted to avoid all human contact. But a late appearance for breakfast had happened to coincide with a mime-show, from the other end of the room, of Immelmann presenting Colonel Bauer with his document case. Immelmann concerned; Bauer indifferent but then registering the concern and wondering where he'd thought his case was and wandering off; Immelmann becalmed, unwilling to sit, glancing around the room, catching her eye. *What is natural now?* Then Bauer was back with reassurance and Immelmann's case, and the mistake was rectified, and Bauer sat down with the cheeriness of a man who has done a good deed for an influential subordinate before breakfast. Immelmann sat, still looking out of sorts.

Clearly he had found his key, or a spare. Clearly nothing had been linked to Hathaway, otherwise... surely they would have confronted her by now. Wouldn't they?

Gerta had not appeared for breakfast. Hathaway had spent the day hiding in the library; had returned to her room to retrieve a thick letter to her uncle from within the pages of a book; had put the letter out for posting; had retired to her room until dinner.

There had been more guests at dinner; the talk had been of the next day's shooting. Hathaway had buried herself satisfactorily among strangers; with their chatter untouched by previous events in the house, with their fresh air of a world outside, she felt the previous evening receding in time and immensity.

After dinner, in the drawing room, she watched the cards again, until the obtuseness of the woman in front of her became too frustrating. She turned away and found Gerta immediately in front of her.

For a moment, they waited, watched each other.

Then Gerta said, 'Transgressions?'

Hathaway felt herself smiling faintly. 'The things of a night.'

As if a password had been offered, and accepted. Gerta's fingers brushed her wrist, and they moved apart.

Hathaway had gone to bed early; slept long, slept well.

Then this morning: a white sky over the land, breakfast, the house bustling for the shooting, and a memory of duty – a desire to be clearly rid of it. Catching the servant crossing the hall: 'Pardon me, did my letter – the letter for England – get off all right yesterday?'

And the servant's empty face: 'But there was no letter to England in the basket, Fräulein.'

Flora Hathaway's world lurched sick and scared.

An hour of mist, a treacly nauseous dream. It had all been arranged; everyone was going out to watch the shooting. The men had gone out first, with loaders and dogs. The women followed: Frau Auerstein and the older women in carriages; the younger women walking. Hathaway walked among them, trapped in a platoon of waterproof capes and tweed. The faces all seemed the same: solid-handsome, cold, assured. They chattered like men: curt, boisterous, hard. An army as ominous as any that picked up a rifle and marched for the Kaiser. *I should enjoy this company.* At any moment they would turn on her, Kurfürstendamm-tailored impeccably mannered harpies, and tear her to pieces. And then they would walk on, haughty and athletic, and challenge their men to do as resolutely with their guns.

If they had stopped her letter, they were onto her. If they had stopped her letter, she was cut off.

Gerta walking close by her in the pack, hair pulled back and face fresh in the cold, moving easily in jacket and skirt that hugged her tight at breasts and waist and hips; another von Waldeck painting would have been sold to equip her appropriately for these occasions. *Does she know?* She turned and smiled at Hathaway, timid, genuine. *She does not know.*

Run? To where? *Ask for help?* From whom?

From Gerta. What could she do, and what would she do, whose duty had brought them to this place?

They reached the assembly point after a quarter-hour, a clearing on the edge of scrub and thickets: a crowd of Germans, immaculate and impressive and armed, and one hunted Englishwoman.

Cautiously, as if she might not be noticed, Hathaway looked for the faces she recognized.

To her horror, she could tell immediately as she saw them one by one, a first catching of the eyes, which of them knew about her. Immelmann first of all, a gun carried alert and easy, a cold stare and then looking away. *He knows.* Eckhardt, less comfortable with his gun, did not know. Colonel Bauer was holding his gun tense, as if the Grenadier Guards might be coming through the undergrowth at any time, and he glanced up and saw her and his face hardened and he murmured something to the man beside him and the man stopped checking the breech of his gun and turned to look at her. Not a man she recognized; they were due to join a party from at least one other estate – or was this a confederate summoned from Berlin? Regardless, the two of them knew. Otto Auerstein seemed not to know.

Heinrich Auerstein was the centre of a group of half a dozen, newer guests or acquaintances from the other party, his gun held by a loader. As she watched, he happened to look and see her, and his eyes iced and died. Auerstein was the Old Testament in the bracken, civilization and hospitality violated and unavenged.

―――※―――

At Pickford's request Ballentyne had breakfasted with an Italian journalist, and then spent three hours of the day in a seminar with Serbian officers. They were mostly young, and it made their earnestness rather appealing, and their wild-eyed bloodthirstiness rather alarming. They were hungry, like boys just out of short trousers, for anything that would enhance their seriousness. And they hated Austria and everything apparently Austrian, and spiced their talk with empty threats of what they would do to that vast empire when they had the opportunity. As a scholar and an Englishman – and a man well past thirty – Ballentyne was treated with veneration.

⊰══⊱

The German forests, timeless and endless, vast trees and barbed-wire undergrowth, fir and thorn and beech and pine each with their mysticisms, a realm of shadows and sounds that slipped between worlds. For one patch of eastern Germany, one part of the forest was an angry scrubland, mixing trees and thickets and paths and clearings, a maze of clutching brambles and no straight paths. In the middle of one clearing, surrounded by hunters, Flora Hathaway waited at bay.

There was to be little shape to the hunt; the habits and discipline of German sportsmen would ensure that no mistakes were made. The thickets were dense with birds.

A silly hope that it might not be real, that she might not have got herself into this horror. Then the sight of her boots against the earth, the sheen on the leather as it settled uneasily in the mud and the yellow reedy grass. A call, a shifting among the men, a gathering and a preparing. Somewhere in the thickets she could be lost; she too could become prey.

She must stay with others; she must not become isolated. They would not— But where was Gerta now? In her focus on the men who knew her as a spy, Hathaway had lost sight of the one person who might defend her. But anyone else would do; they would not dare—

But again, what accidents might not happen in the maze of trees? Around her the hunters drifted, unfamiliar faces and always the sharp shine of gun barrels. Intermittently, a face she recognized – Immelmann, Bauer, Bauer's companion – watching her; perhaps waiting for her.

And then a surprise so unlikely that her first physical instinct was that something worse had happened. It took a second for her brain to catch up, to look at the face again, to recognize it.

London. Distant civilized London; a man to whom she'd been

introduced. A soldier who would be her 'liaison'.

Major Valentine Knox, here in the German forest, the same clothes and the same stiff sureness of Immelmann and the others, gun held easily under his left arm and watching everyone.

For a moment she assumed that, by some further distortion of her world, he had become one of her hunters. Her heart hammered at her, bewilderment and the possibility of safety, and she had to restrain herself.

Now he'd seen her too. But no sign of recognition. *This is not a time for your games, you bloody man!* Holding herself, working for balance on the marshy soil, Hathaway began to drift towards him.

Now he too was moving, not towards her but on an intersecting course. He'd acknowledged someone else, was moving to them, introducing himself, and she saw it was Eckhardt. By picking someone from the Margaretenhof party he'd guaranteed an introduction to Hathaway when she joined them.

And so it was. Compatriots introduced; a pleasantry about the power of German diplomacy even among the English; Eckhardt summoned and moving away.

'I never thought I'd say it to a British soldier, but I'm very glad you're here.'

'I take praise where I find it, Miss Hathaway. First off, let's stand and sound like we've just met; tone and volume more important than what we say; a whisper is far more suspicious than any wo—'

'They know that I'm – I'm a – a spy.' Knox's eyes widened, flicked over her shoulders. 'I got hold of some documents two nights ago – reports – I put the details into a letter for London, but the letter was taken before it left the house.' Her eyes were pleading, urging him to understand how she felt.

A conversation of espionage, in full view of their enemies; a murmuring deep in Germany.

'The letter was in cypher?'

'Yes, and I returned the documents.'

'Good; so they may not know what, if anything, you read or did.'

'But why stop the letter if they didn't suspect me of something?'

'Suspect is better than know. Doubt they'll do anything desperate.'

'Major, I won't pretend I'm not scared.' She glanced around the clearing, the circle of hunters; forced a smile. 'When everyone's got a gun, it seems likely that something's going to get shot.'

Knox hefted the shotgun in the crook of his elbow, smiled hard. 'When there are guns on both sides, both sides will go a little more carefully.'

'No, Major!' She was genuinely alarmed. 'That's madness. That's as bad as—'

'So, Miss Hathaway!' She jumped. Otto Auerstein striding towards them, hatless and hearty in the morning. 'Are we ready for a little sport?'

A whistle shrieked.

✦══✦

Count Paul Hildebrandt was straight off a long journey and in ill humour.

'He overbalanced you on the train, and he overbalanced you last night.' Heinz-Peter Belcredi pulled away from the tone. 'I could not have come a moment later.'

A kind of relief. 'That's right! Really, Count Paul, my responsibilities are not in this area. I should be—'

Hildebrandt's hand grabbed his collar and wrenched him forwards, and a knife appeared in front of his eyes. 'Your responsibilities are now what we say they are. You should be fulfilling them more effectively.'

A squawk: 'I am not – not even a—'

'Oh, but you are.' Hildebrandt released him, and he stumbled backwards. 'We are sworn to support you in the realization of your ideas, and you in your turn must shape your work to the strategic interests of our people.' The knife had disappeared again, replaced by a cigarette. Hildebrandt reached forwards and straightened Belcredi's collar. 'There is no longer such a thing as an occupation of peace and an occupation of war. Every action, by all of us, must be calculated towards the defeat of our enemies.'

He let out twin streams of smoke from his nostrils. 'By finding you, your colleague Mr Ballentyne reveals too much. He will reveal his confederates, and then I will kill him.'

✦══✦

It had been such a silly distraction, and now Hathaway had contrived exactly the situation she feared.

After the whistle and a formal word from Heinrich Auerstein, the group had dispersed into the undergrowth by different paths; some had loaders with them, some – like Immelmann – chose to hunt alone. The clearing emptied within moments, leaving just the servants who would prepare a luncheon. For a few moments the only sound was breathing, and the snapping of twigs underfoot, and the occasional friendly comment, and then the first gunshots began to crack among the trees.

Hathaway had set off with one of the women from the Margaretenhof party, and a male acquaintance of hers from among the neighbours: mixed and neutral company. Knox was deliberately walking not with her, but ten yards or so behind and in sight; Hathaway had indicated the people she was most worried about, and Knox had fastened himself onto Immelmann. When she wasn't in conversation herself, and in the lulls between shots, she could hear the murmur of the two men's voices: cautious, professional, the verbal sorties by which men tested their ground.

The trees swallowed them all. Hathaway's female companion avowed the equal physical fitness of women, which made her admirable if occasionally dull company, and the man was happy to treat his gun as ornamental only, which made him at least quieter than some. From the off, Immelmann and Knox were shooting frequently and fast, the blasts interrupted by brusque compliments and comments. *Discussing pistols, or boasting about their battleships, or whatever it is that men talk about.* Half an hour passed. Other twos and threes of the party occasionally emerged onto their path; polite words, and then dispersal. The rattling of unseen gunfire.

Then, when Hathaway next glanced over her shoulder, a bend in the path had obscured the men behind. She slowed, not wanting to be separated from her two companions, still wanting to be sure that... But the path remained empty.

There had been a fork in the path shortly before. For some reason Immelmann must have been tempted the other way; it would have seemed odd for Knox to leave the German to follow her – suspicious, even. Perhaps he thought it better to watch Immelmann. In any case, Knox was gone.

Her two companions were ten yards ahead now, and she started to walk faster, and then there was a voice from behind. The Austrian count, waving something, 'Is this your –?' something she couldn't hear. A few steps towards him; he was waving a glove. No, it wasn't hers, and he walked away, and Hathaway turned to catch up her companions but they had disappeared, turned back but the Austrian had disappeared too.

Alone on the path, she took a few tentative steps forwards, then lengthened her stride. The main path was easily followed; her companions couldn't be more than thirty yards away; she'd be with them in— And Colonel Bauer stepped onto the path in front of her.

She gasped, at the surprise more than the predicament. He held his gun two-handed, across his chest. Closed, which meant it was ready. Another startle, rustling in the undergrowth beside her, and she turned to see another man pushing his way through the bushes towards her: the man who had joined Bauer that morning.

Expressions dead, guns ready, watching her.

What could she say? What could they say, given what she had done? Bauer's dead expression. What would they say, before—

A crack like a branch breaking, and they were all three startled, and another crack before they'd begun to look for the sound. Two shots had come out of a tangle of trees, and now a rustling above them and they didn't know where to look and something thumped to the ground in front of Bauer and something crashed into the bracken nearby. Hathaway's eyes had veered from the other man to Bauer, bewildered and tense, and then they dropped to the path. A bird, crumpled and bloody.

More rustling in the undergrowth, the breaking of sticks as someone tramped through, and the foliage hardened into a third figure. 'Anyone see – Ah, gentlemen; miss. See a couple of my bag fall hereabouts?'

It was Knox.

He stepped onto the path, nodded to each of them, saw the bird on the ground. 'Gosh, there he is.' He looked up at Bauer; held the gaze long. 'Good thing you didn't get hit, eh?'

'Yes,' Bauer said.

'There's another in the bracken there.' Hathaway pointed.

Knox took a cartridge out of his pocket and slipped it into the shotgun.

'Well that's not bad, is it? Two birds with one whatsit, eh?'

Bauer stepped off the path into the trees, resuming the direction he'd been taking, and was gone; his companion did the same.

Hathaway breathed out. 'That was deliberate, I take it.'

A rough smile. 'Bit of showing off helps sometimes.' He loaded another cartridge, and kicked the second carcase out of the undergrowth onto the path. 'Reasonable enough for you to head back for luncheon now, enjoy the picnic and declare you've had enough sport for the day. Even if they were making a try for you then, I doubt they'll manage another chance.'

'How did you come to be at the Margaretenhof?'

'You reported to London that you were here. Easy enough for me to detour to the area, and relatively easy to get an invite to your neighbours. Friends of friends of friends. Come and see how you were getting on.' A flapping in the treetops and his head rose and swung and the gun snapped shut and followed. But one bird, at least, would escape for now; Knox watched where it had gone, holding the pose a moment longer.

She watched him: the lines of barrel and arm, the instinctive pivots of elbow and shoulder, the narrowed eyes one with their target. A man in his world.

Face and shotgun dropped again. 'Chance for a bit of sport,' he went on. 'And now, I'll see about getting you away from here. Just bumped into each other; mutual acquaintances to discuss. Invite to supper, and why not stay on, etc. Get you back where you ought—'

'No.' It surprised her as much as him. More measured: 'I'm staying.'

'Look, I admire your pluck, Miss Hathaway. But—'

'Do you call your other... professional acquaintances "Mr" so-and-so?' Knox frowned. 'Or are you stuck with women only? Is there a colonel who meets the men?'

Knox looked older when he was exasperated. *Lord, is it I who makes men old?*

'You were about to say that this is no place for a woman. Something like that.' Knox's chest swelled in a breath, and as he released it his body and face seemed to harden and she saw the life come into his eyes, hungry. *This is how he looks in the moment before the battle.* 'Perhaps you and your friends should have thought of that before sending me here.'

But the expression didn't change. 'Yes, *Miss* Hathaway. I was going to say something like that. I do think women are different; and I treat 'em so. You can call me funny names, or chain yourself to railings, or whatever takes your fancy. My attitude doesn't depend on yours. It's a way of the world I happen to believe in; my idea of civilization, and I've fought for it.' His focus widened to their surroundings for an instant, then re-concentrated on her face. 'Listening to your friends here, looks like I'll be fighting for it again. What I was also going to say – and I'd say it to anyone, man or woman, about to let blood get the better of brain – is this: I've done more than my share of damn' stupid things; dangerous, reckless; things you might sneer at. But I've always done them for something that I calculated worth while. Calculated, you hear? Calculated cold. It can be an admirable thing to risk your neck, and I think everyone's capable of finding something they care about enough to do so; but it's stupid to risk your neck when the game's not worth it.'

She searched the face; it didn't move. 'You're sure you weren't sent out by the old men to pat me on the head and tell me not to do anything unladylike?'

'I'm sure. Miss Hathaway, please believe that the game is real. I might think it's not appropriate for you to be here; but here you are.' His eyes swung round them again, some instinct of hunter or soldier. 'When the old men sent you out here, they did so knowing there was a risk. Miss Hathaway, they wouldn't be surprised if you didn't come back. But they'd be disappointed if they didn't get anything in return.'

'Calculate, you say.' Her head came up. 'Two nights ago I read the private dossier of the chief of the German Army. Italy has specified the military support she will give to a campaign in Alsace. The Kaiser has been encouraging the Austrians to fight Serbia now, to stabilize their empire and before Russia is stronger. The German Army are pushing for war, soon, because they think they've a better chance now than in two years' time.'

He was impressed, and she enjoyed it for a second. 'I'll jot down what I remember and try to slip it to you this afternoon. Do you know, you're the first man who's ever told me to calculate more rather than less?' He didn't know what she was talking about. 'I will see you anon, Major.'

'I hope so, Miss Hathaway.'

→═══←

'Bit of cloak-and-dagger, I'm afraid, but they take this sort of thing damn' seriously, and who's to say they're not right?'

And then Pickford was introducing Ballentyne to Captain Tomić, sharp-featured and not a word, and Captain Tomić was leading Ballentyne away from the Miša House where he was supposed to be lecturing, through a heavy unmarked door which was locked behind them and which seemed to have led into a different building, down a flight of stairs, out another door and across an unlit narrow street and in again and through another connecting door; and eventually he was shown into a darkened room and pointed to a chair. He sat.

'Thank you for coming, Mr Ballentyne.' Captain Tomić was standing guarding the closed door, but Captain Tomić had not spoken. 'Please excuse the melodrama.' As his eyes adjusted, he made out a man seated behind a table. The only light in the room, a glimmer from a curtained window, was behind him.

Slavic, speaking slow but solid English. Ballentyne nodded, waited.

'You have information about an Austrian visitor to our country.' He nodded again. 'I ask you to share it. To repeat what you know and what you evaluate, with your scholar's mind.' A big man; surely. Not tall, but substantial. 'I can only assure you that your co-operation is in the interests of the great friendship between the kingdoms of England and Serbia, for the destruction of our enemies.'

Ballentyne had been in enough Balkan conversations to know it wouldn't be the done thing to pay too much attention to the nuances of this friendship or this suddenly shared enmity. He repeated his story with the same clarity he'd given Pickford, adding judgements from his meeting with Belcredi the previous evening.

The shadow stayed silent until he had finished. He then asked a series of shrewd questions about the nature of the villages in Albania where Belcredi had been, the sort of people he might have met in Bosnia, and what if anything Ballentyne knew of the ethnically Albanian Muslims in Serbia. Ballentyne was uneasy now, his loyalties to his Albanian villages and the great Anglo-Serbian friendship gently in conflict; but he pressed on honestly.

Silence again. Then decision: 'This man will be watched more closely – also into Austria, if he goes on there. His past movements here will be discovered. We will make investigations and take precautions in our south. When the war comes, England will find Serbia fully ready.' There was the impression that Ballentyne was expected to pass this on to the King, or at least to Mr Asquith. 'Thank you very much, Mr Ballentyne.'

Ballentyne was back in the Miša House, in his seat on the platform, at one minute before seven.

He'd no more than glanced at the front row when he'd entered the room. As he settled to 'The village: an ancient society meets the twentieth century', hand on the pipe in his pocket as ever, he began to take in more of the audience. Twenty-five of them, perhaps; even thirty. A flicker of pride. Mainly older, mainly genteel-looking. A couple of wizened eccentrics. A clutch of Serbian uniforms, including Captain Tomić. Expatriates eager for any taste of community and culture, and a few Serbs anxious to prove themselves European.

In the third row, sitting at the end, was a man of about his own age with dark hair, looking up at Ballentyne with the suggestion of a smile; and Ballentyne's head and heart seemed to freeze and his hand clenched on the pipe and for an instant he was gaping silent.

It was Hildebrandt.

<hr />

Thomson's knock on the door was exact to time again. The old man watched him come in, sit, prepare his words. Not a chap to be rushed.

'That request of yours,' he said eventually. 'We've turned every man in the records clearing office upside down as you suggested, and they're all clean as whistles.'

'The procedures, then. Somewhere in the system. God's sake, the enemy is actually able to interrogate our own records.'

'I've gone through it myself, sir. Not a chink of daylight.'

'There must be. I put four names into that office, and into no other office. The enemy heard about it. Somehow the request was known to be sensitive. Somehow it leaked.'

'Don't see how.'

'Whoever it is is able to make requests for information too. Look harder.'

An intake of breath; restraint. 'That's all very well, sir. But... Look, if you could give me – just me – those names, I could re-trace the check myself. Try to spot anything out of the ordinary when it went through the system.'

'Double or nothing, eh?'

'With respect, sir, it sounds like you don't have much left to lose.'

'No, Thomson. I don't.'

＊＝＝＝＊

As Ballentyne began his conclusion, Hildebrandt's hand slipped into his jacket pocket. *He has a gun.* His voice distant, muffled. *He actually contemplates assassinating me here.* A glance at Pickford, but the older man registered nothing of his alarm. *How can they occupy the same world?* On the old front line between the Habsburg Empire and the Ottoman, these good souls sat unwitting around that lethal smile, the smile of the knife.

Intermittently, Hildebrandt would nod discreet approval of a point Ballentyne made; once he tapped mute applause on his thigh.

The pressures of twentieth-century life not themselves a direct threat to the villages. *Must get out.* But economic and social changes could weaken the traditional structures of the village and leave it vulnerable. *Give me a door; give me a yard; give me a second.* Was this unavoidable? Was this undesirable? *Hildebrandt is the twentieth century, and he will destroy the world of these old souls.* A breath; a mad notion; a breath. 'But, ladies and gentlemen, I am reassured when I look at this audience, that there is a world of people who are themselves most civilized, yet who are sympathetic to the unique world of the highland peoples. I hope I may count on your agreement.' Polite 'Hear! Hear!'s from the audience. 'Will you uphold the obligations of our European civilization? Will you stand as representatives for all that is best in our world, and offer it to the weakest?' A few more 'Hear! Hear!'s, and 'Yes, indeed!'s. 'You gentlemen at the back – soldiers of free Serbia – will you protect the rights of all your citizens, whether they are in Belgrade villas or the far hills?' Uncertain glances among the handful of officers, then nods. 'Will you pledge it, ladies and gentlemen? Do you offer your word to the impoverished peoples of our Continent? Will you show them that this new century offers a new opportunity to spread civilization, and not an obsession with its destruction?' Louder agreement, bass rumbles and shrill echoes. 'Here is a paper. Will you sign?' Louder agreement. 'You, sir, will you come forwards?' The man in the front row half standing, uneasy but caught. 'You officers, will you as our hosts show us the way? Come forwards and sign!' A hesitation, Ballentyne's heart hammering, and then the man in the front row was stepping in and one of the officers after a glance at his colleagues was hurrying to the front – 'Come then!' – and half a dozen were standing and a gaggle began to build around the table at the front and Ballentyne slipped to the side and through the door and there was a key and he locked it and ran.

⊷═⊱

Elation at his ruse, blood thumping in head and chest, dodging down the alleys; eventually a café. A table, a chair, his head in his hands a moment, and Ballentyne ordered a *šljivovica*. It disappeared, and he ordered another.

I am thought to have a brain, and I am not using it.

He sipped.

A man sat down in front of him. Ballentyne gave a silent gasp, and then a kind of growl.

Hildebrandt caught the waiter's attention, pointed at Ballentyne's glass and held up two fingers. Then he folded his hands together on the table.

'Rather inspired, Herr Ballentyne,' he said at last. *Still the damned pure vowel sounds.* 'Rather amusing. But you really have no idea of following and being followed.' A self-satisfied smile. 'You gave poor Belcredi a scare, but you've been watched all the way.' *Which confirms you and Belcredi are confederates.*

The drinks arrived.

Hildebrandt made to speak, then tried a sip of his drink, and grimaced; a scowl of accusation, as if it had been some new trick by Ballentyne.

'Could we begin – as men of logic – by agreeing that you are indeed an agent of the British government?'

For a moment Ballentyne still thought it wasn't true. He hesitated, and Hildebrandt's face opened in wonder.

Ballentyne cut him off. 'As it happens, when we first met I really wasn't.' Disbelief. 'But now I am.' Hildebrandt shrugged. 'Do you know something? It doesn't matter any more. I still haven't much to tell you, and you, I imagine, still don't care. I find you are my enemy, and I find you are the enemy of my country; and because that means so much to you, it turns out that it means more to me than I thought.' He gulped at the firewater. 'You... You're hatred; and violence; and inhumanity.'

Hildebrandt was placid. 'You have been a country for – what? – a thousand years; Germany less than fifty. Your empire dominates the world; ours is merely a tenant on the barren spaces you did not care for. You really think your dominance was achieved and sustained by nothing more than... than tea and cricket and "Fair play, old chaps"?'

The waiter was hovering nearby, and Ballentyne beckoned. 'I'm hungry. You?' Hildebrandt shook his head, amused. Ballentyne spoke in stop-start Serbo-Croat, then turned back. 'I don't care about countries and empires; I care about human men. All I know is that I've travelled to the darkest, poorest, most primitive parts of this Continent, and I've never met a man as base as you.' This touched Hildebrandt, somewhere in his pride. 'I don't especially care who rules the world, but I know that a man like you means only death to it.'

Something of Hildebrandt's polish had faded. 'You are the tool of a corrupted empire; you are my enemy; and shortly I will kill you.'

Ballentyne watched him. A man who could not be stopped.

I have no identity to protect me. I am become an outcast.

'Yes,' he said. 'You probably will. Like you killed that boy in the village. You'll kill and you'll keep on killing because that's who you are.'

'Your optimism about the twentieth century is a delusion, fit only for those old fools back there.' Ballentyne nodded. 'Ours is a different approach to the world, and it will triumph.'

The waiter appeared behind Ballentyne, and muttered something, and then Hildebrandt sensed movement behind himself and glanced back and found two figures pressing close against his shoulders.

Ballentyne shrugged. 'Different approaches to the world, Hildebrandt. You don't speak Serbo-Croat, and I do. I told the waiter that I was an agent of the British government here to help Serbia, and that you were an agent of the Austrian government trying to organize a coup.' Hildebrandt's eyes went wide in disbelief, anger. Ballentyne saw his whole body tensing, preparing, saw the hands slip under the table. 'Don't! Think first, man.' He breathed long, trying to hold himself. 'Little test of your mettle, now. I'm walking out of here. Smooth talker like you, you can probably negotiate your way out. Or you can kill me; and these men will certainly tear you to pieces.' Hildebrandt's eyes were hard, steady, mind working. *It's inhuman.* His hands were under the table. 'Up to you, old chap.'

A breath. Slowly, Ballentyne stood. Hildebrandt's hands under the table. Ballentyne turned and walked to the door, shoulders tense; step by step.

<hr />

Ballentyne disappeared into the city; into alleys that the police did not know, into a community that lived apart. The Albanians of Belgrade, like their ancestors in every place, existed in parallel to the official structures of society. They followed its laws as much as was required of them, but they knew that the only law they could depend on was their own.

Ballentyne knew a café, and he went there immediately; he knew a name, and he mentioned it discreetly. Within seconds he was in a private room; within fifteen minutes he was talking to a man he had never met but knew he could trust; within an hour he was in a house in the Dorćol quarter, enjoying the taste of coffee in the Turkish style and the highland accent, and chatting politely about everything in the world except why he was there. It would never be asked.

The Austrian Embassy had their spies in the Belgrade police, and they started enquiries. They learned nothing. Hildebrandt had a handful of men circling the city and trying to pick up trace of the Englishman. No trace was found.

... in sum the least significant of the men I set up and
knocked down in the Cape; so little to him there wasn't even
sport in it. He'll have disappeared back into the safety of
his gentleman's club where he no doubt makes a brave story
of it all. If you're ever looking for a good hand, Mynheer, I
trust you'll remember those of us who did stouter service -
on both sides of the lines. F. J. D.

Krug sat more distinctly upright; it increased his distance from the paper.

Such was the opinion of Duquesne.

Duquesne was a braggart; probably something of a fantasist. It was one of the reasons Krug had never sought his opinion of the man they had fought in Africa – and why renewed contact was a risk to Krug's anonymity.

Duquesne said that the Englishman had seemed scared of him. Which more likely meant that he had been suspicious of him. Duquesne had said he was dull, pedantic. Which meant, Krug knew now, that he was intelligent and thorough.

Duquesne said that he had acted hastily. Which meant, Krug remembered, that in the crisis he had been capable of daring.

Duquesne said he hadn't had influence among the British commanders, never seemed to have been considered. Which meant that he had kept himself apart, acted unofficially and in the shadows even then. A habit that would only have increased with experience.

Duquesne said that he hadn't had the spirit – the Boer's word had been cruder – to be a real soldier. Which meant that he might have been an unusually subtle soldier.

Krug placed his two hands deliberately over the paper, effacing Duquesne and his bravado. He had nothing from it.

And yet he had corroboration, hadn't he? Of features that still would not resolve themselves into a face. A man of great patience and great daring. A man preferring to act outside all regular structures.

What game are we playing, old fox?

'I was followed; I am sure.' Belcredi was wide-eyed.

Hildebrandt was tilted back in his chair, cigarette halfway to his lips. 'How would you know?' It completed the journey, and he lit it. 'As it happens, today you are right.'

Belcredi pulled himself up in the chair. 'You boasted that you would find Ballentyne, and you have not. My patrons in Germany and Austria would—'

'Your patrons would no doubt send expensive flowers to your funeral. Your idea is powerful enough to outlive you.'

A knock, and a man entered. He walked round the desk, handed Hildebrandt a telegram, murmured in his ear for a few moments, then left.

'Albanians...' Hildebrandt said slowly. Belcredi scowled his incomprehension. 'That is how he has done it, is it? You are followed by Albanians. It seems Ballentyne trusts his mountain men more than he trusts Serbian Intelligence or the British Embassy; he's probably right...' The last phrase vague, as he pulled open the telegram. A grunt. 'I am summoned back to Vienna. We are ordered to keep Ballentyne under observation, but nothing more; he is now part of something larger.'

'You don't have him under observation, do you? You—'

'I do not have Ballentyne, little man.' A smile through the smoke. 'But I do have you.'

<hr/>

Sir, [HATHAWAY] met as arranged. Suspects enemy aware of role. Encyphered letter intercepted at house. Gist follows. Italy General Staff visited Berlin May. Promised 2 Corps + ? Cavalry Divisions Alsace. General Staff doubtful of Italian, Turkish, Roumanian reliability. Want prompt action before second thoughts. New French and Russian service terms and Corps also encourage General Staff action sooner. Quote could not defeat Russia after 1916/17 unquote. [MOLTKE] encouraging Kaiser. Pushing universal conscription. Kaiser met Austria [FRANZ FERDINAND] in Bohemia. Agreed

quote something must be done about Serbia unquote. General
Staff fear Austria distracted in Balkans weakens eastern
campaign against Russia. [MOLTKE] has told [CONRAD] Austria
must delay Russia enough for Germany to win in west. Gist
ends. [HATHAWAY] refused return ticket.

[SS G/1/894/17 & D/3/449 (AS DECRYPTED)]

'Just got that. Takes a second to flash across Europe. Takes a day to get
up Whitehall.'

'Never mind, Colonel.' The old man was still in the paper. 'In the end
we must depend on the calibre of our people. Knox got to Hathaway, and
Hathaway is clearly flourishing.'

'Good show. Her information is Grade A. It'll be circulated immediately.'

'Yes. But not in this form, please, Colonel. No source, no names.' With
finger and thumb he picked up another paper by a corner; it flashed white
as it caught the sun from over his shoulder. 'I received her encyphered
letter this morning.'

'Oh. So Knox's summary was wasted.'

'Not my point, Colonel.' He laid the paper gently down again. 'It
was intercepted, and then it was released again, with all that precious
information in it. I can't see the German police or Intelligence letting
that go.'

'Perhaps they were just checking it; couldn't see the cypher.'

'If they're willing to intercept a letter in a private house, they're more
than guessing. If they'd an inkling of what she'd got – and they must know
whom she's talked to, what opportunities she's had – there's no chance
they'd let it go. No...'

'You're thinking about this Spider chappie again.' The colonel didn't
sound impressed.

'I am thinking two things about him, Colonel. First, that if he intercepts
and then releases the letter, he is playing a typically dark game. More to
do with his own power and interests than any one nation. Second, that
he is onto Miss Hathaway.'

'I had Ballentyne, Herr Krug!'

Krug gave it limited consideration. 'And once again you did nothing with him.'

'Had not your telegram—'

'Exactly so.' He contrived a mollifying smile. 'Your energy and your reflexes do you credit, Hildebrandt.' Hildebrandt didn't look mollified. 'My thinking changed. I have been guilty of... lack of perspective. We heard of Ballentyne first and I sent you after him. We have continued to treat him as a unique case.' He turned away; the shoes tapped across the floor, and the high ceiling dropped back the echo. His fingers drummed once on his desk. 'This was a mistake. There is more going on here. More that I do not understand. A hasty action would compound the mistake. For now, we may leave Ballentyne to play with Belcredi.' The eyes swung round sharp. 'As long as your people do not lose track of him.'

'Your instructions were clear, and I gave them clearly.'

'I am reassured.' A step forwards. 'I felt I needed you here, Hildebrandt. My arrangement with Colonel Nicolai, this great union of our capacities, is close to fruition. It is the time for circumspection, for clarity, for strategic thought. I feel... I feel I am close to unlocking the last door at the heart of British Intelligence.'

'Berlin is thinking of war.'

'And I, more than any man in Europe, will have the power to give Berlin victory. I will control the board, Hildebrandt; it would be imbecility to become obsessed by the fate of one pawn.'

A house in Belgrade, though Belgrade was unaware of it: a doorway from a back street, a frontage that blended into the shadows, dirt and crumbling masonry outside, scrupulous order within.

Two men talking quietly: careful calculations of deference, implicit respect.

'You told of a highlander, that was seeking a foreigner.'

Silence. Truth is contingent.

'I might have information. Or I might not. It depends upon the nature of the matter. I have the duty of a host to a guest.'

A nod at this, earnest. A moment's thought, and then the matter was described; insubstantially, allusively.

Silence again. The logs shifting in the stove as they burned. 'Very well. You may pass word to the highlander.'

<hr />

Krug at his desk. The sensual lines of its legs were merely something for his shoe to tap at irritably; its antique sheen was covered with papers, which he was no longer reading. He was staring into a photograph.

It wasn't a good photograph: more than ten years old, creased, the fuzziness of a more primitive camera with impatient subjects. A posed group of a dozen men, some in British Army uniforms, some in unmarked clothes; behind them a shed, and beyond the shed the landscape was flat and arid. Most of the men were looking at or at least towards the camera, proud or indifferent.

One face was not looking forwards; it had happened to turn as the shutter had clicked, and it was only a blur.

Krug's finger stroked the face very softly; then he stopped, uncertain, as if the stroking might make the blurring worse.

What game are we playing, old fox?

'Herr Krug?'

Krug's head snapped up, for once off-balance.

Hildebrandt was standing by the door; Krug glared at him, then sniffed. 'Come, Count Paul; sit, have a cigarette.'

Hildebrandt's boots echoed over the parquet; the face alternated pale and shaded as he passed the tall windows; he sat, watchful.

'You're an active fellow, Hildebrandt; you probably hunt, don't you?' Hildebrandt didn't reply; took a cigarette, tapped it, lit it; watched. 'Too much boisterousness for me. Sometimes one waits for the fox to break cover; sometimes one must make one's guess and ride at it. Do I have that right?'

Hildebrandt shrugged. All intelligence work was metaphor; and he could spot a rhetorical question.

'Europe is boiling. The British watch it with one eye. The other eye is worrying about Ireland, which is also boiling. The British have their spies: these new offices, for counter-espionage and for foreign work. New structures, new energy, everyone running around.' He touched the photo. 'And somewhere, in the shadows...' He was silent.

'You mean the Comptrollerate-General?' Hildebrandt had difficulty with the syllables.

'And I'm not even sure who you are.' It was addressed to the photograph; he looked up again, and the voice came with him. 'Do you see the page of Chinese script in the frame over there?' Hildebrandt glanced over his shoulder politely. 'Merely an affectation of connoisseurship, you may think.' He shook his head. 'A reminder. They are very wise philosophers, the Chinese. Of all peoples, perhaps the most naturally gifted for espionage work. Next to them, Europeans – with their energies, their enthusiasms – are like... like little children. One of the greatest of those great philosophers teaches us about "doing by not doing". You get it, Hildebrandt?' Hildebrandt tried to look thoughtful. 'I ask myself: what is the Comptroller-General for Scrutiny and Survey doing, by not doing anything?'

The German shifted in his chair. 'Perhaps he can't do anything; perhaps he is superseded by these new departments.' Krug tutted at this, waved a dismissive hand, shook his head. 'These three agents, what they are doing is not very different—'

'They are Comptrollerate-General agents!' Krug's fist hovered over the table; he caught himself, opened the hand flat, laid it soft on the papers. 'You're right. What they're doing is nothing unusual – even that wonderful young woman. She could hardly have expected such an opportunity; an unforeseen side effect of her otherwise unremarkable tour through Germany. Yet they are each impressive in their way, and they are each the choice of that man...'

Something began to warm in his face. Hildebrandt waited.

'And it is the more likely that they have seen him.' The voice was quiet, hungry. 'Think of it, Hildebrandt. With the rest of the British apparatus busier, he is quieter. We see more of them; we see less of him. It is only by the brilliance of my network that I am even aware these agents are his. No grand machinery; no chain of command. It is surely more likely that they – some of them – have met him; or know something of him, at least.' He was in the photograph. The eyes up again. 'If I could talk to one of these people. If... If I could turn one! But which?'

'Why choose?'

Krug's face opened in delight. 'Hildebrandt!' He waved a finger, mock-scold. 'You surpass yourself.' He scanned the desk. 'Ronald Ballentyne, the hunted. James Cade, the embarrassed. Flora Hathaway, the vulnerable. We have these people where we want them. We shall... issue some invitations.'

⊢══⊣

MOST SECRET S.I.B.

Circulation list 8

Periodic visit by ******* to the office of the Director of the German Imperial Railways (Ruhr Department) reports planned line expansion/redevelopment work Mannheim, Karlsruhe (S. District) and Trier, Koblenz, Aachen (Central District).

Visit also reports new logistic assessment by General Staff. Each of G. Army's 40 Corps will require railway transport as follows:

Officers 70 cars

Infantry 965 cars

Cavalry 2,960 cars

Artillery & Supply 1,915 cars

total 140 trains + additional 140 trains for supplies.

Report refers to companion report detailing provision of same, and planned deployment by route and time.

[SS D/3/1/319]

⊢══⊣

Osman Riza called on Cade a few days after he had contrived the disappearance of a body. The same as ever, as he sat upright in the guest chair: neat; careful. A bird considering a nut.

'Dear friend, I come with an offer – a suggestion. And yet please to forgive me if I suggest that there is an element of... of obligation in the matter.' Cade's open face more watchful, the smile flatter. 'And I'm sorry to raise that distasteful business at all, but... Well, you will of course recall the gentleman whose help I sought when... when...'

'When we found a corpse on my carpet with his head blown in. Mr... Silvas.'

Pained smile. 'Quite so. Well, Mr Silvas has an interest in you.'

Cade felt the kick of nausea. 'Oh, aye?' A deal gone south; your cheque cashed and a cargo of one-legged trews on the quayside.

'As someone active in commerce in Constantinople himself, he had been aware of your work before – before the incident. Since then he has taken the trouble to learn more about the firm of Cade & Cade, and about your dealings here.'

So where was the bite? *I'd expected more from you, Riza.*

'He – he would like to meet you. He would like you to visit him.'

Cade scowled. 'And, ah, now that he has... information that could embarrass me, I should expect him to make certain demands. Money?'

'Mr Cade, no! No, I am sure not.' He seemed sincere, too. 'I believe he wishes to explore the possibility of a business connection. Just an exploratory deal at the first – to see whether the two of you are suited.'

Could it be this straight?

'I'm always interested in a deal, you know that.'

'Dear friend, I must be candid with you. This is a powerful man. More powerful, perhaps, than you are used to in your affairs. But a man of business nonetheless. It is...' – Riza was wriggling for the words – 'it is not a matter of embarrassment. But he does have now... he does have an *expectation* of you. That you would be... open-minded, in considering his offer. It would – it would not do, Mr Cade, to disappoint him.' Riza leaned forwards. 'I urge you to visit him.'

Cade chewed on it. 'He truly wants a business deal? As in, an arrangement beneficial to both parties?'

'I believe it.'

'Well enough.' He didn't like the sense of compulsion, but if the ground was level then a Cade would come out even at least. 'I'm going to need a pile more information from you, my friend, about this fellow.' Riza nodded cautiously. 'Where is this to be? Here?'

'No, Mr Cade. You are... invited... to Vienna.'

<hr />

'Your brother the Austrian is packing.' It was a joke among the Albanians, who here too thought Ballentyne and Belcredi amusingly alike, two fair Anglo-Saxons of an age and build. Ballentyne didn't find it funny.

'Any idea where he's going?'

'Vienna, it seems. While he is here we will not lose him. But if you want to follow, you must be ready now.' Ballentyne nodded, and stood. 'He sent two telegrams.' Two papers were handed over; Ballentyne didn't ask how they'd been acquired.

One was to the offices of the International Cultural Exchange in Sarajevo, informing the manager of when Belcredi would be arriving in Vienna. The second was longer.

TO: HVE VIA ATHENESINSTITUT BERLIN.
FROM: HPB MOSKVA HOTEL BELGRADE. OUR FRIENDS
INSIST I TRAVEL VIENNA. FURTHER DISTRACTION TO
OUR WORK. EXPECT RETURN DAYS AND NEW PROGRESS IN
FERTILE GROUND HERE. YOUR CAUSE AND YOUR SUPPORT
NEAREST MY HEART.

[SS X/72/N/3 (Copy, translated)]

Ballentyne shook his head at it, and pushed the message into his pocket. He held up the first. 'Why tell Sarajevo when you arrive in Vienna?' It was addressed to the paper. He looked up. 'If he arrives in Vienna at 6 p.m., when does his train leave?'

'One hour.'

'I need a smart lad with fast legs.'

Sir, at last a shadow of our young friend [presumably R.
Ballentyne, from context]. Assume has been hiding among
Albanians here but active. Following BELCREDI to Vienna. By
his envoy I have intercept messages of same. Will forward. I
have given name of reliable friend.

[SS G/1/891/14 (DECYPHERED)]

A knock, a word, and Colonel Mayhew was in the old man's doorway.
'Duval's disappeared.'

The old man's eyebrows rose a fraction. Mayhew closed the door behind
him. 'I say "disappeared"; we've an idea where he's headed, but the point
is that he's slipped his leash – he's rogue.'

The old man considered this. 'Mm. That presupposes that we ever really
had control of him.'

'I expressed my doubts, you will remember.'

Thin smile. 'It was noted, Colonel. Do we know what's prompted this?'

'No. As we ordered, he met Frosch, the shipping man. My man Lisson
saw him later that night, and he reported back one or two useful details
that he'd got from Frosch. The Larne incident. Should be on your desk
any time.'

'I hope so. Then what?'

The old man was looking even older, Mayhew thought; more tired, more
dusty. 'Lisson got a message mid-morning that Duval wanted to meet at
noon. He never showed, and it seems he'd paid a lad to send the message.
He'd hooked it hours earlier.' There was something like amusement on
the old man's face, a hint in the lips. Mayhew didn't like it; something
pitying. 'A body of pillows under the sheets in case the maid stuck her
head in first thing, bag still there, but he was long gone: back stairs or out
the window in the small hours. That's another hotel bill unpaid, too; my

287

man's hopping m—'

'Yet you know where he's going.'

'Indeed.' Mayhew looked even more stiff than usual. 'Interceptions from the Russian secret police and German Intelligence: they were both watching Duval.'

'Goodness. Popular fellow. And where, Colonel, is he going?'

'Vienna.'

Something changed in the old face; it was the first time Mayhew had noticed the slightest loss of control – the first suggestion of real emotion. 'But how?' The eyes, the voice were far off. 'How did he get to Duval?'

'I've – I've lost you there.'

'You never had me, Colonel.'

Mayhew waited, uneasy.

'Yesterday, Cade reported through the embassy that he was off to Vienna to pursue a business opportunity. This morning I received a message from an acquaintance in Belgrade reporting that Ballentyne was following a trail he had picked up in Albania and then Serbia, and that the trail was leading Ballentyne to Vienna. Just before you arrived, I received a letter in the usual style from Miss Hathaway; her German friend has proposed an excursion. You can guess whither, can you, Colonel?' He straightened Hathaway's letter on the desk in front of him. Tapped instinctively at the other papers. 'You see the pattern, I take it. In each case our agent believes they are heading to Vienna on their initiative. The... coincidence is not credible. They are being lured there. But Duval – I don't see how Duval has been lured. Perhaps if we knew more.'

Mayhew had the point now. His hands fidgeted; he wanted action. 'Can't we stop them?'

'I doubt it. And... I don't want to.' The old man's eyes were frozen solid. He steepled his fingers together slowly, as if making a house of cards out of them. 'I wanted to provoke a reaction. I have done so.' The voice was calculating; cold; lost. 'I had not believed it would be so complete, so inclusive.' He let out a breath, long, thin, a whisper of wind across the floor of a ruined church. 'But we have no choice now.'

Mayhew was far away; and irritated. 'What – what does any of this mean?'

'It means the Spider is hungry. He has watched the flies, and now he is ready.' He looked up. 'I wanted them spotted, Colonel. I wanted the Spider to notice these agents. I wanted him to show himself.' The voice dropped again. 'If it's Vienna, it's one of two men. Hermes wouldn't be able to operate effectively there.'

'Spider...' Mayhew was still grappling with the folly of the old man's scheme. 'Wait; you said "you wanted". Respect your ideas and so forth... I've taken your advice, sir – naturally recognizing your, er – but – but...'

The old man considered him. 'Colonel, I think we may be reaching the point where this business exceeds your responsibility; best perhaps if you take a step back, now.' A dead smile. 'Prudent, too.'

'But... but I'm—'

'A loyal and senior officer of Military Intelligence, Colonel, and rightly respected as such. If it helps, I will arrange that within ten minutes you receive confirmation from Sir Henry Wilson regarding the... circumstances.'

'You mean General Wilson knows—'

'General Wilson knows very little of this, nor does he wish to. But he does know that there are powers behind him; greater than him.'

'We're supposed to be getting away from this old-fashioned amateur stuff. New departments, clear responsibilities.'

The eyes snapped up, and the voice. 'Believe me, Colonel, I am doing what I can to help those new departments through their rather fraught infancy. I strongly suspect that thus far they have been responsible for little more than drawing attention to Duval, perhaps to Hamel, who now lies at the bottom of the Channel, and to who knows what else.'

'I'm – ah – not following.'

'No, Colonel.' Behind the desk, in the dust, the eyes were again cold and far away. 'You're not. It's relatively simple: I have staked the future of British Intelligence – our ability to shape the affairs of Europe – on those four lives. I need to speak to Major Knox, now.'

⊹═══⊹

Agron Balaj had always been the other one.

He always seemed to be standing with his brother when things were happening, understanding a moment slower what those things were. The two Balaj brothers, Burim and the other one. The two Balaj brothers standing in front of their father, Burim getting screamed at, getting punched, the other one watching and worrying and trying to understand.

Agron thought slower because he thought deeper, that's what no one seemed to realize; he laughed to himself about it. Wandering through the village with his brother, oh, there's unlucky Burim, and the other one, and Agron watching it all and thinking deeply, hahaha.

They all thought he was simple; his father thought it, Burim thought it, everyone in the village. They said so, to his face, and they didn't worry that he would hear. Because he was simple, so it didn't matter; hahaha. He knew. His thoughts weren't simple, oh no; quite the opposite, they were complicated. His thoughts flowed, and wandered, and stopped, and considered, and walked off on their own path, down the river to the market, or over the pass, because sometimes he was on his own, he wasn't just the other one, although usually he was, down the river to market with his brother, through the fields, over the pass to the Kelmendi.

Agron got into trouble with his brother, and people disliked him with his brother, but his brother usually got the blame, because he was just the other one, hahaha, seeing it all. Sitting in the Kelmendi village by the fire, a very warm memory that was, somehow warmer than others, sitting with his brother and talking to the Kelmendi and to the foreigner, not a nice man but polite to his brother and that made him think. They'd sat nearer the fire in the Kelmendi village, that's why it had been warmer. The foreigner wanting to talk about their village, and listening to his brother's complaints, and then business and arrangements and money, none of it with him, except suddenly he'd told them about the gully near the mill and how easy it was to hide there and the foreigner had looked at him first because he was surprised that the other one could speak at all, everyone had said he was simple, and then looked at him with smaller eyes; and Agron knew that the foreigner knew that they were both men who thought deeply, hahaha.

Agron Balaj had always been the other one, until the day when he did not go with his brother to the market, and instead his brother's wife went and his brother did not return, and Agron became the only one.

The wife, that was strange; he'd thought a lot about that.

Agron had never exactly enjoyed life with his brother, just being the other one, second, forgotten, might as well wander the paths for ever, no one talked to him, no one even blamed him, but there was something. Some feeling about being with his brother; not a feeling of being with his brother but a feeling when he wasn't with his brother. Uncomfortable, when he wasn't with his brother, when he was walking along the edge of a field and someone spoke to him and they weren't speaking to his brother because he wasn't with his brother, and he had to look. So much harder to think then, much more uncomfortable.

The woman changed all that. A woman, not like his mother, not noise and curses and knowing he was simple and being the other one. Just a woman, a face, a body, different shape and different smell, and watching him as he ate the food she served, breasts in the blouse as he was trying to eat, hips moving near him as he tried to work. And his brother became different too, sharper, less relaxed, less with him.

Agron thought deeply about it all. He heard them at night, hahaha, heard his brother's animal noises, heard nothing actually from the woman except maybe if he listened closely some grunt of discomfort.

And one day his brother needed someone to go to market with him, and Agron couldn't be with him, and so she went, and came back alone, and Agron became the only one. His mother gave up on life that night, barely grieved for Burim, just disappeared into her bed and did not bother speaking to Agron, the only one, because he was simple.

So Agron's life became silent. His mother like a ghost, and his dead brother's wife who stayed in the house and continued to serve him as she should, breasts and hips and watching him and never a word.

Agron liked the silence. His thoughts seemed to flow more strongly and clearly in the silence. Wander the paths over the mountains, flow like the river in spring. Hahaha.

One night, shots near the Balaj house on the edge of the village, the village waking in alarm, hearing a scream. Shots could have been ignored easily, the scream less so. Adem and the other men found Besa huddled in the house babbling of bandits, but not before they found the body of

Agron lying in the doorway.

Agron Balaj, who had betrayed his sister-in-law's brother to death, was dead; his cursed, unlucky family was extinct. Besa returned to her mother's house, to the rest of the village. The Balaj were forgotten.

Vienna

A guidebook, open on a train seat and ignored:

> Vienna is the city of the world's civilization, for its development
> through the ages has reflected, and indeed has led, the develop-
> ment of man from primitivism to culture. First a settlement of
> the gold-obsessed barbarian Celts, it then felt the influence of
> Roman order; likewise the mediaeval epoch gave both its trad-
> ing energies and its superstitions, and was in time supplanted
> by the baroque, which has ornamented the city with so many
> of its present jewels. These refinements made it natural and
> right that the city should become, at the start of the nineteenth
> century, the capital of a great and multifarious empire, and the
> centre of world diplomacy. The Imperial Age added grandeur to
> Vienna, and brought to its finest elaboration the development
> of man's cultural taste. The work of L. Beethoven, J. Haydn and
> W. Mozart proved only the foundation of later refinements in
> music and art and the intellectual sphere. By the beginning of
> the twentieth century, this city of two millions was the temple
> to which looked, as if by natural impulsion, fifty millions of Im-
> perial subjects of the greatest diversity in race and religion and
> quality, and beyond them the world.

Vienna is where, by diverse routes and through suburbs of endless
squalor, Europe's railway lines meet.

⊹══⊹

A screaming of whistles and wheels on points and a baby clutched
uncomfortably in its mother's arms just opposite, and Major Valentine

Knox gritted his teeth and stared into the night and tried to will the train onwards by anger alone.

It didn't work, and the unchanging rumbling of the wheels only increased his frustration.

Confusion. Inefficiency. Chaos. The tedious journey back through central Europe. A message pushed into his hand as he stepped off the train at Strasbourg. Racing as instructed to meet Colonel Mayhew in Paris. And in Paris there had been no Mayhew, just the old man.

Knox had remembered the old man from his first briefings with Mayhew. One of the last of the old amateurs; given an office to keep him happy until he got round to dying; tolerated in the margins of the new operations, occasional ideas and worthy homilies, because Britain's long history was what distinguished her from a lot of these continental countries and Britain respected her veteran warhorses. Such had been Knox's assumption, confirmed with murmurs by Colonel Mayhew when they'd taken a whisky and soda together before the major set off on his travels.

Except Mayhew seemed to have stepped out of the picture now, and when Knox had slipped into the room at the back of a bicycle shop by the Canal Saint Martin – not a rendezvous on the official list for Paris – it had been the old man, standing in the gloom, who'd given him a sandwich and a flask of brandy and his instructions.

Nothing of the duffer about him, and Knox realized afterwards that most of his previous recollections of the old man had been assumptions, and vague. Now there was only clarity, and a kind of coldness that even Knox, with his experience of battle and of espionage, found unsettling.

Four agents had been sent into Europe. All four were now in danger. For each there were hints – likely point of arrival, forwarding address, possible contact – but no more. The train for Vienna left in thirty minutes and Knox would be on it. It was naturally desirable that Knox try to protect the four if he could.

But it was not the priority, and this had been the point when Knox's irritation at the amateur toing and froing in Military Intelligence business had been replaced by unease; by the sense that there were things he did not know, and habits of battle that even he had not learned.

There was a man. A spy; the greatest of the spies. The old man's words: *He is the whisper in the ear, the eye at the keyhole, in Paris and Petersburg and a dozen other places, and wherever there is violence he is the man supplying the bullets.* The objective of the four agents had been to uncover details of this man – confusion again for Knox, trying to recover his original orders, the certainty offered by the new offices in London – and now this man had lured them all to Vienna.

Knox had tried to reimpose some discipline, something of himself, on the conversation: what then were his orders regarding this master spy? And the old man, matter-of-fact: *If we came closer to war, and if I could be more sure who he was, and if I could reach him, I would have him killed. He is that dangerous.* But the old man did not know, and for now Europe was at peace and the scandal could not be tolerated, and the old man seemed to like the situation even less than did Knox. A final reflection: *He is the minotaur in the labyrinth; he is the spider in the web.* And a reminder to Knox to keep his strength up, and confirmation that Knox had a pistol with him.

Knox caught his face in the compartment window, saw the tension around eyes and jaw; and then, oddly – a flash of imagination – the faces of Ballentyne and Cade and Duval, and Hathaway, observing his tension with their different styles of amusement.

Won't seem so bloody funny when... No. Inefficient. The enforced inactivity must be used for planning. *And eventually even this train must reach its destination, and Valentine Knox will be unleashed.*

The baby opened its mouth again to scream.

◁━▷

Sir, Nicolai departed this morning unknown destination
though timing and station suggest Vienna. Objective to
quote finalize details diplomatic wedding unquote.

[SS D/2/114 (DECYPHERED)]

Vienna.

In Belgrade, Pickford had disappeared. Potentially, Pickford and Ballentyne between them would reveal the music teacher in Vienna.

The old man adjusted the position of the paper on the blotter.

And a little joke from the notoriously humourless Nicolai. Nicolai's machine and the Spider's network united.

The Spider would have access to Germany's chain of agents in Britain...

<hr/>

Krug was reading a newspaper when Hildebrandt showed in Colonel Nicolai. He stood, and covered half of the distance to the door to meet his guest, still holding the newspaper.

Handshake; bows. It was Nicolai's first visit to Krug's office in Vienna. Not his sort of place, but what he would have expected. Over-pretty; decorations fiddly.

Searching for an adequate greeting; *small talk*. He gestured to the newspaper. 'What is happening in the world today?'

Krug beckoned him towards a chair. Then he brandished the newspaper. 'Forgive me a childish pleasure, Colonel, but it is always amusing to see one of one's little interventions echoing around Europe. The pebble in the pool, and the ripples, if you will.' Nicolai nodded. 'In this case, we may jointly take the credit, I think. Grey in London has been forced to deny in his parliament that there have been negotiations with or obligations accepted to Russia.'

'He lies.'

'Of course he lies, Colonel. Technically not, perhaps, but essentially yes. And I can think of few men in Europe for whom a lie could be more uncomfortable than the British foreign secretary. Such a very careful man. Now he will be discreetly cursing the generals for putting him in this position. And the Russians will be cursing this new piece of perfidy from the British. And those negotiations will have been retarded.' He smiled, and placed the newspaper on the desk. 'We have done a good day's work for our masters, Colonel.'

A knock, and a servant brought in three glasses of wine. Hildebrandt sat at the side of the room.

Nicolai glanced at him, then looked at Krug.

'You will say that I am a pedantic Prussian, Herr Krug' – polite denial on Krug's face – 'but I would like to return to the question of security. Both in our general procedures, and... so to say...'

'The distinct protection of our individual networks?'

A little smile. 'Exactly. Thank you. Count Hildebrandt's reassurances about your rigorousness regarding security have been the most important reassurance to my superiors.'

A nod. 'I am pleased to hear it. As you imply, we must be able to benefit from each other, without in any way jeopardizing the careful systems that we have each built.'

'It is well put, Mein Herr. For example, I will not ask to know the identities of your individual contacts—'

'Although there may be occasions when it would be appropriate, in which case I would be content to share them with you, personally and alone, so that you may better judge the material.' Stiff nod from Nicolai. 'For the most part, I will continue to use my contacts as best I can to support you in any problem you care to put to me. It may be possible on rare occasions for German Intelligence officials to contact them direct, but...'

'Unnecessary and best avoided.'

'Thank you. For my part, Colonel, I do not seek direct contact with your networks.' Nod again. 'But perhaps it would be convenient if I was able to put questions or messages into your networks via your regular embassy channels.'

'I have secured approval for you to have a code designation that will demonstrate to any of my officials in any German embassy that you are a trusted person, for whom any legitimate business not obviously detrimental to the German interest should be transacted. This designation does not reveal your identity, but it is distinct from the usual designations of German Military Intelligence headquarters.'

'Why, Colonel, this is excellent. An ideal arrangement, and I'm grateful for your efficiency.'

'Should there be any disruption or irregularity in the system, my intermediaries in the embassies have orders to break off contact and institute the regular procedures to change all codes.'

'I am pleased to hear it. I should say from my side that none of my contacts knows my identity and the full extent of my activities, and that none has known or will know if a particular question or request is on behalf of the German government or not. I am confident that no action against any one of my contacts can mean a threat to me – or, now, to my partners.'

Nicolai considered it all, and nodded. 'The Imperial Government is satisfied,' he said, heavy. It was a phrase he clearly enjoyed saying. Krug contrived a bow.

Nicolai sipped his wine. 'Hildebrandt says you have an operation under way.'

A glance from Krug to Hildebrandt, and a moment's consideration. 'A little entertainment I have devised. And I confess it gives me great satisfaction. I have lured to Vienna, Colonel, three agents of the British Comptrollerate-General for Scrutiny and Survey. Three! Never before has that... that shadow had such substance; never before have I had my hand so firmly on it. One is an old friend of Hildebrandt's, whom he will meet again with productive results for us all. One is an agent from Constantinople. The third...' – pause for effect – 'is an old acquaintance of yours, Colonel.'

'Ah yes, I wondered about the coincidence. The Englishman from Berlin, no?'

Now the glance between Krug and Hildebrandt was confusion. 'No, Colonel. The woman from the Margaretenhof. What Englishman?'

'The man we were tracking. He who met the woman. Our agents have noted him in St Petersburg, and now travelling here. They report to me that he is also being watched by the Russian secret police, and by the French, and now presumably by your Austrian police too.'

Krug had lost his mask. He was thought, and it brought out the lines and character in his face. 'But surely not... He too? What game is this?' Again to Hildebrandt: 'You know my attitude to coincidence.'

→≡≡←

Vienna is where, by diverse routes and through suburbs of endless squalor, Europe's railway lines meet. At precisely 6 p.m. the Paris express slowed to the buffers amid an explosion of steam and the first banging of opening doors. One man was out before the rest, eyes set and striding hard. High above him, a click and the straining of a spring, and the clock chimed the hour.

⇥⇤

Cade

The station clock struck six, and Cade checked his watch against it.

A fraction slow. He adjusted and began to wind the watch, the tiny sawing of the mechanism nagging at him.

Have you lost your way a shade, Jimmy?

The death of Muhtar, and the mysterious Silvas, were facts. And they were history; nothing more. What to make of Vienna?

Trade. He drained the glass, felt the beer's fizz in his nose and head, and cracked it down on the table.

As he walked across the concourse towards the exit he saw a man being escorted by two policemen; clearly under arrest – as they came nearer he saw a third policeman behind with pistol drawn. He'd noticed the escort first – the rifles high, the uniforms – and it was a moment before curiosity drew him to the face of the prisoner, when they were only yards apart, and he saw that it was Major Valentine Knox.

Cade stopped. A thump into his back from someone behind, a glance from one of the policemen, a glance from Knox, dead-faced, and it was the hammering of Cade's heart that urged him into movement again.

Knox and his guards were thirty yards off, heading for a set of offices built into the side of the station. He watched the group into one of the doors, saw it close.

It couldn't be coincidence.

Move, you daft bugger! Standing there like a fart in a storm. Move. Don't draw attention. Get clear. Get things straight. *Cades don't rattle.*

Things weren't much straighter by the time he reached the Hotel Stefanie a quarter-hour later. But he knew he had to meet Silvas, and he knew Knox was irrelevant to that, and at the Stefanie there was a message for him: Elisabethstraße; seven-thirty.

Wash. Clean shirt. Ginger himself up a bit. They were serving a fizzy water in the bar, and he ordered one. A flash of his conversation with Riza, whenever it had been. Keep the nut clear.

Perhaps Knox's presence really had been coincidence. It was seven o'clock as he came out of the bar and made for the concierge's desk. Bit grim to see him being banged up like that.

There were a couple of girls heading for the desk at the same moment, and he gave them a second glance. His own age, perhaps; frocks smart, well-cut, nothing too fancy; one was a glorious golden thing, the other darker, more subtly handsome. *Someone's got his blood back, eh Jimmy?*

They were speaking German. He'd only ever learned enough for polite correspondence, but it served for the gist. As they all three reached the desk together the blonde was talking about needing something – or someone – and then... Then she'd switched to English: 'or perhaps Major Knox.'

The dark girl said something and the blonde was talking to one of the fellows behind the desk and he was saying something back and Cade got none of it.

Cades don't rattle. Cades don't rattle.

Some extraordinary coinci— But no. There had to be a reason why Vienna had suddenly become a reunion of the Knox Appreciation Society.

He couldn't begin to think what.

Faintly, through his own unease, a sense of something wider. The blonde had moved away from the desk but the dark girl was still there. Cade, a desperate instinct, murmured: 'If you're acquainted with Major Valentine Knox, you need to listen to me, right now. I'll be across the lobby.'

He handed over his key, got directions to Elisabethstraße, and turned away.

Across the lobby there was a display of mementoes – chocolates, lithographs of notable Viennese, chinaware adopting styles of the city's Roman past – and he stood in front of it.

His body was electrified. At any moment a hand on his shoulder, a whistle, arrest as a confederate of Major Knox.

There was no link between him and Knox. But what if—

Movement beside him. A glance gave him a glimpse of her profile, staring into the trinkets.

A breath, swallowed. *She doesn't want to commit herself.* Friend rather than enemy. 'What did—'

'One hour ago, Major Knox was under arrest at the station.' He leaned forwards to examine the detail on an urn, then turned and strode away.

It was twenty-five minutes through a pleasant evening to Elisabethstraße. Fashions conservative, but affluent. Shopfronts unimaginative, but of unquestionable quality. Money in Vienna, no doubt about it.

He'd done what he could.

A side street only a couple of hundred yards from the palaces. A door like all the others. A plaque: *Adriatisch Handelsverein.* Adriatic... trading union?

The door opened promptly to his knock. A uniformed footman, stair carpet thick as he climbed, wall-mounted electric lights: discreet money. Would he excuse a slight delay? Would he take some refreshment?

A couple more minutes. Then fast feet on the stairs – the first discordance with the calm – and words in German: 'His death is not a problem; but a lost chance, that is all.'

Had he heard the words right? Cade frowned; sipped his fizzy water.

Another minute, and then the uniform was back and beckoning to him. But as Cade got to the door there was a young man hurrying across the landing ahead of him, knocking at the double doors that dominated the space and then sticking his head through. Cade, behind, heard something about 'an Englishman, asking for Valfierno', and then from within the double doors there was a blast of angry German and the young man was backing out and glancing at Cade and hurrying away.

The doorman knocked, Cade checked his tie, and then he was in.

A man of about his own age, dark-haired and good-looking, was already halfway across the room to meet him. 'My dear Mr Cade.' Strong but not fulsome. 'We are most grateful you have come. A pleasure, sir.' A single handshake, firm and held for a moment, and released. 'My name is Paul Henschler.'

More refreshment? No. A cigarette? This time he accepted.

Unfortunately Mr Silvas could not be with them. Cade produced gracious regret, wondering if Henschler was the real name, wondering if there was a Silvas, wondering if he was watching somehow. Pleasantries exchanged, and Cade studied the man in front of him: a sharpness, a decisiveness, yet the sense that business wasn't his natural environment. He seemed somehow too strong for trade alone. And he was studying Cade just as Cade was studying him.

Furniture good but not showy; a telephone on the desk. Prosperity and activity.

Henschler began a polite interrogation of Cade & Cade. The ownership. How much of the business was cloth and dry goods. Whether they had shops. Involvement of partners. The German had done his homework.

'What prompted you to open an office in Constantinople, Mr Cade?'

He'd tried to make it sound conversational, but it came out blunt.

'Couple of things, really. An experiment in putting ourselves further up the supply chain, and cutting out the middlemen of continental Europe. And, personally speaking' – smile – 'the chance to see a bit of life.' Henschler nodded.

Cade took the opportunity to reverse the interrogation. What sort of partnership did Silvas envisage? Why were they interested in someone new to Constantinople? Presumably for the potential trade with Britain, no? And more about their business. Henschler and Silvas dealt in import-export, with some investment activity; they were active throughout the Austrian Empire, with good links in the Balkans, and some into western Europe. On the specifics – the nature of the ownership, whether the stock was traded, the relationship with those markets – Henschler's answers became general, even uncertain. He might be a decisive figurehead, but he was not a businessman.

The telephone rang, and Henschler answered it. His eyes stayed on Cade. Words in German, then a smile: 'It is Mr Silvas himself. He wishes to greet you.'

Cade stood and took the apparatus.

'Mr James Cade? I'm delighted that we have the chance to speak.' The voice had the usual distortion, as if coming down a drainpipe in a blizzard, but Cade got the accent, and the courtliness. 'I was disappointed that we could not meet; I trust you are seeing the best of us, regardless.'

'Very pleasant and impressive welcome, Mr Silvas.'

'It would be such a pleasure if we could co-operate, Mr Cade. I have gained such a positive impression of you. The little... difficulty you had was so tiresome, and I was delighted we could help you through it.'

'That was – that was very kind of you.' Henschler was sometimes watching him talk, and sometimes consulting a handwritten list on the desk.

'When I have an idea, Mr Cade, I don't tolerate obstacles. Now my idea is to work with you.' More of the same; final pleasantries, and then the connection was all blizzard, and he handed the apparatus back to Henschler.

The dark fellow replaced the receiver in its cradle, and glanced up. 'You see, he does exist, Mr Cade,' and at that Cade had to laugh. *Still wouldn't trust you an inch with a tuppenny bit, but professionals you surely are.*

'As he said on the telephone, Mr Henschler, it'll be up to me to decide on your proposal.' Henschler nodded. 'Or... do you feel that I am under a certain... obligation to you now?' He had to say it.

Henschler gazed at him. Then sniffed. 'Facts are facts, Mr Cade. We need not invest them with emotion. You'll be taking a business decision.' Cade started to nod. 'And yet... Mr Silvas can be a persuasive – even aggressive – businessman. You'll strike a hard bargain, no doubt, but I dare say you'll be working with us in the end.'

The threat was there. But it seemed that the worst he'd be getting was a genuine deal that he might not otherwise have chosen to take up – and perhaps a few business snippets to keep London happy. He said: 'I'll look forward to the bargaining.'

A knock, and a man approached Henschler and leaned close. Henschler kept watching Cade. Murmuring from the man, and at the end of it, distinctly, Cade caught the phrase, *'Er ist tot.'*

He is dead.

He'd heard that clear enough. And this was something different to what he'd overheard on the landing, and Henschler's reaction was different: acceptance – no, satisfaction. Still watching Cade.

A kick in his brain; a memory of his twenty-five-year-old self. Glasgow docks, a lantern-lit office, a man a foot taller than him and broken-nosed, an errand from his father to overcome a hold-up with the off-loading of some cloth from a freighter, a test of young James's mettle. Then, a man had

303

come in with bloody knuckles, bragging to the broken nose that someone wouldn't be obstructive any more, and broken nose had kept on looking at Cade, and Cade with bowels like jelly had tried to hold his pose of suavity and gone hurrying back to the old 'un babbling of criminals and cut-throats. And the old 'un, matter-of-fact, like he was commenting on Jimmy's school report: 'Aye, boy; but did ye get oor cloth out?'

Do nothing criminal yourself, but do not be surprised that there are criminals.

The man across the desk was watching him with calculation, and Cade wondered if his expression had showed that he understood.

This was not Scotland, and the name of Cade & Cade was not known here, to police or to whatever ruthless men ran the front lines of trade. He, too, could very easily end up *tot* and few would know and the few who cared were far away. Cade was back in a Glasgow shack, with the sick instinct that common sense alone would not save him.

⊹═══⊹

Duval

The station clock struck six, and it drew Duval's attention up the inside of the building. Another Viennese barn. Lord, but they did grand here, didn't they? All very stable and do what you're told.

Another train had come in while he'd been drinking; two – there seemed to be two streams of people heading away from the platforms, and the concourse was filling with those waiting to leave. It was like the flushing of the city; the old lot out, and a fresh rush of people in.

At the station offices to the side – Duval fancied himself a bit of an expert on railway administrative arrangements now – policemen were herding someone into a doorway. He felt a moment of sympathy. Outside the offices, a man had stopped and was staring. *That's right, old chap; meditate on your sins.*

Another journey across the boundaries of the world, another new city, another new start. He sent his bags ahead to the Grand, and walked. Every building in the city seemed self-satisfied. But, here and there, something sprightly in glass or ironwork, as if gypsies had come out of some distant part of the empire to dance for the bourgeois.

Frosch the smuggler had told him that among the many poses and impostures of the man who called himself the Marquis of Valfierno was one secret pleasure. He had installed himself, or been installed, as the figurehead of a conservatoire of music in Vienna – 'He has no ability for any instrument, that one! No, like a monkey with a violin! But he loves music and loves to think of himself as connoisseur. Ah, such a charming life!' – and because of this pleasure, and because the woman he called his daughter liked to play, he was often to be found there.

A doze, a clean shirt, two glasses of wine – nice crisp white the Austrians did – and it was past seven when he arrived at the Conservatoire. He'd paid off the taxi early. Had to go carefully.

The front of the Conservatoire was a set of high, heavy-curtained windows bracketing a discreetly signed door. Mustn't seem to loiter. At the side there was an alley, leading to a cobbled square behind the building. Duval crossed the square into another shadow, and looked back.

At the rear of the Conservatoire, on the ground floor, a single room stretched the width of the building and projected into the square. Apart from the framework of iron and wood – rather elegant – it was all glass. Through the glass he could see a highly polished wooden floor, a chandelier, some plants and a grand piano.

There was another alley leading back down the other side of the Conservatoire. Halfway along it he found a side door, open a crack.

Half-open doorways are an eternal enticement; and an eternal unease. Perhaps...

From inside he heard voices. One had a German accent but was talking English; the other wasn't English but nor, presumably, was he a German-speaker.

'What do you mean "delayed"?'

'The other woman, the German, came first. She was supposed—'

'I know what was supposed to happen! Where is the Englishwoman?'

'She is coming a few minutes later; that is all we were told.'

A burst of angry German, then English again. 'I cannot wait! All our timings have been thrown.'

'Just a few min—'

'I must get to Porzellangasse, to the Englishman. Or Belcredi will have lost him, or shot himself in the foot or surrendered or some such.'

'And if the other—'

'Just keep the women apart! You have the drug; use a gun if you must. You: come with me!'

The door was yanked open and Duval had pushed himself back against the wall and the man who emerged turned the other way, towards the main street. A tall man, dark-haired, pulling on a hat and striding hard; he was followed by another.

Duval held himself for a frozen moment longer.

From somewhere above him, he could hear a piano.

An Englishwoman walking into a trap. An Englishman in more immediate trouble. The key chap was the dark-haired one – presumably the German – and he was heading to Porzellangasse. *Move.*

The German looked like he was going to walk – obviously it was close – but Duval flagged down a horse-cab and thrust gold at the driver and urged him to Porzellangasse, and the cab lurched forwards before he could sit and the hooves were rattling over the cobbles.

They reached Porzellangasse inside a minute. He had a head start on the German. But so what?

A bell clanged somewhere and the cabman swore and Duval heard the cab shifting away as a tram lurched round from behind him and began to moan along Porzellangasse.

He began to follow it, looking for inspiration. The houses smart but not grand. A hundred yards ahead, the tram swayed around a bend. Duval pressed on, glancing at the occasional plaque, peering at windows. The street was empty in the dusk now.

The bend was not a sharp one, but from his pavement it had been enough to obscure the other half of Porzellangasse. As he turned the bend, immediately, twenty yards ahead, there was a man pausing in front of a doorway. Checking a number beside it, looking up at a window; reaching for the bell.

The clothes were wrong. They were a traveller's clothes: tweedy, hard-worn. A man from out of town.

An Englishman?

The door opened and the man disappeared.

Duval walked on towards the house. A glance at the number – 33 – and the windows told him no more than it had the other man. But like those of the Conservatoire, the builders of this house had thoughtfully set it beside an alley; many of the houses had the same – access to gardens, or mews, perhaps. Duval slipped into its darkness.

The alley stretched the length of the houses. He edged forwards. At the back of the houses the alley continued between six-foot walls, presumably enclosing gardens. Another few steps in the gloom, and now he heard voices.

They seemed to be coming from inside the house, but that was only possible if there was a window open at the back, over the garden.

Another few steps forwards, and Duval tripped on something and fell headlong and crashed into a dustbin. The greatest possible clattering, lid on bin and there must have been a second bin and that was clattering and he was scrambling to his feet and trying to free himself from metal and stench and gaping round himself, and immediately he saw that what he'd tripped over was the body of a man.

Gasping, heart-lurching confusion and he vaulted back over the body and ran, the way he'd come, squeezing past a tram as it swung round the bend in Porzellangasse and away. He didn't stop running until he'd two more turns and two blocks behind him.

Then out into a main street again, and slowing and trying to recapture his breath. *Now what?*

Keep moving. On a corner next to a milliner's, a beggar woman pushed a flower at him. He took it without thinking, found a coin and laid it on the grimy hand, and hurried on wondering whether the coin was too small or too big.

By a fountain, he stopped and smoked a cigarette. The Conservatoire. That was why he'd come. Besides, Englishwoman in trouble there. Decent thing. He pushed the flower into his buttonhole; it was too large, and sagged sadly on his lapel.

He took a deliberately roundabout route; seemed the thing to do, on this night of strangeness. It was around half past seven when he contrived to find the back way to the Conservatoire, through an archway and into the cobbled square. As he emerged into it, hungry for shadows, he found a motor car parked beside him, shuddering with the vibration of its engine.

No driver; must be nearby though. The car's bulk helped shield him, and he watched the Conservatoire. With evening closing in, even the few lamps inside made the glass room shine; the square was dark around it, as if the salon itself had become a lantern. Now, from wherever it was, he could hear the piano more distinctly.

Inside, vivid in the brightness, there was a woman, and Duval's heart kicked. The girl on the train?

But no. Something about the way she held herself was different, and even from across the square the face seemed wrong.

The Englishwoman?

What am I doing here? He started to move across the square, pressed against the wall, fingers feeling stone and mouldings and doorposts, wanting to wrap the shadows around his shoulders. The notes of the piano fell singly out of the sky onto him, footsteps, heartbeats, fingers brushed over his hands.

The girl had stood, was pacing. By the time he got level with the glass conservatory, her back was to him. An instinctive consideration of her figure.

Get her attention? A tap at the window; a warning. But what could he say? And how would she react to a face leering out of the night at her?

He moved past the brilliance of the conservatory into the darkness of the alley again.

And then something revolted in him. While a city murmured and glowed with life, while trams raced and men hurried on decisive errands and handsome women paced brilliant salons and somewhere someone played the piano – and it was impossible to play the piano without a human feeling for another human, even if it was a feeling of longing or of absence – while all this life rose and fell in chords around him, he was skulking in an alley.

He had come to define himself by how much he could not exist: by not being seen, by running. He had come to seek the shadow and not the light. It was the wretchedness of the spy, and it was making him a non-person.

He must act. He must be.

He stepped to the side door, and knocked.

A moment, and then footsteps inside.

He realized he still had the fugitive's hunch, and straightened himself. Clean shirt; buttonhole.

The door was pulled open quickly, and a face emerged expectant and then confused.

'Good evening. I wish to see the Marquis de Valfierno, please.' *Should have used the front door.*

Hesitation.

'Bitte – bitte warten sie hier.' And the door closed again.

Valfierno's name meant something.

A few yards away down the alley, the glow of the conservatory. He moved towards it, moth to flame. Didn't want to startle the girl; wouldn't mind a look at her face.

In the weeks out of place there had been glimpses of rightness. A woman calling herself Anna, hungry for life and finding it in him. The glances of two handsome women crossing a Berlin square. A kiss in a train corridor, peaches and defiance.

The piano notes in the air; he looked up. At the top of one of the buildings on the square, right at the corner where it glowed pale against the dying sky, a pilaster flared out under the eaves. A whimsy; an elegant way to take the vertical line of the pilaster and unite it with the projection of the roof edge. And a swan's neck of a curve; something that could not be designed, something that could only be felt.

A window lit up in the wall below the eaves, and a woman's shoulders and head appeared in it, naked. *Her?* Of course not. But as the woman in the window looked upwards, neck stretching and skin warm as if he could feel it under his fingers, for an instant the curve of her throat under her chin matched exactly the curve of the moulding outside.

An impossible, unrepeatable flash of harmony in the universe, an absolute beauty, and Duval felt a cold thrill.

Hathaway

The station clock struck six, and Hathaway thought: order.

She said, 'Oh, do stop reading the guide, Gerta.'

The Teutonic approach. Gerta finished reciting about the fifty millions of imperial subjects and their great diversity, and obediently closed the book.

But the clock, when Hathaway glanced up at it, was an ornate queenly thing with tracery on the face. Austria was not Germany.

The invitation had come from a university acquaintance of Gerta's, forwarded by telegram to the Margaretenhof: too long since they'd seen each other; a series of lectures in Vienna on 'Science and Art in the Age of the Machine'; the acquaintance would be busy a lot of the time, so if Gerta had any other friends she could visit, or any companion... A chance to get out of the Margaretenhof, out of Germany.

A man stopped in front of her, and glanced back over his shoulder towards the platforms. Odd gesture. In a station, one was either going to the platforms or coming from them, and one could normally be pretty sure which. A high-buttoned jacket in the Austrian style; a narrow-brimmed hat with a glimpse of a feather in the band.

Now the man set off again, but on a new course, between the café and a news-stand, presumably towards some side exit.

'Tell me something I really want to see,' she said in English.

'I fear, dear Flora, that you want to see the paintings of Klimt.'

'I do want to see the paintings of Mr Klimt, if they're anything like their descriptions. It interests me to see how men see women.'

'*Entschuldigung, sehr geehrte Fräulein.*' Another man had stopped, this one right in front of her, and she looked up into his face. '*Sprechen Sie Englisch?*'

She nodded. 'Thank goodness,' he went on, and she could see the tension in eyes and stance. 'I'm looking for... for a friend of mine. He came this way and now I can't see him. Wearing... a jacket, a... greeny-browny sort of jacket.' Unconsciously he was miming buttons high on the chest. 'And... and a hat. Oh, a...' – he mimed something close to his head – 'a thin thing, not much brim. With a—'

'A funny little thing with a feather?'

'Yes! Yes, that's the chap.'

'He ducked down this way.' She pointed between their café and the news-stand.

'Splendid. That's really – really a great help. Thank you.' He touched his hat, and started to move, then stopped. 'Your English is… well, exceptional.'

'You're most kind. I'm from Derbyshire, but we had a good travelling library.'

For the first time she saw him relax: just an instant as he understood, and laughed once, and life sparked in his eyes and mouth. Then it was gone, the eyes hard, and he touched his hat again and the same to Gerta and was off through the crowd with long strides.

Hathaway watched him go, with curiosity.

'Ah,' Gerta said mournfully; 'and now alas we have no interest in Klimt.'

'Gerta: you're about to be vulgar.'

'Can you blame me?'

'Just a typical Englishman.'

Gerta nodded in the direction the man had gone. 'If that' – she hit the word – 'is a typical Englishman, then German propaganda is wrong indeed, and I have been holidaying in the wrong places.'

'Dozens like that in every college. Long-faced and sad-looking and incapable of considering a woman – let alone her body – in any natural or healthy way.'

'Perhaps he instead should go to see Klimt.' She found her purse. 'I think he looked at me in a most friendly way. I at least would appreciate him.' She put a pair of coins on the table.

'You're welcome to him.'

'And did you think that story of losing his friend really made sense? No.' Gerta stood, and glanced again in the direction the man had taken. 'You English abroad: really a most unusual breed.'

There was a message at the Hotel Stefanie. Gerta's acquaintance had got them tickets for a performance of Mahler songs that evening; a rare opportunity; they should certainly go; they would be collected at the hotel at seven. The lift doors released them back into the lobby as the clock above the lift tinkled the hour.

'Only the good God knows how I'll get along with Martine,' Gerta was saying.

They made for the desk. 'We're not seeing much of her anyway, I think you said.'

'No. We should have arranged other escorts. If you had been more friendly to that man today, perhaps. We need him.' Gerta placed her key on the desk, then pulled herself to artificial erectness and said in English: 'Or perhaps Major Knox.'

'It's you who likes these dry Englishmen, Gerta. I need—' But Gerta was telling one of the staff behind the desk about a problem with her tap, while Hathaway rummaged in her bag for her key.

Afterwards, Hathaway would suppose that she had noticed the man nearby, who had happened to be moving towards the desk as they were. Another sober-coated businessman. In truth she was only conscious of a presence adjacent to her, and then words that were more surprising because they came without introduction: 'If you're acquainted with Major Valentine Knox, you need to listen to me, right now. I'll be across the lobby.'

He handed over his key, asked directions to somewhere, and turned away.

Hathaway was still frozen there. Key half out of bag, head not daring to turn, brain racing.

She handed over her key, and turned. Across the lobby: she could see him looking at some kind of display.

This is a trap.

They had not got her at the Margaretenhof. No doubt German Intelligence were active in Austria, and powerful.

Had it been a Scottish accent? Was it less likely that a German agent would have picked up a Scottish accent?

She began to walk across the lobby. Gerta was talking to someone at the front door. Nothing wrong in walking across the lobby, surely; nothing wrong in an exchange with a stranger; the name a misunderstanding, perhaps.

On the table, a plaque declared that an orange jug was *Stil Erste Jahrhundert*.

'What did—'

'One hour ago, Major Knox was under arrest at the station.' He leaned forwards to examine the detail on an urn, then turned and strode away.

Why had Knox been here? The souvenirs blurred in front of her. What was she trapped in?

Amid the chaos of her thoughts, the impossibility of Knox being restrained.

If I cannot step out of the current, I can at least divert its course.

Gerta was at the top of the steps, a man in a frock-coat beside her. 'Gerta, I find I am... not yet ready. Please go on ahead; I'll follow in ten minutes.' Intensity of gaze; a woman seeking a woman's understanding. 'You gave me the address before.' And she turned and walked back into the lobby and hurried up the stairs to her room.

She splashed some water on her face, and sat in a chair. It was too narrow, and the seat of her dress bunched up around her hips. She gripped the arms, and released them.

If there is a trap, I cannot know it. Ergo, it is futile to try to avoid it. I am effectively alone here. Ergo, I cannot think of aid or sanctuary.

I have been afraid before.

The cab rattled and jolted through the city; the hooves and the wheels and the cobbles between them made a constant chattering that battered her head. She tried concentrating on the city as it softened in the dusk. She tried concentrating on her thoughts. Neither was comforting. She slumped back against the upholstery.

A scolding of girlhood. She sat up again in the carriage. Discipline. Defiance. She would not—

The cab stuttered to a halt. The driver was peering past the horse's head at something. 'What is it?' she asked. Being rude to Gerta's acquaintances was not her intention.

'Can't see. Some accident maybe. There's a tram further up.' Hathaway stretched up from her seat. They were in an anonymous residential street, and past the outlines of the driver's shoulder and the horse she could see a huddle of people staring down at something. 'You're better walking, Fräulein.'

I have feared something, and something has happened. Walking towards the huddle, she had the uneasy sense of a dream: of observing a tragedy that was supposedly happening to her and yet seemed to have left her unharmed. She tried to listen for the sound of her boots on the cobbles; to find something real.

Perhaps ten people, a cross-section of Viennese pedestrians, and all the faces were sickened and unable to turn away, and through the shifting of hats and shoulders she could see a body in the gutter, someone in shirtsleeves bent over it.

The tram was thirty yards off, and empty. Its solitude, gleaming subdued under the street lamps, seemed like shame.

Hathaway took a breath, and peered over the shoulders. She knew that she would see her own face on the body.

It was worse. There was no face, only a mess of gore. That was the nightmare – the effacement of her self, the final loss of identity – and she coughed out a cry and pushed out of the huddle and hurried away along the street.

She walked the rest of the way to the Cäcilien Conservatoire. Air. Control of herself.

A uniformed footman let her in. *Of course; I am on the stage of an opera.* A clock on a mantelpiece showed seven thirty-five; she was only five minutes late, despite everything. Then there was another man, in evening dress, tip-tapping down a staircase. The Fräulein was most welcome. There had been some confusion about the time. The performance was at eight thirty, not seven thirty. The other Fräulein had gone for a little supper with one or two others; if the Fräulein would wait for a few minutes, he would find out for her where they had gone.

Mirrors and gilt and second-rate portraits of Austrian musicians and Hathaway had been led to a conservatory at the back of the building, its glass walls and ceiling presenting the city as if in an aquarium. The buildings that rose up over her, lamplit backs with weird shadows, were a suitably unreal backdrop.

The door had closed behind her. She sat.

And she thought: *It is not I who am looking on. I am the other side of the glass; I am the subject.*

This, then, was the trap. Gerta's acquaintance somehow, perhaps unconsciously, complicit; Gerta and she separated. The doors were locked.

She forced herself to move. To be an actor, not a prop. Back and forth, feeling her body's movement, feeling feet and thighs, holding her head poised.

I fear pain; the pain of death. That is rational; but I can do nothing about it.

I fear embarrassment; the weaknesses of woman, the proof that I am weaker after all. I must be strong in what I am.

I fear my own hypocrisies. But if there be hypocrisies, they cannot be erased; I am on this path, a spy for a system that I have scorned.

Voices through the door. Instinctively, she pressed close. 'There is a British agent out there,' said the voice. 'You know what you must do.'

She pulled away from the door. ·

I fear that I may be insufficient in what I have proclaimed; that I may be wrong. That in the end I shall betray what I have believed in.

But that at least is undetermined. I may yet be everything that I can be.

It came as serenity. And when the door opened, and a man walked in with a pistol pointing at her stomach and told her that the time had come, Flora Hathaway actually smiled.

Then the world shattered around her.

※

Ballentyne

The station clock struck six as Ballentyne stood in the queue to leave the platform, eyes fixed on the hat a few yards ahead of him.

Enough of running; enough of concealment. He would now be the hunter. The only way to end it was to track it to its source. A stab of cold in the fug of the station, as he thought of Hildebrandt.

Belcredi was a dozen places ahead in the queue. Two policemen quizzing each traveller, and Ballentyne thought of the highland ritual of questions for visitors. *Ceremonies performed by the natives of the country to disarm strangers of their magical powers.* Belcredi's hat – Austrian thing, perhaps; made him look like a fisherman – marked him nicely. The queue shuffled forwards. The policemen at the gate were indifferent. Belcredi was waved through. Shuffle forwards.

Vienna seemed German – policemen, procedures, the sense that he was on dangerous ground. But the people were more varied: the stronger bones of Slavs, suits a little shabbier and nattier; a few faces with the faintly darker skins of Albanians or Greeks; and one or two costumes that might have come up from Constantinople.

Forwards. Papers out. Belcredi's hat was twenty yards ahead now. '*Papiere.*' Ballentyne handed his pass to the policeman. '*Englisch?*'

'*Ja.*'

The paper was passed to another policeman standing adjacent, who looked at it then up at Ballentyne. 'A moment please, Mein Herr.' The accent was thick.

'But... yes, of course.'

'You come from...?'

'Belgrade.' Shifting so that he could look for Belcredi without seeming to ignore the policeman.

'Your visit here is for...?'

'Oh... Tourism.' Thirty yards. Other passengers were being waved through past him.

'You stay how long?' The ponderousness was nightmarish.

'A week, perhaps.' He couldn't see the hat any more. Straining up over the bobbing sea of the things. 'Look, is this...?'

The policeman's face dared him to finish the thought. 'Routine, Mein Herr.'

'Of course.'

'Where will you stay?'

'The Bristol.'

'Enjoy your visit to Vienna, Mein Herr.'

He was pushing past and trying not to start running, legs striding hard, ducking and swerving through the buzz of people and hopping over cases. In seconds he was at the point where he'd last seen the hat.

But now it was nowhere. He stared towards the main exit, glanced left and right.

An inconsistency on the edge of his brain – English – two women at a café table on the edge of the current of people, and he thought they'd spoken English.

He mustered what he could remember of his German – gesture of politeness – and yes, the woman did speak English. He tried to seem calm, felt the strain in every muscle. She'd seen him! And he hadn't taken the main exit. The risk of stopping and asking had been vindicated. Now he registered the faces at the table: the companion was a glamorous thing; the one doing the talking less so – sort of handsome, healthy-looking. He contrived a compliment about her English.

'You're most kind. I'm from Derbyshire, but we had a good travelling library.'

A second, and then Ballentyne saw the ridiculousness of it all: himself, chasing shadows; two English visitors colliding in these bizarre circumstances; the accent and the humour flickering warmly and so out of place.

Belcredi. And he was off again. The side exit came out at the top of two or three steps, looking over a street. How many people? Too many people. He forced himself to scan the crowd slowly. Nothing but hats. Ignoring the obviously female. Looking at colour. Brims. Styles. Every hat in Europe was gathering and bouncing in this one Viennese side street.

Except one. He scanned the street, one hundred and eighty degrees, twice. Belcredi's little feathered thing was not there. Every other possible hat – hats everywhere – almost no one without a hat—

One bare head fifty yards away stepping up onto the pavement.

Got you.

Ballentyne was down the steps and plunging into the crowd.

In the middle of this great city of culture, two men were playing a child's game. But this time Ballentyne felt more confident: any place Belcredi touched was a place of significance, a place that London could use.

He undid his jacket, felt his rucksack companionable as ever. He began to feel the tides of the crowd, to navigate them, fixed on the man ahead. He adopted motor cars and carriages and news-stands and trees and doorways as his allies, and the ebb and flow of people.

Belcredi was heading southwards. By the Augarten, he had half turned and was talking to someone, but Ballentyne was absorbed in the window of a hat shop. A minute or two later he happened to look back, but Ballentyne had crossed the street. In Taborstraße he approached a line of cabs, and Ballentyne got within half a dozen yards of him.

In Stephansplatz, Belcredi slowed, began to look into shop windows, sat for a few minutes on a bench staring up the cathedral, ludicrously tall in the squeeze of buildings around it, its zigzag roof tiles sharp against the dusk. Ballentyne lurked nearby; bought a box of matches; considered tobacco.

Then he was following down an alley, and two idiots started scuffling and he couldn't get past, and he had a last glimpse of Belcredi silhouetted against the entrance to a square ahead and by the time he'd pushed through and reached the square the Austrian was gone.

The square was a kaleidoscope of carriages and motor cars and people in the darkening evening. Ballentyne had had his man for all of twenty minutes. He felt alone, in this enemy capital, and stupid.

He took a horse and cab to the Bristol. It felt foolish, clip-clopping through this capital of elegance; a sophistication he could not live up to.

Pickford in Belgrade had given him a contact here in Vienna; Belcredi might yet be traced. He dumped his rucksack, and started to climb into another cab. 'Porzellangasse, *Nummer 33.*' Then he realized he wanted to walk. The change and his clumsy miming failed to impress the driver, who gave him cursory directions and, when Ballentyne tried to asked how long it would take, flicked out all his fingers from the reins, which might have meant ten minutes or 'Clear off'.

A policeman was arguing with a pavement artist; neither could conjure much energy for it. Ballentyne set off. It was hill walking, of a kind. A rough idea of destination; triangulation from occasional way points, offered by passers-by or shopkeepers. Halfway through his journey Vienna's churches began to chime seven, and the bells echoed around him, from peak to peak.

Funny old business. Uncle James: *Funny old stick, Ronald.* And now funny old stick Ronald was an outcast, fugitive and intriguer in a foreign land. An instinct for solitude, for reflection, had led him to the hills. A sense that people were other had led him to anthropology. And that had led him to the villages, to people at their simplest.

Porzellangasse. A white plaque on the corner above his head, elaborate black script. A nothing sort of street.

Trying to uncover the secrets of others; moving among them, yet distinct from them. Still the one distinguished by who he was not, and what he was not.

The light had leached out of the sky, and the city felt gloomy in spite of the warmth. In the mountains, always the promise of an open door to a visitor; a fire; a good meal; a hand on the shoulder and people who would welcome you precisely because you were a stranger.

There was a bend in the street, but Number 33 was before it. Somewhere ahead, the whirring of a tram. A plaque by the door said simply 'Corio'. No one around. He rang the bell.

He realized that Isabella had been right, just as the door opened.

A servant. His name, the request to see Herr Doctor Corio. Half a dozen steps to a half-landing, highly polished dark wood and framed pages of musical scores on the wall, then the staircase turned back on itself for another half-dozen steps to the top.

Belcredi was pointing a pistol at his chest. 'Ah, Ballentyne; you make excellent time.'

After the jolt, Ballentyne found himself oddly unperturbed. The Austrian anthropologist had become a part of his disrupted world; distasteful but unavoidable. After Albania, after Serbia, even the physical threat was becoming tiresome rather than frightening.

'This how you do your research, is it, Belcredi? Breaking into other men's studies?' Life itself seemed rather wearying.

Something flickered in Belcredi's face. 'You are the fool here, Ballentyne. You have acted completely according to our plan.'

'Happy to help.' Isabella had said he needed to belong.

'We knew you would lead us to the house of your contact here.'

'He's dead, is he? Strangest ideas of anthropology you have.'

'Your friend was not here when we arrived. But do not worry; we shall have him yet.' He waved the pistol in Ballentyne's direction. 'You were supposed to lose me a little earlier. Tenacious Ballentyne, eh? You forced a little change in our plans.'

'The police; at the station. That was arranged?'

Belcredi grinned and nodded.

'The men in the alley too?'

Grin and nod. Ballentyne scowled. 'Clever.'

'I lured you' – the verb was drawn out pleasurably – 'to Vienna. We judged that once you lost me here you would make contact with your associates. We were going to follow you, but when you thoughtfully gave the address to the cabman, you gave us the opportunity to come here ahead of you. Avoid any tricks. And better to get you in off the street; all this running is so tiring, I think.'

'You're out of condition. Too much politics, not enough fieldwork.' Was Belcredi really alone?

'Your old friend Hildebrandt will be joining us shortly.' A flicker of fear; the memory of fear. 'He is anxious to see you again.' That eternal evil smile. 'He would have been here now. But your temporary persistence meant he had to divert to take care of... certain other business. You will not be the only British agent captured this evening. Perhaps not the first to die, either. We shall see.' Again the smile.

A breath. 'It sounds as though the company'll be better on the other side anyway.'

A mighty clattering from outside, metal on metal, and they both flinched; Belcredi spun towards the window, and Ballentyne jumped at the stairs. He took the half-flight in one, floundering off pictures and crashing into the wall at the bottom, legs and elbows burning, and the air was a roar and a shattering as a bullet smashed one of the frames over his head; pushing himself off with aching arms, stumbling down the rest of the stairs and flinging a fist at the servant as he emerged, feet hammering behind him and another shot, grappling with the door and wrenching it open. *I want to belong; I am not done living.* And he leaped for the pavement and then the street, and there was a shrieking and a clanging and a blazing light and the world was a tram and it swallowed him.

⊰•⊱

Knox

The station clock struck six, but Knox didn't hear it. He was first out of the train, eyes set and striding hard. His attention was entirely on the immediate physical factors in his world: the bodies, the faces, the luggage, the windows from which his progress might be watched; the interruptions, the threats. The thinking had been done. The old man had named a contact in Vienna; a music teacher. If he hadn't got away already he was at risk, and the old man wanted to limit the damage from whatever chaos was now unfolding. Also, if by chance he was still in Vienna, a useful ally. After that, locate the four agents: protect if necessary; learn from everything.

There was a handful of policemen at the end of the platform. Two came together to form a funnel for those coming off the train. A couple in front of Knox were waved through.

He relaxed himself. Awareness. Watchfulness. But best to lose the expression and posture of a British soldier coming to wreak havoc.

The gap between the soldiers narrowed, and then closed. A pair of uniforms, of blank determined faces. Edgy; they knew him for a threat. Someone close behind him.

'Mein Herr, will you come with us, please?'

There was a click behind him, a revolver being cocked.

Not a question, then.

He looked around the faces. All determined; all waiting for the danger. A handful of them, weapons ready, in a crowded civilian environment.

He nodded. Cold smile.

No checking; no questioning. They knew him.

Two uniforms came tight beside him, the third behind with pistol at his back, and they set off at a march across the concourse.

It looked like the old man had been right, then. Vienna was a trap, and for him as well.

Cade. James Cade just a few yards away on the concourse, gaping. *Get away with you, man. Get well clear.* Then Cade was past, and he was being steered towards a door that opened in front of him and closed quickly behind; a corridor, the sound of the boots different. Another uniform in front of him, another grim face, and the escort stopped and the man was rummaging in Knox's jacket and pockets; his pistol was removed like it was a dead rat. Another door, and a bare waiting room.

The door closed behind him; a lock clicked.

Table; two chairs. One window, high, only mesh protecting it but too narrow for shoulders. Filing cabinet, empty. A print of the Emperor Franz Joseph, looking pretty disapproving.

He sat, facing the door.

They may have some idea who I am and what I am. But they have nothing on me here.

He pulled out a cigarette, and lit it.

Frustration. Mission interrupted. Wondering what was happening to his agents. Need to focus on immediate problem.

Waiting for me. Knew of me. Vienna was a snare indeed, and it turned out he wasn't the gamekeeper, but just another rabbit. *So what is happening to my agents?*

Time passed. *Escape?* He'd kick through the door panel all right, but there was no telling who was on the other side. For now play innocent; keep 'em confused, gauge the situation. Feign some kind of seizure? It might come to that. Escape a last option.

The door opened, and two men stepped in: one the chap who'd taken his pistol off him – officer of some kind perhaps – and the other a guard.

The officer looked at him; frowned. *You like to sit this side, don't you, old lad?* He sat with his back to the door. Knox said, in English: 'Can you please tell me why I have been arrested?'

'You know why.'

'I sincerely don't. Some misunderstanding perhaps.'

'We know who you are.'

'Well that's good. I know who I am, too. But it still doesn't explain why I've been arrested.'

'You have not been formally arrested.'

'Kidnapped, then.'

'You are an agent of your government. A spy.'

'Pardon me, I am a soldier of His Majesty. I wear a uniform.'

'You are not wearing a uniform now.'

'I'm on my holidays. I was told Vienna was very lovely.'

'You take many holidays in Europe, I think.'

'I like to travel.'

'Why do you carry a pistol?' Life in the eyes; he was pleased with that one.

'I've been attacked by robbers in... Turkey twice, Italy once, and France once.' He smiled. 'Never before in Austria.'

The officer didn't get it, or didn't bother. He considered Knox for a while, and then his face wrinkled in indifference. He stood, and walked out, and the guard followed.

The door was closed and locked again.

Knox gazed at it.

You're not interested in me at all, are you? Doesn't matter who I am or what I'm doing. All you want to do is hold me.

He stood. Either they were waiting for someone else to come and take him. Or they were doing something else and they didn't want him complicating it.

He rechecked the window; tried to imagine the squeeze. Tested the door handle; tapped at its panels. *What is happening to my agents?*

He paced. He visualized the map of Vienna in his head. Played and replayed actions and itineraries for the moment when he got past the door. Every five minutes he did twenty press-ups. Blood flowing. Ready for the whistle.

After five repetitions of this he'd had enough. They were clearly prepared to keep him as long as it suited them. That, by definition, could not suit him. *What is happening to my agents?* Stuck in this room he was neutralized; passive. No options, no opportunities.

Time to break their rhythm. He moved to the door, felt the panels again. A series of actions, as many as possible to be completed before they put him down: kick through panel, reach for key or if no key create wider hole, get through door, subdue anyone between him and external door, through external door, run through station, no dawdling, keep running until first moving transport appears whether tram, carriage, horse or indeed old man on bicycle. However far he got, he would have changed their plans and created new opportunities for himself.

He stepped back from the door. Three deep breaths. *Punch anything that moves. Put it down.* He raised his foot and brought it back. Another breath.

The lock clicked and the door opened, and the officer was in the doorway. 'You are free to go.' He seemed disappointed.

Knox got his heartbeat under control, then stepped into the corridor before they had a chance to change their minds. 'My pistol?'

A sniff. 'You do not have the necessary permit. There is a procedure—'

'Keep it. Way things are going, you'll be needing a decent firearm.'

He left. Closed the door behind him. Instinct to hurry; to run! A fraction of a second with his fingers still pressed against the door behind him. *Bit sudden, wasn't it?* Something had happened. Something was about to happen.

He dropped his bag at the left luggage office, partly because he didn't want the burden and partly because it was a natural next step from there to the lavatory adjacent, which as he'd hoped had a window that did accommodate the Knox shoulders. A moment later he was through and out and pushing into the Viennese evening.

Walk to first corner. Run for two more changes of direction. Then look for transport where there was no chance of it being a stooge. Through the warmth and the grandeur, among top hats and frock-coats and elegant dresses and furled parasols, a man in a foreign suit dodged and swerved and ran. He picked up a cab on Heinestraße, got down at the Rossauer Barracks, as the clocks were chiming seven. He walked the rest of the way, zigzag and double back.

He was thirty yards along Porzellangasse when its silence was interrupted by a noise somewhere behind him. A thump of some... A loose paving slab? He didn't turn; walked on. He stopped at a house that didn't have a number, peering for it. The shuttered window was mirror enough to show a figure on the other side of the road, a little behind him, now stopped as well.

Knox walked on. Hadn't been followed; sure he hadn't been followed. So the man – perhaps there were men – were waiting here. Which meant they had the address. *Not good...* He was now marked again; his movements restricted at what looked like an increasingly crucial time.

Number 33.

He walked on; didn't hesitate. But there was an alley adjacent, and that might serve... He ducked into it. Nice and gloomy as night came on. A short way along it there were two dustbins. They'd have to do.

Ten seconds later a figure appeared at the alley entrance. It hesitated, a shadow against the lamplit houses opposite. It was looking for Knox's shadow walking away down the alley, and could not see it.

The figure came into the alley. Cautious. Careful. Five yards; three yards; one yard, and then Knox launched himself upwards, shoulder into stomach and driving the man back into the wall. A roar of discomfort, and Knox was wrenching himself free and looking for the mark. The man staggered, caught a breath, came near upright and Knox punched him full in the face, pushed his head back against the wall and jabbed for the throat. The man dropped, retching for a breath that would not come, and Knox picked his moment and kicked him in the head.

Now the man went still. Knox gave it a moment to be sure, then sank to his haunches beside the body. There was breathing, shallow and far away. He'd be unconscious a good while. Knox was about to rise, but on a whim rifled through the man's jacket. No papers, but there was a pistol, which he took.

It felt very much like his pistol.

He knelt closer. 'One day soon, old chap,' he whispered, 'you're going to come across Valentine Knox in a fair fight. He'll be ready.' This time the pistol went in an outer pocket.

Then he stood and set off down the alley at a jog. The house of the music teacher was somehow a focus for the enemy; under observation at least, or they had something more in hand. He had to come at it from a different direction now. Ten yards brought him into a cul-de-sac; fifty yards down that brought him to a side street. He forced himself down to a fast walk – a few people around him now in the dusk – and followed back towards Porzellangasse. He crossed straight over it into another side street, and looked for the turn that would bring him round in the direction of Number 33 again.

From somewhere, a faint clattering burst into the quiet of the evening; instinctively he thought of his dustbins, but ignored the thought and hurried on. Turn. The Viennese town planners hadn't been as logical as an English spy might have hoped, but he was heading in the right direction at least.

A gunshot.

No mistaking it, even at a distance. Then another. He began to jog again.

It took only a few minutes to work back to Porzellangasse, and he came out roughly where he'd aimed: on the opposite side to Number 33, a few dozen yards away.

But now there was a crowd near the house: gawpers, gathered around something, and it only confirmed the presumption that the gunshots were somehow his business.

There was a woman hurrying away up the street, and for a moment something about the set of the head seemed familiar. Instinctively he started to move, then stopped himself with a hiss. *Enemy ground; no distractions*. But what if— Again the restraint. What if it wasn't her?

He quartered the ground before stepping out of his shadows: to his right, a motor car, the driver inside; nearby, a tram, stopped, dark, empty; beyond it the gawpers, perhaps one dozen; beyond them Number 33. The tram? Was the commotion to do with the tram, rather than with the gunshots? *Speculation*. Once again he looked up and down the street, concentrating on the shadows where other watchers might like him be lurking. Then he moved out towards the crowd; fair cover, at least.

The crowd were gathered around a body. Head smashed in, poor devil. The tram it had been, then. There was a dark-haired fellow tending to the body – No… Not tending, checking. Hands pulling at the jacket that had half covered the distorted torso, rummaging. Then he found something – Knox couldn't see whether it was a paper or a mark of some kind – and turned to someone behind him and hissed 'Ballentyne!' and Knox became ice.

He looked again at the jacket; perhaps it did seem familiar. He forced another look at the obscene face, trying to conjure a living Ballentyne out of the tissue. *You poor bastard… And like this*.

The dark-haired chappie was up and his associate was saying something to him, and now Knox was re-considering him. *Then you, sir, I presume, are the enemy*. He mapped the face; handsome sort of Hun. Now the man was snarling at the associate. 'I can't!' he snapped in German. 'I have to see the damned Scotsman.'

Cade. Ye gods, had the trap worked so well?

Now the man was pushing out of the crowd and striding off, the associate hurrying behind, and Knox knew he had to follow them. The old man's priority: the enemy network, not the agents. Knox shook his head, but moved to the pavement and began to shadow the two men. Seconds later they were at the motor car, though, and climbing into it and it was turning and accelerating into the evening. And Knox was left in the street, no one left to follow, the body of a dead agent abandoned in the gutter behind him.

Come on, damn you. At the end of the street he found a cab, and within minutes it had him at the hotel where Cade had reported he'd be staying. *Trace Cade. A chance to find both him and the dark-haired Hun. Two birds.* He forced a smile for the clerk. 'Good evening; I'm supposed to be meeting a friend who is staying here: Mr James Cade. Now I worry he thinks we are meeting in the city.' The clerk's finger began to run down the register in front of him. Upside down, Knox saw that one of the most recent entries was Cade. 'Ah, yes of course! Mr Cade.' Finger tapping the name. The one below it looked good and Teutonic. Von something. 'I beg your pardon, sir.' Von Waldeck. Knox looked up. 'I didn't connect the sound and the spelling. I'm afraid he has gone out, sir. I remember now. Perhaps half an hour ago.'

'Did he say where he was going?'

'I don't remember, I'm afraid. He may have asked directions, but I – I don't remember.'

Von Waldeck? 'It is quite important.' Uncomfortable shrug from the clerk.

Running out of avenu— *Hathaway's friend, surely.*

He glanced down at the register again. The name below Von Waldeck was Hathaway.

'Another question, then. We were hoping to see another pair of acquaintances in Vienna as well. Miss von Waldeck and Miss Hathaway.'

'Oh yes, sir. They are staying with us.' Sympathetic. 'They are also out this evening.'

'You don't, by any chance—'

'Oh yes, sir! I took the message myself.'

Another race through Vienna, and now he hardly cared about concealment. A gold piece thrust at the driver and a roared order. Whatever the enemy plan was, it was happening now. The trap had been sprung. The hooves clattered over the cobbles like a fusillade, the cab lurching and swaying dangerously on the turns; at last, an Austrian who could be kicked out of complacency. Duval – God only knew where Duval was. Ballentyne was dead. Cade was presumably in the hands of the enemy. But Hathaway...

Knox had something to prove. The old man had let his agents be lured into enemy territory, and he'd known and accepted the risk as he did so. But Knox had thought he was protecting them. He'd swanned around Europe acting the uncle. Now, to lose all of them... And to lose Hathaway, who'd doubted his qualities and then needed him, Hathaway who'd pressed on deeper and deeper into enemy country. 'Faster, damn you!' And the cab careered across a square in a storm of horns and whistles and shouts.

He stopped it at the entrance to the street, and walked the rest of the way. No sense just getting arrested again. When he saw the Conservatoire across the street, he checked his watch by some habit of precision: seven forty. An alley opened beside the building; might prove useful. He kept walking, scanning the façade. Nothing out of the way about it: elegant; pocket grand; shutters on the ground floor and no signs of life above.

Another alley ran along the other side of the building. *That'll do.* He wasn't just going to be a spectator this time. He crossed the street, glanced again to see if the façade was showing life at all, and ducked into the darkness.

For a moment it was total. Then he saw a trace of light at the end; presumably a window at the back of the Conservatoire. Gradually, hints of the buildings in the square beyond began to clarify. He started to walk down the alley, one careful step at a time. A doorway became apparent in the side of the building; he kept on past it, watching as if it were a drowsy snake. Now the window at the end showed itself as part of a conservatory. He shut one eye to keep his night sight, while with the other he watched for life behind the glass. Nothing. He started forwards again.

And at once he went stumbling over something on the ground, something heavy but oddly yielding. Immediately he was scrambling forwards on elbows and knees a few feet, seeking out the darkest shadow he could find, against a buttress on the left-hand side of the alley. There he tucked himself small and started to look around.

Nothing at door or window. Thirty long seconds he watched.

Seen at ground level, the thing he'd stumbled over was more clearly a body. Still uninterrupted, he scurried over to it.

Unconscious at the least; then he felt at the neck. The cold told him before the absence of pulse. The body was slumped face down, and he wrestled it over onto its back. Now his hand was wet.

Another glance at the door, and he risked a match. The first thing it showed was that his cupped hand was scarlet. Whoever it was had been shot – no, more likely stabbed – in the back. Shielding the flame as best he could, he moved it over the face.

He let out a long hiss.

Life had at last caught up with David Duval; come up behind him in an alley. Restlessness and daring had somehow brought him to the enemy citadel; and here his chancer's luck had left him. A flower in the buttonhole. The face was young, and strangely serene.

Knox laid his palm over the face, and closed the heavenward eyes, and did not feel the match burning his fingers as it expired. Then he was up. For a moment he was going to knock on the door and start shooting, but managed to restrain the urge. Instead he walked into the square at the rear of the building, and the first thing he saw was a woman's back through the window and he knew it was Hathaway.

An instinct to get her attention, but then what? He had to get decisively in or, preferably, get her safely out. The door? What was she doing in there, anyway? Did she know the danger?

He walked on into the square, keeping to the limited shadow by the wall but not otherwise bothering to conceal himself, looking all around as he went, taking in the other buildings, the parked motor car, and then the back of the Conservatoire. He was looking for signs of activity, and ways of entry; and he saw neither. Just Flora Hathaway, standing alone and thoughtful and rather proud.

He had a pistol, for God's sake. But what then? Shoot patterns in the glass? Smash a hole and expect the opposition to wait patiently as he clambered in or tried to get Hathaway to clamber out? He could pick them off one by one, but if there were more than six he'd have achieved nothing. He paced, glaring from the gloom towards the luminous prison. Just a pane of glass between them. Like a bird in a cage. And even if he did break her out?

Only one option. And by the time he saw a door inside the conservatory open, saw a man come in with a pistol pointing at Hathaway, saw her lift her head, Knox was in the motor car and halfway across the square with the accelerator pedal hard to the floor. They only heard him in the instant before he hit and the car had reached maximum speed and he adjusted the wheel a touch to aim for the gunman and ducked his head and the night exploded in timber and glass and noise.

Then he was up out of the seat, shards and splinters cascading off him as he slid over the bonnet looking for the gunman. But the man was down, thrown between car and wall and back again, and unmoving. Now Knox turned to her. 'You all right, Hathaway? Come along.' And he was in front of her. Shocked; he could see it. He put his jacket around her shoulders, gripped her arm and began to lead her towards the wreckage of the window.

'Stop!' It came harsh from the doorway, a man hurrying in with pistol drawn.

Knox pushed her farther towards the window, and then his hand dropped from her shoulder, and he edged away from her. Another man was in the doorway behind the first, and they stepped forwards together. The pistol followed Knox. 'All right, old chap; I'll come quietly.'

The second man was surveying the chaos of the conservatory: the grotesque anomaly of the car wedged among the plants; the fragments of glass everywhere. 'This evening has become...' He shook his head. Then he looked at Knox, and seemed to relax. 'But it ends well. You are the soldier, aren't you? An additional prize for us, and our success is complete.'

The man with the gun waggled it at Knox. 'Lift your hands.'

Knox obliged. 'You can't be expected to realize it, I suppose, but she's more of a threat than I'll ever be.'

They didn't get it. The gun stayed on Knox, and their attention stayed on Knox, and it was still on Knox when Hathaway pulled his pistol from the jacket around her shoulders, considered the mechanism a moment, and shot the gunman in the chest.

The other man stared at her, and back at Knox, as if to complain at such a trick, and then her second shot hit him in the shoulder.

Knox took the pistol from her and grabbed her arm again and began to drag her out with new haste. 'Now we do have to— Can you run?'

She stepped swiftly through the gap into the evening; he was looking back at the door as he followed her, gun ready. 'I claim the right to try,' she said, kicked off her shoes and hitched up her dress and set off across the square.

It wasn't an outcome he'd fancied, having to escape through the streets with a woman in a frock and taking pot-shots at policemen if they came too close; it threatened only one outcome in the end. But no choice now. They were out of the back of the square in seconds; she was breathing evenly – healthily – but he could hear the hiss when her bare foot hit a rough stone and once she slipped and gasped. They took the first turn they came to, kept running. Knox put the pistol in his pocket. The second turn, and ahead were the lights of a main street and he slowed them to a walk, took his jacket off her shoulders. 'Normal as possible now,' he said as they came into the lamplight and were among people again.

A cab came near the kerb and Knox was waving at it and reaching for the horse's bridle as it neared. They were up, and in answer to the driver's question he hesitated. 'Heldenplatz,' Hathaway said, and the cab swung away from the kerb and off. 'Not too close, and should have plenty of people.' She was right. They crossed the square, he grim-faced and she stumbling more, and into another cab. This time Knox directed it to the Hotel Stefanie.

'No doubt you... Is that wise?' she hissed.

'No choice. Something I have to check.'

She sat back. She didn't like it. She was also, obviously, cold; and the evening was starting to catch up with her. 'I'm sorry I can't give you my jacket for now. Shirtsleeves too odd.'

'I understand.'

'Is there anything essential in your room – truly essential – or incriminating?' She thought a moment, and shook her head. 'You can't go back up there, I'm afraid.'

'I understand.'

At the Stefanie, Knox told the driver to wait, and helped her down to the pavement.

'Knox: your hand; you're hurt.'

'Not my own. But a friend of ours, unfortunately.'

'Oh – oh, I'm sorry.' Of course; she wouldn't know any of it.

Then she seemed to sag a moment, and he reached for her shoulder. 'Are you—'

'I shot a man!' she hissed at him, venomous.

He stared into her eyes. Then nodded. 'Two men. If you hadn't, they'd have killed me; perhaps you too.' She considered it; she wasn't convinced.

His eyes dropped a moment. 'A boy,' he said, looking up again. 'A boy, in the Cape. The first person I killed. For an instant I felt like a god. Inside a minute I couldn't remember if he'd even been holding a rifle.' He shook his head. 'Sometimes it's necessary. Pray that it... that it never becomes easy.'

A deep breath. A nod.

'Listen: you walk to the desk; you're asking for a man named James Cade. James Cade, yes?' She nodded. 'Whether he's come back; any idea where he might be.' *Lord knows what I do if I get an answer.*

She nodded again. 'James Cade. And you?'

'I'll be in the doorway. If there is anything awry – the slightest thing, Hathaway, the slightest subtlest thing that feels out of place – you turn around and walk straight out again. If someone moves on you...' He patted his pocket.

'In a crowded hotel lobby?'

'Yes.'

'Have you noticed you've stopped calling me "Miss"?'

He scowled. 'Battlefield rules.'

She nodded, and turned. Then stopped, and looked back. 'Thank you for getting me out.' He grunted, and she was away.

It took her fifteen steps to cross the lobby to the desk, and each one hammered in his chest. His eyes moved constantly around the room: every face; every hand movement. And always back to her slender figure, farther and farther away.

The desk. She had to wait for the chap to finish with someone else. Knox's hand hovered near his jacket pocket, unnaturally still.

Now she was talking. The clerk checking something. A reply. She was talking again. *Come on, woman...* Another reply. Now she was saying something else. *Come on.*

She turned. She started to walk back across the lobby. Fifteen steps, as to the gallows. She wasn't looking at him; wasn't looking at anything in particular. *Good girl.* Five steps away and he moved back onto the pavement and checked the cab was still there. And she was out, down the steps, and he was handing her up into the cab.

'Taborstraße,' he said to the driver, and they were away.

'Taborstraße?'

'It's near the main station.'

'You're not suggesting we head back into Germany. You're not that cold.'

'In one door of the station and out the other. Italy. What about Cade?'

'The clerk wasn't sure himself, but he thought Mr Cade checked out of the hotel about ten minutes ago.'

'Checked out?' She nodded. Knox frowned. 'What were you gassing about at the end?'

'Checking they do room service. On that basis, I said I'd pay off my cab, and asked him to have a light supper sent up to my room.' He grunted approval. 'Knox, if we've a moment to breathe, could you tell me what on earth's going on?'

'Very well.' He breathed out, long, and he knew that at last the night was catching up with him. 'An old man sent four agents into Europe. Now they're all gone, except for you.'

333

The Spider

The sky over the English Channel was white, and the water reflected its emptiness. Not a warm morning, but there wasn't a wind either; nothing to suggest life. It was too early in the season for trippers, and Knox found himself alone on the beach. A mile of grey shingle in either direction. It was as if the world had stopped.

Purgatory, wasn't it? Where you waited. Between life and death.

Europe on the brink; crisis of empire, fiends plotting chaos, agents being sent on desperate missions: Valentine Knox had known – somehow he had always known – that this would be his time.

He hadn't expected to spend it in a boarding house in an anonymous town on the south coast.

He turned, parade ground-style, and began to march along the shingle again. Sky and sea white; beach grey; the land a low brown smudge off to his right.

Orders. Barred from even entering London. Quarantine.

What happened when you botched the job. Not much he could have done, but no excuses. On his watch. Take one's medicine.

But like this?

He'd overheard the landlady say she thought he might be a German spy. *Might as well be.* Still had to ask his help to get her blasted cat down off the roof.

Mess revolver; honourable way out. But that wasn't his style. Little Val just kept on going. French Foreign Legion, perhaps. Better yet, take the mess revolver and head back to Vienna; unfinished business. Or just keep marching straight ahead; straight into the bloody sea.

A sound from his right: high and indistinct, and for a moment he thought it was a bird call. Again: 'Major!'

It was the old man.

Where had he even come from, that he was suddenly standing there, suit blending against the slope of shingle?

They walked along the beach together; like a pair of geriatrics off a charabanc tour. Knox glanced sidewards occasionally, trying to catch a glimpse of the face under the tweed hat; trying to guess at the age.

'I'm washed up, is that it, sir?' Knox's first words; back straight. 'Tainted now? I do understand, believe me.'

'If that was the case, Major, you'd currently be on the troopship for Calcutta and a new assignment in Indian Army stores.'

'Sir, I realize that—'

'Knox, your prep school virtues make you a fine man and a brave soldier, but we've no time for that sort of stuff now. If you're not boiling angry at what's happened, and what's happened to you, and if you're not as a result determined even more coldly to fight this to the end, then you're no use to me.'

Knox stopped; it sent the old man a step ahead, and he stared after him. 'If that's how it is, it might be a start if you'd tell me what's actually going on.' The old man seemed to consider this; a surprising suggestion that might after all have merit. Knox set off again. 'For an opener – pardon me, sir, but – well, where do you fit into the department?'

'The Secret Intelligence Bureau, you mean? M.O.5? The new Military Intelligence apparatus? I don't.'

'I thought you were a colleague of Colonel Mayhew. That he reported to you, or you—'

'A convenient misunderstanding.'

'But I work for Colonel Mayhew.'

'No, Major, you don't.'

'Well, I was working for him, at any rate.'

'No, Major, you were not.'

Knox felt that his brain had emptied like the sky.

'You were working for me, Major.'

'The colonel—'

'The colonel is a worthy and able officer of the new Military Intelligence departments. It suited me to have everyone – with one exception –

thinking that this was a Military Intelligence operation: everyone in Whitehall; everyone in Berlin. And you.'

Lost. Knox stopped, with a crunch of the shingle; pulled himself straighter. 'Do I get to know? With two of my agents dead?'

The old man considered him a moment or two; appraised him.

'Major Knox, for the last six weeks you have been working for the Comptrollerate-General for Scrutiny and Survey.'

He set off walking again, as if uncomfortable at the indiscretion.

'I've never heard of it.'

'I am relieved to hear it. Ninety-nine in one hundred officials in British government service, including those who think they deal in intelligence and counter-intelligence, have not heard of it. Or if they've heard of it, they've had a most inaccurate view of what it does. The same, I'm happy to say, is true in Berlin.'

Knox was losing his way, in the featureless sky. 'And this operation?'

'The secondary motive was to identify a leak. For there is a leak – I've seen it even more clearly during these last weeks – and it has tainted my own organization. The primary motive was to prompt a reaction. Flush out that great brain that I told you of in Paris: the Spider, if you'll pardon my schoolboy fancy; last flicker of my professional innocence, if you like.'

'And you didn't mind if the agents were identified.'

'Not at all. Once they'd got going – had a chance to get up a bit of steam – I wanted them identified.' His pace slowed a moment, and his voice was somehow more sympathetic. 'You – ah – you were the guarantee of that, Major.'

'I beg your pardon?'

'Major, as I say, it is my hope and aim that our new Military Intelligence departments will grow strong and effective. But – promising start, and all that – so far they're floundering around like first-week platoon commanders. Since 1911 I have become increasingly sure that the Germans have a very good picture of their operations; they're perhaps not actually infiltrated, but I'll bet that of the bods that Cumming and Mayhew and their Secret Intelligence Bureau think are their contacts in Europe, a handful are working for everyone including the enemy, and one-third to one-half are well-known to Berlin.'

'That would mean—'

'Knox, you'll have been spotted as soon as you stepped off the boat at Calais. Probably while you were still walking along Queen Anne's Gate. If I'd wanted those four agents to remain truly invisible to the enemy, the very last thing I'd have done would be to give them a liaison officer from British Military Intelligence.'

Knox exhaled heavily; bewilderment and self-restraint. 'And this – this scheme cost two of them their lives.'

'Yes, Major. It did.'

Knox watched him; it seemed that each time the old man opened his mouth Knox had to re-evaluate him and everything he himself thought he understood.

He grunted. 'I gave Miss Hathaway a speech about the ruthlessness of the men in London: wouldn't mind if she didn't come back, long as they'd got good use out of her.' Something like a chuckle in the throat.

'That's the spirit.'

'The Comptrollerate-General? That was the name, sir?' The old man nodded, looked the question. Knox grunted. 'Just that it proves your point about the leaks in our system. Shows they were definitely onto poor Ballentyne, from the start.'

'Interesting. In his case I told two men he was en route for Albania for me: a chap in Belgrade, and the secretary of the British ambassador in Rome.'

'No, before that. When he was in the field a couple of months back. Some German agent grabbed him, gave him a bit of a going-over; this German had twigged that you'd recruited Ballentyne, wanted to find out more.'

The old man stopped. 'But that's im—' He caught himself. 'Pardon me. Neither you nor Ballentyne is – was – a fantasist; so it is not impossible.' He shook his head. 'But certainly improbable. Dates. Exact dates.'

'You'd have to check with the legation in Albania when he was there, and presumably with the Ports Office about when he came back. I only had this from him in passing.'

'Mayhew said that Ballentyne had been complaining that people were always suspecting him of spying.'

'No, sir, it was more specific than that.'

'Exact words. Precision please, Major.'

'This German named the – the Comptrollerate-General.'

'The exact name?'

'Sir.'

The old man hissed his frustration. 'This detail should have been reported. That's the kind of casual, Wednesday afternoon sports approach to...' He subsided.

'With respect, sir' – Knox grunted uncomfortably – 'you're conducting business at a seaside boarding house.'

And the old man actually chuckled, grim. '*Touché*, Major. Perhaps I should just retire here.'

'And neither Colonel Mayhew nor myself had heard of the Comptrollerate-General. Didn't know the significance. Just another bureaucratic what-not.'

'That is the general idea, Major. On this occasion it has not served us. But if they knew then...'

'Can't expect the Hun to be dumb brutes all the time, I suppose.'

'This wasn't the Germans. Not their style, either. No, this was the Spider.' He began to stride forwards again, with new energy. To himself: 'And in London...'

Knox didn't follow; he knew he was being left behind now in more ways than one. 'And me, sir? Now?'

The old man stopped, turned to him. 'You wait, Knox. Here.'

Knox nodded; deep breath. 'Thank you for coming, sir. Before you go: thank you for taking the trouble.'

The old man took a step closer, and they faced each other across the shingle. 'Knox, I didn't come all this damned way to tell war stories and pat you soothingly on the shoulder.' The voice dropped, but it still carried, and it was cold. 'The man who learns what you have just learned is either a man exceptionally trusted, a man in whose future I interest myself. Or he is a man who knows too much. A man with no future at all.'

Knox nodded, hesitant. 'Even with this operation finished – even though it failed—'

'The operation has not failed, and it has certainly not finished. I set my bait – those four individuals, so intriguing to him – and he took a bite and he got away.'

The ruthlessness left Knox alone again, in a world empty of warmth, empty of landmarks. 'And now?'

'We are on the brink of war. And our Intelligence apparatus is more vulnerable than it has ever been. We're gambling with the empire now, Knox. Against the greatest of the spies; and he will take the greatest bait. The only bait we have left, now, is the Comptrollerate-General itself.'

⊹⸺⸺⊹

'Hildebrandt, I must spend a week or two in Sarajevo. My office there relapses into its former Ottoman habits too quickly, if it does not feel my hand upon it.'

'And no doubt a convenient place from which to monitor both Constantinople and Belgrade.'

A smile. 'Quite so. And indeed Vienna.' Krug sat back. 'We have a message from your friend Belcredi, I think. I have not read it yet.'

Hildebrandt smiled. 'Not urgent. It confirms that he bolted in shock at Ballentyne's death – he doesn't put it that way. He's gone back to Serbia, to carry on his work there.'

'Ah, the plan of that extraordinary von Einem woman, for the Muslims. It intrigues me.'

'Only a test, he says. A test in the Balkans; the real game will be ensuring Turkish stability; the prize will be the Muslims of the British Empire.'

'There's a kind of grandeur to the idea... I should like to meet your Belcredi some time.'

'He will continue to send reports to your International Cultural Exchange address in Sarajevo. I hope that's not inconvenient, if you are there.' Krug shook his head. 'It's simpler when he is in the region.' A smile. 'He doesn't like having to report on intelligence channels. I think it upsets his academic ideals.'

Krug snorted. 'A man must stand out in the field if he is to look at the stars.'

Hildebrandt considered Krug's contentment. 'You are satisfied with our work here?'

'The Comptroller-General sent a team of agents against me, and I have smashed it. Smashed, Hildebrandt!' Krug settled back in his chair again, a man replete at the end of a feast. 'Such a coup is rare.'

'You still do not know who is this "Comptroller-General"?'

'But I will. I have shaken his foundations, and now he will show his face at a window. Through the Scottish gentleman, I will turn London which way I choose.'

<hr />

The street lamps had come on, and they glowed fuzzily through the net curtains. Still the old man sat at the desk. In front of him he had dozens of sheets of paper, reports dating back a year, five years – in one case twenty years. Under his hands they circled, orbited, until they found a proper relation to each other. He was drawing the lines between them. The web.

In St Petersburg, Mayhew's man Lisson had got the Okhrana to pull Frosch the shipping agent in for questioning. Frosch had been relieved not to be asked about his recent trades in the Baltic and North Sea, or about certain other activities and contacts in Russia, and happy to repeat elements of his conversation with a rogue Englishman named Duval. *Valfierno. Valfierno's woman. The Conservatoire.*

Hathaway confirmed the Conservatoire.

The old man took a sip of water.

Cade had been encouraged to report his business trip to Vienna. His description of the man who had interviewed him was similar to Knox's description of the man searching Ballentyne's body. Apparently a senior and trusted lieutenant of the Spider.

Ballentyne had been hunted, in Albania and in Serbia, by a German named Hildebrandt. There had been a Count Paul Hildebrandt in Bosnia in 1908 and 1909, assumed to be working with German Intelligence. In 1910 a Count Hildebrandt had been obliged to resign from his regiment: debts; brutality; a man to whom he was said to owe money had died. In a photograph of the Kaiser and the German general staff observing manoeuvres in 1906, there had been a young officer in the background identified as a Hildebrandt – right age, right social profile. Knox could be shown the photograph.

Ballentyne had been following a crank anthropologist called Belcredi, a man with a purpose, a man with influential patrons in German society, a man who reported his movements via an office in Sarajevo called the International Cultural Exchange. In Belgrade, Hildebrandt and Belcredi had been confederates.

On the surface there was nothing to link Belcredi and Hildebrandt with Valfierno, the suspected tool of the Spider. But it was inconceivable that two unrelated entrapments of British agents, centred on Vienna, should happen simultaneously. Valfierno and Hildebrandt and Belcredi, and the Spider.

The old man took another sip of water.

Cade had had a meeting at the Adriatic Trading Union. Records from the Bank of England, and relevant offices in Rome and Constantinople, showed that the Adriatic Trading Union – and its president, named Silvas – did a certain amount of legitimate business; but not enough to make it other than a front.

In 1910 the Adriatic Trading Union had purchased a shipment of rifles, notionally for Portugal; it was thought that they had ended up in Mexico. The guarantor for the purchase had been the Amalgamated Alpine Bank of Zurich.

Two men: Krug and Morgenthal. The banking, the Zurich front, suggested Morgenthal.

Vienna suggested Krug. Morgenthal had financial interests in Austria, and money enough usually to get what he wanted. But the operation in Vienna suggested a level of official linkage that sounded more like Krug. Krug the confidant of great men; Krug the influence-peddler. And Sarajevo? Krug, whose life until the early 1900s was a mystery, but whose mother had reputedly been Bosnian.

In 1913 the Amalgamated Alpine Bank of Zurich had failed. There was little attention or impact, so insubstantial was it. Its few assets were noted as having passed to its main creditor, Kärntner A.G.. In 1912 Kärntner A.G. had been bought by Iris S.A. A newspaper clipping reported the donation by Iris S.A. of three minor Corot landscapes, part of the residue of Amalgamated Alpine, to something called the Hüpfebrunnen Foundation.

Iris S.A. was Krug's public front.

It was circumstantial. It wasn't enough.

Another sip of water.

The Cäcilien Conservatoire was a small concern. Limited assets, occasional events, a few students tutored by men of solid repute. It had been founded in 1909; the Marquis of Valfierno had been put in as president of the trustees in the same year. The organizing force behind the establishment of the Conservatoire was unknown. The costs of renovating the property and buying the necessary instruments had come from a handful of men of profile and worth; there was a list... and one of the men was Morgenthal.

'No.'

The old man said it aloud, to the empty room.

That is it, surely.

Inconceivable that the Spider would associate himself publicly with an organization that he then used for such a dramatic operation as had transpired in Vienna. Inconceivable that the Spider would associate himself publicly with Valfierno. The old man's hands continued to feel their way around the papers on the desk, running his fingers along the connections.

Among the papers, there was a list of the two dozen concerts and events that the Conservatoire had hosted in the last few years. All small-scale, all low-profile; the place couldn't accommodate an orchestra. The list swirled round into the centre of the evolving web.

Among them was a performance of duets by Dussek, to mark the arrival of a new harp. This had been funded by a gift from the Hüpfebrunnen Foundation.

The Hüpfebrunnen Foundation, which had received money thanks to Krug.

The web sprawled over the desk. He could see its strands more clearly now: the strands that had led to Vienna, to the Spider.

A moment of fancy. The office was dark now, the pages and his hands the only things to be seen, stark in the pool of light from the desk lamp. He felt the four agents around him: their faces, their voices, their attitudes.

Flora Hathaway and James Cade. And Ronald Ballentyne and David Duval. The agents he had sent into Europe, to their fates, against his enemy.

During his interview in Vienna, James Cade had had a telephone conversation with some mysterious other, some senior partner. Had the Scotsman actually spoken to the Spider?

Hüpfebrunnen. An odd name, somehow unnatural. In English hop – or jump... jumping fountain.

But there was something else...

Not German, not English; Dutch. Cape Dutch. Hüpfebrunnen was a German rendering of Springfontein.

Springfontein.

Again the memory from more than a decade before: the dust, the sweat, the chaos far out in the African wilderness, and the knowledge of defeat. The nausea as he realized how completely he had been tricked. The understanding that the game had become real. The beginning of a long journey, and the first knowledge of the true capacity of his enemy.

Krug?

<hr/>

Sir, [Admiral BEATTY] was invited to luncheon by [the TSAR] today 15 June [CRONSTADT]. [The TSAR] nervous at current European situation. Persistent questions about reliability capability and intentions of [FRANCE]. Recognized [RUSSIA] had failed to support [FRANCE] in [MOROCCO] 1905 and latter had reciprocated over [BOSNIA-HERCEGOVINA] 1908. Urged [BRITAIN] to give lead. [Admiral BEATTY] raised frankly the subject of [RUSSIA]n quote consuls unquote and other activities in [PERSIA] using information provided on this channel. [The TSAR] uncomfortable. Not clear if discomfort at discussion or at his own lack of control over diplomatic military activities. Quote [RUSSIA] must protect own

defensive interests unquote. Atmosphere around visit of
First [BATTLE CRUISER] Squadron subdued but satisfactory.

[SS R/1/227 (DECYPHER)]

──✦──

The British India Line and the Bibby Line were bringing in a new class
of troopships, but the *Manora* was not one of them. Only twenty years
old, apparently, but when years are spent steaming from Southampton
to Calcutta and back again, crammed with British soldiers and – with a
little more space – British horses, twenty is a lot of them. The hull, once
white, was a sickly cream streaked with brown. Any exposed metal surface
was tarnished and corroding. They were scrubbing at it incessantly, but
couldn't remove or cover the smell of mammals that inhabited all the
interior spaces and drifted out of the vents.

Major Valentine Knox was a solitary spirit on the ship. His rank allowed
him some freedom from companionship and inquisitiveness, but the
checking and re-checking of each other's service history and prospects and
anecdotes are how soldiers make themselves comfortable in their rootless
lives. And a chap can't be a complete hermit. So he'd been obliged to
give some broadly accurate descriptions of his past career – which the
other officers on board knew or could have found out – and some vaguer
references to his recent and current activities, which they hopefully didn't
and couldn't.

The *Manora* came out of the fresher winds of the Atlantic into the
warmth of the Mediterranean – a warmth that seemed to hang about you,
like an over-friendly dog – during the third week of June 1914. Probably
not halfway through the voyage, and Knox knew he was going mad. Never
fancied the sea. Never fancied confinement.

Companionship. Good thing; part of the appeal. *There's Knox again;
never stops marching, does he?* A few similar chaps on board; like-minded.
Round and round the deck, all bloody day. But the endless card games...
God, he loathed card games. *Keeps himself to himself, don't he?*

Knox was on a troopship to India.

On the morning of the 14th of June, the woman who styled herself the daughter of the Marquis de Valfierno was approached in a hat shop on Vienna's Graben by a woman a little older than her, and veiled. This woman stated that she was the sister of the man who had been seen with the marquis and his daughter on a train from Florence to Berlin; the man had come to look for the marquis and his daughter in Vienna, and had disappeared; the sister would not rest until she learned what had happened. The marquis's daughter could say nothing to help, and hurried from the shop. The woman in the veil disappeared.

That afternoon, an innocuous telegram was sent from the Cäcilien Conservatoire to the address in Geneva that had been in the bundle of messages borrowed by David Duval. The same text was then forwarded from the Geneva address back to Vienna, to the office of the Adriatic Trading Union. From there it went to the office of Iris S.A.

On the same morning, an article had appeared in that section of Vienna's *Neue Freie Presse* devoted to business news. It noted that a magistrate in Switzerland had lodged an enquiry with the office of the state prosecutor in Vienna regarding the status of the Hüpfebrunnen Foundation, following a complaint by a party in Switzerland whose application for a grant from the foundation had been refused.

Later that day two messages were sent by Iris S.A. to the same destination. The coding of one message made it impossible to know whether it concerned the daughter of the Marquis de Valfierno and the woman who had accosted her. The coding of the second message was similarly impenetrable, but one name was of necessity transmitted in clear: that of the Swiss magistrate who had lodged the enquiry about the Hüpfebrunnen Foundation.

In Geneva, and in Vienna, these messages were intercepted. The destination of the last two, sent from Iris S.A., was the International Cultural Exchange in Sarajevo.

Krug's office in Sarajevo was a faded version of his office in Vienna. They kept it spotless for him, of course, because they knew him. And the practical aspects – particularly his prized wireless transmitter – were first-rate. But there was something about the city – those centuries of Ottoman lethargy that a few years of Habsburg insistence would not shake; or perhaps it was the dust merely – that made wood tired before its time, plaster paler, stone worn, something that infused the people too. Vienna was bustle; Sarajevo was languor.

He was fond of the place; acknowledged that he sought excuses to return. After Africa, he had done good work in the Balkans; younger then, of course, running here and there. A playground for espionage! The borders kept changing, and no one acknowledged them anyway. No one was loyal to anything beyond his village, and his worst enemies were usually inside it. Such confusion, and such corruptibility. And Sarajevo was the heart of it: warm sedate life, and cool busy shadows where every kind of business was talked in every kind of language.

Its rhythms of indolence, tobacco-doped and coffee-thickened, infected even him. He would stand at the window, thumbs in waistcoat like some complacent small-town shopkeeper, looking over the square and watching the mingling of every complexion and costume, pale edgy Teutons and rolling Turks, frock-coats and pantaloons and homburgs and fezes, and wonder: a great marketplace of information and of power.

On the desk behind him, another small token of those currencies: the representatives of Berlin and London had initialled an agreement on the 15th of June resolving their differences over the extension of the German railway into Mesopotamia; a perfectly obvious compromise setting a limit to the line and giving the British the reassurances about local control and tariffs that they always craved. A fractional easing of the tension between Britain and Germany; but the other side of the coin could be an increase in the insecurity and volatility of France and Russia, should a man choose to spend it thus.

Alexandria was hot – a dry heat, somehow crisp on one's skin, edged with a sandy breeze coming out of the desert and rustling down the boulevards. To Knox, it felt like a place of work, and the heat accordingly a reassurance of duty. The harbour was thick with ships: grey beasts belching smoke and things of wood and cloth that nipped among them, like butterflies around elephants. Amid the mayhem of the waterfront there were plenty of British uniforms. Mostly he was just glad to be on land again, if only temporarily: march where he wanted; dust on his boots.

The place looked pretty European. The façades could have been Paris or Rome – or Vienna. A lurch of memory. Carriages and European dress, and among them lots of natives in their white get-up – sheets and turbans – as if they'd strayed into the wrong play.

Façade it was. Five blocks back in any direction the buildings dropped to single-storey, sand-brick affairs. The stench lurched at one, the rotting of vegetable and animal matter, and the houses became shacks, timber and loose brick and packing crates and sheets.

His instructions took him through a fruit market to another open space, less hemmed in by buildings and less packed with people and noise. The buildings were squat blocks, sand on sand and unembellished with canopies or displays. Half the signs were in Arabic; those in English or French – a flicker of Knox the schoolboy – advertised wholesalers of dry goods, furniture sellers, horse traders. Much quieter.

In a timber merchant's at the corner of the square, he found a man with a shrivelled hand. Arab-looking fellow. Linen suit, but with a cummerbund and a fez.

'I had a teacher once,' Knox said; 'loved to quote the line... what was it? "Hew me cedar trees out of Lebanon."'

The chap looked past him, glanced around instinctively. 'My servants shall be with thy servants.'

'Unto thee will I give hire.'

The Arab nodded, and disappeared into the gloom of his warehouse. A minute later he was back with an envelope. Knox took it, and stepped away.

In the envelope was a paper, and on the paper only an address. A number, a street, and a city: *Sarajevo*.

He read the address three times, checked it in his head, pulled a box

347

of matches from his pocket and watched the paper flare and twist in his hand. He ground the remains into the dust of the warehouse floor, nodded formally to the Arab, who nodded back, and left.

That afternoon a message was received on the troopship *Manora*, on the headed notepaper of the British Military Ward of the Alexandria Hospital. It stated that KNOX, Major V., had succumbed to a bout of what presented as dysentery but could be something worse. His condition and the possibility of contagion meant that it would be a grave risk for him and for the others on board should he return to the ship. His destination unit in India and his dispatching authority in Britain had been informed of this interruption to his deployment – hopefully only temporary.

⊢═══⊣

As the days had passed, so the memory of the unease in Vienna had faded in James Cade's mind.

He'd made the deal, he hadn't liked the ground, and so he'd got out. It meant that stepping out of the train in Constantinople felt like coming home, and that had been peculiar. Pleasant, though.

He was making a life that worked here. Business quietly prospering, private life pleasant. No one seemed to have noticed the disappearance of Muhtar.

Intermittently, he wondered what Silvas's people had done with the body.

Ani and her brother, Varujan, seemed a little more sure of themselves these days. Varujan's business was flourishing. He'd gladly accepted Cade's hints of what it would take to worsen the pressure on Muhtar – some over-generous loans; a short-term loss – and now he was getting the medium-term benefits. He and his sister contrived somehow to give the impression that they had helped Cade, rather than the reverse. He was invited to the house as a family friend; honoured, and expected to invest here and there, to contribute. There was murmuring through the tobacco smoke of possible partnerships.

Ani had grown comfortable in their relationship, and expecting little gifts. *And why in hell not?* She was languid and lovely, and Cade's passion was becoming fondness.

He and Osman Riza finally made time for one of their lunches. Cade risked a second sherry, and they gossiped a little: Riza about the ministry and Cade about the foibles of the British Embassy. Riza passed some new suggestions that the German Mission was making for Turkish imports; and, under a napkin, a sketch of a plan he'd seen in someone's document case in a meeting, for defensive arrangements in the event of war. Just the sort of thing to keep London content.

London content. The old 'un content. Ani content. Constantinople, it seemed, was a grand place, and James Cade was feeling himself very nicely settled.

━━┅═┅━━

The Foreign Office was surprisingly rambling for such a grand exterior, and Hathaway was doubting the directions right up until she reached the door she wanted. Everything was wooden panels; the sun dropping in through net curtains illuminated sleepy swirls of dust. It was the establishment as she'd always imagined it – more so; only now she had the disturbing sense of the power and clarity that could inhabit the maze.

Even once she'd found the door it didn't seem quite right. No sound in this extremity of the building; unnatural, as if she'd slipped into a dream. Nor did it seem right that what she was beginning to understand of the organization behind her could exist in such anonymity. She knocked.

'Do come in, please, Miss Hathaway.'

The old man rose courteously as she came in. He was holding an envelope, apparently closed, and a match.

'How were your parents? Well, I trust.'

'How did you know it was me?'

'Please sit down.' She did. 'You are naturally a punctual person; I have very few visitors, and almost none unexpected. Would you forgive me if I finished a few administrative chores?'

'You... had me watched? Followed to Derbyshire?'

A smile. 'No, Miss Hathaway, I did not. My resources wouldn't allow it in any case. No, I just rather assumed... back home, you know – natural to remind oneself what's what.' He sat, and focused on envelope and match again.

Hathaway nodded; then – an old impulse of impertinence – 'May I ask what that is?'

The old man lowered both objects to the table. 'Well, yes; let's see what you think, Miss Hathaway.' He raised the envelope slightly. 'This, I infer from certain marks and certain aspects of the internal addressing, is a report. From a man in Constantinople.' He paused, professorial.

'And you habitually burn reports from your sources without reading them?'

'A little exercise for your logic, Miss Hathaway. This man – a man of essentially the same status as three others – travelled recently to... a certain European capital. As did the other three.' Hathaway was working hard to control her face. 'The other three suffered harassment and, in two cases, death there.' She saw his lips thin. A pose of coldness; she knew it for a pose. 'This man came out apparently unharmed. Why might that be, do you suppose?'

He was watching her, just like in that first meeting: weighing her; calculating her. She waited.

'This man has previously sent reports – credible reports – from a certain source he has cultivated. Rather useful snippets about German influence in Constantinople. He has another promising source as well. Now, after his Vienna trip, he sends us a new report.'

The old man pushed the envelope to her side of the desk, and laid the match on top of it.

'Now you have all the information that I do, Miss Hathaway. The envelope too.' He gestured her to it. 'No doubt just the sort of thing our politicians and generals would be fascinated to hear of.'

'You doubt this man's loyalty?'

'I do not.'

'So you worry that he is being manipulated. That he has been recognized as an agent, and left as a channel for false information.'

'I do.'

'You could read the contents; evaluate their credibility.'

'The envelope is before you, Miss Hathaway. You are intelligent and politically alert. Evaluate by all means.'

She reached out for it. Wary, watching his eyes; they were blank again.

She picked up the envelope, by one corner, and held it loose. 'I have... some idea of the sophistication of these people. The report will be credible regardless.' He said nothing; the eyes said nothing. 'If the report makes one assertion, one must suspect it. Having suspected it, one must suspect that one's opponent wants one to do just that, and that the assertion might after all be true.' Nothing. 'Two outcomes are likely: either one's unconscious preferences – one's existing assessment, one's preconception – will influence the evaluation; or all evaluation will be paralysed.'

Two sets of eyes gazed cold at each other. Hathaway struck the match, and waited for the flame to take before dropping the envelope into the wastepaper bin.

Now something flickered on the face. 'Thank you, Miss Hathaway.' The eyes dropped to the desk, and he began to read a document.

There was a newspaper framed precisely by the corner of the desk; Hathaway began to read it.

＊＊＊

On the morning of the 22nd of June, a steamer edged her way close to the wharf of the Romanian port of Constanta. It was an embarrassed approach, made with coughs of smoke and much shuffling of the water. The steamer was black, a battered beetle squirming and belching her way along the wharf. Seen against the white walls of the houses, against the mosques and the cathedral with its lively stripes in the stone, she was a foul thing.

Shyly she found her berth, and the crew began to moor. Before the first rope was tied, a man had stepped from the deck onto the dockside, a small rucksack on his back and a stride hungry for land.

Major Valentine Knox had come back to Europe.

＊＊＊

'Miss Hathaway.'

Hathaway focused. 'I beg your pardon. Just something in the newspaper. It's— Would you object if I took this page?' He shook his head. She pulled out the page and began to fold it carefully. 'A woman called Bertha von Suttner has died; yesterday. She was...'

'The Austrian. She won the Swedish prize for peace.'

'I met her.'

'Yes. I recall. She made an impression, I think.' Hathaway hesitated, and then nodded with something like defiance. 'And her death must seem a kind of symbol.'

'Symbolic, perhaps, that one of the most remarkable people of the age is given only a note at the bottom of the seventh page.'

The conservatory. The woman in the chair, her crown of hair, her bulk, her implacability, her sharpness. Staring out into the darkness.

The old man watched her.

'I didn't expect you to love the idea of war, Miss Hathaway. Leave that to the arms dealers and the poets. But, given the likelihood of war, I hoped you would make a rational analysis of which outcome would best guard what you care about: your family, the possibility of the realization of certain ideals; then I expected you to apply your mind to securing that outcome.'

'Pretty speech, sir, and as shrewd as ever. But the logic is uneven. Your actions may give us advantage in war, or mitigate its effects, but they increase its likelihood nonetheless.' She looked at him bleak. 'Even I. My jaunt through Germany, my little games of adventure. I was a message to Germany; a confirmation of her prejudices and fears, and in response there will have been some countervailing action, some countervailing actress, to confirm our prejudices and fears and further increase the likelihood of war.'

She shook her head; a flash of Gerta in her mind. 'It should be possible for two people to reinforce sympathy, not fear.'

He nodded, very slowly. Then: 'It falls to very few that they may change the world. Some have the character and the opportunity to change their place in it. After sixty years, the number and variety of men – better men – that I might have been is large indeed. But I find myself in this room.

352

In this Europe.'

'As do I. That's your implication presumably.'

'I don't ask your motives in being here. Nor do I tell you what your motives should be for what you do next. If they lead you to assist me, I may know that it would be of benefit to me, but I could make no assertion about its effect on you. You are alone.'

✦

Knox hadn't been to Belgrade before. Gloomy sort of place. Good-looking women.

He was on the edge of the battlefield now. The old man had been clear on the point. Serbia's interests were close to Britain's, but that went for nothing in this part of the world. Vienna worried about Belgrade, and Vienna was correspondingly active in Belgrade. Within the Spider's web. Ballentyne had been in Belgrade, and it had been from Belgrade that they'd lured him.

In enemy country, you must take it for granted that you will encounter the enemy. Do not look for the observers, because it only makes you more easily observed. Be alive and stay alive.

Knox walked the side streets on feet that seemed to echo through the world, a world made of porcelain. He heard the stones moving against each other, knew that if he broke his even anonymous tread they would explode around him.

A bar in Skadarlija; a phrase to the barman.

Then wait.

He sat on his own, sipping at a beer, for an hour. He was alert to the room, to the rumble as a finger moved across a table, the creak as a head turned, the thump of a closing eye. But he did not seem to watch it. A man on his own, staring into nothing.

He knew that the whole room was watching him; the whole world.

No tricks; no games to pass the time. His whole consciousness, his whole existence, was concentrated in this room; concentrated in muscle and sense; concentrated in the terrible and extraordinary phenomenon of being alive in this body in this moment.

After an exact hour, half the beer undrunk, he got up and left.

Neither age nor success takes from a man his insecurities. Indeed, the more years and the more power he acquires, the more he feels he has to lose. A man never loses the instinct to show his neighbour his latest acquisition, in the hope that this time at last he will receive the respect that is his due.

By the 23rd of June 1914, the Royal Navy's Second Battle Squadron had gathered in Kiel. At its heart were four dreadnought battleships, the *King George V*, the *Ajax*, the *Audacious,* and the *Centurion.* They were superlatives. Only buildings had ever been built anything like as big: the dreadnoughts were the cathedrals of the new century, monuments to man's technical ingenuity and to his aspiration to a power transcending anything else human, a power touching the almighty. In the last week of June 1914, the last week of the last summer of the world, Kiel hosted the most powerful men, and the most powerful weapons, in existence.

The voice seemed to come at the old man out of the fog, and his stick was up and across his chest ready for defence or attack before he'd absorbed the words. It was still braced there as the voice solidified into the figure of Thomson – solid indeed – stepping forwards onto the path.

St James's Park was a cloud of greys: the trees and shrubs, Thomson one of them, were darker shadows in the fog; the lake might not have been there, but for the far-off splash or squawk of a duck. Thomson made one wide circuit of where the two of them stood, before coming in close and speaking.

'We think we have him. A clerk in the Ports and Consulates Office. Name of Palmer.'

'Ports and Consulates...' A long sigh. 'I see...'

'It was your tip that did it. The reason why this chap Ballentyne was picked up, and none other. When you asked for the whereabouts of the four, his name went into Ports and Consulates because he was thought likely to be abroad.'

The old man held up a hand, like a marker post in the fog, straining for clarity. 'Hathaway. The Spider got onto Hathaway... when we ran a search on Auerstein.' The hand closed into a fist, and dropped slowly. 'Ideal place to have a spy. The Spider would know if we were flagging people coming in or out.'

'And the offices are close enough for this chap Palmer to be able to pop across and check the general files. He would also have been able to start the enquiry about your man Duval, or whatever his name was.'

'Can you prove it's this man Palmer?'

'We're turning his life upside down. But... no. No, we can't.'

The old man swished at the grey with his stick, and the fog swirled around the tip.

⊢══⊣

Twenty-four hours later, Knox returned to the same bar, said the same thing to the barman, and sat nursing a glass of the same brand of beer for the same length of time. He knew that the whole room was watching him; the whole world. After an exact hour, a little of the beer undrunk, he got up and left.

In the street, he heard the whispering of the shadows. Hesitated, then set off on a roundabout route towards the doss-house where he was bedding down.

As he moved, he had the sense of someone appearing in the doorway of the bar behind him. But no steps followed him. They wouldn't, not if they were any good. Just a signal, if anything.

Sure enough, something wavered in the blackness across the street as he walked. Something flickered briefly in the pool of a street lamp and then was gone.

He walked on.

Fifty yards further he turned right; the street was narrow – almost an alley – and it was darker and sounds echoed louder. Immediately there were footsteps behind him. Their pace was forced; they were catching him up. Then a shift in the shadow in front of him – they'd got in front of him; that was smart work – and immediately they had him between them.

Knox stopped. Felt the night with his fingertips, steadied his feet on the cobbles. Waited.

Expected and acceptable. The figure in front said in English, 'Good evening.' Knox nodded.

Then a wrench at his collar, the man behind trying to pull his jacket down around his shoulders. Not acceptable, and Knox was driving backwards against the man behind, still driving as the back of his head smashed into the man's nose and he sent him stumbling; only then did he turn, the momentum becoming a backhand that kept the attacker stumbling away, and Knox found his balance and with dancing feet sent two straight punches into the man's face. Around to the other man, ready for—

There was a pistol one foot from his forehead, cocked and steady.

'You come with us, or you pass the rest of your life on this spot. You come with us, you come with us on our terms.'

Knox straightened his jacket. 'After you, old chap.'

<hr />

Yet another corridor in Whitehall, panelling and tiles that carried distant footsteps, like hints or memories. 'Pardon me, sir.'

The old man turned. 'Mayhew. I trust you're well.'

'Well enough, thank you.' The colonel came closer. 'Not wishing to stick my nose in, of course, but we picked up something that might interest you.'

'You're most kind.'

'Kiel. We're keeping a particular eye, because of the fleet being there. There's a set-up called the Baltic Design Bureau. Never noticed them, never meant anything, until your man Duval went through. Because of him, we got the idea they might be some sort of front office for part of the German Intelligence machinery.'

'I remember.'

'We intercepted a wireless message addressed to that office. It reports that other sources – presumably German spies in Britain – have confirmed that one of our seaplanes participating in the regatta at Kiel has the new engine configuration. It says that a man named von Cramm will be arriving to manage the situation.'

'Manage it, eh? And von Cramm.'

'He was bound up with that business of Hamel; we never proved that von Cramm sabotaged Hamel's aeroplane, but...'

'Quite. I have suspicions enough of Herr von Cramm.' The old man absorbed it all, considered it, then looked up. 'Some preparations will be necessary. Thank you, Mayhew. Public-spirited of you.' Mayhew nodded.

The old man turned away, then stopped. 'Colonel: Duval didn't make it.' Mayhew's uncertainties, suspicions, flickered in his face. 'He died.'

'Oh. Sorry to hear that.'

The old man turned to go.

'Doing his bit, what?'

The old man stopped again. 'Yes. Yes, he was.'

<hr />

Knox's hands had been tied immediately, which effectively stopped him running as well as resisting. The cord bit into his wrists, unnecessarily tight, revenge from the man he'd knocked down. He'd been escorted a few hundred yards through back streets, then pushed up into a carriage – again, more roughly than was necessary. Then the world went dark, a bag pulled over his head.

He relaxed his limbs; concentrated on sounds. The presence of his two escorts, shifting and breathing near him; another man – driver, presumably; a horse breathing, and then they were rolling forwards. There were five minutes of swaying through the streets; he assumed back streets, for discretion, and tried to gauge changes of direction. Then they had stopped.

Pushed down out of the carriage, hands gripping his biceps and steering him. 'Step!' But it was too late, and he was stumbling forwards and his escorts were pulling him upright and swearing at him. 'Down steps!' And this time they were more careful with him, holding him as he took the steps one clumsy pace at a time. Wooden staircase.

Odd smell. Sort of thick; sweet-sharp.

Steered along corridor, through door, then he was pushed down into a chair.

After a second, he knew there were more people in the room. His escorts behind him, and another body — no, two bodies — breathing and shifting somewhere in front of him.

He waited. Trying to keep the blood flowing in his fingers; flexing the muscles in his feet and ankles.

'Who are you?' English, but spoken by a foreigner. Accent thick. One of those in front of him. Heavy smoker.

'That depends on who you are.'

Someone moving closer in behind him. 'You are not in a position to play games.'

Knox said, carefully, 'When fortune smiles it is easy to be brave.'

Silence.

He listened for movement; nothing.

Then, from the man in front again, 'Adversity does prove the warrior soul.' Pause. 'Do you now condescend to answer?'

'I am Major Valentine Knox. I am an agent of British Intelligence.'

Another pause. Then a word, and his arms were being pulled and twisted and there was a blade at his wrists and he flinched and suddenly his wrists came free. He hissed his discomfort as the blood started to flow again, tried to massage the wrists without too much show of pain. Irritated at his own discomfiture, he pushed on quickly: 'I seek a meeting with the man known as Apis.'

Everyone shifted at once. Then settled. Waited.

'That name is a fantasy only.'

'I deal in fantasies.'

Again silence. The smell: was it malt? A brewery?

'What would you want to say to this Apis?'

'To ask his help.'

'The British Empire needs the help of little Serbia?'

'In Serbia's interests as well.'

'The British do not care about Serbia. You do not care about the Serbs of Bosnia, suffering under Austrian tyranny. You use us when we are useful to your strategy, then you forget. You are not present in this region; you are not active in this region.'

'My presence says otherwise.'

'You have come; you will go. We will be left alone again.'

'To depend on the promises and the restraint of Germany, and Austria, and the countries you fought last year.'

'Perhaps.'

'Good luck with that.'

'Perhaps you don't know our resilience. Our diplomacy.'

'Perhaps you don't know that on the 26th of May the Kaiser met the heir to the Austro-Hungarian throne and urged him to deal with Serbia now.'

Silence.

Eventually: 'There was an Englishman named Pickford.' Knox waited. The name he'd been given by the old man. The contact here, the man Ballentyne had been in touch with. 'He was found dead.'

'I see.' They wanted more. 'If you know who he was, you know that my organization would not have wanted him dead.'

'Oh, we don't mind that he's dead, Major. But you people are obviously unhealthy. Accident-prone.' The idiom was uncomfortable. Pause. 'Dangerous to know.' Now the voice was closer. 'We would think very carefully before associating with you.'

'I represent a man who represents an organization as old as your nation. A man who represents an ancient friendship. A man who knows the three Truths.' He could feel the uncertainty now, hear the thinking. He hoped he'd remembered the dates aright. 'The Truths of 1804, 1815 and 1903.'

Something changed; some signal, and now there was movement all around him again. The disruption of air, the tap of steps towards him – and past him, and then the door closing.

Silence. No movement now, no presence.

Then three steps towards him, someone standing over him, the sound of breathing – and then the bag was pulled off his head.

To: Ports & Consulates Office

From: SSO

A representative of this office with highest authority is travelling to SARAJEVO on exceptional liaison business. He

will be travelling as MARSDEN. (For operational reasons, he
will not arrive before 29 June earliest.) Given the diversity
of those he will be trying to meet, and the urgency and
sensitivity of his mission, he may contact you directly
and at short notice requesting information. You are hereby
empowered, on the authority of this department under FO
I.iii.2, to respond directly and with all promptness.

The knock at the door was soft, single. Krug finished the sentence he was writing before acknowledging it. A clerk entered, carried an envelope to the desk, and left again all in silence. Envelopes even for the movement of messages between rooms of the building; a moment of satisfaction at the order of his world.

The message was a transcription of another message. The details copied, and smuggled out of an office in London and delivered to a post office for collection; collected by other hands, and – depending on the sensitivity and urgency of the information – either cabled from London or taken to a house in Gravesend and radioed from there; and thence by a series of stages the message would come into his hands wherever he was.

As soon as he saw the originator's designation, Krug was sitting forward. The same as before...

The paper as if electric. He saw a creased photograph in his mind. *I have never been this close to you...*

<hr />

Knox was glad of his jacket, thick like his army rig and hard-wearing for travel. The evenings got cool quickly hereabouts. The last of the sun still clutched at the hilltops to the west, but here in the valley everything was blue-grey shadow and no warmth. The village was a huddle of houses tucked in a bend of the river, and the veranda where he and his companion sat – a timber creeper-wrapped framework projecting from the front of a house, two benches – was the only place to get a drink.

'And now, Major, you fulfil your share of the bargain.'

His companion was called Rade. Pronounced as two syllables. First name, apparently, and that was all he'd given. A compact, watchful sort of chap.

'Seems odd you needing me to get across the border,' Knox said. A petulant remark, and he knew it; didn't like the fellow's tone.

'As the colonel promised, we deliver you to the border, and our courier will meet us on the other side and deliver you to Sarajevo. For the border, British Intelligence must show its ability.'

Meaning that British Intelligence must show one of its very few assets. It had indeed been the deal with the colonel, a bull of a man with shaven head and waxed moustache, always in shadow and always watching and calculating. Knox had needed to get Serbian Military Intelligence on his side, to avoid the risk of being stopped as he passed through Serbia; and he needed them to get him to Sarajevo, which Comptrollerate-General assets could not guarantee. The old man had been clear on each point.

'Some sort of problem with your network, is there? I'd have thought you'd be back and forth across the border daily.'

Some of the mischief went out of Rade's face, leaving a dead smile. 'We are, as you say, very active. But after some recent activity – someone was a little casual with his security – the Austrian authorities became more interested in our arrangements on the border. For a week or two now we do not use these arrangements.'

Knox took a sip of his firewater. Filthy stuff, but welcome in the evening. Cartwheels rattled somewhere behind them. 'Seems I turned up at the right time, then. Help you across for whatever you need.'

The mischief was back. 'Meaning: what I am crossing into Bosnia for?' Knox didn't rise to it. 'We're both too polite for those questions, eh, Major? Anyway, I'm just a messenger boy.'

The river was the border. This side of it – the remaining fifty yards of mud and shacks – was Serbia. The other side – one hundred yards of water away – was Bosnia–Hercegovina, the newest acquisition of the Austrian Empire. The river was what Vienna, and Berlin, looked across when they considered how finally to deal with defiant, mischievous Serbia.

A few hundred yards away was the bridge.

'Excuse me,' said a voice from the shadows beside them. Rade looked stung; Knox had been expecting it, but it was still a jolt. 'I heard you talking in English; are you with Dr Grant?' A slight figure in the gloom, face obscured.

'No,' Knox replied. 'I'm on a walking holiday. I am interested in butterflies.'

'It is not the best season.'

Knox nodded to Rade, and stood. Rade finished the last of his firewater, and followed. He'd been unperturbed by the exchange and the outcome. *Old hand.*

The figure led them down a track beside the house, to a horse and cart. The horse was a weary grey, with a glorious multicoloured blanket over its back. The cart was open for the driver at the front, but the rear was sheltered by canvas.

'I am curious how you do this,' Rade murmured. 'Someone trying to enter who has not already an exit stamp on his papers is checked very closely. If the papers are forgeries, I hope they are good ones. I think the colonel told you I would be a big prize for the Austrian police.'

'Don't you trust us, old chap?'

Rade looked at him as if he were insane, and Knox chuckled.

Their guide gestured them up into the back of the cart. Clambering into its gloom, they found a pair of moth-eaten overcoats and hats, and a mound of blankets. 'Put on the clothes.' They did so, and slumped down with their backs against the driver's bench, and their guide covered them in the blankets so that only glimpses of face showed. 'You are too sick to move or speak,' he said. 'Do not move. Do not speak.'

He climbed up onto the bench, and chivvied the horse into movement, and they began to sway and bounce along the track towards the bridge.

At the near end, the Serbian policeman came near and saw the driver and nodded the cart past. The tone of the wheels changed: sharper, clearer as they swung onto the bridge.

Knox felt his heart in his chest; felt his pistol in his pocket. He couldn't see anything except a window of Serbian forest shaking and dwindling behind them. Ahead, somewhere behind his shoulders, Austrian sentries were waiting. The dwindling dusky forest, the noise of the wheels on the bridge, and the crossing seemed to take an age.

Then shouts, and then they were stopped. Words of challenge to the driver that Knox could not understand; a murmured reply, calm. Then boots, and the unique rattle of rifle and sling against shoulder. Something began to glimmer through the gaps in the canvas and then the open back of the cart blazed white and a lantern was thrust in.

Mumbled words, and the lantern swung away. The boots receded. More words, and the cart jerked into movement again.

Enemy country.

They bounced onwards, slumped in the back and unmoving, and Knox through half-closed eyes saw a town around them and then the houses shrank and they were into open country.

After a mile, darkness only, they rolled to a halt. A moment later the figure was at the back of the cart again. 'Out now,' he said, and began to pull at the blankets. 'Keep the coats and hats.' He thrust a handful of papers at them. 'If you need. Not for long.'

Rade looked at them warily. 'Forgeries.'

'Two men crossed the bridge yesterday, too sick to speak. Two men crossed back today, too sick to speak. The papers are good.'

'Won't those two men need them?'

'They were not too sick to speak; they were too dead to speak. Their papers outlived them. Do you know where you are?'

Rade looked around in the dusk. The cart had pulled in beside a fork in the road. He nodded.

They shook hands with their guide, and tramped off into the gloom. Ten minutes' walking brought them back into the outskirts of the settlement, where Rade led them to a single-storey house. The door opened to his knock, and he murmured something and something was murmured back, and they were in. The man holding the door was too tall for the room, and solid. 'Welcome to imprisoned Bosnia,' he said to Knox, and with an effort he wrestled the planks of the door back into their frame.

＊＝＝＝＊

Off Kiel the ships sat massive against the sky, monochrome and ominous. The bunting and the brass band music, intended to enliven their presence, only emphasized their implacability. Thousands of Germans – princes, officers, sailors and civilians, dressed in the brightest feathers and the dirtiest rags – watched the monsters and considered their own fears. Around them buzzed smaller ships, magnifying the dreadnoughts by their own tininess. The waters of the Baltic seethed with their traffic, but the battleships were impassive. Intermittently, an aircraft – for many, the first they had ever seen – would buzz across the sky, minute and frail against the clouds.

Two pairs of eyes considered the aircraft more expertly.

'You are determined to proceed with this plan, Mein Herr? If it is a matter of revenge, we have surely—'

'It is not revenge. That action was a necessary intervention to stop German secrets reaching England.' Von Cramm watched another aircraft disappear into the clouds. 'The British still owe me an air machine.'

+≡≡≡+

Knox and his two companions – Rade and a lad now guiding them, Dragan – walked most of the day, away from the road and up into the hills. This was the route they had decided on, it seemed, to minimize the chance of being seen and stopped by the Austrian police. Rade wasn't all that solid, but seemed fit enough; the lad looked a rather frail specimen: city-raised; a student. Knox didn't walk as fast as he might have done. But they were proud, and fit enough to last the day without difficulty. Late in the afternoon, they came round the top of a hill and began to drop quickly into a valley. Shortly afterwards, a town was visible below them.

Halfway down the valley, their way now clearly a path, the Serbs insisted on stopping in a hut – a low thing of stone, with planks for a roof; presumably once a sheep pen – until dusk. Knox approved of the precaution. They passed around a flask of the local firewater, and ate some bread. The lad, Dragan, quizzed Knox on his knowledge of Serb history. Did he know how long their people had been in this place? Did he understand that the border between Serbia and Bosnia–Hercegovina was only an accident of the past, a detail of Ottoman and Habsburg jostling, an unnatural barrier between brothers? Did he know of the oppression of the Serbs in Bosnia–Hercegovina, now forced to live under the Austrians? Even worse than the Turks!

Knox knew the outlines of it, and wasn't sure that Dragan's version of the story would give him much that was reliable. But he let him chatter and boast, with occasional wiser embellishments from Rade, and injected sympathy or surprise when it seemed appropriate.

When the sun dropped behind the surrounding hills, they set off down into the town, and five minutes after reaching the first houses they were being ushered in through a front door by a man whose furtiveness and anxiety were perhaps understandable but certainly calculated to draw attention, had anyone seen his beckoning and his glances around behind them. Immediately there was supper: bread and potatoes and beans and more firewater. Knox was not introduced to their host, which bothered neither of them. The talk, over an intricately embroidered but much stained tablecloth, seemed to be of families and of politics. Knox ate in contented silence.

Immediately the food was finished, their host chivvied them up into an attic room, where mattresses and bedding were ready. He seemed happy to get them out of his own sight. The two Serbs continued to pass the flask around, and to lecture Knox or – when his polite interest was insufficient – each other on history and politics. Eventually the firewater made them drowsy and, after some last murmured invocations of God and country, then they were asleep. Knox checked the door, his kit, his pistol under the pillow; then he took a second look out of the window to remind himself how it would work as entry or exit. At last he too lay down. A glance at the two faces, now deeply asleep.

The gruntings and shiftings of men asleep together; a lifetime of barracks and tents. There was a kind of comfort in it: familiarity, companionship. But the lad, Dragan... he was almost young enough be his son.

Must beware foolishness. Old buffer trying to be one of the boys, twenty years too late. Embarrassing. He glanced again at the two of them, and smiled. Fit enough and wise enough for this generation yet. Never seen himself as a general, anyway, bustling staff and unbroken nights. He slept.

The morning came with shouts and a bayonet.

On the 23rd of June the commander of the British Battle Squadron had been received by the commander-in-chief of the German High Seas Fleet, on board His Imperial Majesty's Ship *Friedrich der Grosse*. Admiral Sir George Warrender was later received by their Imperial Highnesses the Prince Henry and the Princess Irene, granddaughter of Queen Victoria and sister-in-law of the Tsar of all the Russias. Their flawless English was much commented on. The prince – the emperor's brother and a grand admiral, the inspector-general of the Germany Navy – then visited H.M.S. *King George V*; the prince and the dreadnought shared a grandmother, of course.

On the morning of 24th June, Grand Admiral Alfred von Tirpitz arrived in Kiel and received his British guests on board His Imperial Majesty's Ship *Friedrich Karl*. The British officers got a first look at the man they had seen so often in photographs, the creator of the new German Navy as rival to the Royal Navy, his distinctive dome of a head and his elaborately forked beard; Tirpitz talked in English of the weather, of his memories of Plymouth, of the experiences of his daughters at Cheltenham Ladies' College. There were final discussions about preparations for the ceremonial arrival of the Kaiser that afternoon: the salute by naval guns; the aerial formation of assorted British and German aircraft, the gestures of exchange and fraternity.

Shouts and hammering and a slam and more shouts, and Knox came awake wild to see a bayonet pointing at his throat. The instinct of shock, the instinct of resistance, and then the control. He breathed. He considered the bayonet and the face behind the bayonet; a boy, almost, as wide-eyed as the man on the other end of the bayonet had been. Knox looked away from the tip to the rest of the attic. Another uniform was waving another bayonet between the two Serbs, Rade wild and Dragan still gaping and scared. Behind the two uniforms, a third, reviewing what he had just captured. He snapped words into the room, in a language Knox didn't recognize. He repeated them, and pointed at Rade. Rade said something back. The officer in charge didn't challenge what he'd said, but didn't seem convinced either.

Knox was suppressing consideration of whether their host had sold them. First point: the Serbs had said that police checks – harassment – were frequent; this seemed like a check rather than an arrest. Second point: the possibility of resistance or escape. The lad with the bayonet didn't look strong or sure of himself, and Knox fancied he'd have a fair chance of getting under the bayonet once the lad started to relax, and then it was all to play for. A bayonet on a rifle makes the bundle a deal more cumbersome, especially in an attic room. But he couldn't be sure how his two companions would react, and if there was a chance to avoid having to attack a man wielding a bayonet it was usually a good one.

These were the deductions of seconds. Knox tried to relax himself; tried to read the officer's face. Wondered if one of his companions would try anything stupid. Now the officer was kicking at Rade's rucksack. He bent down to it.

Rade's face turned quickly towards Knox. 'Do nothing!' he said in German. 'This happens sometimes. It is routine.' The officer's glance followed Rade's.

Why the hell had he spoken in German? Perhaps he knew the officer was Austrian; perhaps he thought that giving a calming message in the officer's language would help to convince him they were not a risk. But the immediate and natural effect was to turn the officer's attention to Knox. He stepped to him. 'Who are you?' he asked in German.

'I'm a tourist,' Knox replied in the same. 'An anthropologist. I'm British.'

The officer stuck to German. 'Your name? Your documents?'

'My name is Marsden. Here.' Deliberately, Knox lifted the fold of the jacket beside him and pulled out his identity paper.

The officer considered it, and then played with the name. 'Ma- Ma-res... Maresden.' He looked up. 'You will wait here. You must not move.'

They did not move. One of the policemen stayed in the room, rifle and bayonet standing loose in his hand beside him. The officer and the other left. Knox and his companions could have rushed the sentry, but the tension had gone out of the room and it didn't seem necessary. After fifteen minutes, Rade and Dragan were starting to probe the policeman with little comments, which he tried to ignore but then started to answer. After twenty minutes they were having an intermittent conversation. The officer was back inside thirty minutes, with Marsden's identity document and permission to leave.

⊰≡≡⊱

To the north of the main port complex at Kiel there was a harbour separate from the rest. The evolution of Kiel as a city and naval base, and the development of ships with ever greater draught, had left it behind. It was used as an overflow berth for vessels that didn't need deeper water or more advanced dock machinery.

In the week of the regatta of 1914, the harbour was loaned to the British for their use. Alongside a floating jetty, a seaplane bobbed. It was a gawky insect in Royal Naval Air Service markings, with its high wings and its floats, unnatural against the backdrop of warehouse walls and scrubland.

In the cockpit, von Cramm was reconfirming his familiarity with the essential controls. They hadn't even needed to whistle up the fuel cart. Something flickered on the edge of his vision, and he looked up to see a figure trotting along the quayside towards the jetty – a figure in a British uniform. 'Quickly!' he hissed to two engineers standing by. 'Untie the machine!'

'There is not time, Mein Herr; not with the engine too.'

'You know what to do, then.'

The two engineers were standing back respectfully as the British officer – a naval uniform – climbed down onto the jetty and hurried towards them.

Nearing the seaplane, he slowed as he saw the body of a British sailor slumped on the jetty.

He glanced at the engineers, then up towards the cockpit. 'Good morning.' It was not friendly. 'Mackay, Royal Navy. I must clearly tell you, sir, that you are not supposed to be in this machine. I must clearly tell you that no arrangement has been made for a German inspection of this machine, and that if you do not climb down from it now you will be in breach of all protocol agreements concerning the regatta. And I'd be obliged if you'd tell me what's happened to my sentry.'

'I am about to take off in this seaplane – Commander, is it? – Commander Mackay. In the fraternal spirit of this regatta, to participate in the display welcoming the emperor. So charming, these exchanges of equipment, no? Your sentry and one of my engineers had an unfortunate misunderstanding, and I regret to say that there was a lapse in discipline.'

Mackay glanced back. 'Is he dead?'

'Merely unconscious. When he regains consciousness, he will not remember anything to contradict what I say.'

'I don't believe you.'

'What you believe is irrelevant. Even if your sentry tries to contradict the German account of this incident, your high command will not contemplate making a controversy out of the story of one confused sailor, when set against the magnitude of this week's activity.' A smile, cold. 'And its fraternal spirit.'

'And me? You planning to knock me out as well?'

'No, Commander.' A sound from behind him, and Mackay glanced over his shoulder to see a pistol pointing at his spine. He turned to von Cramm again. 'If you do not walk away from this jetty immediately, my colleague will shoot you and your body will be weighted and thrown into the harbour here, and you will become an unfortunate footnote to the European pageant that continues over your corpse.'

'You can make me disappear, but not an aircraft.'

'Its loss will be explained easily enough.'

The officer looked around the empty waterfront. Inspiration: 'There's a reason why the support boat and mechanics aren't here. An intermittent fault with the engine, which they can't diagnose or solve; they got leave to push off and watch the regatta until a specialist fitter can get here. I must warn you—'

'Oh, come! Now you become desperate – though your little story will serve us well. Ask yourself whether this small disclosure of British technology to Germany is really worth your life, and then step aside.'

A minute later – Mackay watching intently from a distance – the engine coughed and growled and became a roar; two minutes later its pitch rose to a whine, and the seaplane began to accelerate over the water until, as it came clear of the harbour mouth, the last clutches of foam dropped away from the floats and it was airborne and rising gracefully towards the sun.

***

A pair of cigarettes: Krug's danced in the air as he spoke; Hildebrandt's rarely moved, shrinking in regular draughts of great strength.

'Berlin thinks that Austria is too indecisive, Herr Krug; too accommodating. If Serbia is to be destroyed, it must be quickly. Austria's duty is to fight Russia.'

'Her duty?'

'European war is no longer a game for dilettantes, Mein Herr. Strategy must be European or it is nothing. Austria must hold Russia while Germany wins in the west.'

'Germany must win quickly, if Austria is not to be overwhelmed.' Hildebrandt nodded. 'Berlin worries about Serbia as much as Austria does, Hildebrandt. Your masters fear for their links to Constantinople and beyond; their precious railway.'

'Berlin would be delighted to see Austria smash Serbia. But this constant hesitancy and change keeps Austria weak and strengthens her enemies.'

'You want such a war, Hildebrandt? France, and Russia, and all?'

'It will not be my choice. But I will be ready for it.'

Krug smiled. 'Good, Hildebrandt. That's good.' The telephone jangled. Krug lifted the receiver and listened. Then: 'Was he? But... Good. That's good. The name again?... Very good... No – no further action. Thank you.' He replaced the instrument. A smile. 'He's on time, it seems.'

Hildebrandt nodded. Another suck at the cigarette. 'Herr Krug: after everything, you do not want war?'

'A war of such a scale?' A spasmodic shake of Krug's head, distasteful. 'Chaos. I prefer my conflicts elegant, manageable. If Europe destroys itself, who is left for poor Krug to do business with?'

***

'Herr Colonel, I regret that I bring you bad news.'

Colonel Walter Nicolai looked up; his neck stiffened and his head came higher and the eyes went colder – it passed for an instruction to proceed.

'Herr Colonel, I regret to report that von Cramm, the pilot, has crashed in the British seaplane that he was flying.'

Nicolai smiled. Behind the smile, a laugh pulsed in his throat.

'Herr Colonel?'

'When you understand, Tretsche, you will wish to share in my satisfaction. The news you bring is not tragedy. It is confirmation of a very neat little comedy. Von Cramm did not crash. That is just the report that has been circulated. He has made a controlled landing in the air-machine. Our engineers are examining the prototype engine that it contained. The British will be presented with the burned-out wreckage. Von Cramm will go away to recover from injuries that are reported to be very serious.' Again the laugh beat in the throat. 'But he will make a fast recovery.'

'Please forgive me, Herr Colonel, but you do not understand. I was aware of this plan; you will recall that I was present when it was discussed earlier in the week. Something went wrong, Herr Colonel. The machine crashed into the sea. The British Navy are recovering the wreckage. There is no doubt that von Cramm is dead.'

When His Imperial Majesty Kaiser Wilhelm II arrived in Kiel in his yacht *Hohenzollern*, every ship in the British and German fleets fired a twenty-one-gun salute from her main armament, and the Baltic heavens thundered. A Zeppelin airship drifted overhead, regal among the circling aircraft. The atmosphere of celebration and grandeur had been little affected by one British seaplane crashing into the sea – great drama overlooks its minor accidents – and His Imperial Majesty received Admiral Sir George Warrender and the British captains.

On the 25th of June, wearing Royal Naval dress uniform, the Kaiser visited Sir George, and the British orchestra played popular German tunes. This day was the formal opening of the regatta. His Imperial Majesty challenged Sir George to a race.

German officers were invited to see the British ships. They tested the mahogany furniture, the leather armchairs and sofas, the real fireplaces; they considered the ten main guns on each ship, contemplated the effect of a projectile thirteen and a half inches wide fired ten miles.

By the 26th of June the streets of Kiel were a cheerful mix of British sailors and German, and the city's inhabitants were happy to celebrate such a lucrative tide of enthusiasm flowing through their shops. The city had been a power for seven centuries, a place of trade and a place of maritime power, and it was only appropriate that they should host the spectacle. The British travelled free on German public transport, and there were sports competitions between teams from the two navies.

Admiral Sir George Warrender offered an open invitation to his opposite, Admiral Ingenohl, for German sailors to tour British ships. Only the wireless rooms and the gunnery-control stations of the conning towers would be off-limits. Admiral Ingenohl did not feel able to reciprocate, and so the invitation was declined – with polite regret and quiet satisfaction from both sides.

In one amusing incident, a dinghy sailed by Lord Brassey and one of his sailors from the yacht *Sunbeam* strayed into Kiel's submarine dock. It was not clear how he had managed to find his way so far, and the authorities were obliged to arrest his lordship. His lordship was a friend of His Imperial Majesty the Kaiser, however, and freed in good spirits in time for dinner with him. The sketch map he had carried had disappeared, the last trace of David Duval's daring swallowed by the waters of the Baltic.

Later that evening, on the other side of Europe – a Europe of warmer skins and more varied costumes, a Europe where two civilizations met, a Europe where the traditions of the Continent's greatest cities mixed with those of its rawest mountains – Major Valentine Knox came through the Miljacka valley into the city of Sarajevo.

⊷⊶

The Sub-Committee of the Committee of Imperial Defence:
'Gentlemen, is there no useful conclusion we can draw on Ireland?'
'We're waiting to see.'

'They're all waiting to see. Meanwhile they're arming.'

'The PM has had to be extremely shrewd on this one. Constructive ambiguity in the text. No one's quite sure what the arrangement for Home Rule will be.'

'The PM's pardon, but he's been too shrewd by half. Both sides smell a rat. If they're tolerating his bill it's because they're expecting it to be overtaken by civil war.'

'We have increasingly clear reports of the nationalists trying to buy arms. They saw what the Volunteers did at Larne, and they want the same.'

'The difference is that one lot are essentially patriots, the others essentially anarchists.'

'Gentlemen, whatever our views on the merits of their causes, we surely cannot be happy with a flood of arms into Ulster. There's little difference between one Briton and another firing rifles at each other.'

'Have we *any* useful intelligence on this?' Silence. 'Any that colleagues are prepared to share?' Silence. 'The objective of our new departmental arrangements was the facilitation of efficient co-operation, not competition.'

'Chairman, the question is more perhaps that we have no useful security options. We do not have a neutral force with a realistic chance of keeping the peace.'

'Which brings us back to the politicians.'

'Smoke and mirrors. He's merely delayed the crisis. Perhaps only weeks.' Papers were straightened. A pen tapped nervously on a blotter.

'Lighter note: the picture's a little rosier on the Continent, I should say.'

'The signs from Kiel are certainly good.'

'We agree. The foreign secretary is rather pleased.'

'That's naturally our main concern in the War Office.'

'Gentlemen, if I may venture a generalization, the European situation – and I'm also thinking of Persia, where the Russians have behaved themselves better in recent weeks, and of the Baghdad railway accord – is rather less tense than it has been at not a few points in the last fifteen years.'

'Fat lot of good that is if we have civil war in our back garden.'

The battlefield. Major Valentine Knox had only known open battle – an enemy with a uniform and a rifle trying to kill you – in southern Africa, as a young infantry officer. The thirst. The sand. The wretched thorny scrub. The faces of his men, sweating and stubbly, watching him and appraising him and waiting for his command. Blood: soaking scarlet on the khaki of uniforms; thickening to a dark paste in the dust.

But the principle was the same here: the terrain; the enemy; the objective.

He was up and out early on the morning of the 27th. He'd considered dawn and dusk; and rejected them. Solitary prowler conspicuous; telltale sign. So now he sat in the window of a café, among the first of the morning clientele wanting a hot drink before the working day started.

The terrain seemed harder now – cobblestones and walls – but there was much more cover than he'd known on the veldt: trees, doorways, alleys, streets clogged with café tables and pedestrians.

The enemy could be any of those pedestrians; that was the snag.

The objective was just across the street: the office of the International Cultural Exchange. Three storeys. Rather elegant, you'd say. Fancy stonework around the windows; plaster painted yellow. They went in for colour here; the buildings were a mix of yellow and pink and grey. Front door in the middle of the façade, two steps up to it, push-button bell to the side. That surely wouldn't be his way in.

There was another door, in a side street. Much more his cup of tea. Except that the security seemed good. He'd still been in his first café when the side door was opened to allow a cleaning woman to enter. He was sitting at a table in a different café, wearing glasses and reading a different newspaper, watching the side street from the other end when the door opened again and the woman began to ferry sacks of rubbish into the street. It only took her a few minutes, and at least once in that time a head popped out of the door behind her. Cap of some kind; doorman, perhaps, but keeping an eye on her as well. When she left at around eight, the woman didn't close the door behind her, which meant that once again there was someone there doing the opening and closing and, presumably, the locking.

Knox shifted position again: another vantage point, a different newspaper, a hat. He saw the doorman – nightwatchman? – leave, and be replaced by a chap in a smarter uniform who fussed around the front step for non-existent shortcomings in the cleaning, then shut himself inside. He wondered at caps and uniforms.

Around half past nine – from the bow window of a restaurant a little way down the street – Knox saw a closed motor car pull up for a moment outside the front door; the chauffeur went to ring the bell, but it opened as he got there, and then a figure in frock-coat and hat stepped from car to doorway and was gone. The door closed and the car puttered away around the corner. Knox wondered where the chauffeur spent the day. Knox also wondered about the man in the frock-coat.

After that, he began to explore the surrounding area. He allowed himself no more than half an hour at a time inside a quarter-mile radius of the objective. He came and went by different routes and with adjustments each time to his appearance. He tried to gauge the rhythms of the building, the times when there were many people nearby and when there were not. He found the angle that enabled him to confirm the wireless aerial on the roof of the International Cultural Exchange.

He had no intention of meeting any of the occupants of the building. But later in the afternoon, as he was turning out of the street in which the International Cultural Exchange was situated and making for the river, an instinctive glance over his shoulder at the ground where he'd have to fight, his shoulder barged into another man's, and they were both instinctively poised and then stepping back and nodding a courtesy and moving on.

And Knox thought: *I know you.*

The man in the street searching Ballentyne's body. Probably the man who'd interviewed Cade. *Just the type of smooth-looking Hun you'd want for an enemy.*

While Hildebrandt strode on towards the office of the International Cultural Exchange, Knox sauntered away into the city. He would not return to that district again, not until morning.

Sarajevo

St Vitus, so the story goes, freed the emperor's son from an evil spirit. But because he would not recognize the pagan gods, the emperor – Diocletian, who built his palace in Split, near his old home – had him killed. At the moment of his death, in boiling oil, pagan temples in the area were destroyed by a great storm.

For the Serbs, St Vitus's Day means the Battle of Kosovo, in 1389, when their prince led a coalition of Balkan peoples against the invading Ottomans. Given the choice before the battle, by an envoy from heaven, of the celestial kingdom or the earthly, the prince chose the former; like all proud rulers, he knew that the risk of war was better than the certainty of shame. The prince was killed in the battle, and his army was destroyed, but they stalled the invasion for a while. So the story goes.

St Vitus is the patron saint of actors and comedians. In mediaeval times, it was thought that dancing in front of the statue of the saint would bring good health. But the name of St Vitus was given to a sickness, an uncontrollable and apparently inexplicable physical frenzy.

St Vitus is celebrated on the 28th of June.

+≈=≈+

Valentine Knox walked alone through the streets of Sarajevo, the first of the light paling their pastel colours. The shadows still waited thick, in doorways and alley entrances.

The city was coming awake as he walked, with street sweepers crossing in front of him and waiters carrying tables out onto terraces and maids opening windows, the houses taking their first breaths of fresh air. There seemed to be more flags out this morning, and along the river the street had been strung with bunting. The fluttering and his solitary stride: a memory of running onto Big Side at the end of the cross-country.

He was in the second of his cafés in time to see the side door being opened to admit the cleaning woman.

The countdown had started.

In front of him the window, a shelf running along it. He saw the trench parapet, parched strands of thorn in the sand. Felt the shifting of his men beside him, felt the sun on his neck, heard the men breathing, heard himself breathing, heard his heart.

The door opened and the woman stepped out with the first of the rubbish sacks, and Knox heard a whistle and he was up and out of the trench and moving.

A casual trot to another alley, then he was sprinting hard, because these were the seconds where failure waited, *first place, Knox V.*, slowing and out into the main street and swallowing his breaths. As he came past the front of the International Cultural Exchange, he rang the bell and strode on.

As he turned into the alley a third rubbish sack was on the ground by the door and the woman was disappearing inside. *One more. One more will be enough.* His jacket came off and he draped it over his shoulders and began to slump and stagger, a beggar in his natural environment, boots trudging through rubbish and slime. The doorway was five yards away, and three, and now he could see that it was open still, and a sack swung out in front of him.

If the woman saw the beggar nearby, she didn't acknowledge it. Doorman should still be checking the front. The sound of feet in a corridor and he was pulling his jacket on properly – a breath – and he was in.

From one pocket he pulled a cap, from another a screwdriver and spanner, staring around for – and then he was bent down over a pipe. He heard the woman come and go behind him. There was a line of pegs in front of him, and beside them another door, frosted panels, and he was through it and into a lavatory.

Footsteps in the hall again, heavier. The doorman returning to lock the side door. The footsteps dwindled.

No thinking. Out fast; the coat and the cap went onto a peg, revealing a tweed jacket and a collar and tie. Trousers out of socks, and from an inside pocket a piece of paper. At every stage he had to look right enough. A breath, and he was through the door and into the corridor. At its end a more solid door, with felt on the inside. That was the border between the servants and the quality. He edged around it. Chequerboard floor, walls finished smooth, a window, and then another. This was the main hall. Another inch showed a glazed partition, and through it the front door.

He edged further, and saw the edge of a table, set back opposite the door, and then on the table a pair of legs.

Still too early for the doorman to be relieved; that might be a chance. He could rush the man, but he wasn't desperate enough for that yet. The alternative was just to—

The bell rang. Immediately the legs swung off the table. Knox pulled back farther. The doorman came into his vision, opening the glazed partition and then unlocking the front door. Someone else? But no – the doorman was accepting something.

Postman. Knox was out into the hall and crossing it, head down into his piece of paper. Movement to his right on a staircase: the cleaning woman, coming down with a bucket. Head down and keep going; the doorman would see the woman before he saw Knox and that might... The door in front of him – no key – and he was into another corridor.

He heard the glazed door rattle shut. With his door open an inch, he saw the doorman cross the hall again and drop a pile of envelopes on the table. The woman was by the door leading to the servants' area, and now the doorman walked over to her. He said something, and then mimed it. *Are you done?* The woman hesitated, nodded. Another mime? *You are going now?* She shook her head, pointed to the back part of the house and mimed scrubbing the floor. The doorman gestured her through her door, and she went. Knox thought: you had to be poor indeed to be a foreign immigrant in Bosnia.

Then the doorman locked the servants' door behind her, and put the key on his table, and Knox winced. So security-conscious that they didn't even give the servants the run of the place. More importantly, that was his escape route, should escape become possible.

The legs swung up onto the table again.

With the sense of safety disappearing far behind him, he turned. This was a mirror of the servants' corridor running parallel along the other side of the building. But this side was smarter: tiled floor, finished walls, the doors glossy and brass-handled. Offices for junior staff? He didn't want to risk trying every door.

Then he saw the trunking. A few inches thick, it ran from floor to ceiling beside a door at the end of the corridor. He saw it because he was looking for it: a wireless room and a transmitter mean electric cables, and electric cables installed more recently than the main wiring of the building mean trunking.

A bell rang somewhere behind him. Knox was looking through the crack again in time to see the doorman unlocking the door to the servants' wing, and disappearing through it. A few minutes later it opened again and a different man came into the hall. It was the daytime doorman, in his uniform. He locked the servants' door, and put the key on the table.

Knox waited for the doorman to sit, but he didn't. Instead he picked up the envelopes from the table, and set off up the stairs.

Knox gave him a few seconds to get clear, then he was back into the hall, across to the table and picking up the key, on to the servants' door and unlocking it and putting the key back on the table. *A chance, at least.*

He was halfway back across the hall when the servants' door opened behind him.

It was the cleaning woman. He'd assumed she'd have gone, but here she was, staring up at him, alarmed. Part of Knox's mind was noticing that she was a younger woman, handsome in her way, skin a little darker, and still she was staring. He had to trust that she wouldn't question a man, wouldn't question a man in a suit.

She lowered her eyes, and hurried up the stairs and, as he watched, through a door on the landing. Knox kicked himself into movement and was back through the other door and heading for the wireless room.

<hr />

When Hathaway walked into the office, the whisper of a dress against the panels, eyes always considering the office as if for the first time, the old man was staring out into the park.

He didn't turn round, or say anything.

'It is today?' she said at last.

'It is today.'

She realized that he wasn't actually looking into the park, but into the net curtain, deep into it, where its fog became a fine lattice, and then beyond.

He half turned, and gave a formal nod of greeting over his shoulder. 'Now,' he said, 'there is only Valentine Knox.'

'There could be none better.'

He turned again, a flicker of interest in the eyes. 'I would trust your judgement on him more than most.'

'War is passion applied to unreason. Knox, at his best, is passion applied to reason.'

The old man considered it, approved it, and merely nodded again slightly. He turned away.

'And if he's captured? If he fails?'

'If he is captured, Miss Hathaway, then they will torture him. He will tell all he knows about me, about this organization; even Knox will not hold for ever.' He was still gazing into the net. 'If he fails, everything fails.'

＋＝＝＋

The wireless room wasn't even locked. Knox had his penknife and the screwdriver ready, but the door opened with the handle only. First he checked the door opposite – a filing room – and then he was back across the corridor and in.

Knox was familiar with wireless and had used it before, but the old man had insisted on him spending an hour in the company of a little goggle-eyed chap from the Post Office who'd told him more than he would ever need, or probably remember.

It meant that the room felt immediately familiar – the layout, the different pieces of equipment – and without having to think he was switching on the apparatus and getting the satisfying humming and glowing.

His priorities now were exact. Each second increased his chances of capture. So the maximum had to be achieved in each second. He was sitting at the transmitter, setting the frequency.

It was a simple message. The first word was a designator, to alert a man waiting in London – and, in case the transmitter here was not as strong as anticipated, men waiting in Venice and on board a cruiser in the Adriatic – that this was the message they were waiting for. He'd no need for acknowledgement; the old man had been clear that they would be there.

The message contained only three other words.

Knox adjusted the frequency so that if someone disturbed him now it would not be known. Then he was searching the immediate area around the transmitter for a list of regular frequencies. There had to be one, and an operator might leave it close at hand as a matter of routine.

But in this office, only strict security was routine. The habits of the doorman had taught him that. Which made his job harder, and capture more likely. Immediately he was up from the chair and quartering the room, just in case the list had been left on another surface. But it hadn't, of course, which meant it had to be in the wooden cabinet on the other side of the room. He was at the lock with his knife a second later, using the screwdriver as a lever and ignoring the damage to the woodwork. The phase of concealment was past.

As soon as he was in he began to work methodically through the documents inside. Three shelves, piles of papers and books, and he guessed at what they were – messages recently received, records of messages sent and received, and so forth – and started on a pile of small ledgers.

It would not be quick, and Knox knew what that meant. Something inside him kicked; a lurch of disappointment.

He straightened, and continued through the books. He must either have sent the message or be out of the room; either way meant the faint possibility of success. To be caught searching was failure.

As he finished skimming each of the ledgers, he threw it aside. *Faster.* There were two or three lists of what looked like frequencies, but the destinations were in code, and a part of Knox had to respect the mania for security. *Faster.* Another ledger thrown aside, bouncing off a desk and flapping to the floor. Then another, a cursory rummage through the piles of papers. *There is still a faint chance of success in this.* Papers flying over his shoulder and fluttering down. Inside five minutes the cupboard was all but empty, and Knox was slipping out of the wireless room and across the corridor.

＊＝＝＊

Krug arrived at the International Cultural Exchange at half past nine, as usual. The routine was set, and congenial to him: a cup of coffee; the international newspapers; the post. His secretary brought in each, silently and at the expected time.

And then his secretary confirmed his appointments for the day. The anthropologist Belcredi was due at ten o'clock. Count Hildebrandt would be present today, and at Herr Krug's disposal. Herr Krug would visit the Austrian minister in Sarajevo at four o'clock in the afternoon.

Krug felt well. A pleasant day – not too hot. The city *en fête*, though he would be avoiding the noise and the ceremonial. A scheme in hand to entrap another of the Comptroller-General's agents – and this one, it seemed, more knowledgeable than most. His world was functioning as it should. He sipped contentedly at the coffee. Sweet, but not too sweet.

＊＝＝＊

The world of Hans Martić was not functioning as it should. He considered himself lucky in his work as wireless operator in the International Cultural Exchange. The pay was good, the conditions were not onerous; he was lucky to have a job, let alone one that used his skill. Sometimes he wondered whether the messages that he passed to the clerks for decyphering contained only diplomatic secrets – might there not be something criminal in all the subterfuge? – but he'd seen enough officials and uniforms around the place to be clear that he was on the right side.

He liked to arrive between nine and nine thirty in the morning. To be ahead of the day, as he put it. Have the equipment warmed up, his lists ready, for the start of business. Ready for the chief's command, or the message coming in. But today the city was chaos, because of the parade, and he was at least fifteen minutes late.

He knew in a fraction of a second that it was all wrong. The door to the wireless room – his wireless room – was only half open when he saw the first of the papers lying on one of the tables, and that was surely not how he'd left it. As the door opened farther there were more papers – papers everywhere, and the ledgers too! – thrown around the room. He was gaping, sick, wondering how it was his fault, wondering whom to tell, and the door wasn't even fully open when something shoved him in the back and he was stumbling forwards and the door closed and when he turned there was a pistol pointing at his head.

'*Deutsch*?'

Hans continued to gape.

'*Sprechen Sie Deutsch*?'

Hans nodded.

Knox nodded back at the man. 'All right then.' German it would have to be. 'First, the rules. If you speak, if you resist, I will kill you. Please believe me.' He pushed the pistol against the man's forehead, hard, and the man froze, eyes crossing up at the barrel. 'You do believe me, don't you?' A desperate nod, the barrel scratching against the forehead.

'Good.' Knox took his handkerchief. 'Open.' And stuffed it into the man's mouth. 'Get the list of frequencies for your regular contacts.' Hesitation, and Knox clutched the man by the back of the head and started to push the pistol against his eye. The man staggered away and flapped at the ledgers on the floor until he found the right one. 'Now sit.' The man sat. Knox took the curtain cord that he'd borrowed from the filing room, and tied the man to his chair.

He pulled the handkerchief from the mouth. 'Decypher the list. You will realize that if I can get in here, I can also tell if you are trying any tricks.' The man nodded. It was the best Knox could do. Simply asking for the German Embassy frequency would be an invitation to deception; if the man didn't know what he wanted, under pressure he wouldn't be able to produce credible bogus answers for all the frequencies. The man started to recite the destinations: offices in Vienna, in Berlin, individual offices in other cities.

The German Embassy in London was 'Sergius', near the bottom of the list – a recent addition. Knox made the man repeat the list; again, the best he could do to check he wasn't being tricked.

He stuffed the handkerchief back into the man's mouth. He reset the frequency to that for his listeners in London, Venice and the Adriatic, and transmitted details of the frequency used for the Germany Embassy in London. Then he turned the dial to that frequency. 'Now, send the following message, in clear. You're doing the transmitting because you're faster and they'll know your fist. But believe me that I know enough Morse to know if you're playing games.' He pushed the barrel into the man's ear. 'You do believe me, don't you?' Nod. 'Right then. First his designation, and yours, as usual. Go!' The man's hand trembled over the transmitter key. 'Relax, my friend, and you might live.' The hand flexed, settled on the key, and started to tap out the letters.

—✦—

When the summons came, Thomson was quickly into the old man's office in Whitehall. If he was surprised to see a woman in there, he didn't show it. Handsome-looking female; seemed a bit anxious.

The old man fluttered a message slip at him. '"Marsden apparently expected."'

'Ah...' Grim smile from Thomson. 'The gentleman in the Ports and Consulates Office has been indiscreet.'

'I used the name of Marsden in no other message, to no other office.'

'"Apparently" expected. The arrangement was that your man would say "certainly" if he could.'

'That is true.'

'This is certain enough for you?'

'This is certain enough for me.'

—✦—

Knox dictated the second message slowly, a word at a time, wanting to check his own memory of it, wanting no mistakes, wanting the operator to feel that every letter was being monitored. There were substantial pauses.

It was finished within a minute. When the words stopped coming, the man slumped back in his chair. And took a long breath.

'I think you misplaced your coat,' said a voice from behind him.

Knox couldn't restrain the startle. Another long breath. Very slowly, he raised the pistol over his head, then out to the side.

'That's good.' Speaking English; accented. 'Lay it on the floor beside you, stand, then kick it back towards me.' Knox did so. 'Now you may turn.'

He turned. Dark hair, handsome; pistol in one hand, rock-steady, and Knox's coat in the other.

Vienna; the tram; Ballentyne's body. 'Hildebrandt, I believe.'

The eyes widened. 'You have the advantage.' He didn't act disadvantaged.

'I saw you in Vienna. Ransacking the body of a friend of mine.'

Again the interest, then a rueful smile. 'Poor Ballentyne. We never did have the conversation I had promised him.' The smile widened; inspiration. 'Now I can have it with you instead.'

Valentine Knox wasn't familiar with fear, but he wasn't a fool and he wasn't without imagination. He looked at Hildebrandt, and knew him for a killing gentleman.

'The unlocked door was our alert. We're rather strict about security here. Then, the coat didn't seem right.' He threw it at Knox's feet. 'I have kept the tools; I don't think you need further encouragement to foolishness.'

'They weren't mine anyway.'

'Mm. Would you kindly release my wireless operator?'

Knox did so. 'No hard feelings?' he said, as the man stood and slipped away as fast as he could, the chair scraping on the floor.

'Get Kopp!' Hildebrandt snapped in German. 'Tell no one what has happened. Then come back here and resume your routine.' The man nodded, and hurried out. 'You have unsettled him,' he went on to Knox. 'And he was quite a good operator.' He looked around the room. 'You have been busy, I think. Did you find what you were looking for?'

Knox smiled.

'And your message?'

'My mother. Likes to know where I am.'

A polite chuckle from Hildebrandt. 'You've no idea how much that British coolness amuses me.' He leaned forwards. 'It will not endure, my friend. Not in our cellar here. Down there... it will be very hot indeed.'

MOST URGENT. SERIOUS... AGENTS... NEPTUNE
CONSOLIDATE... ALTEMARK MINOS HARM... ALL MUST REPORT
TO EMBASSY.

[SS X/72/165 (TRANSLATION)]

Krug had been looking forward to his meeting with Belcredi. He had his own ideas on the inclinations of the peoples of the Balkans and the Near East, and wanted to test the anthropologist a little. And Belcredi's patrons in Germany – particularly the woman – were influential indeed and would bear cultivating.

Belcredi was rather late, and when he was shown into Krug's office the most obvious thing about him was a swelling under his cheek. 'My dear sir!' Krug began. 'That looks...'

His guest, embarrassed, mumbled an explanation about his tooth. Krug had to control a smile. He'd thought Hildebrandt's description of the man's haplessness rather overdone, but he did seem rather a fragile element. Which might be useful... Hardly the man to shape a masterstroke in the Near East. Krug offered him a chair, commanded coffee, and began to muse on how he might supplant him and improve his own position among Belcredi's patrons.

They had only started on the pleasantries when the telephone rang. Polite irritation on Krug's face, but he answered quickly, and his guest saw the face change immediately. Surprise, and this time the emotion was genuine. A few half-words, and then Krug snapped an order, and replaced the earpiece.

He contrived a smile, but couldn't disguise his haste. 'You must excuse me, my dear fellow. A rather urgent matter – in my wireless office. Would you mind returning to the waiting room for a few minutes?'

His guest looked a little irritated, but did as asked. It was more than a few minutes before he was back in Krug's office, but Krug had recovered his poise. 'Again, my apologies. A small—'

'May I ask what?'

Krug hesitated.

'It seems you have controlled the situation, anyway.'

Krug smiled. 'Indeed. I'll tell you, my friend. Since you have been so involved in our activities against the British – on top of your own, more civilized work. The British, as you know, sent agents against me in Vienna. Or rather, they thought they did. Instead, they fell into my trap, and you played your part in our success. They seem to have become desperate, and they sent another man – here.' Krug stirred his coffee. 'I had warning of it, of course, thanks to my network in London. Quite an impressive fellow, apparently. He was earlier than expected, but we have him anyway. I have now taken steps to rectify the little damage that he managed to do.' He took a sip, and found that it was cold. 'Hildebrandt has him in the cellar now, and will encourage him to tell us all that he knows.' There was something like real discomfort on Krug's face, and then he suppressed it. 'Then he will die.'

'I would like to see this man.'

'Really?'

A shrug. 'I have met at least one British agent. Perhaps I know him. Before he...' An uncomfortable smile. 'It is amusing to see a proud man who learns his mistake.'

Krug smiled. 'You're right. Let's have him up. Hildebrandt likes it in the cellar, and such places, but then his suits are so much cheaper than mine.' He rang for his secretary, and gave the instruction.

A few minutes later, there was a knock at the door, and Krug called the invitation. He saw Belcredi stand and edge away from the door as it opened. The first man in was Major Valentine Knox, hands tied behind his back and face cut and bruising; the second, pushing him and holding a pistol casually at his side, was Hildebrandt.

Both of them saw Krug first, and then saw his guest. When they saw his guest, both of them gaped stupid.

❖

There was no regular postal service to the island of the Counts di Lascara in the middle of the Adriatic. But at two or three ports, a boat going in the right direction might be persuaded to make a delivery there.

On the 28th of June a steamer anchored off the island; just long enough for a man to row ashore, and pass a package to a boy who'd come to see what was going on, and row back again.

Isabella di Lascara found the package on the doorstep when she returned from riding. It spent another half an hour on a table, while she washed. Deliveries were rare, but there was little in the world to interest her.

Inside the package, when she finally opened it, she found a pair of man's slippers, which she did not recognize as being in the Albanian style, and a pipe.

<hr />

'Ballentyne!' For once, Count Paul Hildebrandt's control had gone.

And from Knox: 'Good Lord...'

Hildebrandt's surprise was long enough for Ballentyne to have the pistol out of his pocket and up level. 'Drop it!'

Anger had replaced surprise in Hildebrandt's eyes, but too late. He put the pistol on the floor. Ballentyne pulled a wad of cloth from inside his cheek. 'Untie him.' It took a few moments for Knox's hands to come free, and they did so in obvious pain. 'Over there.' Ballentyne gestured Hildebrandt away from the door, until both he and Krug were covered by the pistol.

Knox flexed his hands, rubbed the wrists. Then he stepped forwards and punched Hildebrandt in the face. The German staggered back against the wall, and came away with the clattering of a picture and a bleeding nose.

Ballentyne said, 'Feel better?'

'Much.'

'You—' – Krug was clutching for reality – 'You are Ballentyne?' And a glance of vicious accusation at Hildebrandt.

The voice was quiet, flat. 'I don't seem to have any identity any more'– the memory of sending the package to Isabella; a final bid to belong – 'except that I was faster than your friend Mr Belcredi. He got hit by the tram, not I. In the few seconds before the people from the tram made their way back, I got his jacket off and laid mine over him.'

Hildebrandt: 'And the reports that were sent in the last weeks?'

'A bit overstated. I've been trying out some ideas of my own among the Muslims of south-eastern Europe. You'll get no tickle from them for a while. I knew this place had some kind of significance for Belcredi; I knew if I didn't follow the trail to the end, I'd never be able to rest easy. I've spent the last few weeks brushing up my German and trying to get to y—'

'Halt!' A shout from the door, and Ballentyne started to turn and then saw Knox's urgent eyes and reaching hand and managed to stop himself. The man in the doorway had a pistol of his own, and it was pointing at Ballentyne's chest.

Ballentyne laid his pistol on the floor and stood, empty. The man in the doorway shifted round until he could watch both the Englishmen.

A great breath, and the life came back into Krug's face, and the control. The scale of the chaos had only fuelled his appetite to dominate it. 'So we are back where we started,' he said. 'With a bonus.' He glanced at Ballentyne, and then to Knox. 'You: what is your real name?'

'I am Major Valentine Knox; British Army.'

'Sent here by the Comptroller-General for Scrutiny and Survey, yes?' Krug's triumph.

Knox said nothing.

Krug breathed it in. 'Major, I must commend you on your daring, your... *élan*. It is only when we look for a word for an empty quality, that we learn what the French have given Europe, no? Your... resilience. And yet I must inform you that it has been futile.' He pointed. 'I knew of your advent. I knew of your mission. I wanted you here. You were here a day earlier than we were warned of, which was why you managed to get in here, but that did not matter.'

He smiled. 'You have about you the air of the martyr. You think you have done your duty, and may die proud.' He shook his head. 'You have done... nothing. My operator has told me what you sent – that desperate, nonsensical message. What did you think? That you would so confuse the German Embassy, the German network, that they would all be persuaded to reveal themselves? What were those meaningless words, anyway? "Neptune" and "Minos" and so on?'

Knox looked at him for a moment, then shrugged.

Hildebrandt said quietly, 'They are words in German Military Intelligence code.'

'But do they mean anything? In this context, in this order?'

'No.'

Krug shook his head again, pitying. 'In the end, rather a feeble stratagem. You hoped to provoke an excitement in the network, no? To make the agents reveal themselves somehow? It has had the opposite effect to what you intended. We immediately warned the German Embassy about the violation of our codes here – your pillaging of our documents – and the compromise of security. Even if you knew something of the German code, you have lost it because already that code is being changed as a result of your adventure here. The German network in Britain is even farther from you than when you started. It is out of your reach.'

Knox's face, as watched by Ballentyne: stone, refusing defeat. Then from somewhere deep a flame, burning in his eyes and then warming his whole face. The shoulders pulled up even straighter.

The door pushed open wider, and the cleaning woman stepped into the office.

The five men saw her as a woman, as a servant; they saw the headscarf, the swirl of skirts, the loose smock and the chemise beneath. And because they saw all these things and nothing more, and because it was the day of madness, they took an extra second to see that when she pulled her hand from the folds of her clothes it held a pistol.

Even the guard, the one man with a weapon ready, could not truly see what was happening. The woman had time to glance at each of the faces in turn. The pistol swung with her eyes, and then pistol and eyes hardened at Hildebrandt, and by the time the guard had his own weapon up she had pulled the trigger.

It clicked. It did not fire.

The pistol in the guard's hand, a 1912 Model Steyr, was less fallible than its nineteenth-century forebear. It cracked once, and the woman was flung to the ground.

Again, the five men stood looking at her, and not seeing.

'Who – who is she?' Krug, trying to deal with this final insult to the order of his office.

Ballentyne crouched over her, laid his palm on her forehead, and when he looked up again Knox saw that his eyes were moist. 'Her name is Besa,' he said. He looked at Hildebrandt. 'When you came for me in the village, it was her brother that you murdered.'

'She came all this way – for that?'

'Amazing, isn't it?' Ballentyne said. 'That someone should still care about a single life.' He looked down at the woman again, at her beautiful face, now pale. Her eyes flickered, winced. She clutched at her stomach, clutched for his hand.

He let her hold it as she weakened, let her pull it against her body. Felt the last warmth of her stomach; felt the butt of the second pistol, tucked into her waistband under the loose shirt.

Her eyes came open again, wild and urgent and lovely. Ballentyne smiled at her, and murmured a word in a language that only they could understand, then stood and the pistol came up with him. Yet again, the guard was caught; he found himself staring into the void of the ancient muzzle while his own weapon was down. Beyond the muzzle, the features of the Englishman were a blur.

Ballentyne swung round to face Hildebrandt, and shot him between the eyes.

A moment of shock, as they all realized that this time the pistol had fired, realized that Hildebrandt was now lying broken and still on the floor. And then the guard's pistol came up and Knox flung himself forwards and there was a shot and a roar of pain, and Knox had the man by the throat and was driving him to the floor and punching him in the face, punching him and punching him until he was still.

When he came up, one side of his face was a scorched mess, the eye closed. 'It's a simple rule,' he hissed. 'You fire at the one with the weapon.'

Ballentyne closed the door and locked it, and bent over the woman again. Her breathing was shallower, fading. He glanced up. 'You above all should understand the idea of duty.' He looked down at Besa again. Her eyes crept open. He smiled sadly; nodded; said a word.

A smile flickered on her lips; he bent further, and kissed her forehead, and waited until the last breath had escaped.

He covered her face with the headscarf, and stood.

Banging on the door, shouts.

'Send them away!' Knox said, hard. 'It is under control. Do it!'

Krug was lost in the mayhem.

'Do it!'

Krug called something. A question from the other side of the door, and this time he snapped back angrily, and there was silence.

Knox said, 'How on earth did she get here?'

Ballentyne shook his head. 'I don't... The Albanians in Belgrade? Perhaps the first time I was there, they sent word. I was there again recently. Thanks to them, she will have followed me to Sarajevo last week. Earlier, perhaps.'

'And then got in this morning?'

'She wasn't interested in me. All along she hoped that I would lead her to Hildebrandt. Some time in the last few days, she found him; got work here, or replaced the usual woman. Somehow, today something changed; she was able to do what she hadn't been able to do before: get into this part of the building.' Knox frowned. 'Today, she came to the end of her journey.'

Knox turned to the man behind the desk. 'And you,' he said, 'must be Mr Krug.'

Krug nodded.

'The Comptroller-General for Scrutiny and Survey sends his regards. "A greeting from Springfontein", he called it.' Krug's face was bleak.

He sat, heavily, gathered himself. 'This little bit of chaos does not alter the failure of his operation.'

'Bit of bad news for you there, old chap. I only properly understood it when you described your reaction to my activities this morning. British Intelligence has always suspected who the link-man is for the German network in Britain. But there's been no way of identifying the members of the network. Arresting the link-man would only break the chain. Everything I did this morning – throwing the papers around, sending that nonsense message, with a few words of German codes that we've picked up in recent months – all built the idea that your security was compromised. It prompted the German Embassy, and through them the link-man to the network, to do what seemed like rigorous procedure but was actually exactly what we wanted.'

Krug was white.

'How will the new code be sent to the network? Some innocent-looking commercial pamphlet? It doesn't matter; what matters is that when the link-man goes to the post office, he will be jumped on by a lot of policemen, and on the envelopes in his hand – all in one go – will be the set of names and addresses that we couldn't have dreamed of getting had it not been for you. Special Branch'll roll up the whole network whenever they choose.' Grim smile. 'Your German partners aren't going to be impressed.'

Krug was staring into the ruins of his Europe. He looked up, searching for defiance. 'You could kill me, but you would not get out of the building alive.'

'You could call for help, but you would die.'

'You suggest that we stay here for ever, Major?'

'Stalemate.'

The telephone rang.

It continued to ring. Knox said, 'You'd better answer that. No tricks, no alarms.'

Krug picked up the apparatus, and listened. He said almost nothing, but as he listened his eyes were quickly wide and he was gazing at the two Englishmen.

Eventually he put down the telephone again. It took him a moment to gather the words.

He looked at Knox. 'You came over the border with a Serbian, yes? Was his name Rade Malobabić?'

'I didn't get the surname.'

'He is the head of Serbia's network of spies in Bosnia–Hercegovina – a notorious man.' Knox was indifferent. 'The strictest watch was being kept for him at the border, but somehow... Did he say why he was entering Bosnia?'

'He said he was delivering a message.'

Krug nodded, bleak. 'It was a message of command: to his agents gathered here in Sarajevo. Just a few minutes ago they assassinated the heir to the Austrian throne.' Faced with the chaos, he seemed very small. He saw farther than Knox and Ballentyne, still poised over him; but even their faces showed glimpses of what must follow. 'The crisis that no one of the European powers could create has been created by a handful of peasants. They have brought the world to the precipice.'

Author's Note

I t's a matter of record that on the first day of the First World War, the British authorities rounded up a string of German spies across the country. For all practical purposes, the German espionage threat in Britain ceased to exist, and it was not re-established. It was the first great coup for London's new Intelligence arrangements (its immediate impact was to allow the British Expeditionary Force to link up with the French Army unreported and thereby help to block the German advance), and arguably their most significant contribution to the war.

Implementation of the Third Irish Home Rule Act was postponed because of the outbreak of war, and then overtaken by the 1916 Easter Rising, by the armed resistance to British rule, and finally by civil war.

The German scheme to exploit Muslim sentiment in the Near East was only delayed by the death of Heinz-Peter Belcredi. The story of his sponsors' subsequent more dramatic efforts, culminating in the Battle of Erzerum in 1916, is best known in its fictionalized form as one of the great tales of British adventure, Buchan's *Greenmantle*.

Albania's German king reigned for a total of six months, before unrest, the changing calculations of his international backers and the approach of European war made his position impossible. One hundred years later, the international community continues to meddle and manoeuvre in south-eastern Europe.

Conclusive technical explanations for the failure of Gustav Hamel's aircraft and that of a British seaplane piloted by a German officer during the Kiel Regatta have never been advanced – or, at least, have never been made public.

The evidence suggests that Eberhardt Krug was still alive towards the end of the First World War, living in a kind of retirement in Switzerland. The details of his activities and death are not clear from publicly available records. It's probable that the archive of the Comptrollerate-General for Scrutiny and Survey has more to say on this extraordinary man.

The archive may also fill some of the gaps in the subsequent histories of those who survived the Comptroller-General's great gambit.

James Cade's career seems clear enough: he was prompted to return home early in the conflict, with Constantinople increasingly uncomfortable (and, the correspondence would suggest, with his mother increasingly insistent); he fought in 1915, and was wounded; Lloyd-George's assumption of the premiership in 1916 brought a new style to government, and Cade was given a senior administrative position making use of his organizational skills; he returned to business after the war.

An anonymous donor (one may only guess at their gender) paid for David Duval's discreet memorial plaque at Golders Green Crematorium, in north London; the pamphlet on the history of Golders Green, full of such anecdotes, says that once a year for ten years after his death a rose was placed next to the stone.

Ronald Ballentyne's activities during the war aren't immediately evident from the regular records. The documents of the Comptrollerate-General archive may have something to say on this; the stones of an island in the middle of the Adriatic may have more. Perhaps one can only speculate whether the Countess Isabella's home offered him a place comfortably to disappear from the world, or a base from which to engage with it.

Academic records and her very discreet public profile show just enough of Flora Hathaway's activities to suggest that there's a great deal more to be known. The archive of the Comptrollerate-General appears to be the place to find it.

Hathaway apparently burned almost all of her papers. Among the very few mementoes that she kept and that survived her is a telegram of invitation, to the wedding in February 1915 of Major Karl Immelmann and Gerta von Waldeck. It's highly improbable that she attended, but a pencilled tick on the telegram hints that at the very least she replied. Major Immelmann was killed in 1918; his infant son died that winter. Gerta's subsequent career – as a civil engineer in the Middle East, and then as the author of a briefly very fashionable set of meditations on spiritualism and desert peoples – brought her some public renown.

The military career of Valentine Knox in the first half of the war is a matter of record – and of legend; as was described in the introduction to *The Emperor's Gold* (retitled *Treason's Tide* in paperback), towards the end of the war Knox had become Comptroller-General. The archive that he himself began to re-gather should hopefully reveal more of his activities, and perhaps offer an explanation of his disappearance after the war.

But the identity of the man who was Comptroller-General for Scrutiny and Survey in the period leading up to the First World War, the man who gambled with the future of British Intelligence in order to save it, remains a mystery. The archive shows the name he was using during the Boer War, and shows that it was a cypher. Speculation about who he might have been involves credible figures (Hozier, Melville) who moved in the margins of the ever shifting structures of British Intelligence; but if the archive of the Comptrollerate-General doesn't reveal his secret, nothing will. He has drifted back into the dust of Whitehall. Indeed – for such is the nature of the dust of Whitehall – in a sense, he's still there.